Who was this freak? Why the costume? Was he dangerous? Or worse, did he see her break into the car? Whoever it was stared at her for what felt like an eternity, standing still as his dumpster backdrop. The black voids of his eye sockets bore into her.

Lucy checked her mirror a final time, ready to tear out of there. But when she looked up again, the figure was gone.

Her stomach flopped. *Fuck this,* she thought and yanked the stick hard into reverse. Then a *tap-tap-tap* hit the driver's side window. Lucy froze. Her eyes turned to the sound, but her head stayed glued forward. Her hand blindly found the crank for the window and rolled it down only a few inches. The costumed freak leaned forward, its white, raven mask filling the opening.

"Excuse me, miss. I seemed to have been given the wrong time and location for a very important event. Would it be possible to procure passage in your vehicle? Your assistance would be vital." The voice behind the mask was clearly male, yet different; he spoke with an accent she couldn't quite place.

"Sorry." She shook her head. "No passengers tonight." Smirking to herself, she began to draw the window up again.

The man put his giant hand on the glass and pushed down. Lucy heard the wheels inside the mechanism struggle under his strength.

"My apologies, I forgot to introduce myself. I am Doctor Emidius, and the survival of your species may depend on my timely arrival."

"Pff, I bet," she said. *Just another crazy then.* Lucy's fear eased; she knew how to handle crazies. . . . Don't.

WORLDENDER

NICK NIKOLOV

![FFF]

FFF

SCIENCE FICTION

WORLDENDER
by Nick Nikolov

ISBN (hardcover) 978-1-989071-17-5
ISBN (paperback) 978-1-989071-18-2
ISBN (ebook) 978-1-989071-19-9

Cover art © Tessa Barron
Cover design © Bear Hill Publishing

Published in North America by Foul Fantasy Fiction, an imprint of Bear Hill Publishing.

www.foulfantasyfiction.com
www.bearhillbooks.com

*To my parents, whose unconditional support
made the pursuit of dreams possible.*

WORLDENDER

VENICE, ITALY
APRIL 22, 1640 AD

The luxurious and dismal personalities of the city met on the street in celebration. They glided and danced around each other, concealed behind masks to evoke either fear, humor, or arousal.

High above, the light of the stars seemed to shine down exclusively for the revelers' merriment. But one of the jovial lights blinked violently and sped straight down toward the dancers. Moments later, the star flashed and disappeared into the black abyss of the night sky.

On a more peaceful night, keen-eyed observers might have noticed the light was actually a dark object, hurtling toward the buildings surrounding Piazza San Marco. Those same spectators would then see the object latch itself to the damaged roof of Canpanièl de San Marco. But tonight, no one observed, watched, or otherwise witnessed anything outside the realm of festivities. In the square, all dressed in their most colorful clothes, the people were preoccupied, doing their best to meld into each other, forget their troubles, and let go of their pesky prejudices.

As the crowd danced and colors blended, the object's sides opened, and three circular containers drained of a viscous, orange liquid. The liquid oozed out and fell on top of three street performers dressed in monochrome colors. As soon as it touched the masks hiding their faces, it began to eat away at them. The liquid numbed the skin's nerves, corroding everything on its path to the nearest open orifice. A fourth tar creature slid out of the craft and plopped on the ground impotently. Within seconds dancing men and women stomped on top until it became mushy paste, nearly indistinguishable from the thrown up oranges by the side of a nearby column.

The masked figures touched by the slime froze for a moment. Their elegantly flowing movements turned to twitches. Nimble limbs swayed and staggered like a master puppeteer had given the strings over to their grandchild. The three figures ambled forward like a toy boat pushing through a congregation of autumn leaves on a river's surface.

Another shooting star zipped above the heads of the people in the plaza. Those capable of semi-coherent thought acknowledged the event by raising a cheer. The blazing object stopped in place, lost its luminescence, and hovered out of view to those below. It made a sharp and distinct turn toward the plaza. Invisible to the human eye, the black structure landed atop a square-roofed building overlooking la Piazza. The side of the structure opened, creating a pure white sheet of light from which a broad silhouette stalked out. A faint sliver of starlight illuminated the figure's frame revealing hard, brown, rhomboid shapes like that of a snake running up and down its arms and body. The creature took two strides that easily covered twenty feet of roof and stopped in front of the stone railing.

The new arrival peered down to the torrent of people. Turning from the crowd, its attention fixated on a burly man sitting nearby, vomit staining the collar and belly of his near-bursting shirt. The man's back leaned against the stone railing.

He had an almost empty bottle of aqua vitae in one hand and in the other a long cane. Beside him, a woman in a state of half-undress, rested on the man's lap, face-first toward his pants. Both of them breathed the steady rhythm of sleep. The figure moved closer and touched the man's white, raven-like mask with its scaly fingers.

The snakeskin was swallowed beneath a black coat that hung loosely just beneath the shins. A neckpiece engulfed the figure's throat that reached all the way to the jawline where it became stark white, forming into a long-beaked bird mask with two deep black circles for eyes. Finally, a hood materialized over its forehead, draping dark eyes in shadow.

A light blue shimmering screen appeared on the figure's forearm, and a message decipherable only by the creature flashed:

Active camouflage synchronized.

The message disappeared, and more writing streamed down faster than any human eye could detect. The screen showed an internal summary of malfunctions, the biggest of which were local language synthesizer and biological agent scanner. The figure's head moved forward sharply as if uttering a curse, but no sound of frustration came out. The only noise up on that rooftop came from the snoring man and woman. Not being able to speak wasn't such a hindrance, but the mobile scanner was vital. The figure had made sure to scan the crowd below before venturing out, so it knew the parasites had embedded themselves into three street performers, dressed in black and white-striped matching suites.

Inputting the preset into its forearm screen, the location of the three infected was marked in the augmented reality the figure saw through its round eyes. The targets were on the move, and so was the figure. It leaped over to the nearest house and, without slowing down, continued to jog to the edge of the next. It jumped and jumped, again and again.

As the targets grew ever closer, the reality that the figure's visors showed changed to its mundane nature. Losing the last of the scanner's functionality made the figure lose balance just as it landed. Its near seven feet of bulk fell on the roof and slid until it reached a railing. The figure grabbed hold with one hand and vaulted its whole body over it. Now, it flew down toward the ground, coat flaps whipping from acceleration. Hitting down, the figure cracked the tiles beneath its feet and startled two men walking a few paces away. One of the men fell in a pile of garbage while the other stuck his back against the wall.

The figure dusted itself off, gave a courtesy nod to the fallen man, and ran headlong into the festive crowd.

Shoving past the revelers, the figure reached the first infected, grabbed him by the neck, and spun him toward its white mask. The figure used its free hand to slip a small, white cylinder into the infected's mouth. The figure threw its arms around the man in a wide embrace. A brief flash of white incinerated the infected's brainstem and all other soft tissue. The black garments partially shielded those around from the dangerous luminescence.

Those surrounding the street performer slowed their celebration and shifted their focus to the odd occurrence. Necks craned, and masks peeked from behind stylish fans. Moreover, the plague doctor didn't emit the pungent odor of lavender, nor did he carry the customary cane used to prod the dying from a safe distance. Such pointed interest from a plague doctor spelled disaster.

The Doctor released the infected pied jester, and he slumped to the ground like a sack of rotten fruit. A woman next to him screamed, and more witnesses soon joined her. The translator inside the figure's mask flashed the same word over and over.

Plague. Plague. Plague.

The disguised figure cut its way through the crowd without sparing a glance at the frenzied people or the corpse on the ground. A wave of panic swept through the revelers. Scanning the fleeing people, the figure caught a glimpse of another street performer seventy-eight feet away. The infected pushed a woman with an intricately decorated mask back toward the nearby columns. The Doctor tried to rush forward, but the mass of people thickened and pushed it back. The infected man cornered the woman near a column and raised his fingers to her mask. Using the magnification allowed by the suit, the Doctor caught sight of the tiny sharp tendrils extend from the infected's fingers and stab the eye-opening on the woman's mask. A moment later, she began to convulse.

The counterfeit doctor tilted its head and jumped into the air, cresting over the crowd and catching the nearby second floor's railing. The infected continued to execute his primary function. He didn't even notice the figure, which used the railing to perch then push itself toward him, landing directly on top. The Doctor slammed the infected into the ground, and with a single swift movement, shoved another cylinder through his mask and teeth until it met throaty resistance. The Doctor used one gloved hand to press the man's face into the cobbled stone and the other to muffle his cries. Another brighter flash followed. The infected's eyes became two columns of pure light, leaving black scorch marks after it faded.

The figure stood and examined the infected's victim. Two red streams trickled down her intricate mask from where the tendrils had exited the eyes.

Standing a good foot above the crowd, the Doctor searched

for the last street performer. A growing circle of people backing away drew its attention. Black and white stripes danced in jagged bursts across the atrocious shifting form that had once belonged to a man.

With not enough room to jump, the Doctor grabbed railing after railing, clutched columns and windowsills. The long way around to the street artist took far too many seconds. The infected performer clutched the shoulders of the slowest woman in the crowd, toppling both of them to the ground. The figure landed on the paved square.

Too many people blocked the way, so the Doctor grabbed at shoulders, tearing at pristine outfits until the mob parted. Like a rock falling into a lake, the fake doctor pushed through the staggering celebrants, who rippled away in waves. Just as the Doctor reached the struggling bodies on the ground, tendrils plugged into the hollow eyes of the woman's vermillion mask.

Opening its coat, the Doctor took a cylinder and drove it through the back of the infected's head. The flesh bloomed in red and orange, viscera hitting the white mask, sliding downward, leaving a pale, diseased trail. The woman beneath him still struggled, but that would soon come to an end.

The Doctor set its chest over the cylinder and bowed its head down. It wrapped its coat like the wings of a dark bird around the bodies. The explosion of light illuminated the square while the last of the revelers escaped.

The Doctor stood, bowing its head in mourning. When the required time passed, it climbed the buildings until it reached the ship. At the top, it took one last look at the ruined tower where the containment ship had fallen. Shaking its head, it stepped into the vessel.

With the passageway closed and sealed, the figure tapped on

a console and wrote a message:

Location secured. Specimen holding failed. Local life forms infected. Quarantine and purge completed. Requesting exfiltration permission.

A reply came a few seconds later:

Received. Retrieval team sent. Exfiltration permission granted for agent Emidius. Safe journey.

The figure, agent Emidius, grabbed the ship's controls and was in orbit 24.5 seconds later.

DAY -1

I-YAO

ONE

Dead drops were Lucy's favorite way of making money. Nice and simple; you go to the specified location, leave the package there, then get paid.

Her phone blinked in the dark, alerting her that she had reached the right place. The target building across the potholed street stood shrouded just beyond the dim street light. Thick iron bars weaved a protective mesh on all first-floor windows. The façade's plaster was the color of faded paper left in the rain and put into a forgotten folder at the back of a dusty shelf. Burn marks marred the windowsills on the upper floors where a fire had ravaged not only the inside but out as well. Lucy's eyes finished surveying, noting the rickety metal steps on the side of the building she could use if things went sideways on the job. Clicking her tongue, she circumnavigated a soiled mattress slumped over the curb and crossed the street.

No one else seemed to be around, but that just meant the look-outs knew what they were doing. Lucy exhaled sharply, picking up her pace, and trotted up to the lumbering man texting on his phone, missing every key while pretending not to notice her approach. He gave a glance to the pack she carried and gestured with a thumb to the door behind his back.

"Second floor, 2F," he said like there was something in his throat that he was trying to spit out.

Without a word, Lucy went through the door. She caught a glimpse of the ketchup stain above her right knee as she climbed the stairs. Her wardrobe for the night had been coordinated with the information that she was doing a dead drop. So, she wore her stained sweatpants and favorite hoodie. A hoodie that most adults possess—it's the one you like so much you can't get rid of, even if it makes you look a bit like a bum.

Up the stairs, she turned right and found another man lounging on a wall opposite a door marked '2F.' Stepping closer, Lucy raised both of her arms and widened her stance. The man pushed himself off the wall and diligently patted her down for any concealed weapons. She didn't have any. Not that this job was supposed to warrant them. The search finished, the man opened door 2F and beckoned her into a living room thick with cigarette and pot smoke. On her right stood a low, glass coffee table with handguns set on top of it. Near each gun sat a man—all three eyeing her. One rested on a couch that faced her directly, another on a chair so small its legs buckled beneath his considerable weight, and the final one, judging by his demeanor, was the one in charge. He sat on a lounge chair facing the front door. A hulking fourth man walked into the room from what appeared to be a kitchen area and gave Lucy a hungry once-over.

"Frank, frisk her," the man in charge said with a glowing joint resting on his smirking lips.

The six-foot-two mass of muscles nodded, giving Lucy a lusty stare. He came up behind her with a quick and agile step. She rolled her eyes, raised her arms, and spread her legs again.

Frank prodded her boots first, moving his hands along her calf and shins, then slowly, too slowly, ventured up her legs, his thumbs lingering on her inner thighs. Once his palms reached her butt, he squeezed, and Lucy bit her cheeks. Moving up, he checked her hips, belly, arms, and the brim of her jacket. The other men watched with triumphant smiles on their faces until the whole process was done. Frank stepped away and gave the man in charge a nod, who puffed a ring of smoke in return.

Lucy took this as a sign, unslung her backpack, and threw it to the man giving the orders. He caught it and began working the zipper.

"This one looks dangerous to me, Frank," the man said while digging into the bag. "That chest looks mighty suspicious. Have another look for me, will ya."

"You got it, Mike," Frank said, and Lucy saw his smile in her head even before he turned to face her. She gritted her teeth. Looking past him, she watched the smoke as it danced into the air and focused on its banality to calm her nerves before returning her attention to Frank.

About 4 inches taller than me, she judged now that he was close, *so that would mean just about clavicle level.*

Frank pushed her arms up again then put his hands on her hips. Lucy felt his breath brush her hair and cheeks. Dragging his palms, Frank put both hands on her breasts, squeezed once, and then smiling like a child in a candy store, continued up.

At least I'm getting good money to get felt up, she thought as her indignation swelled like a dead whale about to blow its guts across the beach.

Frank's middle fingers brushed the bottom of her neck. Lucy's hands snapped back, catching each of his thumbs in her firm grasp. *Hopefully, I don't get too much cash docked for teaching this asshole some manners.* She pushed the thumbs forward.

The man yelped, then began moaning. His posture wavered, and he almost dropped to one knee. Not satisfied, Lucy increased the pressure and kneed him in the groin. Frank grimaced and fell to his knees, hands up, prostrated before her. She pressed her lips together to keep from grinning.

The two other men snatched their handguns from the table and leveled them on Lucy. The leader, Mike, just stared at her with black eyes through the halo of smoke around his head. If she wasn't making a point, she could have broken Frank's fingers and ducked into the kitchen behind her before the others could chamber a round. However, she didn't know the layout of the rooms, so antagonizing these armed men was ill-advised. *Well, antagonizing them even more . . . .*

"No need to get antsy, boys. I just don't like to be fondled in such large company," she said with a humorless smile on her lips.

If these assholes get even a whiff of weakness, I'm out of a job, or worse.

"I'm not gonna do anything bad to Frankie here. I'm just showing him how not to treat a lady."

Lucy looked at Mike, who nodded to his men and went back to rummaging through the backpack. They left the guns on the table but stayed poised, leaning forward, ready to get up if commanded.

"Mike," Frank whimpered, looking like he was about to vomit, "she's going to break my fucking fingers!"

"That's your fault, my man, you underestimated her, and now you need protectin', which is what I fucking pay you for," Mike said, shaking his head in disappointment. "Now, what to do?"

His eyes remained fixed on Lucy while the tips of his outstretched fingers came together rhythmically. A police siren wailed from outside, and guns were pointed at Lucy again. Mike's fingers froze just as they were about to touch.

"That's not me. Police are bad for business. Mine and"—

Lucy tugged Frank's fingers, and he moved closer to Mike—
"yours." She tilted her head and gave him a pointed look just to
drive her argument home.

"Up and at 'em, boys, we're outta here." Mike stood up,
backpack in hand, and stepped off toward the kitchen behind
her. Lucy caught his eye as he passed; his empty stare froze like
black ice.

The other two stood and followed. Lucy looked down at
Frank and gave him a devious smile.

"Think before you act next time," she said, then broke both
of his thumbs.

Frank screamed, and Lucy left him. She dashed to the window
at the back of the living room that led to the fire escape and the
alley, but her heart sank when she noticed someone had glued
the latch shut. "Fucking paranoid thugs!"

Glancing around, her eyes landed on the stressed tiny chair.
It would do. She grabbed it and began hammering the latch,
hoping that it would give in time. Heavy footsteps of men
wearing bulky police gear stampeded down the hall just outside.

"Shit." She gave the chair one final strike with everything she
had.

The latch swung, and both the window and door flung open.

"Freeze!"

The window smashed into brick and shattered. A piece of
falling glass cut Lucy's arm beneath the shoulder as she climbed
out. She grabbed the railing and shot up the steps. One flight
up, she looked down and saw a broad figure burst out after her.
The person was wearing a black vest with white letters at the
back, which read: W.A.T. She didn't have to see the S to know
who he was.

"Hey, stop!" He emerged fully and spoke into a small mic

attached to his ear. "Suspect heading to the roof. In pursuit."

Lucy continued up, taking a few steps at a time. The fire escape swayed as more feet landed upon it. A metallic sound came from the alley below. Someone had released the emergency ladder, adding more vibrations to the groaning structure.

Just my fucking luck. The cops show up when I'm this *close to having enough cash. Keep it together and run.*

She made it to the top and found the north lip of the building, regaining her bearings. *The bike should be that way.*

The rooftops were dark and silent. Her speeding heart and the gravel beneath her feet were the only sounds in the night. Someone made it to the rooftop; flashlight beams bobbed around, searching for her. Lucy crouched down and shuffled over to a drainpipe at the edge. Sliding over in the darkness, she came close and inspected it. Rusty on top but sturdy. She judged it was about thirty feet down; her stomach tightened at the thought. Lucy looked up and surveyed the nearby buildings again. The nearest adjacent building stood no less than twenty feet away—definitely not jumping distance.

"Shit," she grumbled and took off her jacket.

Not giving herself more time to chicken out, she quickly tested the brace holding the top of the pipe to the wall and crested the edge. She looped her jacket just beneath the mount. Using it as a safety fasten, she descended. All her muscles tensed as she fought to stay close to the wall.

Lucy had only shimmied down a couple feet when something above her head snapped. Her whole body seized. And she fell. The next brace proved more resilient than the first, and Lucy slid down the rest of the way. She slammed into the wall. Her forearms and elbows hit first. Then her chest and stomach. Air rushed out of her lungs, but she managed to hold in a cry of pain. Tears made her vision blurry, but after a few blinks, she looked down. She was halfway there.

A shout came from the rooftop above. "Stop!"

Something dangled over the edge. A sub-machine gun trained on her form. Returning her gaze down, she continued her earthward waddle.

Either they shoot me, and I get down, or I get down, and they shoot me, but I am getting down!

Resolved, Lucy pushed herself forward and hugged the pipe. A burst of bullets came from above, one ricocheting off the metal mere inches from her face.

"Fuck this."

She put her forearms, biceps, and hands over the jacket and let gravity do the work for her. Someone else made it to the edge above; he yelled something, but Lucy didn't understand the words. Her feet hit the ground like meteors plummeting to earth. For a moment, she forgot how to walk, but her legs remembered. Jacket still held tight in her hand, she swayed in the direction that led out—out of the darkness.

Reaching the edge of the alleyway, she peeked outside. Nothing was familiar. *Wrong street.* She turned on her heel and ran back to the drainpipe.

Dashing past it, she left the alleyway a few moments later. This street she knew. It wasn't far now. As she crossed to the other side, she noticed spinning lights in her periphery, blue then red, and they were getting closer. Ducking inside another alley, she put her back against the wall and waited. The red and blue light stopped a few feet away, and police stepped out of the cruiser. Lucy hastily tied her jacket over her lower hips and stalked deeper into the darkness, away from the flashing lights.

Once she was on the other side of the alley, she walked out

onto the street, forcing her breath to steady, trying to look as normal as possible. The dumpster she needed was just beyond the crosswalk on her left. Running over to the other side, she found a pile of papers that breathed. And stank. Covering her nose, she kicked the pile's boots. It stirred and moaned.

"Stars' fallin' from the sky, Lucy. It's bad news, I tell ya. Boom, Boom." The pile shuddered.

He must have heard the shots . . . or is he just rambling again? In too much pain to care, she sucked air in through her teeth. "Where's my bike, Bernard?"

The pile raised a hand.

"S'over there, Lucy, jus' like I promised." Bernard gestured imperiously.

Lucy stepped back and dug through the trash, moving an old coat, several bottles of wine, a large brown TV box, and a few newspapers. Finally, at the bottom was her bike. Nothing special in design, just a standard twenty-one gear mechanism at the back, curved down handles on the front, with thin wheels for speed on concrete. The body's deep red color got lost in the darkness, and that was just what Lucy needed now. She picked it up and moved it into the light of the streetlamp. Nothing appeared damaged, and the gear mechanism spun with ease. She let the bike lean on a nearby wall and returned to the talking garbage pile.

"Good job, Bernard." She knelt, reaching into her pocket and pulling out two banknotes. "Here's a bit extra for the hard work."

A grimy hand appeared and took the notes, rubbing them between index finger and thumb. Satisfied, the hand vanished under the pile. Lucy smiled and shook her head. She never knew if Bernard was really drunk or just using intoxication as camouflage.

On her bike, Lucy wheeled down the street and merged into traffic. Upper right arm pulsing with pain from the cut, elbows buckling each time she had to make a turn, stomach still aching from the hit, she smiled and picked up speed. Today she'd gotten away from the police, and tomorrow she'd get paid.

I think I need to discuss an increase in my hazard pay.

In the morning, she'd hurt all over, but for now, she was victorious and off the clock.

* * *

Lucy sped through the night streets, a wave of green lights urging her on and allowing her to keep a quick pace. When she neared her apartment building, she debated whether to go into Mr. Wilson's store and grab some booze, but it was nearly midnight. She could spend her night cleaning the dredges from a few older bottles. Looking down at herself and seeing all the blood and bruises, Lucy thought it might be for the best.

She turned to face her apartment building.

The midnight darkness gave the bricks a sickly, diseased glow. The windows, now all dark, looked like wounds, their panes weathered and decaying. The six-story stood like a shambling specter, a pale shadow of its origins, desperate to avoid its inevitable, terminal end. Lucy blinked once to chase away the terrible vision.

Crossing the street, she reached a stairwell which she climbed to the front door. To go in, she had to lift her bike vertically in front of her and squeeze through. She took a right turn on the second floor, walked down the hallway, and opened the door marked '231.' Complete darkness greeted her from the other side. Lucy plunged her left hand in and clicked the light switch.

Nothing.

"Greeeeeat." She rolled her eyes.

She clicked the switch a few more times to make sure it was really dead. The light stubbornly stayed off. The darkness coming out of the room devoured the pathetic amount of light the hallway provided. The doorway seemed like an underground passage an archeologist might find fascinating, not a door to someone's home. Lucy left the bike on the wall next to the door. Entering the portal of darkness, she reached for the phone in her pants pocket. Desperately, she decided to give the switch a final chance to disperse the darkness. She clicked it on again. Light bathed the apartment. Her head dipped low with relief as most times when something got broken in the building, it stayed broken. She made a mental note to search on the Internet for how to fix a broken light switch. If she couldn't manage, then she'd ask Mr. Wilson for help.

That'd make him positively giddy, she thought as she gathered her things from the hallway.

Leaving her keys on the small kitchen counter, she went into the bathroom. Fatigued brown eyes looked back at her through the mirror. Dark circles underneath made her look like she hadn't slept in days, and her usual warm caramel skin appeared gray in the light of the feeble bulb. The pain in her arm made her frown, small dimples forming beneath her high cheekbones. She turned the faucet on and splashed some water on her face and neck. The coolness refreshed her.

With the pleasantries out of the way, Lucy began the work in earnest. She scrubbed the skin beneath her cut using a bit of soap until the blood flakes washed down the drain. Once the skin was clean and fresh blood was oozing down her arm, Lucy opened the stand above the sink and got some disinfectant out. Spilling copious amount of it on the wound, she winced, breathing heavily. Stars appeared behind her eyelids as her jaw muscles contorted. *That's enough of that.* She bound the wound with gauze, tightening it around the arm with the help of her teeth. When the last of the red liquid had swirled away down the drain, she walked out.

Getting her leftover vodka from the fridge, she took one step out of the kitchen and found herself in her living room. Right next to her stood an ancient couch that she inherited with the apartment. According to legend, it came straight from her landlord and could be unfolded to accommodate guests, granted those who dared sleep on it could brave the very real possibility of tetanus. Leaving the glass on the table, Lucy crashed down on the lumpy couch cushions and leaned back. She relaxed her muscles as she tried to decide what food to order. Something at the bottom of her vision caught her attention. Tilting her head down, she focused her eyes. Directly across the couch, leaning on the wall between the bathroom and bedroom, stood a TV stand sans the TV, which the previous tenants may or may not have stolen. Her landlord wasn't clear on the matter. What caught her attention was the blinking red light on the old answering machine that came along with the couch and the vacant stand. The machine blinked in a nervous rhythm. Messages were waiting to be heard.

Lucy leaned forward, got her phone out of her pants, and dialed a nearby twenty-four-hour Chinese restaurant. When someone picked up, she ordered her favorite, a number thirty-three, from the dinner menu. After the conversation was over, she locked her phone, crossed her arms on her thighs, and stared at the blinking light.

The only person who'd leave a message is Valentina, and ten times out of ten, it isn't anything good.

Lucy left her cellphone on the table and walked over to the stand, picked up both landline phone and answering machine, and walked back to sit down on the couch.

"You have one new message," a female voice spoke from the antique speakers on the answering machine.

Lucy pressed play.

"Hey Lucy, it's Val. When you get home from work, you really need to give me a call. I'll stay over until at least ten . . . bye."

The hesitation before the end of the message gave Lucy pause.

Sighing at the thought of another painful task, she speed-dialed her mother's house.

"Hi, Val, it's me." She leaned her cheek on her hand.

"Hi, Lu. I'm sorry for making you call this late, but it can't wait."

Lucy tensed, her face and lips slacked down into a frown. Before Valentina could continue, another voice cut her off.

"Is that Lucy? Ooh, can I talk to her?"

The line went quiet for a moment after the sudden outburst.

"Lucy, is that you?"

Lucy sighed, hearing the new voice, a load falling off her chest.

"Yeah, it's me, mom. How are you doing?"

"Oh, dear, it's wonderful here. The weather is all nice and warm. All the humidity was killing my poor legs. But today, it's nice, warm and dry."

Her mother sounded happy, and Lucy pictured her in a colorful sundress with a big beige hat. The thought made her smile.

"Did you and Val go somewhere? You know you're not supposed to go far from the house alone."

"Of course I was with Val, dear. It's no fun to go anywhere without company." Her mother's tone was instructive, like the one she used when Lucy was younger.

"Great, that's great, mom. So what did you do?"

"Oh my, it was wonderful. We went on the bus, had ice cream, and went to the hospital. There we didn't have to wait at all, we just went straight to a room, and a very handsome doctor asked me a few questions, and then he did the strangest thing."

Lucy's eyebrows furrowed. "Really, and what was that?"

"Well, he took out this funny-looking little hammer and started hitting my legs and arms. Then he smiled and said he needed to do more tests."

"That's great, mom." Lucy squeezed her eyes shut and pulled at her face. "I'm glad you enjoyed a day out."

"The best thing about the doctor was," her mother continued, "that he had eyes like your father, dear. Clear as the sky, very beautiful."

"Mom, dad's eyes were brown, just like mine," Lucy said, her lips forming a small, sad smile.

"Oh, yes . . . well, they were beautiful nonetheless—"

"Okay, okay, Linda," Valentina's voice cut off her mother, "let me speak to your girl a bit. It's already late there, and Lucy has work in the morning."

Linda complied with reluctance in her voice, "Okay. Goodbye, dear, and don't talk to strangers."

"Bye, mom. Don't worry, I won't." The phone passed hands, and Lucy's words were lost as she said, "I love you."

"Linda, I'm gonna go in the kitchen to talk to Lucy a bit." Valentina's voice came muffled like she had her palm over the speaker. "You watch the show and tell me what happens, okay?"

Lucy heard her mother agree or say something similar to an

agreement. Reclining on the couch, Lucy waited for Valentina to reach the kitchen.

"So, as you heard, we were at the doctor. And um, I don't—I don't know how to say this."

"Just tell me what happened, Val. It's okay," Lucy encouraged. Valentina took a breath.

"Well, your mother had her yearly exams, and after getting the results back, her doctor had a suspicion she might be getting worse, so he recommended a specialist we could go to. We went there today," Valentina paused.

"He told me that the disease is getting more aggressive, that he'd need to change Linda's medication," her voice cracked. "I'm sorry, Lu, I know money is tight for you. The medication he recommended costs twice as much as the one she's on now."

Lucy imagined the tears well up in Valentina's eyes.

"It's alright, Val," she said softly, "I'm gonna figure it out. I'll go to the bank and change the amount on the monthly checks. You guys just stay safe, okay."

Silence gripped the conversation now as neither one knew how to continue. Lucy didn't want to end their talk this way, so she spoke first. "Thanks for taking the time out of a workday to take her to the hospital. I really appreciate it."

"Nonsense, just coming before and after work isn't close to enough, but it's all I can manage . . . ." Valentina's voice became quiet.

"Most people wouldn't do half as much. I want you to know your help is invaluable to my mom and me, okay. Never forget that."

Another pause in the conversation followed.

"Can I ask a favor, though?" Lucy closed her eyes and massaged her temples. "Could you please call the doctor tomorrow and ask him to send me an email with information about the new meds?"

"Sure thing, Lu."

With as much cheer as she could muster, Lucy said her goodbyes and listened to the tone. After a while, she closed the line on her side as well. Leaving the phone on the ground, she swiped the bottle of vodka and made her way to the kitchen. On the counter she found a book titled 'Advanced Biology' and on top of it lay a piece of paper. The first line read 'Admissions Application.' She gazed at its letters, eyes unfocused. After a few seconds, she crumpled the document, still looking at nothing. When the paper stopped collapsing in on itself, Lucy threw it at the trash can next to the TV stand. She tilted the bottle up, but a knock on the door stopped her.

She opened the door to a small, middle-aged man. "Good evening. Your total is 14.99." He handed her the plastic bag.

Lucy searched her pockets. Finding three five-dollar bills, she gave them to the man and snatched the bag. "Keep the change."

A head shorter than her, the man glared upward. "How generous," he said in a flat tone with a practiced, fake smile.

Lucy watched him pocket the money and closed the door. She sat down on the couch and ate her food mechanically. After finishing her meal, she reached for the bottle, opened it, and drank until she no longer could.

DAY 0

TWO

Lucy lurched forward, and the bottle resting on her lap fell to the ground. The thud of the thick glass hitting wood snapped her fully awake. She'd had a nightmare in which the sky was falling. Its vastness washed over her, stars pelting her face, painful as bee stings. Then she woke. Rubbing her eyes, she shook off the feeling of dread. Her gaze rested on a spot of decaying wallpaper along the ceiling. Water had made its way down from the floors above, leaving its sickly, yellow mark. Lucy grabbed the phone off the table and checked the time. Her gut sank. 7:23 AM.

"Shit."

Salvaging whatever she had in her fridge into a makeshift breakfast, she quickly ate, then threw her clothes into a hamper that sat next to the bathroom door. Yesterday's bloodstained sweater and pants spilled over the brim. She'd have to get those washed very soon, and that meant she'd have to go to the laundromat.

Problem for tomorrow, not today, she thought as she stepped into the bathroom.

Flipping the light switch on, she searched the medicine cabinet for a hair tie. Her hair wasn't long; it reached just below the midpoint of her neck, but she didn't have time to wash and dry it this morning, so her solution was a quick bun. Putting her hair up, she pushed the mirror back and took a lingering look at her body. She poked at the bruises painting her breasts and ribs. The blue spots looked like someone had thrown balls of paint at her defined ab muscles. Curious, she edged back to get more of her in the mirror, then sucked in her stomach. The spots moved, and her eyes bulged from the discomfort. In the reflection, she noticed a dark welt that had managed to escape the previous night's inspection.

Just great.

She let out a deep sigh and twisted her upper body. Stopping mid-motion, she placed her palms on the healthy parts of her hips.

No. I'm not doing that.

The mirror showed her walking out of sight, while usually, she lamented the loss of voluptuousness around her backside from all the bike riding. Today she had won over body negativity, her powerful thighs taking her out of the visor of the judgemental reflective surface.

After a quick shower, she put on clean clothes. Taking a deep breath, she let the remaining stress of the night before fly away then went back to the living room. Picking up her phone, she dialed her boss over at the *Cher Ami* courier service. The line rang several times, but no one picked up, so Lucy left a message.

"Hey Boss, I need work pretty bad. My shift at the shop ends at noon. Call me back, or I can swing by the office, whatever works. Bye."

Lucy grabbed her keys, opened the door, and reached for the light switch. She thought about leaving the light on just in case but immediately thought of her electric bill. The bulb over her head went out, then she closed the door and locked it.

Lucy checked her clock. It said 7:57 AM. She ran to the

stairwell, sat on the railing, and slid down.

"Good morning, Mrs. S!" Lucy said as she sped toward an old lady, hidden behind an armful of paper grocery bags.

Mrs. Smith almost tripped and fell but regained her balance at the last moment. "Good morning Lucy, aren't you late for work?"

"Yes, very," Lucy answered while jumping from the railing to make the turn downstairs.

Pushing the door open, she got to the street in a few strides. While she waited for an opportune moment to cross, she rechecked her phone. 7:59 AM.

"Might just make it in time."

The cars in the closest lane stopped moving. She dashed past them. The other lane's cars were packed so close together that Lucy had to slide over the hood of one, the man inside bellowing at her. With a final nimble jump, she was inside the store.

Mr. Wilson leaned in front of the counter, watching the wall-mounted TV. "What's the time?" he asked without looking away.

"7:59—oops, it's eight o'clock now," Lucy said, glancing at the screen of her phone.

"Almost had you this time, eh?" Mr. Wilson continued to focus on the TV.

Lucy would bet a sizable sum that he had a smirk beneath his mustache. When he finally lifted his head to look at her, his gaze lingered on her bandaged arm, concern knitting his brow. He shifted his eyes back to the TV without comment.

"Better luck next time." She smiled and followed his eyes to the television.

A well-dressed young woman sat primly behind a scrolling news ticker. "Now joining us live is Dr. Shields from the department of astronomy and astrophysics of Roan University."

The camera panned right.

"Thank you for having me," Dr. Shields replied, flashing a warm smile at the newscaster. He wore a plaid jacket with a blue sweater underneath and horn-rimmed glasses, completing the stereotypical college professor look.

"Now, doctor, did anyone expect these meteors last night, or were they a freak occurrence?"

Meteors? Bernard said the stars were falling. Is that what he meant?

"Well, in most cases, if an object is on a collision or near-collision course with Earth, it is followed with great interest by the astronomical community. However, due to the sheer amount of objects floating up there"—the doctor's right index finger pointed up to the ceiling—"some may slip by unnoticed, as was the case this time."

Lucy turned her head to ask if Mr. Wilson had witnessed the occurrence but saw how concentrated he was, so she kept quiet.

"No one knew these exact meteors were coming our way?" The newscaster shifted back, her hands resting on top of the giant glass table in front of her.

"No. Unfortunately, these particular objects weren't monitored. They were obstructed by other bodies, such as planets or larger celestial formations," Dr. Shields explained. "It's quite fascinating, actually." His face lit up, and he leaned into the table.

"In what way?" The newscaster crossed her fingers.

"Well, first, the objects had to have been traveling toward something else instead of Earth. The orbit of our planet around the sun is the only reason the objects even came this way. What's fascinating is how they avoided being pulled off course by any other celestial body in the system and wound up here."

"I'm sure the viewers want to know . . ." The newscaster waved her hand at the camera and continued in a gravely dramatic tone, "is there any danger to us or to the planet?"

A small smile rose on the man's lips. "Right now, NASA and other agencies around the globe are tracking several large objects, which could potentially cause an extinction-level event," Dr. Shields paused, still holding his smile. "But none of them are on a collision course with the planet."

Pleased with himself, he leaned back into his chair as the newscaster turned to face the camera. "I hope you're right, doctor. When we come back . . ."

"Whew." Lucy sighed and dragged the back of her hand across her forehead in an exaggerated gesture.

Mr. Wilson, too engrossed in the broadcast, gave no reaction, so she shrugged and went to the back of the store to get her work clothes. She grabbed her trolley and rolled it through a steel door and into the alley. The building was Mr. Wilson's home; he just used the first floor as a convenience store. So the "loading dock," as he liked to call it, was a filthy back alley with barely enough room to fit a truck going in reverse. Lucy shielded her eyes from the brightness of the world that made her head spin. She spotted the supplier backing up toward her. Pushing her trolley onto the street, she stood and waited at her usual spot. The truck stopped, and the driver's side door opened. The edge of the door bonked against the building wall as a man slid out. He turned sideways and walked like a crab to reach her.

"Morning, Lucy," he said after making it out, a bright smile on his face.

"Good morning, John," Lucy tried to match his cheerfulness.

John was a head taller than her and wore faded blue jeans and a shirt with sleeves. The sleeves made her eyebrow twitch. It was the first time she hadn't seen him in his usual sleeveless denim jacket. With that much skin covered up, he looked like a tanned businessman instead of the day laborer she knew and expected.

A small platform lowered until it was level, followed by the lift. Lucy pushed her trolley onto it. John pressed another button, and the lift began to ascend. He grabbed a handle by the side and leaped in next to her with a swift, agile motion.

John began loading. "Did you see the light show yesterday?"

"You mean those meteors?" She narrowed her eyes.

"Yeah." John nodded, then, with a sharp exhale, got a box from the floor and left it on the trolley.

"No, I was working in the city, but even if I was home, the view from my apartment is . . ." Lucy paused to search for a proper word to describe non-existent. "Limited."

"Hmm, too bad, it was exciting. Maybe you can catch it on the net, seeing as how you don't like TV."

'Can't waste money for' is closer to the truth, she thought but did not correct him.

John finished loading and pressed the button that lowered the lift. Halfway down, he proffered the clipboard Lucy needed to sign. She grabbed it, left her signature, and it was back in his hands before they reached the ground.

"Well, you'll have another chance to get an eyeful. There's supposed to be a new one in a few days." He gave her another bright smile that wrinkled the tanned skin around his eyes.

Lucy frowned. *Damn peppy morning people.*

"What do you mean?"

"Well, something else's traveling toward Earth. People say it'll end the world."

"Bullshit." Lucy raised a skeptical eyebrow. "I just heard an astrophysicist say the exact opposite on TV." She pointed with her thumb over her shoulder.

"Don't know about that." John shrugged. "It's what I read on the Internet, and you can't put too much stock in that most times." His eyes went wide to signify that Lucy should be careful online.

Having grown up on the Internet, John's comment made her lips form a straight, taught line.

"Whatever's going on, I plan to watch the skies myself, so we'll just see." John put the clipboard to his forehead and made a curt goodbye gesture.

She nodded and pushed the trolley up the ramp and into the dark storeroom, leaving it in the corner. After unloading, she brought a box of apples back to the storefront and began stocking the fruit stand. Clients steadily poured in. Soon enough, the store was filled with the light buzz of human presence. She didn't look up from her work until an old and squat lady waddled in.

"Good morning, Mrs. Anselmi," she heard her boss call from the front.

The old woman returned the greeting and started to "browse" the store's inventory, even though she always bought almost the same items every day. People might wonder why a woman would go to the store every single day to buy the same things when she could buy in bulk, but for Mrs. Anselmi, going to the store was something much more than shopping. For her, it was a social function. The old lady walked the aisles searching for items while every other customer in the store mysteriously finished their business and left. When Mrs. Anselmi couldn't find herself a target, she made her way to Lucy. "Good morning, dear. You look a little rough around the edges. You sleep alright?"

"Just over-exhaustion, nothing to worry about." Lucy gave the woman a weak smile.

"You be careful girl, you may be young and strong, but you ain't invincible. You gotta take care of yourself." She waved a wrinkled finger in front of Lucy's face then paused.

Here it comes . . . Lucy tried to keep her laugh contained.

"Or you should find someone to take care of you," Mrs. Anselmi added with a mischievous wink.

"Thanks for the advice, but I'm still looking for Mister Right." Lucy batted her eyelashes, doing her best impression of a stereotypical movie princess.

"I mean," the old woman continued as if Lucy hadn't said a word. "You're too pretty to be working all hours. Just find a nice boy with a steady job, and you're set."

Proud of the indispensable advice she'd just given, Mrs. Anselmi winked once more. "Now be a dear and give me the usual."

The usual being an apple, an orange, and two lemons. Lucy made a point of not doing this for customers, but Mrs. Anselmi's height only allowed her to reach the fruit at the bottom of the stand. Not to mention, the electronic scales were something beyond the old lady. While Lucy weighed the produce and put it in a bag, the woman prattled on about her neighbors' cat, which Lucy mostly tuned out, but by sheer instinct, knew when to nod and make intelligible sounds as if she were listening. When the work was done, she handed the bag over. Mrs. Anselmi thanked her and made her signature waddle toward the counter in search of new frontiers of conversation.

Before the shop owner had a chance to acknowledge her return, the old lady continued, "Is your home okay? Did it get hit by any of the meteors from last night?"

"I'm happy to report no damage to the house or my person, ma'am."

"Hmm, that's good to hear. Yours is the best store in a sixteen-block radius. If anything happened to it, it would've been such a loss . . ." Mrs. Anselmi veered off, "to the community of course."

Mr. Wilson waited a moment to see if the speech had ended. Lucy moved away from the stand to get a better view.

"Thank you for the kind words. But you know, the people on the news said that all the meteors burned out inside the atmosphere."

The old lady made a dismissive sound with her mouth and waved her hand.

"You can't believe everything you hear on the news, especially on the channel you're watching." Mrs. Anselmi turned her head to the television, grimaced, and made a face that suggested she might spit at any moment.

Lucy kept watching. Mrs. Anselmi caught her gaze, and her face went flaccid a moment later.

"I'll keep that in mind," Mr. Wilson said after the old lady turned toward him once more.

She passed him the produce and other items, and he began scanning. Handing her the bag, he chimed, "Good day!"

Mrs. Anselmi turned around, but instead of going toward the exit, she waddled back to Lucy. The old lady grabbed her right arm just above the elbow and squeezed.

"You be careful out there. I have a bad feeling about these falling rocks." The woman's eyes locked with Lucy's, and deep within them, there was the unmistakable glint of terror.

"I will." She patted the woman's hand.

Mrs. Anselmi nodded with satisfaction, walked to the door, and opening it, disappeared into the light.

Lucy returned to her work only to see the stand nearly empty once more. With a sigh, she went to the back for a resupply.

From the backroom, she heard someone in high heels walk through the door.

Who wears heels this early in the morning? She peeked around the corner.

A short woman with a stylish black and white dress spotted Lucy immediately and blew her an air kiss, accompanied by a wink.

The woman strolled past the counter and gave the man behind it a smile that could instantly land her a movie role. "Good morning, Mr. Wilson. May I talk to Lucy for a second?"

"If you don't disrupt business or get in her way, yes you may, young lady." Mr. Wilson said with his stern fatherly voice.

The woman turned on her toes and strutted toward Lucy with the rhythmic *clack-clack-clack* of her heels. Lucy deposited another box of apples in front of the stand and waited.

"Hi there, Sarah," she said with all the cheer she could muster. Her head had almost stopped pounding.

"Mornin, Lu!" Sarah smiled and gave her friend a tight hug.

She was so short that even in heels, her head only reached up to Lucy's chest.

"Make yourself comfortable," she said to Sarah and dragged the box of apples to the front.

Sarah looked around to see if there was anything she could use as a chair. She saw an empty stand next to Lucy, used on Saturdays and Sundays when they had more clientele. Lucy referred to them as stands out of work ethic, while in fact, they were just tables covered by a cloth. Sarah gave the stand a critical look, and upon finding nothing that could stick to her immaculate dress, she turned around, raised her butt, and plopped on top like a toddler.

"So, what brings you here so early in the morning?" Lucy

asked after she arranged all the apples in place.

"I'm meeting Damien in a bit for brunch," Sarah said while her dangling legs swung back and forth.

"Ooh, Damien." Lucy's eyebrows rose. "This one's lasted pretty long. Don't tell me you like-like him?"

"Oh, I liked-liked him so much last night you wouldn't believe it!" Sarah fired back, not about to be outdone. "And speaking of sexual encounters . . ."

Lucy shot a sharp look to Sarah, who snapped her mouth shut. "This is a family-friendly store. Keep it civil, or else Mr. Wilson will revoke your lounging privileges."

"No worries, message received." Sarah's hand rose up, and she waved.

Lucy turned around to find a young boy standing at the end of an aisle. The boy's mother held a box of cereal in one hand and his wrist in the other. The woman was engrossed in reading while her son was engrossed in Sarah. She smiled at the boy, and he put one foot out toward them. His mother tugged him away, and they disappeared down the next aisle.

"I can be family-friendly. Did you see that?" She turned her head to Lucy and smiled devilishly.

Lucy didn't comment.

"Sooo, what I was trying to say before I was rudely interrupted . . ." Sarah tilted her head and arched her eyebrows.

Lucy rolled her eyes.

". . . I think I found a nice, shiny, potential, new boyfriend for you!" Sarah's lips curled into a smug smile.

Lucy could almost feel an exclamation mark fly at her face from the amount of energy her friend exuded while talking.

"Can you skip a study session, so I can arrange a date?"

"Studies are on hold for now." Lucy's voice dipped low as she reached for an apple.

Gripping the fruit too tightly, her fingers cut through the rind, and the apple exploded in her hand, the inside oozing brown and rotten. She threw the apple in the discard bin behind the stand and went to wipe her hands on her apron. Sarah coughed and handed her a tissue.

"Thanks," she said and wiped the remains off her forearm.

"I can help, Lu. My family can help." Sarah's eyebrows softened, and her eyes glistened.

"I don't need help, Sarah." Lucy's tone was flat.

"No, you don't *want* it."

I don't want to argue either, she felt like saying but continued cleaning up in silence instead.

"You gonna tell me what's up?" Sarah pressed after a few awkward moments.

Her voice was soft and caring. People rarely talked to Lucy like that.

"It's my mom. Her meds aren't working, so she needs something more expensive." Lucy bit the inside of her cheek and stared at the pyramid of apples she'd stacked.

"I may have to go back to that shithole town and work full time there so I can take care of her." Lucy's fingers balled into a fist, nails digging into the skin of her palm.

Sarah got off the stand and hugged Lucy tight.

"Be careful," Lucy's voice cracked, "you're gonna mess up your dress."

"Fuck the dress," Sarah said, not letting go.

Lucy hugged her back until a blond woman walked into the store.

She pushed herself away from Sarah. "Take a seat. I'm gonna be busy for a bit."

Her friend nodded and sat down on the counter. The blond woman wore grey yoga pants and a red sports top with a matching grey jacket. Her hair was tied back in a ponytail, and a handbag dangled from her left elbow. "Good morning, Lucy," she said.

"Mornin', Mrs. Rayburn. The usual?" Lucy automatically went to her position at the back of the stand.

"No, not today." Mrs. Rayburn picked up an apple and inspected it. "The gym I go to is very exclusive. It has a separate kitchen area where you can cook if you like, or make shakes and such."

At the edge of her vision, Lucy saw Sarah roll her eyes.

"But the problem is that the fruit and vegetables they provide are . . ." Mrs. Rayburn paused to find the right word. Behind her, Sarah mouthed the word 'shit.'

Lucy stifled a laugh, and Mrs. Rayburn turned her head to Sarah, who was now admiring her nail polish and swinging her feet.

". . . unsatisfactory," the woman finished.

Lucy shot an angry glance at Sarah, who smiled, then pantomimed zipping her lips shut. Mrs. Rayburn pointed to the fruit she wanted, and Lucy bagged them. "Anything else?"

"No, I think that's all. Thank you."

"Oh, I almost forgot," Mrs. Rayburn said as Lucy handed the bag over. "Did you remember to do what I asked? The party is tomorrow, and I want to try those fruit recipes."

Lucy nodded. "I talked to the delivery man this morning, and he assured me that only the best products will be delivered tomorrow morning. You can pick them up whenever you like after 8:30."

"Thank you so much. I'll see you tomorrow." Mrs. Rayburn

smiled, turned around, and walked to the counter.

"Look at you, miss accommodating!" Sarah smirked and laid her hand over her heart.

"Well, she doesn't want her son's birthday party to have processed sweets. She found some recipes online, and now she's making desserts exclusively out of fruit." Lucy shrugged and came back around to the front of her stand. "So, she wanted me to ask the delivery man for—"

Sarah raised her right hand to stop her.

"Only the best products. Right?" Sarah bobbed her head up and down.

"Right," Lucy answered and looked around to make sure the topic of discussion had left the store.

"So did you?"

"Did I what?"

"Did you ask the man for the best products?"

Lucy shook her head. "Of course not."

Sarah tried her best to put on a sad face, but the soft grunts escaping her nostrils wouldn't allow it. "Why not?"

"Because there is no such thing as the best products. I've been to the farm, and I've seen the sorting process. Everything that isn't up to the shipping standard doesn't leave the property," she paused to catch her breath. "Essentially, everyone gets the best products, and if Mrs. Rayburn wants to believe hers are better, I'm not gonna waste my time convincing her otherwise."

Sarah burst out laughing.

"Okay, okay, quiet." Lucy looked over her shoulder. "Mr. Wilson will throw us out."

Sarah brushed her eyes and checked the time on her phone. "So on to business then. Damien has a friend who he—"

Lucy arched her eyebrow and stared her down.

"Damien *and I*," Sarah corrected, "think he would be a pleasant dinner partner for you."

Lucy sighed and crossed her arms, fingers tapping her bicep in a wave-like rhythm.

"Come on, Lu. We're going to this restaurant opening tonight. If you're not working, you can come with us." Sarah took both of Lucy's hands in hers. "You deserve a night off." Swinging her arms, Sarah's eyes opened as much as possible and actually glistened.

Command performance. Lucy marveled at the onslaught of cuteness her friend could manage.

"I can't skip work now, sorry. The answer is no." Her tone was unequivocal.

Sarah's face went sullen; she pouted and raised her downcast eyes to meet Lucy's. Defiance sparkled in her gaze. This wasn't over, and she would try again. Lucy wasn't sure when Sarah would strike, but she did not have the luxury of a night out right now.

"Well"—Sarah pushed out her chin and hopped off the table—"since you're so busy, I guess I'll leave you to it."

"Yeah," Lucy's voice came out half-whispered, "bye."

Sarah gritted her teeth and spun in place so fast her hair flew in a flurry, settling in front of her shoulder. The sound of her heels seemed louder on her way out, and Lucy watched the closed door for a few seconds until a new customer arrived. Even though their meeting ended on a sour note, Lucy still felt refreshed after seeing Sarah, who always seemed to make a bad hangover a little better.

After 10 AM, the shift died down, and two hours later, Lucy went to the back room and changed into her street clothes. She walked back into the store and grabbed a few things to keep her fridge at home a comfortable degree of bare. Upon Lucy laying her groceries out on the counter, Mr. Wilson set a piercing gaze on her. "No liquid courage today?"

Heat crept across her cheeks, and she dropped her eyes to her feet. "Nope, none today."

"Good, very good." Mr. Wilson sounded pleased, or at least not overly disappointed.

"I wanted to ask you something."

"Mmm?" His shoulders squared on Lucy.

"I've got this problem with the light or with the switch. I'm not sure—"

"We can go check it out right now." He reached behind to the ties of his apron. "I'll close up for fifteen minutes while we figure it out."

Lucy's stomach dropped, and she waved the bags in her hand. "You're working right now. I don't want you to close the store because of me!"

"That's one of the perks of being your own boss." He winked at her. "You can do whatever the hell you want."

"I don't want to be a bother," Lucy said, sliding back. "I'll let you know if I need help."

Before Mr. Wilson could say anything more, Lucy was halfway out the door with the words, "Thanks. Bye."

It was warm and pleasant outside. Lucy could feel the salty breeze on her neck and arms. She crossed the street and stopped at the bottom of the stairs leading into her apartment building. Taking her phone out of her pocket, she saw that it was 12:05 PM. Her other boss still hadn't called, so she decided to wait another minute to see if he would. Her eyes bore into the turned-off screen. The roar of a large car engine made her fingers lose their grip, and her phone tumbled down. Good thing she had a sturdy screen protector because a fall from that height meant a new phone, and she wasn't the least bit inclined for such expenditures right now.

Glancing away from her, thankfully, intact phone, she saw the source of the commotion. It was her asshole neighbor and his asshole friends. Four of them were inside an old, recently-restored Mustang. Catching her gaze, the man behind the steering wheel gave her a confident smile and revved the engine once more. The sound assaulted her ears. Wincing, she tilted her head back and frowned. Her neighbor seemed to enjoy her reaction, so he continued his offensive auditory attack until people shouted from nearby windows. The other three men inside the car cheered as if that were a big achievement. The man pursed his lips, simulating a kiss. Lucy's upper lip quivered, but she wasn't in the mood to pick a fight; she flipped him off and went up the stairs.

Her boss still hadn't called even after she came inside and sat down on her couch. Dialing his number, she waited for a few rings before he picked up.

"Yeah!" He sounded angry.

"Hey Boss, did you get my message?"

"Yep," his tone was flat, "but we better discuss this face to face. I have to drill some work ethics into your colleagues, so come by in an hour." He hung up without waiting for her reply.

Lucy exhaled loudly and turned on her whirring laptop to check her email.

First, she saw the usual spam about winning the lottery, royalty beseeching her to help them with their inheritances, and the everpresent penis enlargement ads. Scrolling down, she found the email she was looking for from a physician named Dr. Boden, apparently. The email mostly repeated what Valentina had said last night. Her mother's condition was deteriorating fast, and more aggressive treatment was suggested. The doctor stated that if the family wanted, they could still use the old treatment plan.

Valentina must've told him about our money situation.

Lucy clicked her tongue and drew her lips back in displeasure. The doctor continued to explain that if the treatment wasn't changed immediately, her mother might suffer a 'terminal complication.'

"That's that then," she said under her breath.

With a grim look in her eyes, Lucy read on. Skimming through the doctor's remorse that the problem wasn't found sooner, she reached what she was looking for, the name of the new medication. Lucy copied and pasted it into a search engine.

The first few links spat out were sponsored and promptly ignored. Looking further down, she saw articles about studies done with the drugs. At the end of the first page of the results, she found some online pharmacies. Their prices weren't far off from what Valentina had said.

So double . . .

Lucy clicked on the second page. The prices were the same. The third one was no different. Fourth, fifth, sixth, she continued looking to the tenth. With each page, her heart sank more. The noise from the laptop began to irritate her, so she slammed the lid closed. The whirring quieted down, and a few seconds later, there was only silence. Lucy felt like the emptiness inside her was streaming out, infecting the room, but she wasn't going to stew in self-pity. She clenched her fists, and a few heavy breaths later, she shot upright, in need of movement. Grabbing her bike off the rack and slinging her backpack on, she left the apartment to wander the streets. After half an hour of this, she set her course to the *Cher Ami* courier service.

The building had been sky-blue once, but now the elements had scraped off the soft colors. The only trace of the original hue was vertical stripes on the façade. It looked like it had been on the losing side of a fight with a wild animal. Lucy glided through the large parking/unloading zone. Dismounting, she opened the double-winged glass door and pushed her bike inside. The front desk was a gray oval, and behind it sat a blond woman wearing a pink blouse and black thick-rimmed glasses.

"Hey Melissa, Boss still in?" Lucy asked as she leaned on her bike seat. Somewhere deeper inside the building was the echoing bellow of a man.

"Patrick's in the back . . ." Melissa pursed her lips, "as you can hear."

"When isn't he?" Lucy said with a smile and made her way to a door on the right. "Can you buzz me in?"

"Mhm." Melissa complied and returned to shuffling papers.

Lucy pushed her bike inside and closed the door. She wheeled it through a dark hallway, leaving it at the rack, and walked toward the yelling. Rows of packages on shelves stretched for tens of feet in front of her, and at the end loomed two tall doors. Lucy went through the one on the left. Inside, along each wall, bikes in repair perched upsidedown on workbenches. Shelves full of reserve parts and tools lined the room from floor to ceiling. At the other end of the shop was the door that held back all of her employer's screams, and when she opened it, they rushed at her like a tsunami.

The room was filled with boxes, leaving only a narrow path between the giant mounds of packages, which she tried to traverse without disrupting the sleeping mountains of paper. Their arrangement seemed so perilous that a single breath could cause an avalanche. She managed to reach the middle of the room, a small island of concrete not covered by boxes where three people stood marooned. A large black man, arms like small barrels, towered over the other two men he was shouting at. Lucy had been on the receiving end of such a loud lecture, and she knew she had to wait for it to end. She also wanted to hear if the giant had added some flavor to the speech from the last time she'd heard it.

"So when you say you can make the run in thirty minutes, you'd better make the run in thirty fucking minutes." Her boss waved his right index finger at the others.

"Because what's needed is discipline and reliability." His finger stopped waving, and his wrist bent each time a word needed punctuating.

"Discipline keeps you in shape, aware of what you can and can't do. And reliability keeps me"—his voice rose so high that windows rattled from above—"in the *fucking business!*"

"When you go outside these doors," he said, his finger pointing at two large doors leading out, "get this through your fucking skulls and never forget it. You are upholding the standard and work ethic I've built." The man hit his chest with his open-palmed hand.

"My reputation and honor are on the line. Don't fuck with my livelihood!" He seared the point into the two men with a smoldering gaze that jumped between them.

There was a brief silence while the giant man waited for his words to sink in. Neither of the others looked him in the eyes.

"We're done. Go," her boss dismissed them with a wave of his hand.

The two men made a swift turn in place and went for the door. Both hung their heads low. No one said anything as they passed Lucy. The giant man had his back turned to her, but Lucy could hear him panting from strain.

"Honor, Boss?" she said when she heard the door behind her close. "Don't you think that's a bit much?"

He looked at her over his shoulder, his left eye visible and bloodshot as he spoke. "What we do to survive has no bearing on principles, Castle."

"It's okay to do bad shit as long as we don't mean it, right?"

"I think so, yes." He rose to his full height, running a hand through his hair, and turned around to face Lucy while leaning on the edge of his desk. "Speaking about bad shit. What the fuck happened last night?"

Lucy shrugged. "You tell me."

"According to my sources, a certain early twenties courier had a run-in with the special weapons and tactics unit of our city's police force."

"Hardly," Lucy dismissed. "They just saw me running away from a dead drop that turned out to be anything but."

"Someone snitched."

"No shit." Lucy paced back and forth now. "You know it wasn't me."

"Of course." He nodded, his eyes swinging back and forth, matching her movements. "That's not the issue, though. Everyone's spooked now, so no more deliveries on foot."

"What? Why?"

"Because," he raised his voice to remind her to keep hers down, "if SWAT was there, then that means they're tryin' to catch a big fish, and they get the big net out for those. You don't wanna get caught in it now, do ya?"

"No." She stopped pacing and pouted in place. "So, what's the play?"

"My people, including you"—he stabbed a finger at her—"are laying low. So you only get nice and clean bike jobs for now until you hear otherwise."

Lucy opened her mouth to complain and explain her situation, but the slow rise of his eyebrows made her reconsider.

"Melissa's holding something for you. Go get it, and get on with your shift." He dismissed her with a flick of his wrist.

Lucy went back to reception, where Melissa handed her the schedule for the day. Scanning the meager amount of addresses and package sizes told Lucy that none would be profitable. Looking back up, she saw Melissa push an envelope toward her. Inside it was a few hundred dollars stacked in small bills.

"Hazard pay," Melissa answered the unasked question.

Lucy nodded and went into storage to get as many packages as she could safely carry. Opening the glass door, she pushed the bike outside and hopped onto it. Fifteen minutes later, she was scouring the city again in search of addresses.

THREE

Deliveries finished, Lucy headed for home. The world pressed down on her more than usual, and she just wanted a drink. She remembered her vodka was gone but didn't want to cause another worried look on Mr. Wilson's face, so she went to a corner store on her way back. She bought the cheapest vodka that she could stomach and went home.

After hanging the bike on its rack, she set the bottle on the counter and opened it. Before Lucy could take a swig, there was a knock. Her eyes shot to the door, and she froze. Another knock came, but no one announced themselves. She set the bottle down, then glided to the door, making no sound. Looking through the peephole, she saw a man standing too close to identify, his face just out of view.

It could be one of the goons from yesterday. The thought made her look right, to where she kept the kitchen knives.

She shook her head, attempting to shoo away her paranoia.

There's no way any of those idiots know where I live. It's probably one of the neighbors.

Lucy softened her posture and relaxed her muscles, then grabbed the knob and turned.

Her eyes took in a familiar man, holding two large bags. "Hi, Damien." Attention shifting down and to the right, she added, "Hey, Sarah, couldn't take my answer lying down for more than eight hours, eh?"

"You need a break, and that's that." Sarah crossed her arms and planted her feet.

"Oookay then." Damien took an exaggerated step inside. "I'm just gonna hop over this tension real quick and wait for you ladies to settle *this,* whatever it is."

Lucy saw the look of determination on Sarah's face. She wasn't going to budge. Stepping to the side, she let her friend in. Sarah gave her a quick nod of acknowledgment and gracefully drifted by, the scent of her perfume leaving a pleasant trail behind her. The dress she wore clung to her body like a second skin. It was pale white with elegant, black, diagonal lines flowing down her shoulder and chest. She made the three strides necessary to reach the couch. Her mere presence there, sitting on the old fabric, made the piece of furniture more appealing.

Damien's eyes were glued to Sarah as well, and when he looked at Lucy after she'd closed the door, an understanding smile appeared on his lips.

"Babe, would you get the light for me," Sarah asked as she rummaged through one of the bags. "I can't see anything in here."

Lucy raised a hand, stopping him. "It's out of order. It broke last night, and I haven't had a chance to fix it."

"Want me to take a look at it?"

"Not really. I'll handle it."

"Geez, let him be useful, Lu," Sarah said, grabbing both bags then standing up. "Let's go." She gestured with her chin toward Lucy's bedroom.

"I have to clean up first." Lucy cringed.

"Stop stalling. You've never once cleaned for me before. Now come one, chop-chop." Sarah gently put her fingers on Lucy's waist and spun her around.

"You have any tools by chance?" Damien's eyes darted all around the room.

"No, sorry, but there's a janitor's closet at the end of the hallway. Maybe you could find something there?"

"Cool, I'll check it out." He smiled and went to the door. "You ladies have fun beautifying yourselves."

When the front door closed behind him, Sarah had already pushed Lucy into her bedroom. Looking at the strewn clothes on the ground and the wide-open doors of her wooden wardrobe, she bit her lower lip. That was the surface-level messiness she wasn't too embarrassed about, but her eyes darted to the window, where the rust had nearly melted the sill. Just above the fading window was the leaky culprit—a large, pale in color spot on the ceiling. Sarah's incessant pushing made her trip on a pair of jeans. Before her gaze could become level again, her eyes lingered on the small hole near the corner where her vanity sat. She'd filled the hole with quick-drying cement and hadn't bothered covering it up with any kind of finish. Lucy almost tripped again, so she stopped allowing herself to be pushed around.

"Knock it off already. We're here." She turned to face Sarah. "What is this?"

Sarah tried to look confused, but Lucy tilted her head and stared her down with intensity.

"Fine." Sarah rolled her eyes. "You're too stubborn for any other tactic to work. That's why I'm here." Both arms, holding bags, drew up by her side like giant wings.

Lucy thought for a moment, then nodded in agreement.

"Glad we're on the same page." Sarah gave a curt nod as well. "Now, let's see what we can do here." She sidestepped Lucy, straightened the top cover of her bed, then turned one of the bags upside down.

Lucy's eyes went wide as a waterfall of beauty products poured out.

"Did you drag *all* of your makeup here?" Lucy asked, struggling not to let her jaw slack.

Sarah tilted her head so much that her cheek almost touched her shoulder. "Please, don't be absurd. These are some things I can spare."

Sarah left one other bag on the bed, and the final one, she set on a clean patch of floor. Straightening her dress, she clasped her hands before her belly. "I know you've got a whole thing about accepting charity"—her right index finger rose, stopping Lucy from speaking—"*which* this is not. This is simply me helping a friend out, so you can't say no to it, and that's that." Her chin rose, and she pursed her lips, looking expectantly at Lucy.

"Fine, fine, you win. We'll go on your stupid date."

"I'll have you know"—Sarah stabbed a finger at her—"no date I orchestrate is stupid."

"Nice word choice there. You know, your subconscious might be against you manipulating the love life of a friend."

"I sincerely doubt that," Sarah said as she leaned over the bag on the bed and drew something out of it.

A dark, gem-studded dress made it onto her covers. When Lucy moved her head, the stones sparkled in different colors, and the fabric looked like someone had managed to transpose the night sky onto silk. Lucy couldn't resist it and ran a finger along the edge, confirming it was indeed the expensive woven fabric.

"I can't take this." Her hand jumped back as if it were hot to the touch.

"Nonsense, the dress was made for you. I can feel it." Sarah's eyes glowed with an almost mystical light. "Just try it on, and then we'll decide. Please. For me?" Her voice jumped up an octave.

Lucy stopped protesting and slid into the dress, taking the utmost care as she did. It barely reached the middle of her too-large thighs, and she immediately regretted giving in to the proposal of a date.

"Perfect fit." Sarah nodded her head as her eyes shamelessly took her friend in. "When I wear it, it's under the knee, but I think you can make this work. Just look at those legs!"

"That's why I don't wear things like *this*." Lucy gestured at the sizable portion of muscular thigh from her knee to the hem of the dress. "People just stare."

"So what? You work out, big whoop. Don't tell me you don't like the way you look?"

"That's not it," Lucy struggled to describe what her problem was. "It's just, I'm not sure it looks that good. You know?"

"I'm sure I don't. . . ." Sarah came in close and evened out a few edges on Lucy's hips. "Since I don't have amazing legs like you. I learned how to flaunt my very average legs, and the feeling is amazing. I recommend it one hundred percent." She winked and stepped back to give Lucy another once-over.

"I'm just like a fairy godmother." Sarah clasped her hands together and shook from giddiness. "Here to whisk you away to the ball. A ball with a hot stud, of course." She waved one hand at Lucy and looked at her from under her lashes.

"Speaking of said stud—"

"First, take a seat, then the scoop." Sarah tapped the red leather of the small revolving chair.

Lucy sat down, and Sarah grabbed her chin and began to move it in the mirror. Eyes focused and lips taught, she looked like a skilled painter scrutinizing the quality of a canvas. Nodding to herself, she ducked out of the confines of the mirror and grabbed a few products. Black letters caught Lucy's attention. Looking down at the gap between the vanity's mirror and the flat surface regular women used to keep beauty products on, she saw her framed award certificate. Even backward, she could read the words at the top—*Award for Martial Excellence.* She nearly forgot about the framed proof of fighting prowess, kept out of sight because she didn't want the reminder of the things she could no longer afford to do while sending money back home. Returning to Lucy's field of vision, Sarah opened a silver case to inspect the contents.

"So," Lucy said with inappropriate amounts of impatience, the memories of her neglected hobby fouling her mood.

"Don't rush me. Beauty takes time, missy."

"Not that." Lucy's eyebrows jumped. "I mean about the date. Any information on the person I'm meeting would be appreciated."

"I don't know much myself. I've only met him a couple of times. All I know is he's the head of his team, oh, and that he's brilliant, according to Damien. He's also polite and good-looking, in my humble opinion."

Humble, huh? Lucy smiled at Sarah's usual lack of humility.

"They went to the same high school, and Damien's a good judge of character, so you don't have to worry. At least give him a chance, yeah?"

"Sure, I will."

"Now, eyes closed, I'm going to work my *magic.*" Sarah fluttered her fingers in front of Lucy's eyes.

She rubbed something cold and creamy all over Lucy's nose, cheeks, forehead, and chin.

"Eyes open."

Lucy opened them and saw Sarah with several products in hand. She looked at Lucy's brows, then to her products. Deciding on a few, she threw the rest back on the bed.

"So, how is your study fund coming along?" Sarah asked while she worked on Lucy's eyebrows.

Lucy couldn't see a way to deflect the question. Since she was stuck here for a while, she decided to talk. "Well, as of last week, I have money for roughly the whole tuition."

"Closed again."

She felt a soft surface rub her eyelids and just above them, then to the skin under her bottom lashes all the way to the crease of the eye socket.

"But as of yesterday, my expenses have risen," Lucy continued with a sad smile on her face. "So I have to see how much medicine my savings can afford. As I said, I might have to move back home and get a job there." She kept her face tight, trying not to show any emotion.

She felt nothing on her skin for so long, she reached out for Sarah.

"Stop worrying about me," she said when she couldn't find Sarah's hand. "I'll manage like I always do."

"That's the thing, Lu," a somber voice spoke from behind her. "You don't have to do everything alone."

Lucy opened her eyes. The voice was so fatigued and distant that she refused to believe it belonged to her friend, but there she was, hands frozen in midair, face full of sorrow. Lucy hated the pity she saw in Sarah's eyes, so she clenched her jaw to avoid insulting her.

"Don't look at me like that," Sarah said. "I'm offering you a helping hand, not a handout."

Bah, what does she know? Lucy's anger flared brighter. *What has she ever worked for? The dress, the makeup, the shiny car that drives her around. All those things were given to her by her parents.*

"I get doing things your way. Being high-powered and independent is great, but when is it enough?" Sarah lifted her chin, defying the anger in Lucy's eyes. "Is it really worth sacrificing everything you are just so you can say you did it all by yourself? When does it end?"

Lucy blew out a rough breath that sounded like the release of a strained pressure valve. "It ends when I've done what I need to."

Sarah studied Lucy's reflection for a few more moments, then closed her eyes, a sad smile of concession on her lips.

"Let's drop it," Sarah's ridiculous and peppy tone came back. "There's a ton more to do. Eyes closed."

The glimpse into the real Sarah was over, so Lucy closed her eyes and let the makeup session continue. One of the things she hated most about her bubbly friend was the absurd, over-the-top, girly-girl act she put on. It got her whatever she wanted from her parents and men. Lucy liked to talk to the *real* Sarah—but that Sarah showed itself less and less these days. The obnoxious mask she put on to look defenseless and in need of care stayed on her face longer and longer now. So much so that she seemed to believe it herself. Lucy couldn't stand it, but she respected her hustle.

"I'm nearly done with this masterpiece," Sarah informed, and Lucy heard her leaning on the bed.

She felt something small and sharp move from left to right in a straight line above and below her eyelashes. Sarah finished up her work with the pencil and leaned away again. This time Lucy heard squirting, then hands rubbing. Sarah's finger touched her skin and smeared something creamy all over.

"You almost done there, Da Vinci?"

"Shh, don't distract me, or you're gonna end up looking like a clown."

Lucy kept her mouth shut while Sarah brushed her cheekbones, then moved to her jawline and finally stopped.

"Okay, let's have a look," Sarah said in a tone that made it obvious she was speaking to herself. "Good, good. Okay, great. I have the perfect color for you, so purse your lips and stop pouting."

Lucy did as commanded without comment. Her lips received their coat of paint, and fingers swayed her face side to side once more.

"I think I'm done."

"Took you long enough."

Lucy received a painful pinch on the arm for her remark.

"Great things take time. Now, open your eyes, and let's see if I've achieved the *wow* effect."

Lucy complied and was struck by the person looking back at her. Her reflection was almost unrecognizable. Her eyes were painted in dark purple, and her upper eyelids sparkled, actually sparked! Her cheeks had a slightly pink glow to them. The depth of the color changed depending on the angle of her face. The lipstick was a deep shade of purple, not as dark as her skin, but a softer, fuller shade that made her lips look plump and sensual. She looked at Sarah, a satisfied smile on her face.

"Wow . . ." Lucy said with an uncontained smile.

"Damn right, wow!" Sarah grinned wider. "Let me have a look-see at your shoe collection then."

"Collection's not the right word." Lucy went to her wardrobe and reluctantly fished out her stash. A few pairs of shoes were crammed in boxes, two at a time. Some just lounged at the bottom, missing their counterparts. Lucy threw a backward glance at Sarah. She sat on the bed with a smug look on her face and a brown box on her lap.

"What?"

"Oh, nothing." Sarah's smile grew. "I'm just waiting to see your selection."

Sarah's sarcasm was none too subtle. Lucy opened a box and took out a pair of shoes. Inspecting them, she tugged the left one's heel. It didn't move, so she decided it would hold. The sole of the right shoe had bloodstains that Lucy could never wash off.

"These babies have seen better days," Sarah said, shaking her chin.

Lucy shot her an angry glance.

"Hey, I'm very thankful for those shoes and deeply sorry for what happened to them, but I knew you wouldn't throw them away, and so, I took the liberty of buying you a present." Her fingers tapped the lid of the box in a quick patter. "Here you go!" she chimed, eyes sparkling.

Lucy got the box and set it on the floor. After opening it, she picked up the shoes, holding them between her thumb and index finger. They had low heels and an elegant crimson design on the bottom. Their top looked like a half-finished dome encrusted with rhinestones. Lucy realized what she was holding, dropped the shoes back in, and slid the box toward Sarah.

"I can't take these," Lucy said, shaking her head. "They cost more than I probably make a month from *both* jobs."

Sarah got up and knelt down beside her. "So what?"

"It's too much." Lucy looked pleadingly into her eyes. "Don't you see it's too much?"

"I don't think it is." Sarah raised a finger to stop Lucy's

bubbling words. "The point of today is for me to show you a good time, and I'll be damned if you're not gonna look at least close to as fabulous as me." She waved her hand across her own body to present her outfit. "Now, put those babies on, and let's test out your new look on Damien, okay?"

"Okay," Lucy agreed, still looking at the shoes that only someone with access to an absurd amount of wealth could afford.

Sarah gently caressed her shoulder then walked out. Lucy took a breath in, donned the shoes, and stood by the door for a moment.

"Babe, you done?" Sarah called from the other room. "And why is it so dark in here?"

"Had to stop the electricity to the apartment while I work," Damien replied.

A more distant voice, as if from a radio or phone speaker, droned beyond the door.

"No, no, we won't die of any meteors soon," the faded voice said. "There could be an extinction event caused by a falling object that's big enough, but that's in the realm of speculation and fiction. I can assure you, the world won't be ending today or in a week."

"Well, we disagree on that note, Dr. Shields," a new radio voice chimed in.

"Turn that off, babe."

"But it's just getting good."

"And *we* have places to be, so get your butt over here and help us out."

"What about the light?"

"Nevermind that, just get over here. Thank you, you sit over there." They fussed for a few moments, then Sarah's voice came again, "We're ready, Lu. Dazzle us!"

Lucy took a deep breath, opened the door, and stepped outside. Sarah grinned ear to ear as Damien stood frozen, eyes stuck to Lucy's figure. After a couple of seconds of no reaction, Sarah poked his ribs with her elbow.

"Just wow. Marvelous," he said, looking Lucy up and down.

"What did I tell you, Lu." Sarah winked. "The *wow* effect."

"You've outdone yourself, babe," Damien turned his head to Sarah, then said with a straight face, "I'm sorry, but we need to break up. I'm going to ask Lucy to be my girlfriend."

Sarah flailed her arms at him.

"It's your own fault!" he shouted while defending himself from raining blows.

When Sarah's breath ran out, she moved to the other side of the couch, held her head up, and stared out the living room window. Damien fixed his ruffled shirt, winked at Lucy, and slid over to Sarah's side.

He hugged her waist and started to kiss her neck and ears. "Don't be mad, babe."

"Don't you have something to fix, *boyfriend?*" Sarah's tone was cold as she pushed him away.

"On my way, Ma'am." Damien saluted and got up.

"You look lovely, Lu. Maybe I've created a monster." Sarah said with a smirk, then pulled her purse from the table and retrieved her phone. "Can I take a picture, please? You look so good in that light. It's just magical," Sarah pleaded, her hands holding the phone in front of her face.

"Okay, just one." Lucy raised her right index finger. "As thanks for doing this." She gestured at the dress with her free hand.

"You got it!" Sarah said, ducking behind the phone.

Lucy stood for a couple of seconds, trying to act normal.

Sarah's face remained hidden behind the device.

"What's taking so long?"

"I'm waiting for you to stop being awkward."

The anticipation gave her a sick feeling deep in her gut like she didn't belong in her own home. "We don't have all day here."

"There it is! Smile."

Lucy managed a small smile, then the camera's shutter noise came from the phone, and Sarah leaned forward. The lights flickered on.

"Voila!" Damien shouted in triumph.

"Thanks for the help."

"No problem, pretty lady." He gave Lucy another wink.

"Watch it," Sarah growled, aiming a finger at him without looking away from her phone.

Damien smirked and sat down next to her. And after a few moments, Lucy came over as well, and Sarah handed her the phone. "Have a look."

The picture on the small screen showed a woman standing in a doorway, her hands resting a little awkwardly by her hips. The weak smile on the woman's lips was accentuated on each side by dimples. A pale red glow tinged her lips and made them look more sensual than ever. The lines of rouge seemed to frame the rounder face into an angular and more aesthetically pleasing form. But the most striking thing was the dress with little flashes of light that shined like exploding stars. They made the woman's eyes stand out like hazel beacons. Sunlight fell directly on the right eye, and the exposure made it strikingly bright. The woman's gaze looked piercing and mystical. Her outward appearance had significantly improved, but Lucy saw something else in that picture. She saw a young, well-dressed woman that could enjoy the simple things in life, like going on a blind date that her friend set up. A young woman of opulence and plenty. A woman that looked happy. A woman that was not her.

"It's about time, ladies." Damien's voice snapped her out of the glimpse into a world not her own. He looked at his watch, then to Sarah. They both stood up.

"Thanks." Lucy gave a weak smile and handed back the phone. "Just let me get my stuff." Running her hands over her dress, she realized that it didn't have any pockets.

Meeting Sarah's gaze, she saw a look on the young woman's face that said: *that's what purses are for.*

"I've got an emergency bag in the car." The disappointment in her tone was palpable. "It's not the best for your outfit, but it'll have to do. Let's go, fashion-dummy." She shook her head as she and Damien walked out.

Lucy got her wallet, phone, and keys, then locked the door behind her and followed. Once seated inside the car, Sarah dove elbow deep into the glove compartment. She got a small, jet-black purse with a silver strap and handed it over her shoulder to Lucy.

"Let's get this party started!" Damien said, tapping the roof of the car with his hand.

They pulled out of the parking stall and onto the street in a smooth motion. Lucy stared out the window at the sky. Most of it was dark now, with only hints of leftover light. She turned her gaze forward. Sarah's fingertips drummed away on her phone, humming some melody. The car stopped for a red light, and Damien caught Lucy's gaze in the rearview mirror.

"I think we're gonna have a great time. Rick's a pretty cool guy," he said with a smile.

"I'm sure he is," Lucy said, sounding a bit too uninterested, even to herself.

Damien's left eyebrow arched up.

"You okay? If you're not feeling up to it, we can always reschedule. I don't know if he'll be free again soon, but still."

Sarah stopped messing with her phone and snapped her head up.

"No, no, I just have a lot on my plate. A night on the town should do me good." Lucy held Sarah's gaze in the mirror.

The car started to move again a moment later, and Sarah returned her focus to her phone.

"Can you tell me something about him at least? Sarah was very . . . cryptic."

Damien moved his chin up and eyed his girlfriend. "Was she now?"

Lucy nodded several times, then leaned forward and adjusted her position.

"Let's see. Where to start?"

"It's usually best to start at the beginning, babe," Sarah chimed in sarcastically.

"That's a good idea. What would I do without you?" Damien continued, completely unfazed.

"The beginning, hmm. That was some ten years back. We met in high school. Rick was a bit weird then, still is actually, but back then, we were teenagers, so he didn't fare well."

"Look at you, Mister Eloquent. *Fare well.*" Sarah cackled.

Damien just gave her a sideways glance then continued, "We became good friends in high school. After that, we both went to different universities, so that was a bummer. I went to study engineering. He went to study infectious diseases."

"Infectious diseases, that's oddly specific," Lucy said while looking forward through the front windshield.

"The crazy part," he continued, "is that later we found out, we applied for work at the same place! The CDC."

"My mom knew someone there, so I kinda got fast-tracked, but Rick isn't that type of guy," Damien said with a proud smile on his face. "Nah, he has ideals."

The car stopped at a red light. Damien leaned forward and put his chin on the wheel.

"A man of principle is what you'd call it," he added, flashing Sarah a disarming smile.

"But enough about that. What else? He's a Leo. Doesn't go to clubs. He's at the lab most of the time, always working. I swear to God, it's like he lives there. First one in, last one out. He's a freaking machine. And that, my dear ladies, is dedication. If he wasn't so talented and diligent, he wouldn't lead a team at our age." Damien tapped his left index finger on the wheel as he spoke.

Richard couldn't be more than twenty-eight, twenty-nine years old. Tops, Lucy mused. "He's a team lead? Really?"

"You bet your fine-dressed ass he is." The proud grin appeared on Damien's face again.

"So, seeing as how you're both single, I decided to get you in a room together. See if sparks fly or we die in the cold."

The car was quiet for the next few minutes as Damien searched for a spot to park. Not finding any, he stopped at the entrance of the restaurant.

"I'm gonna go ask where I can park. Be back in a flash," he said and got out of the car.

"Sarah," Lucy moved closer to her, "what the hell are you doing on that phone?"

"Research," she replied, not looking away.

Damien opened the door and jumped in. "Parking's out back, so you guys get off here."

Lucy slid out the door.

"Very strange," Sarah commented, after shuffling out of the car and now looking at the screen once again.

"What is?"

"The fact that I can't find any kind of social for Rick. There's almost nothing online. Except for some boring stuff, like articles and papers."

"So?"

"It's just peculiar." Sarah's eyebrows furrowed as her finger movements became angrier. "Everybody has stuff on them."

Lucy struggled to find the words to explain to Sarah how having published articles is the furthest you can get from boring. Before she could attempt this, Damien appeared from behind the corner and waved them over. They all met in front of the entrance. Lucy was about to ask when Rick would arrive, but Damien raised his hand to hail an approaching man. Her newly acquired heels made her taller than both of her companions, so she had a chance to get a good look at him. He was tall, as tall as Lucy in heels—at least six feet.

His haircut was modest and to the point, black and short, bangs coiffed. The eyebrows, a bit thin for a man, formed straight lines on either side. His eyes were a deep, dark blue; a day's worth of stubble roughed his otherwise smooth face. Just before he reached them, Lucy was able to give his body a quick look over. He appeared too big for a man who worked in a lab, shoulders broad and a sailor's knotting forearms peaking from under a wrinkled t-shirt. She didn't feel an overwhelming attraction to him, but the confidence in his step kept the embers of her interest alive.

Sarah's finger pointed at the sky. "Hey, what's that?" Everyone looked up and saw three bright lights burning their way through the night.

"There weren't supposed to be any visible comets in our longitude, were there?" Damien said to Richard.

"Nope," he replied, staring down at his phone. "Hi, I'm Richard." He held out his hand to shake Lucy's, glancing up to look at her just before their hands touched.

"I'm Lucy."

His hand gripped her firmly as he shook. Lucy respected people who didn't adjust their strength because she was a woman. Holding her gaze for a moment, he looked away and patted Damien on the shoulder.

"You wouldn't believe what those idiots at forecast spending told me just before I left." He pulled Damien forward, and they both walked toward the restaurant, leaving the women behind.

Lucy's eyebrows rose, and she threw a bewildered glance at Sarah, who shrugged her shoulders and followed her boyfriend. Gritting her teeth, Lucy took a deep breath and went inside. A waiter led Richard and Damien, who remained at the forefront, with Lucy and Sarah trailing behind them. Richard continued to complain to Damien about some coworker they had. Lucy had trouble unclenching her jaw, trying to calm down by inspecting her surroundings. Massive round tables filled the ample space, while smaller, more intimate tables hid in the private recesses. Heavy drapes covered every window in the room, but Lucy couldn't tell if there was actual glass behind the curtains or if they were simply decorative. Fastened to the narrow spaces between the drapes, small, circular lights glowed a spectral, pale yellow.

Four waiters stopped at their table as Sarah and Lucy picked their spots. Each waiter pulled a chair back. Once seated, they offered their hands for jackets or coats. Damien took his coat off and handed it to the nearest man. With no more clothes to take, the additional staff walked away. A few menus waited on top of the table. Lucy scanned the dishes and picked out the dryest thing she could think of, terrified of the possibility of a stain on her immaculate dress. Switching to the alcohol section, she picked an adequately priced wine.

"Can I take your drink order?" the waiter asked after a few minutes of patient standby.

Everyone gave their order, and when Lucy's turn came, she stumbled over the long French names.

"Very good. I will be right back with your wine." The waiter nodded and dissolved between the tables.

Off to a great start, Lucy, she chastised herself, then noticed everyone was staring at her.

"Sorry, I got a bit distracted by the menu," she scrambled. "I've never been to a fancy place like this before." Her lips curled into an apologetic smile.

"Eh." The right corner of Richard's mouth twinged. "It's nothing too fancy. We've seen better." He smirked at Damien.

"It's okay, yeah," Sarah moved in quickly to change the direction of the conversation. "Anyway, I was just telling them how exciting your job is." Her eyebrows went upward, signifying which job Lucy should talk about.

"I guess it is," she agreed.

"Sarah said it has something to do with *bikes?*" The way Richard spoke the final word made Lucy's stomach twist into an angry knot. "You seem pretty fit, so great for your body, at least."

It was apparent he aimed to be charming with the smooth smile that spread across his lips, but his words coupled with the unabashed once-over he gave her sent unpleasant shivers along her spine.

This is for Sarah; just power through, she told herself and prepared for a long evening.

"It keeps me in shape for sure, and the wide, open spaces are great. I tried to work in offices a few times, but the walls just box me in, you know?"

Giving him this easy-to-follow conversational lifeline, Lucy sat back and relaxed her shoulders. He nodded in agreement and smiled.

"Speaking of wide, open spaces, that reminds me of when we were in the Caribbean a few months ago. You guys remember, at that beach with the bar?"

"Oh yeah, where you got so smashed that you couldn't even say your stupid pick-up line to that girl." Damien snapped his fingers together, trying to remember something. "The actress, right?"

"Model," Richard corrected with a smug expression on his face.

Lucy furrowed her brows in confusion and glared at Sarah.

"We went on a vacation a few months back. You were studying every day, and I had nothing to do, so daddy offered to take us there since he was flying over anyway."

"What, you don't get enough rest and relaxation at a grand manor on the lake?" Lucy's tone was as flat as her expression.

"If I lived in a place like that, I'd be on the lake every night after work," Richard said, dreamy gaze stuck on the ceiling.

"Amen, brother," Damien nodded.

"I wouldn't call it a lake . . ." Sarah attempted to redirect the conversation.

"The road you live on has *lake* in the name," Richard said, eyebrows raised. "You probably can't relate to people who live on streets that don't reference a landmark they own."

Lucy drew her lips inward, growing more confused by the

minute, wondering why Sarah thought Richard was a person she'd be interested in. Even if she inwardly agreed with his assessment. Richard continued to ask uninspired questions until the waiter arrived with their drinks. Lucy ordered something to eat, doing her best to speed this trainwreck of a date along. The waiter nodded politely then wrote down what the others wanted. Sarah ordered several full courses, and as she did, Damien's face got paler and paler. Once the waiter left, Sarah reassured her boyfriend by flashing a black credit card from her purse—her father's no doubt. Lucy wasn't the least bit surprised that her friend wouldn't be paying for anything she was getting.

The table got quiet and awkward after the waiter left. Damien cleared his throat several times. Richard looked at him and followed his eyes as they darted from him to Lucy and then back to him. Lucy was doing everything she could to stifle a deep sigh.

"You guys have been friends for a long time, right?" Richard's right hand pointed to Sarah, then to Lucy.

"A couple of years, yeah," Lucy confirmed, giving him a half-hearted nod.

"Damien says there's a story there," he continued expectantly.

Sarah's face lit up, and she nodded her head in agreement like a toddler. Lucy didn't usually like to tell the story. But right now, she would do anything to fill the time, and since Damien looked more interested in hearing it than Richard, she thought she might as well.

"I was attending first year at university," she began, "and when the semester was done, there was going to be a small course party. After that, we would go to a bar for the real party."

Sarah put her phone on the table and gave Lucy her full attention.

"So the classroom party, or the boring part of the night, as Sarah likes to put it, ended, and we went to the club." Richard's chin rested on his chest, eyes staring down at his phone.

Bored already? You asked for this story. Lucy fumed but continued, "We got there, and a few minutes after reaching the bar, the men immediately began to annihilate themselves."

"Typical," Sarah clicked her tongue, then narrowed her eyes, her dirty glance stabbing Damien.

He picked up a glass and hid his smile behind it while Richard nodded absently.

"At the bar, all these dudes come out of the woodwork, offering us drinks or to join them. Cindy, one of the girls with me, walks off with a guy, and I don't see her for about an hour. After some drinks, the girls decided we should go to the dancefloor. Just as we're about to reach it, I see Cindy leaning on a column, looking very much out of it. Then this sleazebag nestles close to her and starts talking in her ear. Cindy doesn't say or do anything, so the asshole looks around like a squirrel collecting nuts, slings her over his shoulder, and starts to drag her somewhere.

"I walk over, catching them just before the exit. While I'm trying to wrestle Cindy away from the guy, some giant dude in a black shirt appears and asks what the problem is. I tell him that the sleazebag is trying to kidnap my friend. Sleazebag starts to sweat and stammers to the point of not being able to form sentences. Then I see the giant guy has a sign on the back of his shirt, that says 'Security.' This humongous pile of muscles picks up the smaller dude, opens the door, and actually throws the prick out like a filthy cat." Lucy smiled at the thought, then took a drink while the table chuckled.

"After that, I dragged Cindy to the bathroom and splashed some water on her face, but that didn't help. She looked pretty bad, so I went outside to call an ambulance. Now, when I get outside, I hear noises coming from down the alley. I walk closer and see the same asshole that got thrown out, cornering a girl beside the dumpster. I ask Sleazebag what he's doing. He turns around and says, 'it's none of your business,' even waves me away with his hand. So I came up behind him and kicked him in the nuts," Lucy said, shrugging her shoulders.

Everyone stared wide-eyed. Even Richard lifted his gaze from the phone.

"Oh, come on!" Sarah raised her voice. "That's not what happened."

Sarah looked too happy for someone remembering a traumatic event. Damien's face expressed the exact emotions Lucy expected to see on Sarah's—fright and anger. His eyes jumped from Lucy to Sarah. Richard, seeming to be immensely entertained by the story now, or at least by Damien's expressions, leaned in.

"You're not telling it right," Sarah protested, shaking her hand side to side, a dissatisfied frown on her face.

Grabbing her chair, Sarah hopped it to the side so she could face the guys better. "Lucy, I kid you not, fucking *spin* kicked him in the face! Like in martial arts movies."

"Seriously?" Richard asked, amazed.

"Scouts honor." Sarah's face grew solemn as her right hand rose, her three fingers straight up in the scout's sign.

"Lucy even slipped and fell down in the filth right next to him." Sarah laughed a throaty, vibrating laugh.

Damien was in no laughing mood. The look on his face said he had heard a completely different story.

"Why didn't you call the cops?" Richard asked, chuckling.

"Because I could handle it myself," Lucy grunted, "and I did."

"What if he had a knife or a gun?" Richard continued to

press.

"I saw neither, but I did see Sarah"—her hand sharply jumped up to point—"who was getting attacked."

Their food arrived. The waiters left the dishes and disappeared without a word.

"Helping was honorable," Richard resumed the conversation after the waiters had gone, "but confronting assailants without observing whether they're armed or not is an excellent way to get yourself injured or, God forbid, killed."

"So you're saying I'm stupid?"

"Your word, not mine," Richard lifted both arms. "Naive is the one I would use."

Lucy's teeth ground into each other. Her phone buzzed, and so did everyone else's at the table. All around them, the room began to hum with conversation. The lights flickered for a moment. Lucy unlocked the phone and read the emergency message sent from the town hall. It said that a meteor had fallen on top of a car, no one injured or killed, but the authorities asked citizens to stay vigilant. Looking away, she saw Richard had gotten up from his chair.

His eyes were fixed on the screen of his own phone. "I'm sorry to do this, but I have to go."

Getting several hundred-dollar bills from his pocket, he tossed them onto the table and turned to Lucy.

"I didn't mean to insult you, but if I did . . ." He looked her straight in the eyes. "Sorry."

He strode toward the exit and disappeared.

"Awesome." Lucy sighed and poured herself a glass of wine.

She finished the bottle while the others ate their dinner. Taking a few bites of her own dish, she then felt the night was over and simply stood up and walked to the door.

The car ride back was quiet and sullen. Soft jazz sounds from the radio accompanied the falling night sky. Lucy's vision smeared. Time felt like it dragged behind the car. She closed her eyes so they could rest, and just before she fell asleep, the car stopped. Lucy said her goodbyes and stepped onto the pavement and into the brisk night air, wishing her foul mood would stay in the car behind her.

It didn't.

FOUR

She watched the car drive away, then turned for home, the high heels hampering her movement the entire way. Her first hurdle, getting from the pavement to the sidewalk, almost landed her on her obnoxious neighbor's car. She regained balance and continued in smaller steps.

"Why would anyone wear these stupid things?" Lucy mumbled as her feet throbbed.

A fitting end to the worst night of her life here in the city. She'd take being shot at by SWAT over another date with *Richard* any day. Her lips twitched at the thought of his smug laugh and holier-than-thou attitude.

Her stilted shuffle made her bruised hip twinge, so she shifted her weight, creating the image of the shambling undead in her mind. A few hours ago, she let herself be fooled by a smartphone photo into thinking she could relax—let up for one night like a real person. But this is what happens when you let your goals out of your sight for even a moment.

She could have spent her night making plans to recover her recent losses, now she'd wasted precious time. At least she got a nice bottle of wine out of the arrangement.

Lucy threw a backward glance at Mr. Wilson's shop. It was still open, and she could hear his TV even across the street. The other shops nearby, still usually open at this time, were dark, and the roads had emptied of the regular beaters. Turning her head made it feel light again. Lucy took a second to stand up straight and continued onward. The steps of her apartment had grown since she'd been away, and she needed to hold onto the railing like a life rope to heave herself up them. The front door to the building on her left burst open, and a man walked down the steps. He got inside his shiny, restored muscle car and started it up. Lucy could see the dumb grin on his face as he revved the engine. Grinding her teeth, she spun in place and slowly descended. She reached the car as her neighbor got out; his gaze lingered on Lucy's half-exposed thighs.

"Hey, beautiful, lookin' for a good time?" his words dragged out, full of bravado. Like someone else she'd met tonight . . .

"I could take you for a drive and"—his left palm patted the roof of the car, and his eyebrows jumped up suggestively—"more."

Her hand clenched into a fist by her side. Lucy willed her eyes to focus on his face and the space behind him to stop spinning so fast.

"Stop making all that noise, dipshit," the words hissed out through her teeth.

"Fuck you, bitch." The man's face contorted into an angry mess. "It's a free country. If you don't like it, call the cops!"

Locking the car, he met her eyes again, flipped her off, and went back inside the building. Lucy's blood boiled. A very hazy, lucrative, and illegal plan formed in her head. Her lips curled into a crooked smile, and forgetting the pain in her feet, she turned around and went into her own building.

A few minutes later, she was back on ground level, a roll of cloth under her left armpit and hands gloved. Kneeling by the car, she spread the faded, old roll to reveal several "tools." Not much good for work around the house, but they got marvelous results when applied to locked spaces.

A little rusty from not breaking into cars these past few years, it took her an embarrassing minute to maneuver the slim jim around to the lock pin. Pulling, the pin popped up, and the restored, dark beast opened its door to her.

She removed the steering column and found the bundle of wires she needed, leading to the battery ignition and starter. After stripping the wires, she twisted them together. The car rumbled with a comfortable vibration that went from her feet to her hips. Smiling, she rolled the cloth up and threw it onto the backseat. Remembering her aching feet, she took her ridiculously priced heels off and threw those in the back as well.

Closing her eyes, she let the gentle rocking sway her lower body and relax her mind. Caressing the steering wheel, she thought about the pretty penny a restored model like this could fetch. She knew some people on the bad side of town. A few problems could be solved tonight, and after the one she'd had, she deserved a win. She leaned forward and put her hand on the gear shift.

A boom resonated from above her, and the sky lit up for a brief moment. Lucy leaned over the dash to get a better view. She half expected to find a meteor plummeting toward her newly acquired cash prize, but there was nothing. A black object rushed by in her periphery, drawing her eye down to the back alley. Again, nothing appeared out of place; the alley, housing a large dumpster, was as uninviting as usual. Even so, the hairs lifted on the back of her neck.

Just get the fuck out of here, Lucy. She reminded herself that this was now a crime scene, and she couldn't stick around to get caught. Lucy checked the mirrors for pedestrians. When her gaze leveled in front of her again, the black of the alley shifted. A tall figure freed itself from the darkness. It wore a white raven-shaped mask—everything else blended into the night.

Lucy's heart stopped beating for a painful moment. A thousand questions rushed through her head. Who was this freak? Why the costume? Was he dangerous? Or worse, did he see her break into the car? Whoever it was stared at her for what felt like an eternity, standing as still as his dumpster backdrop. The black voids of his eye sockets bore into her.

Lucy checked her mirror a final time, ready to tear out of there. But when she looked up again, the figure was gone.

Her stomach flopped. *Fuck this,* she thought and yanked the stick hard into reverse. Then a *tap-tap-tap* hit the driver's side window. Lucy froze. Her eyes turned to the sound, but her head stayed glued forward. Her hand blindly found the crank for the window and rolled it down only a few inches. The costumed freak leaned forward, its white, raven mask filling the opening.

"Excuse me, miss. I seemed to have been given the wrong time and location for a very important event. Would it be possible to procure passage in your vehicle? Your assistance would be vital." The voice behind the mask was clearly male, yet different; he spoke with an accent she couldn't quite place.

"Sorry." She shook her head. "No passengers tonight." Smirking to herself, she began to draw the window up again.

The man put his giant hand on the glass and pushed down. Lucy heard the wheels inside the mechanism struggle under his strength.

"My apologies, I forgot to introduce myself. I am Doctor Emidius, and the survival of your species may depend on my timely arrival."

"Pff, I bet," she said. *Just another crazy then.* Lucy's fear eased;

she knew how to handle crazies. . . . Don't.

The man's masked head hung low at her words, then looked back up. Instead of eyeholes, two midnight-black circles reflected Lucy.

"Good evening then." The figure nodded. "I can't afford to waste any more time here."

Lucy closed her eyes and sneered. When she opened them again, the odd stranger was gone. Raising her eyebrows, she released the brake and pulled onto the road. A light fog shrouded the city and reflected the lamps, giving the sky an eerie glow. With scarcely a car to be seen, the homeless ruled the night. Every few blocks, a bin fire, surrounded by huddled urban campers, lit the street. Three blocks down, she thought she saw the raven-masked silhouette against the firelight of one. It was just for a moment before it disappeared.

Lucy shook off the image. She must have let him scare her more than she thought. But a few more blocks down, the hazy peripheral of Lucy's gaze caught the figure once more. Her inebriated mind convinced her not to worry because the figure may just be going the same way. The vague thought that she had gone a couple of miles from her apartment dogged her, but she squashed it. She'd stick to cheap vodka from now on. Leave the expensive wine to the snobs.

Shifting gears, Lucy picked up speed to prove to her subconscious that it was playing tricks on her. Passing the sign that said *I-95*, something heavy crashed onto the roof of the car. The added weight made the Mustang veer too far to the left, and she could barely turn the wheel in the opposite direction and evade a crash. The sound of sharp spikes driven into metal screeched from above her head toward the passenger side. Lucy screamed and made her body small, afraid that whatever was up there was about to pierce the roof. A hand reached down on the passenger side and opened the door. The loud cacophony of speeding air rushed inside. Dr. Emidius slithered through the narrow opening, contorting his body like a snake. Making himself comfortable in the seat, his right hand moved up and hovered above his left forearm. Fingers pranced in the air as if typing on an invisible keyboard.

"Excellent. If we keep this speed up, we may reach the crash site in time." The satisfaction in his voice was palpable.

Lucy couldn't speak. She wanted to ask questions, scream, get out of the car, or be in any other geographical location but this one. Her voice didn't come to her. This *creature* couldn't be human and enter the way it did while Lucy sped through the fog at 60 mph. Her hands shook, and looking back at the road, she saw a bright, red line bisecting the sky. It came straight down, and the trail it left behind looked like a child had chosen the most vivid hue of red to paint against the night.

"Wrong time *and* location," Emidius broke his streak of monotone syllables. "Oh my, it seems my information for this mission is compromised indeed." He followed the statement with a crestfallen shake of his head.

He turned his black-pool eyes toward her and said, "Would you kindly take me in the direction of the falling object, miss?"

Lucy flashed him a glare, breathing hard. It wasn't what he was asking for or his dreadful monotone voice, but the politeness. Her head spun. She was in a nightmare. She couldn't trace back how she found herself in this situation, and much like in a nightmare, she was unable to escape. She tried to focus on something in her surroundings that she could use to calm her mind, but the world moved too fast, and glimpses of the moon behind the overcast sky were far and few between.

"Wh . . ." Her mouth couldn't form the words.

Her hand moved quicker than her mind and found the parking brake lever. She pulled up. The car screeched and spun around to a vomit-inducing halt on the shoulder of the highway. Lucy's lungs couldn't find the air they needed, and her eyesight narrowed to a small tunnel.

"Miss!" Her hijacker bellowed. "Do you not know how to operate this machine? You must get me to that object now!"

She threw him the most defiant gaze she had in her. "Why should I?"

"I would assume that the fate of your world would be motivation enough?" he tilted his head again in what Lucy took as confusion.

"Fuck the world," she snapped back. "There's gotta be something in it for me. If you want me to go anywhere that isn't away, you gotta make it worth my while. And that won't be easy, let me tell ya."

Lucy congratulated herself on her quick thinking and immediately set her gaze on her surroundings. There had to be a way out of here. She could make a run for the ditch and disappear into the night.

"Ah, I see," Emidius gave two short nods, the beak of his mask jumping up and down. "You would like compensation for your service. Understandable."

He plunged his right hand into his belt and got out something round and shiny. He extended his hand and gave Lucy a gold coin. Taking her eyes off the road, she took the coin and looked it over, about to give it back when she realized what it was.

". . . D-do you have more of these?" She placed the coin between her canine teeth and bit.

How does he have this?

Lucy had come in contact with coins like these before on one of her first walking deliveries. Her curiosity had gotten the better of her, so she opened the package and found three coins such as these. Seventeenth-century gold ducats from Italy she found out later with the help of the Internet.

"Roughly about 300 more of these," Emidius said as he tapped the right side of his mask with a gloved finger. "If these do not suffice, I could always get you a more precious metal called platinum. Are you aware of it?"

Lucy gave him a sideways glance. "I'm aware. Let's see it."

As he rummaged through his belt, Lucy looked at the sky again. The falling object was very near now, and it seemed to be headed toward the farms that John brought produce from on the outskirts of town. Emidius got out a 4-inch long rod and handed it to her. Lucy wasn't aware of what actual platinum would look like, so she gave it a cursory glance and tossed it back to him.

The fiery streak fell on the orchard as Lucy predicted. No explosion followed, just the chill air coming in through the rolled-down window.

"Fine," she sighed. "I'll take you, but I'm gonna need all the coins."

This is insane. When does it end, Lucy? Sarah's words echoed in her mind. . . . It could end tonight.

If they're still worth the same price, that's about ninety thousand dollars. I can go to school and buy mom her new meds. I can live a normal life.

"Then it is agreed. You will take me to the landing site in exchange for the sum."

The dancing lights of a police cruiser pierced the night. Lucy looked through the rearview and saw they were still far off in the distance.

Either that asshole reported the car stolen, or they're going to the crash site. Whatever the case, it's a big problem!

More lights joined the flashing dance.

"Fuck!" Lucy popped the car into first and screeched back onto the road, switching gears as fast as the classic would allow.

The exit to the farms was coming soon as far as she remembered.

"Will the vehicles with strobing lights be a problem, miss?"

"You could say that," Lucy nodded. "And they're going the same way as us—or after us."

"It would be best if they are disabled then, correct?"

"Yeah, I mean, uh . . ."

"Understood."

He propped his hand up and began typing in the air. Lucy watched him from the corner of her eye. A blue screen had appeared just above his forearm. Below the screen hovered a keyboard in the same color. Emidius hit its invisible keys. She blinked, and the keyboard vanished. He unbuttoned his coat and pushed its flaps to the side. In place of a belt buckle, a rectangular box flashed once, then a circular opening formed in its center. Emidius grabbed whatever his belt spewed out, then, with the same slithering motion, got out of the open window next to him. He leaned over the side, more than half his body breaking the wind. The noise from the air whipping past him hurt Lucy's ears. His body shivered as if he'd thrown something, then he retracted back inside.

Lucy watched the cars behind them. Nothing happened. Just as she turned to scold him, the night engulfed everything beyond the rear license plate. Lucy glued her eyes to the mirror. The stretch of road behind them had gone completely black.

There was no light from either street or headlights. After ten seconds, cars began to slowly slide out of the night.

"Fuck me, you did it!" she watched him with pure amazement.

"Please, miss, there is no need for profanity."

"Oh, sorry." She leaned on the steering wheel and shook her head.

A few hundred feet later, she took the exit marked *Black Hill*. A flashy billboard behind it read: *Welcome to Black Hill*, and just below, *Home to the best oranges in Georgia*. Between the two sentences was a picture of a young girl, holding an orange and running away from a boy chasing her.

FIVE

With the speed they were going, the lights from the city quickly faded. The immediate threat of pursuers had disappeared, but the danger of the thing in the car remained. Lucy tried to keep her hands from shaking by gripping the steering wheel, but her forearms continued to tremble. The creature sitting next to her was all wrong; she didn't see its chest rise or fall. It showed no signs of respiration at all. Terror rose from her stomach. The thought of being in the dark with this thing bubbled up her throat.

Emidius spoke. "We have to continue going forward for another 3.5 kilometers." His monotone syllables echoed through the shadowy interior.

"I don't know how much that is," Lucy stumbled over her words, "so you just tell me when to stop, okay?"

His suit creaked as he turned his head, and even in near-complete darkness, Lucy saw his mask nod in agreement. The car's wheels left the well-paved road and now treaded packed dirt. The looming orchard branches obscured the moon's light, and Lucy thanked God for the illumination the headlights provided. With each tree that sped by, the orchard began to appear as a giant, thorny hand, reaching forward intending to crush her in its palm. Blinking the image away, she took a deep breath. Her arms continued to shake, but at least her mind was free of the terrible visage for a moment.

"Stop here," Emidius commanded.

Lucy stopped the car before she had a chance to process the words. Turning her head, she saw him wiggle out of the opened window. Lucy leaned on the steering wheel, hands crossed beneath her chin. The absurdity of his exit calmed her tremors somewhat. Once out, Emidius put his mask through the window.

"Wait for me here please, I will be back momentarily. And do not follow. What I am about to do is extremely dangerous, and a civilian not wearing a protective suit"—he gestured to his coat—"would be in mortal danger. My job is to secure the specimen, and if anyone else is present, I cannot guarantee their safety. Am I understood?"

Lucy pushed her head off the wheel and opened both of her hands wide, fingers spread. Emidius watched her for a second, then nodded and slipped back out of the window. The car engine's hum died down, and the headlights showed Lucy that she was alone in the night. Her heartbeat pounded in her ears while her eyes adjusted to the low amount of light. She looked at one of the trees. A single, pale moonbeam illuminated a patch of discolored bark. Disease had turned the mighty defensive layer into a melted, festering hole. The blight on the tree looked strikingly like the patch of wallpaper in Lucy's apartment—one that had been neglected for a long time until stagnant water in the wall broke through.

What if he doesn't come back? The thought choked the air out of her. *What if he just leaves me here, clutching the steering wheel like a frightened schoolgirl?*

Lucy's jaw tightened, so did her hands around the wheel. She was no dupe. Even though terror ran up her arms and spine, the anger boiling in her belly at the prospect of being taken for a fool proved stronger.

I won't let an alien or whatever this thing is ruin my life. I've worked too hard to get here. It promised money. Enough to make everything work, so I can live like a real human being!

Like the rot on the tree, the growing hole on Lucy's wall would never get fixed if no one did anything about it. Releasing the steering wheel, Lucy made her decision and got out of the car.

Wait here, my ass. Diving into the trees, she stalked in the direction of the crash site.

Keeping her distance, she followed the path that the so-called "doctor" had taken. The ground beneath Lucy's feet made no sound. The dirt tried to envelop her feet with each step, and the feeling of imminent collapse stuck in Lucy's mind. Shaking her head, she banished the thoughts of the earth falling away and continued walking.

Lucy soon came upon a clearing. The Doctor had just reached it and was stepping out into the plentiful light of the moon. She circled toward his right. As she got closer, she noticed the clearing was unnatural. It was a few degrees hotter, and the smell of burned citrus wafted through the air. She came as close as she dared until something gooey under her sole drew her attention down. A tar-like, orange liquid writhed beneath her foot. Before she could move it, the liquid coiled around her calf and clung to her skin. Lucy screamed and ran to Emidius. The liquid remained in place, encasing everything under her ankle like a boot.

"What the hell is this?" she yelled, but a focused Emidius didn't respond.

The trees parted on her approach, revealing the subject of the

Doctor's fascination. Embedded in the middle of the clearing was a metallic object.

Good god, is that a spaceship?

It was shaped like a massive teardrop, nestled deep in the upturned earth, steaming like a casserole fresh out the oven. Even thirty feet away, the ground under her feet was warm . . . except on her slime-covered foot. At that moment, all she could think of was Steve Mcqueen in *The Blob*.

Crap . . .

"Hey!" Much closer now, Emidius finally turned his head. "Get this shit off me!"

The sound of snapping branches to the right caught both their attention. Their heads snapped in that direction as another orange liquid stream jumped into the trees. Emidius made a low growl, and Lucy's fear switched targets. He raised an arm, and she backed away reflexively.

"Do not move," he said in an angry monotone and got out three long, black rods.

Lucy rooted herself as the three rods slammed into the dirt around her right foot. A moment later, a blue triangle of light formed around the orange liquid. Lucy looked down; the goo had made it up to her knee. Her eyes went wide, and the terror from minutes ago returned in full force. She watched the thing reach her lower thigh and keep going. The light that encompassed it moved a bit ahead. Emidius tapped away on his air keypad.

"What is this? What are you doing?" Lucy's eyes darted from the light to his rapidly moving fingers.

"I am preparing to amputate your leg."

"Like hell you are!"

Her heart leaped into her throat, where it beat so painfully that she feared it might explode any moment. She tried to pull her leg from the light, but her knee hit the blue wall and couldn't go through. Emidius continued to type into the air, not acknowledging her struggle at all.

No, no, no, no, no.

"H-Hey, look at me. Please. If you cut my leg off, I-I won't be able to help you!"

The dark pools shifted to her eyes.

"The other thing that got away." She waved her hand toward the trees, feeling suddenly feverish and sweating. "You're after that, right?"

He said nothing.

"I-I can help you get it, but I'm gonna need this." She jabbed her finger into a spot of still uncovered thigh.

"Come on! There's gotta be another way you can fix this."

"There is, but that course will cause a considerable amount of pain for you."

"And chopping my leg off won't?"

Emidius nodded and got the platinum rod out of his belt again. He handed it to her. "Bite down on this, so you do not sever your tongue."

Spots on her skin grew hotter as intense beams stabbed the ascending mass. The warmth went clean through Lucy's muscles, leaving double-edge pain on each side of her leg. The invisible piercing rods of light grew in number and soon illuminated all of her skin. The substance bubbled and began to retreat.

Her teeth gnashed on the metal rod, and she lost the ability to hold herself up. With a splayed hand, Emidius propped her up by the chest. The substance on her leg squirmed, moving down. The blue light moved with it. Pulsing, it delivered blow after heated blow to the mass. Each strike making Lucy want to shriek, but the platinum between her teeth only allowed pathetic whimpers to escape. Flaring her nostrils, she endured. The light was just below her knee now. She knelt on her free leg, her breath still heavy, saliva dripping down the sides of her mouth.

Looking down through tear-soaked eyes, she saw that where the light had traveled, her skin had become bright red and blistered like from a bad sunburn. Just under the surface, she imagined the muscle and bone blistered and peeling as well.

At least it's still there, she comforted herself as the light burned the thing away at her ankle.

A few excruciating moments later, it was gone. Emidius released her, and Lucy collapsed to her knees. The Doctor stood up and continued to type. He looked around, then back to the screen. His hands fell by his side, and his dark eyes settled on her.

"In the time it took me to save your leg, I could have completed my mission, sabotaged as it was. Now, it might be too late to stop the organism. You may have doomed your race, miss. I hope your leg was worth that," he said in his monotone, but Lucy felt a sharp sting nonetheless.

He got a pill out of his belt and threw it to her.

"Take this. It will get you up and walking."

Without thinking, Lucy swiped the pill off the ground and threw it into her dry mouth, desperate for respite from the pain still pulsing through her entire body. It left a chalky, bitter taste in her mouth.

Emidius turned in place and lumbered toward the trees.

"What was it?" she yelled just as he merged with the darkness.

"Methamphetamine," the moonlit forest replied.

"Motherfu—"

The pulse of blood pumping in her ears expanded outside

of her and quickened, like the air around her was sympathizing
with her pain. She angled her head to the sky and listened, then
scrambled to her aching foot. She ran into the forest after Emidius
because the sound she heard was not the blood pumping in her
ears but that of approaching helicopters.

SIX

The drug coursed through her body as she hobbled after the Doctor, and although the pain in her leg still plagued her, she struggled to focus on it. Her heart beat too fast. Boundless energy welled up inside her, and she had to expunge it somehow. She blinked and saw Emidius dive deeper into the trees, in the direction the goo had jumped off. The helicopter sounds were even closer now.

"Hey!" she yelled. "We don't have time for this. Choppers are on the way. We have to get out of here!"

Nothing. Lucy stopped in place and listened for a moment. The forest was quiet, but the angry sound of a gravity-defying engine was coming ever closer.

"Fuck this," she said as her upper lip twitched.

Turning around, she ran back to the crash site. She danced around the craft until she got her bearings and made it to the car in a wild run. The ground was clear, so she just had to avoid the trees until she reached the road. Once out, she saw the white mask floating above the car. Emidius stood in place, looking at a now visible screen on his forearm.

"We have to leave," he said with a flat tone that didn't match the immediacy of his words.

"I'd say," Lucy did her best to stomp her feet, but the soft soil prevented her. "Hear that?" She pointed a finger to the sky and whirled her wrist in a circle. "That aggressive noise is a helicopter filled with—"

"A response team from somewhere called the CDC," he enunciated the organization's letters without hesitation.

"What? How do you know that?"

"I managed to intercept unencrypted radio communications from adjacent sources to the response team."

Probably the cops, then. I doubt that if the CDC had a response team, they wouldn't secure their comms.

"Do hurry, miss," he urged as he slid inside the car through the window. "We are fleeing, after all."

Lucy grimaced, the skin on her nose rippling upward. The single speck of irony in his otherwise monotone voice hadn't escaped her notice. She opened the door and got inside. Her mind was preoccupied with the nagging thought that none of this was worth it. Gripping the wheel tight, she shooed those thoughts away. This was happening, and she *was* getting paid.

Lucy knew John lived somewhere around here, and since the way they took before was now out of the question, she decided they would head there. Turning the key in the ignition, the soft rumble swayed her body once again, but this time it brought no gentle relief. Her body was itching to move, jump, race, or otherwise be in motion. She turned the car around and drove toward the destination.

The moon hid behind the clouds, but the headlights showed the road clear enough. The only sounds Lucy could hear were those of the car and the nearing helicopters. Her heart was doing its best to match the rhythm of the flying machines.

I'm gonna die—this is going to kill me. I can't breathe . . . The thoughts in her head became so oppressive, she rushed to break the silence. "You said you intercepted the radio transmission.

Does that mean you know how far off the helicopter is?"

"Heli . . . copter?"

"Yes, the thing that's making the noise. Don't you know what that is?"

"I merely deduced, from your very hostile tone, that what I heard in the radio transmission was referring to some means of transport headed our way. Is that this *helicopter* you speak of?"

He angled his head toward her then his torso turned in a slow and unsettling way.

"Yeah, it flies great distances and can carry enough weapons to wipe out a small village."

"Fascinating! Advanced aerodynamic machines."

"Sure, yeah, cool," Lucy said with mock enthusiasm. "How long until it gets here?"

Her eyes bulged, and the words in her throat came to an abrupt end. She switched off the headlights. Ten of her accelerated heartbeats later, a loud shadow sailed over the road. In the distance, lights cut through the darkness. The moon reappeared, aiding visibility. The junction she needed should be close by. The sea of police cars might reach them before she could find it. Straining to focus, her eyes lingered for a moment on the contrasting, white mask of Emidius, and behind it, the sign pointing to the residential side of the farm. She wrenched on the wheel, the side of the car scraped a nearby tree, but they made it into the junction unscathed. Lucy let the engine die. Moments later, the road was bathed in red and blue. The car glided deeper into the trees as she watched in the rearview mirror.

One, two, three, five, six. The cars she counted continued toward the crash site, and none of them stopped.

Lucy let out a sigh, then gripped the wheel with her left hand and turned the ignition again. About half a mile down, they reached a clearing with a house. The house and its surroundings were dark save for a tiny red pinpoint in the night about six feet in the air.

"Shit." Lucy ducked.

Someone was smoking on the front porch.

"Hey! Get down." She grabbed the Doctor's black shoulder and yanked him down without much success.

The dark figure tilted its head to the right then moved forward. The top of its mask touching the windshield.

Perched there, turning halfway to Lucy, it spoke. "I am unable to move much further, miss."

Lucy caught a hint of sarcasm in his words. Glancing back, she saw the lit cigarette fall to the ground, then the front door of the house opened. She gritted her teeth and got back up in the seat. Turning on the headlights, she drove to the end of the forest, which merged with the coastal road leading to Roan.

Traffic was non-existent here, but Lucy was full of energy; she gripped the wheel tight, and her feet twitched. Twice her shaky foot slipped off the clutch and stalled the car. The pain coming from her burned leg didn't help at all.

"Was there really nothing else you could've given me?" she growled under her breath, cutting the silence.

"Excuse me?" Emidius turned to face her.

Does he always have to look at me like that?

"Don't you *excuse me*. You gave me meth!" Lucy leaned on the steering wheel and began to sway her body left to right.

"You, in turn, compromised my mission and possibly doomed your entire species."

"Yeah, that remains to be seen." She smacked her lips, trying to get rid of the dryness in her mouth.

A cracking noise came from the right.

"Stop the vehicle," he commanded.

Lucy glanced over and saw that his fingers had pierced the dashboard. She complied without a word.

"What?" She turned to face him as the car came to a halt.

Emidius pushed the door off its hinges and stepped out onto the road.

"Hey, what are you doing?" Lucy leaned in after him. "We have to get back to the city and lay low."

"No," he said, and a bone-deep chill went through her body. "What we must do is fix the mistake that we have created, and since it seems you are unwilling to cooperate, I will return to the landing site and attempt to mend this disaster."

Lucy opened her door and followed him outside. "You are *not* leaving! We had a deal. I got you where you wanted to go; now you pay up. Or maybe I should turn around and help the police catch you?"

He closed the distance between them in an eyeblink. Putting his right hand on the side of the car and pushed, the sound of rubber scraping concrete filled the air.

"No one on this planet can *catch* me. Best remember that, miss."

His voice bordered on rage. He seemed to keep the emotion at bay, but the way the car moved to the side like it were a toy, made Lucy's feet almost give out underneath her. She nodded, her teeth clattering.

"Apply this on the burned area." He handed her a small vial of silver paste, his voice back to its typical monotone. "By morning, the pain should be gone."

Lucy took the vial in her trembling hands. *What the fuck did I get myself into?*

"Your name?" he demanded.

"L-Lucy."

"I want to say it was a pleasure to meet you, but it decidedly was not. Since you are unwilling to cooperate now, let us agree upon a place and time where we can meet tomorrow if I am not able to resolve the problem tonight."

"No."

Her response came as a shock to both of them. She wasn't sure how she mustered the courage to decline this creature who was obviously so much stronger than her.

But I did, and here we are. Her recklessness was worthy of a sigh, but she couldn't muster one now.

"And why not pray tell?"

"Not my problem."

"If we look honestly at this situation, we will find, miss, that it is unequivocally your fault that the organism escaped."

"Sure." She nodded and pointed at him with a wave of her hand. "But it's your job to catch it, not mine."

"I see." His posture lengthened. "Am I to understand that you are unwilling to do the honorable thing and help me?" His head leaned toward his left shoulder.

"People that know me wouldn't call me honorable. Best of luck, though." She spun on her aching heel and got back into the car.

After looking at her for a brief moment, Dr. Emidius nodded and turned around. Taking a step into the orchard, he melded with the darkness.

"Then pray that I succeed . . ." Lucy heard him say. She couldn't be sure, but she thought his following words were ". . . or all of you are dead."

DAY 1

SEVEN

The first thing Lucy did when she got back to the city was ditch the car. The walk back in heels was excruciating, but she didn't have the cash for a taxi, and buses wouldn't start running for another few hours. The last mile to the apartment building blurred time and space, and Lucy awoke on her couch. Daylight trickling in through her blinds coaxed her eyes open, and she rubbed her throbbing forehead. Her tired gaze lingered on the area her burn should be, now covered. Pulling up the leg of her sweatpants she didn't remember putting on, she noticed the skin underneath was an unusual, pale blue color.

What do you know, the ointment really did work.

A metallic clang made her shoot up to her feet. She shuffled to the door and grabbed the knob. Another clang. This time from outside, vibrations running through the doorknob and into her hand.

"Enough," she said, swinging the door open.

Sarah stood holding a plumbing wrench as big as her forearm. The weight of the instrument dragging her forward.

"You're okay!" She dropped the wrench to the side and hugged Lucy around the waist.

"Of course, but if you made me lose my deposit because of the stupid door, I wouldn't be," she joked, trying to rid the concern from her friend's face.

"If you opened it on time, I wouldn't have to resort to handling tools."

Sarah glanced at the wrench and shook her hands in the air like she'd touched something disgusting.

"The way you look"—Lucy leaned on the doorframe and smiled—"I'd say you were just coming back from handling tools."

"Very funny." Sarah tilted her head to the side. "Can I come in?"

Lucy closed her eyes and nodded as she stepped back to make room. Sarah brushed by her and sat on the couch.

"Sorry, I can't offer you anything in the way of refreshments," she said, closing and locking the door.

"That's okay. I just have a few minutes anyway. I came down to the shop, but you weren't—"

"Shit." Lucy clutched her hair in her fingers. "What time is it?"

"It should be around 9:30 now."

"Mother—"

Sarah raised a hand to stop her.

"I already let Mr. Wilson know that we were out drinking last night, so that's covered."

Lucy turned around and put her hands on the kitchen counter. Her fingers formed a wave as they tapped on the surface. Last night's events flashed before her eyes.

Calm down. There's no way the government will let anything even remotely close to the landing site leave the farm. That's not my problem. Lucy wanted to feel reassured by this, but she wasn't. Something at the back of her head kept on nagging. As if reality had slipped away.

"I feel bad for last night." Sarah's words slammed her back to the present.

"It could've gone better, yeah." Lucy sighed. "Sometimes, these things don't work out. It wasn't meant to be and all that." She hoped her disinterested tone would tip off Sarah that she didn't want to have this conversation right now.

Instead of replying, Sarah shifted her body to face her. "Do you think I'm a slut?"

Lucy recoiled and narrowed her eyes. "No. Why would you ask that?"

Sarah's expression softened, her posture relaxed, and she settled in for a lengthy discussion.

Goddamn it! I don't have time for this. Why can't we talk about bullshit some other time? Like never.

"You noticed by my clothes that I'm coming back from Damien's place," Sarah began in a quiet voice. "And we had sex last night."

"Just like normal people." Lucy nodded and came closer.

"That's just it. It wasn't normal. Normal for him, maybe." Sarah's eyebrows rose, her gaze remained locked on the floor.

"Meaning?" Lucy dragged her single chair over and sat across from her.

She sighed. "Last night, he asked me if we could try some rough stuff."

Lucy leaned back into the chair, her right arm loose and hanging on the side.

"Like choking and slapping, nothing too violent. The slapping I didn't like; the choking felt great. I've never orgasmed like that. . . . Is that bad?" Her eyes moved up and met Lucy's gaze.

"Too much information, yes. Bad? No—It doesn't mean you're a slut," She leaned forward in the chair. *Let's get this drivel over with*, she thought and continued. "It just means that

Damien has fucked a lot of girls."

Sarah's head snapped back like she'd been struck.

"Come on, don't give me that look." Lucy raised her head and narrowed her eyes. "How the hell else do you think he got so good? Honestly."

"That's exactly my point." Sarah tilted her head to the side. "Afterward, he was acting so cold. What if he's done with me now?"

"No, I believe that's anal." Lucy half-smiled.

"I'm having a crisis here! The holiday I told you about last night. I paid for that and other stuff too. I feel like he's using me. What if Damien's done with me now, and he'll find someone else."

"Well, duh." Lucy's stare was flat. "Of course he's using you. You're filthy rich!" She threw both hands in the air.

"My parents are rich, Lu, not me," the sullen words tumbled out of her mouth.

"It probably doesn't matter all that much to him. The simple fact is that people that don't have money, like me"—she placed her open palm on her chest—"can level the playing field only if we manipulate people who have money. Like you." Her palm separated from her chest, and in a smooth motion, her finger pointed at Sarah. "Just dump his ass and find someone rich, so you don't have this problem in the future."

"I came here for help." Sarah's lips formed a trembling frown. She shot straight up and, with a quick step, went out, slamming the door behind her.

"I did!" Lucy called back, a moment too late.

Running her hand through her hair, she sighed. She'd pay for this conversation later, but right now, she had damage control to do at work.

She got up from the chair and went into the bathroom for a quick shower. While she scrubbed herself clean, she realized that she'd changed her clothes in her drugged stupor.

Impressive work, she congratulated herself.

Going into her bedroom to find something to wear, she saw the sparkling dress splayed neatly on her bed, not a wrinkle in sight. Not wanting the further reminder of the dumpster fire that was last night, she tossed it onto the vanity. After five minutes, she was dressed and out of the apartment. On the ground floor, she checked her phone for the time. The display showed 9:59 AM.

Only a few people were on the sidewalks, but all of them ogled a tall figure dressed in black, wearing a white bird mask. Doctor Emidius stood next to Mr. Wilson's shop. His arm was up in the air, but he was not typing anything, only staring, his head angled oddly. Lucy froze, the pain of last night hitting her full force before being replaced with a torrent of fury. She crossed the street, and he leveled his head to look at her.

"Good day, Miss Lucy. It is not a pleasure to see you."

"Right back at ya." She gestured with her hand to the alley next to the store. "Get off the street. You're drawing attention."

He nodded and followed her into the much quieter side path.

"You're here to give me the coins, right?"

"No." Annoyance colored his even voice. "I am here because your species is in danger, and I still require assistance." His tone shifted from annoyed to disbelieving; the white beak hovered in dangerous proximity over her jugular.

"No deal." Lucy's arm crossed her chest. "This is your mess. You fix it."

"*Our* mess," he corrected, the way he straightened his back and shoulders signaled to Lucy that her words ruffled his proverbial feathers. "The organism escaped because of your interference."

"Yeah, so you say," Lucy shot back. "What about the other one? The one you burned away, along with a layer of my epidermis. You are only one guy, after all. How were you supposed to catch both of those things if they were running around?"

He seemed to be cowed by her outburst. Lucy narrowed her eyes and decided to try something. "You got the one on my leg. Why couldn't you catch the other one without my *interference?*"

"The one that escaped is a class 5 organism with immense camouflaging abilities, capable of mimicry on a molecular level. The one I destroyed had advanced movement capabilities . . ."

"So, it was a gamble which one you went after. If you changed targets and got the mimic one, the other one might've gotten away from you too. Ha!" Lucy smiled triumphantly. "Don't give me that high horse bullshit then. Pay up what you owe me and go fix *your* mistake."

His demeanor changed. Hands hanging loosely by his sides, black circles for eyes fixated on her.

"You do not have even an inkling of my abilities. Five or six similar organisms may be child's play for me. The fact remains that you disobeyed my direct instructions and interfered at the worst possible junction. For this, you are accountable, are you not?"

Lucy lowered her defiant chin an inch. "Okay . . . yeah."

"As we discussed during the early hours of the day, I still require your help. Our agreement stands, I will imburse you the amount promised, and as a gesture of goodwill, I will give you 150 of the coins now and 150 upon completion of my task. Is that acceptable?"

Lucy tensed and got ready to run. No amount of money could be worth handing herself over to the mercy of this *thing* . . .

could it?

"You saw a glimpse of my abilities. Do you truly believe you can outrun or outfight me?"

Lucy raised her hands and moved them around, limbering up.

"You don't scare me. You may be tougher than me, but I'll take my chances, and you can be sure I won't make it easy for you." Lucy cracked her neck and lowered her stance.

He shook his head and said, "Do you have a quarter?"

"What now?" She straightened.

"I require a quarter to convince you of your disastrously wrong assumptions."

Lucy smiled and took out a quarter, throwing it to him. He caught it in his left hand, displayed it for her to see, and then bent the quarter into a half-circle with his index finger and thumb. Lucy blinked, and same as last night, he was standing next to her.

"Agility is one of my lesser physical attributes." He looked down at her and spoke in a much quieter tone.

His left hand moved down in a blur, and a loud crack followed. Lucy looked at the ground and saw a fresh hole in the sidewalk, about the size of the bent quarter. She gulped. Panic gripped her, and she attempted to flee. The figure next to her grabbed her shoulder, holding her in place.

"Now that you have a proper perspective on the matter, would you kindly assist me in completing my mission? You gain valuable metals, and I save your species from extinction. I do not have to be so generous."

Lucy struggled to steady her breathing, but her body would not cease to tremble under pressure of the dark looming figure in front of her. The cool wall of the store touched her neck, and the nightmare creature with impossible abilities blocked the only way out. There were no alternatives for her to pursue. Emidius seemed to pick up on that and took a step back.

"There is no need for fear, Miss Lucy." He extended his right hand. "I would never turn my strength against a comrade."

Lucy nodded, took the hand, and reluctantly shook. She let go, and her muscles relaxed with the distance he had created between them.

"Here is what information I was able to gather." He put both hands behind his waist and straightened his back as if he were a soldier giving a report. "With the help of my instruments, I was able to infer the organism has taken the shape of an orange, which was harvested and consequently transported. Before the last of the vehicles left, I was able to catch a glimpse of an image on the side—two children running in front of a field."

"Okay." Lucy perked up. "That's perfect. The truck belongs to Hilltop Farms. We get morning deliveries from them."

"We?"

Lucy nodded to the shop. "The market. I work here. Maybe we can get this over with fast."

"We can only hope, Miss Lucy. Lead the way."

They both went into the store. Only one customer was inside. He finished paying at the counter, turned around, and jumped at the sight of the Doctor. With a nervous step, the man tip-toed around them and ran out. Lucy prepared herself with a deep breath as they approached the counter.

"Morning, Mr. Wilson, really sorry I couldn't make it on time today."

Mr. Wilson gave her a cursory glance but kept his eye on Emidius.

"No worries, I'm just glad you had some fun. Mrs. Rayburn

wasn't too happy, but I got her sorted." The sides of his cheeks rose in a triumphant smile hidden under his giant mustache.

"Sorry to make you handle that. Did she buy something specific from today's batch?"

"Almost all of it. Had to help her load it all into the car."

"Why did she buy so much?" Lucy asked, feeling guilty that Mr. Wilson had to halt work to help the woman out.

"She was pretty embarrassed about that. Said she wasn't sure how much of the produce she'd mess up until she got it right, but once it was done, the rest she'd donate to charity."

Bah, charity. Probably just wants to show all the other rich soccer moms at the party how generous she is.

"I see," Lucy said. "Well, sorry to disrupt business like this . . ."

Mr. Wilson dismissed her worry with a wave. "Your friend's awfully quiet there," he said, extending a hand. "George Wilson, proprietor."

"Doctor Emidius." The tall figure shook the shopkeeper's hand.

"The Doc and I, we go way back," Lucy jumped in before Emidius could blabber something out of place. "He's here for a costume convention, cosplay, they call it. It's very popular. I promised I'd help him while he's in the city, and I forgot to ask you if that'd be okay."

She knocked her fist on the top of her head as if to check for the tell-tale hollow echo and gave another apologetic smile. Mr. Wilson looked the Doctor over once more.

"Of course." He leaned close to her as the Doctor veered off to explore the items on display. "Be careful around people that throw their titles into unrelated conversations like that. Just some wisdom from an old man." He gave her a warm smile and leaned back.

"Pleasure to meet you, sir. Hope you have fun at your convention. Now, if you'll excuse me." He nodded behind them.

Lucy and the Doctor stepped aside for the next customer. They continued down the aisle and into the back room.

"This is where we store the shipments after delivery. Can you scan for traces of the organism or something?"

"Or something," he said as he walked past her.

He knelt down and got four familiar rods out of his coat. Shivering, she turned away and let him do his business. A few minutes later, he rose and walked out the front door.

We're leaving, apparently.

She waved Mr. Wilson goodbye, and he did the same. On the outside, the Doctor went into the nearest alleyway.

"Any luck?" she asked. *Please tell me this is done.*

"Some, yes. There is a high probability the organism was bought by this *Mrs. Rayburn*. I was able to detect faint traces."

"Traces of what? The organism?"

"If I were able to trace the organism, Miss Lucy, I would not need your . . ." he paused for an agonizing moment ". . . assistance. What I was able to find were traces of fruit harvested from the most likely trees from which I took samples."

"Fruit the organism hitched a ride on?"

"Quite," the Doctor replied with an almost sour note.

Guess he doesn't like to repeat himself. Well tough. Lucy crossed her arms. She was beginning to find this creature very obtuse.

"Okay, so there's a good chance the organism is at Mrs. Rayburn's house. Good thing I know where it is. But before that, we need a story."

"A story?" The Doctor tilted his head to the right and stared at her.

"Yes. We need a reason to visit and most probably a reason to enter. I can come up with something about getting news of the fruit being bad, but you're gonna need to sell it." She pointed at him with her left index finger and nibbled her right thumb.

The Doctor's head kept its maddening tilt.

"I mean, we need to pass you for a police officer or FBI agent. Whatever it is, it should be related to the government."

His head stayed in the same position.

Lucy opened her arms wide and growled, "You need to pretend to be from the authorities!"

The Doctor nodded, finally getting it. "I am a doctor."

All Lucy's energy leaked out of her. "You've told me."

"Can we not just tell her that?"

"Not without credentials and a reason to be there . . . we could say you're from Health and Safety." She sighed, feeling the weight of the task ahead of them. "But we need to forge some kind of identification that can get you through the door."

"What would such an identification look like?"

Lucy grimaced. "Like a transparent rectangular holder thingy about this big." She outstretched her thumb and forefinger on both hands and showed the rough measurements.

"I will need some kind of reference. At least something better than your fingers in the air."

Frowning at his lack of faith in her guesstimation, Lucy got out her phone and did a quick search. Scrolling through a couple of pictures, she tapped on one and turned the screen over, showing it to him. His mask moved down until her phone reflected off his black pool eyes. He held the image in his gaze for a few seconds then his alien screen appeared above his forearm. He typed something, then unbuttoned his coat. The fake ID popped out of his belt buckle, and he handed it to her. An older man wearing a white jacket stared up at her from the picture. Lucy turned it over in her fingers.

"Impressive. It'll do, I think." She gave the ID back to him.

"Lead the way, Miss Lucy."

With that, the two of them walked out into the thin wave of pedestrians.

The Doctor held his hands behind his back and took small awkward steps to keep pace with her. "Would you please show me how you found those images on your device later?"

"I'd prefer you to be gone later." The prospect of him staying made the words in her mouth taste sour.

"So would I." He sidled up closer. "But if I must stay, I would be much obliged for any help you could provide with current-day technology."

"Let's just focus on saving the world right now. After that, I'll show you how to browse all the porn you want, don't you worry."

Half an hour later, they knocked on a pair of grand doors. The knob turned, and Mrs. Rayburn appeared. She wore stylish jeans, her hair tied in a ponytail. On top of her designer shirt, she wore a white apron. Lucy couldn't help but notice the Armani eagle logo embroidered on the corner. She wanted to scoff but chose to flash her shop girl smile instead.

"Lucy, hello!" Mrs. Rayburn returned a charming smile of her own.

A moment later, she noticed the Doctor, and her smile disappeared. Her eyes darted between him and Lucy several times. The subtle movements of her head and body resembled those of an animal in headlights.

"Ahem, I missed you this morning, Lucy," Mrs. Rayburn said with a slight quiver in her voice, "you could've helped me pick out the fruit."

"Yeah, sorry about that. I wasn't feeling well earlier." Lucy put her hand on her pelvis to cement the reality of her discomfort.

Mrs. Rayburn's eyes focused on the spot where Lucy indicated, then she nodded as if nothing more needed saying.

"So, who's your friend?" Mrs. Rayburn asked with a pleasant ring to her voice, staring at the Doctor, "and does he know that Halloween isn't for some time now?"

The laugh she produced was so fake that Lucy almost lost her composure. "Yes, let me introduce you. This is Doctor Emidius. He's a Health and Safety inspector."

The Doctor extended his hand to Mrs. Rayburn. "A pleasure to meet you, madam."

The woman blushed and rubbed her hands clean on her designer apron.

"May I ask, why are you wearing such strange clothes, Doctor?" The smile on her lips was much more genuine this time.

"That's the first thing I asked too." Lucy chuckled, trying to assuage Mrs. Rayburn's concern that the situation was indeed weird.

"He told me that it was a prototype the ministry is testing. Very safe, very cutting edge. Right, Doctor?" she looked at him with her eyebrows raised high.

"Ahem," he made a slight pause, "yes, indeed."

"I see." Mrs. Rayburn nodded. "Are you from the States, Doctor Emidius?"

Lucy's eyes widened as she scrambled to say something.

The Doctor was quicker. "I am from Italy originally, but I moved to the States some time ago to pursue my passion of . . ." he paused once again, "health and safety."

His tone made him sound really dispassionate about his passion, but Mrs. Rayburn seemed content with the answer. Lucy felt eyes on her and turned around. People gathered on the sidewalk to gawk at them. Mrs. Rayburn hesitated for a moment and threw the Doctor a concerned look. He leaned in.

"Just a moment, madam." He did his best to fake annoyance and plunged his hand inside his coat. "My credentials and ministry inspection order are with me. Let me get them out. Ah, my identification first . . ." He got the ID out and handed it to Mrs. Rayburn.

While she looked at it, he continued to search for the non-existent ministry inspection order. Mrs. Rayburn's eyes jumped from watching neighbors to gawking passersby.

Lucy interjected, "I'm sorry about bothering you, but could we talk inside?"

"Yes, that would be preferable." The Doctor nodded and leaned closer still. "I would very much like to avoid panic," he said, his tone heavy and severe.

Mrs. Rayburn's eyes grew wide, and she gulped as more people crowded around. "Oh, yes, of course, come in." She stepped aside. "Excuse the mess, but I've been busy in the kitchen."

Lucy strode inside with the Doctor right behind her. They were in a small hallway that branched in all directions—upward toward the bedrooms, left to a dining room, and right to a living room. The house looked small from the outside, but inside, its true expanse was made apparent by clever design.

"Right this way." Mrs. Rayburn pointed to the dining room ahead of them.

Lucy and the Doctor followed silently, and Mrs. Rayburn continued into the kitchen.

"Make yourselves comfortable," she called back. "I'll be right with you."

Lucy held a palm up to stop the Doctor from taking a seat. He looked at the chair he'd grabbed, and his shoulders sagged. He moved closer to Lucy as she went through the kitchen door. Loud music played from an open laptop on the counter.

"Sorry, Mrs. Rayburn," Lucy said, as her host abruptly closed the lid of the computer, "but we're in a bit of a hurry. We have to do this and be on our way."

"Mmm, yes, yes." Mrs. Rayburn nodded and straightened up. She noticed the Doctor's ID still in her hands, so she shook her head and handed it back.

"How can I help?" she asked once he'd returned it to his coat pocket.

"Well, there seems to have been a problem with today's shipment of fruit. The inspector came in this morning and found some . . . irregularities. Mr. Wilson was so concerned that he sent me over to personally extend his deepest apologies. The Doctor wanted to come and make sure that everyone was okay, that you didn't have any spoiled food, and no one was sick after eating anything. Stuff like that," Lucy finished talking and took a long breath.

She turned to the Doctor and gave him a pleading look.

"Right, Doctor?" Annoyance seeped out of her tone.

The Doctor glanced at each of them.

"Yes, precisely right, Miss Lucy!" he exclaimed in the least convincing way possible. To add to his discredit, he actually bent his arm up at the elbow, index finger pointing to the ceiling.

He looks like a fucking cartoon; Lucy wanted to slap her face at the thought.

"Ahem, yes." She coughed and continued in a flat tone, "Can you show us the fruit you bought, and the inspector can make sure everything is in order?"

"First, please tell me what this is about." Suspicion pulled Mrs. Rayburn's lips into a taut line, making her dimples visible.

"Certainly, Madam," the Doctor said. "The fruit you bought today may not be up to ministry standards, and we have received reports of contamination in several other locations throughout the city. This is strictly routine. There is no need for you to worry."

"Oh, my," Mrs. Rayburn exclaimed, her hand shooting up to her mouth, "If there could be something dangerous to our health, then, by all means, go ahead. Good thing you came when you did; I was going to give the rest to the community center. Sorry, I'm babbling. I put the fruit in that bowl over there." She pointed at a bowl on the counter opposite the door.

"Thank you," Lucy placed a hand on Mrs. Rayburn's upper arm and stared into her eyes.

Letting go, Lucy motioned to the Doctor.

They both walked to the counter.

Emidius reached to activate his screen, and Lucy grabbed his hand. The texture of the suit was like a mix between rubber and fur. She turned to their reluctant host. "Would you please wait for us outside?"

"Oh, yes, of course." Mrs. Rayburn took a final, concerned look around and left the room.

When Lucy turned again, she found the Doctor holding three small rods. Two were in his right hand, the last one in the left. They looked like the same ones he used in the forest, and Lucy surmised they might have several uses besides exterminating dangerous organisms and burning the flesh off young women. The recently healed skin on her leg tingled uncomfortably. The rods lit up with blue light at the top. It, in turn, formed a faint, transparent, triangular field around the fruit. The field began at the end of the batons and ended in a single point just above the highest fruit. Once fully formed, its inside filled up with blue mist that looked like the static displayed by an old, broken TV screen. The field shimmered and swayed for a second. Emidius typed symbols that looked like snakes entwined in different positions on his screen, and the field crystallized.

"What's that? What's happening?" Lucy asked.

Silence again. He continued to type on his screen. Lucy stepped closer and grabbed his elbow.

"Hey, I got you this far, talk to me. Is this going to take long? Do I have to go out and stall?"

"No need." He turned his head toward her. "I will be done momentarily. What I am doing now is setting up a perimeter around the suspected fruit and performing rudimentary tests. As soon as they finish, we can decide how to proceed."

He returned to his screen. Lucy moved closer and saw a stream of information sliding up it. She couldn't understand any of the writing, so she stepped back and watched the hazy field separating her and the fruit.

"Miss Lucy, there was an infected specimen here," he spoke without looking away from the flowing letters, displeasure creeping through his monotone. "Sadly, this is not the primary vector we are searching for. This bears the marks of the organism, but only residue."

He met Lucy's look of confusion.

"This means," he continued, "that one of these fruits was very close to the impact zone we visited last night. There is still a possibility we have found the right place."

"So, what do we do?"

"Now, Miss Lucy, it would be wise to ask Mrs. Rayburn if

there are any other fruits left while I dispose of these." He waved his hand to the bowl.

Lucy clicked her tongue. "Carry on then." She walked by him and left the room.

Mrs. Rayburn wasn't in the dining room; Lucy found her pacing by the front door.

"Is everything okay?" the woman asked.

"Oh, yes. The Doctor's just finishing up."

Looking back, she saw violent flashes of blue light coming from beneath the door frame. Taking two quick steps forward, she placed herself between Mrs. Rayburn and the kitchen.

"The inspector found some possible signs of contamination with one of the fruits, so he's getting them stored and ready for disposal. He assured me everything is according to regulation and is very safe. There's nothing to worry about." Lucy added the last part more for her own assurance than the socialite's.

"Oh, good." Mrs. Rayburn put a hand on her chest. "That's a relief. I'm going to have some words with Mr. Wilson tomorrow!" she exclaimed, striding into the living room and reclining on her couch.

"Mrs. Rayburn, I wanted to ask, is there any more fruit in the house? Anything you might have put away for later?"

"No, that was all I was going to use for the sweets—wait!" Her eyes grew wide. "I gave Johnathan and his friends a couple of oranges earlier."

Mrs. Rayburn jumped off of the couch and scurried past her. Lucy blinked once, then ran to the kitchen door. "Doc, we've got a situation," she yelled on the way.

"Johnathan!" Mrs. Rayburn's shout came from upstairs.

Lucy opened the door.

"There were more oranges," she said after coming inside.

"Mrs. Rayburn gave some to her son and his friends."

The Doctor's demeanor changed in the blink of an eye. He dropped his center of mass and leaned forward. Prepared for a fight, he slipped past her like a shadow. She barely had time to dodge his movement. Saying nothing, Lucy followed as best she could.

By the time she exited the kitchen, the Doctor was making the turn to the stairwell.

"Johnathan!" another desperate cry came down.

Lucy sprinted to the stairs. There was no sign of the Doctor, so she headed up. On the final step, an almost inhuman howl filled the hallway. It sounded like Mrs. Rayburn but more primal and uncontrolled. She followed the screams. The Doctor stood in a doorway from where the terrible and pained cry had come. Beyond him, the sight of a recent slaughter froze Lucy in place.

EIGHT

Mrs. Rayburn kneeled on the ground near the center of the room. Char marks etched the floor around her in a perfect circle, but the area inside it was pristine. The trembling woman grabbed a blue stuffed toy from the ground and clutched it. Swaying backward, she sat on her calves. Her head drifted aimlessly.

Lucy surveyed the room. Blood splatters painted the carpet, toys, and walls. She turned to the Doctor in horror and followed his black-pooled gaze upward.

Oozing globs hung above the unburned circle, each a varying shade of pink. Lucy stared at the pulpy mass for a moment, then returned her attention to the room. It was nearly destroyed. The mattress and sheets from the little race car bed were ripped to shreds as if by a wild animal. A dresser lay toppled on the floor, all of its contents thrown around in torn strips. The trail of clothing led to the window, its upper and middle sash broken in half like something had been thrown out of the room. Still grasping onto the stuffed toy, Mrs. Rayburn suddenly shot up to her feet.

"Johnathan," she screamed, running out of the room. "I have to find him—Johnathan!"

Wild and frantic, the woman went from door to door shouting her son's name.

"I have to investigate." The Doctor stepped into the room before Lucy could say anything.

Lucy had seen Johnathan with his mother at the store. He liked a particular type of candy that she never bought for him. After each denial, his little shoulders would slump, and his feet shuffled. Bile rose in Lucy's throat at the thought that one of the pink pustules on the ceiling could be that lively young boy. She gripped the side of the door frame, her mouth quivering beyond her control. The skin under her nails had turned white. She forced her eyes to focus on the wood grain of the door, to trace the dark lines in her mind and breathe.

Get a grip, she scolded herself. *It's just another dead person. Plenty of those around this city. Every once in a while, they even pop up on jobs.*

Of course they do! her inner voice responded to her thoughts. *But this is someone I know. Shit, I just saw the kid a few weeks ago, and now he may be splatter on the fucking wall!*

The image pushed the bile further up her throat.

Tough luck. They were in the wrong place at the wrong time. It happens, she tried to rationalize. *It's a shitty way to go, but that's life.*

The thoughts in her head only made the bad taste in her mouth worsen. Shaking them off, she noticed the Doctor staring at her. "You need something?"

"Yes, some time alone with the scene."

"I'll keep watch. Just be quick, cuz in a couple of minutes, the cops are gonna be taking over."

He nodded, and Lucy spun in place, finally breaking visual contact with the room of carnage. She had trouble letting go of the wood frame. Her feet gave out beneath her, and she slid across the hallway wall. It seemed that her hand had been doing most of the work of keeping her upright. Her chest rose up and down, ragged breaths shaking her neck and shoulders. The sound of rushing blood filled her ears, but it wasn't quite enough to drown out the wails of Mrs. Rayburn. The woman sounded more and more desperate with each passing scream of her son's name.

She's gonna call the cops any minute now. The thought introduced a new fear into her mind. *Maybe I should suggest it to her, and then we can both wait for them to come. I'll explain everything that happened, and they can fix this.*

She tried getting up, but the terror of the thing looking for clues in the next room made it impossible. The Doctor seemed amicable now, but she was sticking to the plan. Just the both of them, no time or effort wasted by bureaucracy or politics. A small part of her screamed that she was in over her head—that she needed help, maybe more than the world could offer, but the situation was dire. Dire enough for her to ask for help?

No. I'll do it the same way I've always done it. Just me. Well, the Doctor is here this time, but he hardly counts, and all he needs to do is get rid of this thing and leave me alone!

Plus, the cops would bust her for grand theft auto first, and only then, hopefully, they'd ask the right questions and rectify the situation. The game plan had to stay the same. She'd get to the bottom of this with the Doctor and then enjoy her reward.

For now, she'd keep her bets on the thing in the other room that insisted it was a doctor.

Fear somewhat abated, Lucy dared to peek back in. The Doctor stood near the broken window, studying the hole in its middle. She rested the back of her head on the wall.

This is pointless anyway. He moves faster than me and is stronger than any human. She pondered her use of pronouns. Shaking her head, she closed her eyes and rubbed them with her palms. He, it, whatever. This whole situation had her tripping over herself. The bigger issue here was that Johnathan or any of the other kids could still be alive. That's what she had to focus on. She and the Doctor had the best chance of finding any of them alive.

The thought of a lost child that needed her help gave her the resolve she needed. Slowly and with shaking knees, she slid up along the wall. The terror of the Doctor and the dread of the unknown contagion that could wipe out the human race was still there, and, despite it, she stood. Placing her palms on the wallpaper, she pushed off. Teetering for a moment, she found her balance and towered upright.

She moved to the stairwell's railing, grabbed it, and leaned forward. Just as she did, Mrs. Rayburn appeared from the living room and raced up the stairs with blinding speed. She stopped dead in her tracks halfway.

"No, no, no, no! Already checked there. Maybe they ran outside, right?" she asked, voice breaking, looking at Lucy with hope.

"That's right. I'll stay here in case they get back. You go look outside." She did her best to sound reassuring, even flashing the woman a placid smile.

"Oh, thank you." Mrs. Rayburn waved her open-palmed hand at Lucy and then turned around. "I'll be right back. If you do see them, tell them not to move a muscle." She went down the stairs and ran out, not even closing the door behind her.

Lucy returned to the room. Emidius kneeled near the center circle. "Anything, Doc?"

She liked the way 'Doc' sounded. He didn't have to show her an actual diploma or anything, but Doc was neutral enough, and it saved her the trouble of philosophizing about he's or its.

"Yes, as you can see, we were unfortunately too late." He stood up and stalked closer.

Even through the monotone, the way he spoke made Lucy feel like he somehow blamed her for this. He brushed by Lucy's shoulder, pushing her out of the way. She ground her teeth and grabbed him by the elbow. To her surprise, he allowed her to spin him around.

"Don't put this clusterfuck on me. You hear?"

"*I* was not. But you made the statement yourself, so there might be truth to it."

His mask moved down until it was only a handspan away.

"Real mature! You're gonna be petty now? Right now, when God knows how many children's blood has been spilled in that room?"

"Yes, right now," the Doctor took a step toward her. "The child or children that were in that room are dead, but you seem to miss the larger ramifications in play, Miss Lucy," his voice rained down in a hiss.

He loomed over her. The beak of his mask touched her collarbone.

"The blood spilled in that room means that a human being has been infected. The broken window is an indication of the direction it fled. Now, while you prattle on, vainly trying to shield yourself from the guilt you feel for what is transpiring here, a wholly new life form is stalking your fellow man."

His calm, monotone voice had disappeared to be replaced by a razor-sharp accusatory string of verbal knives. His proximity evoked images of a keen beak slicing open her weak, fleshy throat. Instead of being unnerved, she became adamant in her belief that this was not solely her fault.

"This is not on me. The only reason we are late is because you drugged me. After I rubbed the ointment on my skin yesterday, I fell asleep and don't remember anything else!" She stabbed a finger in his chest.

No soft flesh gave way. Instead, it hurt like she'd just voluntarily jabbed a wall, with intent to penetrate no less. Blood rushed all along her body. Her breathing became heavy just as it had a few minutes ago, but this time the force behind it was rage.

"I supplied you with that salve to heal your injuries. The social visit we paid at your workplace was time wasted on trivialities."

"What the fuck do you know about that? That's my job! I have a life beyond this." She made a sweeping gesture.

"And thanks to that, no one on this planet may get to further enjoy theirs."

Lucy had no reply to that. After a few moments of silence, the Doctor took a step back and raised his head to its neutral position. It was as if the exchange had never happened. On the other hand, Lucy realized she'd leaned forward with her arms at her sides as if preparing to grapple with an enemy.

Upon finally getting her breathing under control, she asked, "So, how do we fix this?"

"We locate the infected host and destroy it."

Lucy wanted to remark on his usage of *it* instead of him or her. *He just said it a few moments ago as well. These are not humans to him but new, dangerous life forms threatening the world.*

Even if that were the case, Lucy wasn't on board.

"Don't—"

"Lucy!" Mrs. Rayburn screeched, and the two of them ran to the stairwell. "Did they come back?"

Despite being on the verge of tears, her eyes appeared hopeful as she stared up at them.

"Sorry, no," Lucy said, shaking her head. "I think you should call the police."

"Yes, yes. Dear God, where could they be?" Mrs. Rayburn walked to the window, mumbling. ". . . all that blood." She bumped into the furniture along the way like she had lost her sight.

As she stumbled, Lucy came down and helped the woman take a seat on the couch.

"Can you think of any place they might have gone?" Lucy sat next to her. "The police will ask as well, so you'll be ready with the answer. You won't lose any time thinking."

"I'm not sure," Mrs. Rayburn snorted through occasional sobs.

"Does he play any sports, does he like to eat anything specific, does he have a favorite place to go with friends?" Lucy fired every question that popped into her head.

"The only place I can think of is the arcade. He begs me for quarters every time we go to the store. He really likes the way the machines are painted even though he's not so good at the games." Ripples of anguish distorted her face, and more sobs wracked her body.

"The arcade on the pier?" Lucy didn't feel comfortable questioning the woman right now, but it had to be done.

The Doctor stood at the front door, saying nothing.

"Yes," Mrs. Rayburn answered.

Her eyes lost focus, and the words that followed lost all coherence. Each sorrowful whimper was a painful tug on Lucy's heart.

"I'm sure they're fine." Lucy put her hands on the woman's shoulders and gave them a gentle squeeze. "They might have had an accident and gotten scared, but you should really call the police." She put all the comfort she could muster in her voice.

Mrs. Rayburn just nodded, and her shoulders sagged. She had become a leaky waterbed, slowly deflating in Lucy's arms and leaving her soaked.

"I have to go, but please call 911 now." Lucy helped the woman stand and gave her a gentle nudge toward the kitchen.

Mrs. Rayburn almost tripped on a lamp before disappearing around the wall. Lucy walked over to the Doctor by the wide-open front door. She looked around. Seeing no one, she said, "Stay here for a few seconds. I have to check something out. I'll be right back to get you."

Without waiting for his reply, she continued down the steps and turned left to the alley beside the house. Walking deeper, she reached the fence of Mrs. Rayburn's backyard. Above her, she saw the second story of the house and the hole in the window. Grabbing the edge of the fence, she lifted herself up and inspected the lawn. Noticing a trail of blood and glass, she followed it. A crimson smudge in the vague shape of a child's hand smeared one of the fence's white planks.

Whoever made it out of that room jumped the fence here. She turned her head toward the pier.

With that confirmed, she returned to the Doctor. "Come on, Doc. We're going to the beach."

NINE

The alleyway leading to the shore provided ample shade from the midday sun. That suited Lucy perfectly because Emidius's mask was so white it actually glowed in daylight. They reached the exit, and Lucy raised her hand to stop the Doctor. She took a few steps out onto the pavement and looked around. There was minimal traffic and almost no one on the street. Lucy made two quick hops back into the alley.

"Here's the plan. There's a straight line of alleys we can use to get to the shore, and that's what we'll do. After what happened at Mrs. Rayburn's house, we have to be careful not to draw any unwanted attention."

The Doctor tilted his head in question. "Unwanted attention from who, Miss Lucy?"

Lucy narrowed her eyes, trying to figure out if he was that dense or just pretending.

"The police, duh. Considering the mess that room was in, I wouldn't be surprised if they called goddamn SWAT on me again, and I'm not dealing with that shit twice in a week!"

"I believe we should seek help from the authorities, they should be notified of what is happening at least, so they can better help the populace in a worst-case scenario."

Lucy used her right index finger and thumb to massage both her temples. She clicked her tongue. "I thought about that, but unfortunately, that's not how it works, Doc. We'll only lose time. We were already at the landing site, and now we disturbed a crime scene, that won't look too good for us and once they find out what *you* are . . ." she paused and looked him up and down, "then we'll probably get nothing done. For now, we try our best to do it ourselves. We're already on the trail, and all we need to do is kill this thing, and you're gone, right?"

The Doctor began raising his arms in what looked like an argument, but he decided against it, letting them rest back at his side.

"Good, if we need help in the future, I'll do my best to get you in contact with whoever is necessary." Lucy wasn't sure that would be at all possible, and her tone suggested as much, but the Doctor did not comment.

"Shall we?" He made a simple hand gesture to the street.

Turning around, she surveyed the area and signaled him to move with her. They crossed the street and dove into another alley. As they got closer to the coast, more and more dumpsters appeared along the sun-bleached brick, and where there were dumpsters, Bernard's people would be near. Maybe one of them had spotted an alien-possessed eight-year-old.

Lucy recognized the cardboard boxes they used to make windbreakers that kept them warm at night, but no one was around. Even this tiny amount of "property" of theirs was worth defending. So where were the owners?

As she pondered that, the image of the blood-soaked room popped into her head. *What could leave so much blood and live? If it did live, that is.* She shook her head, exorcising the thought.

She was beginning to think like the Doctor, calling a child *it*. They needed to clear the air.

"Doc," her words flew back over her shoulder to him, "mind

telling me what happened in that room." She motioned with her chin in the direction of Mrs. Rayburn's house.

She prepared arguments to convince him she needed to know.

"Violent redistribution," he replied, his voice lower than usual. "The organism infects a host, merging with it and redistributing its physiology to suit its needs. Some hosts are just not . . . compatible, so when the process begins, the redistribution might become *violent*." The way he said the word made Lucy shiver despite the warm day.

"From what I was able to determine in the room, I would wager that at least one child is deceased and another one is infected."

Dead, the thought made Lucy stumble.

Her breath caught in her throat. She stopped in place and looked out onto the adjacent street. Almost no one there, thankfully. She stood like that for a few moments more. The hope of no one dying evaporated, leaving a void in her chest. Against reason, she'd let herself believe that the kids were okay. Maybe one of them became infected and attacked the others, then they fled. Any other scenario got ejected out of her head. Someone had died because of her. Setting aside that burden for now, she stepped onto the street. Crossing to the other side, they slid into another alley.

She felt a hand on her shoulder after a few steps. The Doctor pulled her back gently and knelt near a pile of garbage. He took out four rods this time and set them at equidistant points around the heap. After the protective field appeared, he typed something on the keyboard and studied the flowing information. Lucy took the time to survey their surroundings. No homeless were around; no one else walked the nearby streets either. The absence of people made her jumpy. The shadows of the day became more sinister, full of hiding dangers and disease. The world seemed to unravel, and the people were the first to go.

The rods stopped buzzing. Their distinct sound pulled Lucy out of the false, dreamlike reality she'd just experienced. She turned around to see the Doctor pushing away some garbage, underneath which lay a small skeleton. Dark burn marks ran along the right arm, from the radius to the humerus, the clavicle, and up the vertebrae, finally culminating at the base of the skull where it bloomed into a black, gaping maw. Light char marks streaked both sides of the cranium as well. Lucy gagged and took a step back to lean on the nearby building. The skeleton's unburned arm lay outstretched toward the alley's exit—a final grasp for the light outside.

Lucy swallowed, tasting the fiery juices that bubbled up from her stomach. The sight twisted her vision. The buildings on all sides seemed to rise from the ground and engulf the sky above. A breath later, the skeleton was buried under garbage again. The Doctor put a comforting hand on her shoulder. Saying nothing, he let her breathe until her composure returned. Or a tiny fragment of it, at least.

Keep it together. I can do this, she thought with resolve and took a deep breath.

"We're not far now, follow me," she spoke with a voice not her own but borrowed from someone stronger and more willing.

One alley down, and they came to the ocean, an endless stretch of soft blue spanning from left to right, the edge of the horizon sparkling. A few minutes later, they were at the pier.

Nearing the arcade, Lucy found her focus, keeping an eye on their surroundings. *Where are the people?* No one stood next to the railing taking pictures. No children scurried the boardwalk making loud, happy noises. Everything seemed still and barren.

Food, bags, phones, and all sorts of other belongings lay on the pier's boards.

The Doctor's mask swayed as he watched as well. Lucy threw him a glance and noticed a change in the way he walked. He kept his pace the same but now had ample caution in his step. His weight had shifted forward.

"Be on your guard, Miss Lucy." He extended his hand back to caution her. "Something has happened here."

"That's an understatement," she said with zero sarcasm.

The entrance to the arcade was a few hundred feet away from them. Lucy and the Doctor moved with sharpened vigilance around the scattered personal effects until they reached the front door. Lucy walked a bit further ahead, to the side of the building.

The scene was the same, personal belongings littering the dock with the noticeable addition of a strikingly bright, green hat, tumbling across the boards with the breeze. Lucy checked the stands. All were empty, devoid of personnel. The wind picked up; cotton candy spinning freely in a giant bowl flew out in little tufts that drifted gently through the air.

"Hello," Lucy yelled. "Anyone here?"

She waited for a few seconds. There was no reply, so she looked around the pink-striped stand one last time. Seeing nothing, she walked back to the Doctor, who stood at the door staring at his blue screen.

"Locked?"

"Indeed," he replied, not halting his tapping fingers.

"Just break it down. I know you can."

"If the host is inside, that could scare it" He met her gaze. "We will need another, more tactical entry point."

"Fine." Lucy moved past him and waved for him to follow.

"Let's go find the back door."

The arcade was the largest and only actual building on the pier. Lucy knew of a wooden staircase behind it that led to the beach, next to it was a grey metal door. Lucy tried to open it. *Locked.*

She took a step back and leaned on the railing, gesturing for the Doctor to try. He came close, and without bracing his feet or relying on his shoulders, he pushed the door forward. Groaning from the strain, its hinges gave way. The Doctor slid the door out and leaned it soundlessly against the nearest wall, then slipped inside. Lucy followed close behind.

The first thing to hit her was the smell. It was thick, leaving a strange aftertaste in her mouth like boiled meat. The walls wept with humidity that didn't match the weather outside. Lucy searched for any other doors, but they appeared to be in a back hallway. The navy blue walls offered no clues as to the children's location. The floor, however, did. Following each step was a squelch, and her soles became sticky. She got her phone out and shined a light. Blood paved the floor as far as the light reached. Splotches of coagulated crimson blotted out the glowing galaxies on the retro carpet, covering the whole surface like a sanguine lake under a hellish blood moon.

"Wha—" Lucy started, but the Doctor turned around with lightning speed and put his hand over her mouth.

If she hadn't seen it with her own eyes, she'd never believed that someone could move so fast. The Doctor raised his free finger to just below his beak, signaling for silence. *There's just so much of it!* The thought crammed itself into her mind, leaving room for nothing else.

Emidius stood in place, holding her mouth shut. Her eyes slid from red pool to scarlet puddle.

The Doctor pecked her on the forehead with his beak, the strange act shocking Lucy out of her stupor. He nodded and removed his hand, his finger still near his unseen mouth. Lucy watched him for a second, then returned his nod, feeling ashamed of her momentary breakdown. He turned, and she followed him deeper inside.

As they got closer to the games room, the hallway filled with sounds from the arcade machines. Beneath the cacophony of chimes and 8-bit chiptune music was the sound of light summer rain and something else Lucy couldn't place, like a bass too low to hear but strong enough to make your stomach twist. The Doctor must have felt it too because he shifted his balance again just before they went in.

Lucy turned off her phone's flashlight to not give away their position and clenched her jaw. Mirrors lined most of the walls, reaching up to meet the exposed steel rafters. Strung along each beam hung rows of human bodies. Some were left in only their underwear, but most were entirely naked, bound by their hands with whatever clothing they must have been wearing. Lucy caught eyes with a lithe man; he couldn't have been older than twenty. He thrashed against his bonds, screaming muffled angry cries for help, staring into her soul. The young woman hanging next to him swayed gently side to side, her head hung down between her shoulders, lips a pale shade of blue. His girlfriend?

Lucy's teeth chattered so hard she pushed her palms under her jaw to minimize the noise. Her blood went cold. Forcing her eyes down, she watched the machine lights reflect off the wet carpet and let her breathing slow to match their undulation. She wanted to run to unbind them, but the best way to help them right now was to get the thing that did this to them. Nerves settled, she brought her gaze back up.

All the people she could see had their mouths stuffed with underwear or other small pieces of clothing. Their blood dripped down their bodies from numerous wounds and fell to the wet floor with echoing plops. The hall sounded like a giant machine made of flesh, trying desperately to move while its fluids spilled to the ground. To Lucy's right, the Doctor had ventured further in without her noticing.

How can he make no sound while walking through all this?

The Doctor seemed to be heading for the center of the hall. Creeping along a row of pinging pinball machines, she made her way in the opposite direction, so they could cover more ground. As she passed one of the machines, it let out a screeching guitar riff, making Lucy squeal like a little girl and fall back into another's buttons. It replied with a Ninja Turtle "Cowabunga!"

Desperate not to draw any more attention, she took a swift left but tripped, landing arms first into a heap of bodies lying on the floor.

No, not bodies. Body parts, she realized.

She snapped back up to her feet and took an involuntary step back. The body parts had been thrown in a corner next to a column. Arms and legs jutted out everywhere. Most had their skin and muscle intact, others were more bone than flesh, black scorch marks marring the ivory color.

All around the heap lay heads, packed tight with the other human remains, unblinking eyes staring, powerless before the unfolding horror before them. Lucy put both her hands in front of her mouth. Retreating, she bumped into another machine behind her. She turned, frightened that it would make more noise, but nothing happened. Above, the blinking red light of a surveillance camera caught her attention. Its vision was now blocked by a dead, middle-aged man, but Lucy's heart skipped a beat all the same.

What if I've been caught on one of them. Her eyes bulged, but she reined in her emotions. *One problem at a time.*

She exhaled and leaned more into the machine, her eyes searching for the Doctor. Across the room, she spotted him. He held a handle, from which a black line coiled around his right arm.

Is that a fucking whip? She wondered as he jumped over the machine in front of him.

Her phone rang. Lucy heard an inhuman growl, then splashing feet. The sound was coming her way, fast. She swiped toward the red receiver, but her sweating fingers ineffectually slid across the screen. The phone stopped ringing on its own.

"Really?" She shoved the phone into her pocket and leaned forward over the machine to peer around the corner.

There stood a young boy, maybe eight or nine years old. Bleach blond hair, soft freckles beneath his vivid, green eyes, glowing in the technicolor arcade lights. She hesitated when she saw him, and that cost her. He rushed her, slamming into her legs and knocking her to the ground. The boy clambered up her legs to her waist. She grabbed his throat with her right hand, saving her left for defense. She squeezed, but it did little to discourage his attack. He clutched her wrist, and she screamed. The child exerted the pressure of a grown man, and she thought her wrist would snap. Then he started to flail, a barrage of hits landing on her stomach and thighs. Lucy clenched her jaw and stared at the boy. He looked absolutely normal, except for the eyes. They gleamed with pure malice. Lucy knew how angry or frightened people fought, but this was something different. The intensity of the attacks suggested that this boy was fighting to survive as if he were a wild animal and Lucy a threat.

I guess I am, she thought and steeled herself.

She let go of his throat and grabbed his left hand with both of hers. Twisting, she felt the arm pop out of its socket. The boy whined like a wounded cub. He slouched to the side, and Lucy used his pain and confusion to slam her palm into his neck, trying her best to use moderate force. The boy fell backward on the floor, gagging and clawing at his tiny throat. Lucy dragged herself farther back. He noticed the movement and propped his body up to a kneeling position. Pinpointing Lucy, he dashed for her.

A shadow fell on the boy from above. Dozens of his bones cracked at once. The Doctor's right knee pinned the boy's lower back to the ground.

Emidius leveled his gaze on her. "Hold it down!"

She crawled over and put her right hand on the boy's back. Her left pushed down on his neck. Despite the numerous broken bones, the child thrashed around with wild vigor. The Doctor hit him once at the base of the skull. His forehead hit the floor, splashing blood in all directions. The flails diminished but did not cease. Lucy pushed down even harder to the point where all of her arm muscles bulged from the strain. The boy continued writhing, but she mostly had him stable. The Doctor's knee kept his lower back immobile as if crushed under an anvil. Emidius used his free hand to rummage in his coat. He got out a small syringe-like device and lowered it down, close to the boy's spinal column. Pausing, he turned his head to Lucy. She doubled her restraining efforts. With a slow and confident movement, the Doctor pushed the needle inside. He drew the plunger back until the syringe was full, then took it out and returned it to his coat pocket.

"You may release it, Miss Lucy."

Lucy let go, swayed back, and sat on her calves. The Doctor leaned forward and watched the boy's face. His right cheek was smeared with blood. The child snarled, clutching for anything. Lucy couldn't tear her eyes from the tiny bloody face as the Doctor's hand grabbed the back of the boy's neck and pushed. Something underneath buckled. The angry struggles ceased; the youthful visage remained, half-submerged under a blood tide.

The Doctor looked at the boy for a couple of seconds. His gloved hand gently touched the blond hair, and his head slumped low between his shoulders.

TEN

"**W**hy the fuck did you do that?" Lucy shouted. The ease with which the Doctor crushed a child's life threatened to burn a hole in her chest. "He was still alive!"

Head tilted to the side, his dark, glassy eyes slowly met hers, reflecting back her own horrified image.

Lucy threw her hands in the air and let out a pained growl, pointing with her open-palmed hand at the boy's corpse. "We could've helped him. You didn't have to go that far."

She tried to stand, but her legs wouldn't cooperate.

"I didn't ask for your goddamn help either. What, you think I can't handle a child by myself?" Nostrils flaring, the breath she drew expanded her chest, fueling the rage that burned away her fear.

"That *host*"—the Doctor stabbed a finger at the limp body—"was trying to eliminate you because it does not seem to have the ability to infect others." The Doctor rose to his full height, filling Lucy's view.

"After I extracted what I needed from it, I eliminated it in order to save lives. That is why we are here." Both his hands rose and swung through the air to encompass the space around them. "We are here to put an end to this so others will be spared suffering. This suffering." He presented the writhing bodies hanging from the ceiling with his arms. Lucy couldn't bring her gaze up to follow. Instead, she kept her eyes on the innocent, bloodied face of the child before her. "If you do not have the resolve for that"—he stepped closer and angled his beak at her forehead—"say so now, and I will release you from my charge. Our agreement will be void."

Lucy wasn't sure what scared her more, the Doctor's poised needle-pointed implement or the horror behind him. She took a few breaths and steadied herself.

I didn't do all of this for nothing! She bit her cheek to keep from saying something she would regret and stared as deep into his black-hole eyes as she could. "I'm okay. I'm still in this."

The Doctor regarded her for a moment. Finally, he nodded and turned his back. Without his looming, predatory presence, Lucy was able to find the wherewithal to stand.

"There's no chance of avoiding the police now. Someone had to have noticed the pier and called it in."

"Indeed, Miss Lucy," the Doctor said, watching the woman closest to him release a convulsing gargle from her throat before going limp. "We cannot hope to circumvent the outbreak, but neither can your government. The devastation the prime contagion managed to cause in just a few hours is not something your species is equipped to handle. The only feasible solution at your current level would be containment. Followed by destruction." He pivoted in place and drifted past her. "Either way, I believe your earlier assessment that bureaucratic procedure will only slow us down. Your authorities will be aware of the situation soon enough. There is no need for us to get them involved at this stage."

"Soon enough? What are you talking about?"

"Several police vehicles are approaching our location, so I suggest we make haste and depart."

Lucy made a quiet, unhappy snarl instead of arguing why he chose not to mention this earlier. "Fine, let's go."

"Not yet." the Doctor raised a hand to stop her. "Your attire is too conspicuous for us to escape unnoticed."

Lucy looked down to her jeans, soaked in blood. Red drips ran down her elbow and pooled at her palms and the crooks of her fingers. The Doctor was right. She couldn't walk out of a crime scene and onto a busy boardwalk drenched in blood. Emidius, however, didn't have a speck on him, although he'd been kneeling in the same puddle she had and killed the boy himself.

"I'll go wash up as best I can. You try to find me some clean clothes."

She ambled in the direction of the bathroom, acutely aware of where she placed each foot. The sound of the Doctor climbing up the rafters reached her as she moved out into the hall. After a few steps, she took her t-shirt off and looked at her bra. The blood had soaked all the way through. Lucy clicked her tongue. Shifting her attention back to the floor, she hopped over a couple of feet lying on the ground. It was too dark to tell if they had skin or muscle left on them. She slowed at the door marked with a woman in a dress, opening it only a crack. She briefly imagined that the alien organism had used it to store human remains, so she listened for low moans or splashing sounds. After ten seconds of silence, she worked up the courage to go in.

The lights above her flickered. Their omnipresent buzzing pressed down on her. *Just like home*, came a sarcastic thought. *You got this.* She turned on the faucet, replacing the buzzing with an ear-cutting squeal. The ice-cold water flowed onto her hands and quickly turned scalding. Relishing the bite of it, she scrubbed. First, she cleaned her hands, then her arms and elbows. The blood had already hardened into a crust at the backs of her triceps, so she peeled off what she could, cringing at the arm hairs that ripped off with it.

She caught her own eyes in the mirror and froze. Her face was splattered with a child's blood, a bright smear across the top of her forehead, clumping at her hairline. The eyes staring back at her were those of a feral beast, its chest and neck painted with crimson war paint.

Turning the hot water on higher, she attacked her face with her hands, scrubbing until her skin was raw. Wiping the water from her eyes, she appraised herself again, skin still red from the burning hot water or the bloodstains, she couldn't tell.

The sound of creeping footsteps came from the corridor outside. "Who's there?" She slid into a low crouch and edged to the left of the door.

There was no answer. Lucy's blood pumped loudly through her ears, and all she could hear was her own shaky breathing. She was imagining things.

It's nothing, she thought and relaxed her balled fists.

The door behind her spoke, and her heart leaped in her chest. "Miss Lucy, are you almost finished? We *are* pressed for time."

Lucy grabbed her clothes from the counter and pulled them on, nearly gagging when she caught a whiff of the acrid stench of her shirt as it slid over her face.

"We really do not have any more time to lose, Miss Lucy. According to data from my landing craft, the police are arriving on the three major roadways as we speak. Judging by their current speed, the approximate time of arrival is seventy-two seconds." He paused a moment before adding, "We have to leave, *now!*"

"You should have said that sooner." Lucy burst through the door and nearly bowled the Doctor over.

"Apologies," he said, his attention on his blue screen. "I had trouble finding something for you to wear and lost track of the police officers."

"Fifty seconds," he announced as they walked to their entry point at the back door.

They stepped out onto the pier. "Thirty seconds."

"Okay. You have the clothes, right?"

"Indeed, Miss Lucy. They are safe." He lifted his right arm, a white bag swinging from it.

"Great." It would be a relief to take off her sickening, crusty attire. "So the cops are coming on the major roadways, and I have to change clothes. Going back the way we came is out of the question." She moved to the railing and narrowed her eyes at the rocky ridgeline in the distance.

She pointed at the beach, tracing her fingers along it to the horizon. "Half a mile down the beach, there's this cave. I can change my clothes there, and we can hide from the police while things cool down. We only need to reach it before they get here."

"Ten seconds, Miss Lucy."

"We have to jump in the water, there's no other way." She gulped as she tried to guess the water's temperature. "You're too conspicuous to walk on the beach. You make your way to the cave on the water. I'll surface on the beach somewhere and meet you there."

"Police have arrived."

"Fuck." She inhaled, ready to throw herself off the pier, but then felt herself being lifted up.

The Doctor held her in his hands like a child's doll.

"What are you—"

"Escaping," he said, then stepped on the railing and jumped into the air.

The feeling of sudden flight locked her jaw, leaving her unable to scream. Squeezing her eyes shut, she prepared for the inevitable rush of water to flood over her, but instead, only the wind whipped her face. She opened her eyes to find herself flying over the waves far beneath.

"Miss Lucy, in a few seconds, I will have to throw you because, with our current trajectory, entry into the water will break your neck and back," the Doctor said as they flew, his tone making it sound like entry trajectories were typical, everyday happenstance.

"While you fall," he continued as their ascent slowed, "you need to keep your hands and feet straight and close to your body."

"I know how to dive, goddamn it!" Lucy shouted just before they began to plummet.

"Excellent."

Without further preamble, he threw her upward.

His forearms and hands pushed her away like someone disposing of fetid meat. Indignity at his callous behavior made her grimace as she ascended. Her momentum faded, and she began falling again. From below, a splash like a cannonball sent the ocean's surface up in a tidal wave. Lucy glued her elbows to her hips and flexed her leg muscles. Her face was locked in a rictus she could not get rid of if she tried until she hit the water and the sensation of a thousand knives slashing her cheeks reset it.

After the initial shock, she gathered her senses and swam up. She breached the surface, gasping for air. Saltwater stung her raw eyes, and she opened them to a blur of blue on blue. Brushing the water away, Lucy looked back at the pier and almost sank back under. It was at least three hundred feet away from her. The beach was equally far.

How far can he jump? Lucy wondered. The Doctor hadn't seemed to be out of breath during the lecture he gave her while they were flying through the air.

She shook her head and tried to see if anyone was pointing or shouting in her direction, but the beach was peaceful. There weren't many people around, it being a workday and all. Treading the water, she observed the beach for a few more seconds. Once she was sure they had escaped unnoticed, she swam toward the cave, all the while keeping the shoreline parallel to her. A few minutes later, her legs began to tire. The water-ladened shoes and soaked pants didn't help her exhaustion.

Nearing the cave, she reached shallow water where she could stand. After a quick scan for spectators, she undid the buttons on her jeans under the water. She took off her shoes, then her pants, finally her shirt, folding them neatly to ensure the bloody parts were on the inner side. Done, she got out of the water and ran to the mouth of the cave. She watched the horizon, trying to spot the Doctor, then stared at the ocean for a few minutes. The sun was high in the sky, so her skin dried almost immediately. She let light warm her body. The pleasant feeling was soon cut short by the primal fear of standing in the open, vulnerable to predators.

With a quick step, she retreated into the shadowed entrance.

* * *

Lucy sat on a rock in the dark cave. The cool surface beneath her sapped away all the warmth the pleasant sun had generated. She watched the waves hit the shore for a while, waiting for the Doctor to show up. Soon after, she got bored and moved closer to the entrance; she sat down in the shade and extended her legs.

Wiggling her toes back and forth, she tried to match them to the rhythm of the surf. When her feet got too hot, she pulled them back inside. Running fingers through her hair, she found it still a bit wet, so she twisted in place and leaned backward on the sand.

The sunlight hit her hard. After a while, she got used to the bright shine and relaxed. She yearned to poke her head out of the nearby rocks and check what was happening on the pier, but the possibility of someone spotting her turned her stomach to knots. When the heat began to reach unbearable levels, she decided her hair was dry enough. Rising into shadow once again, she opened her eyes. For the few moments it took for them to adjust, she couldn't see anything. Shapes returned to her vision one by one. First the walls, then the rocks, and, finally . . . her jeans.

"Oh, shit, shit, shit, shit!"

Getting up, she stumbled and fell. She clawed through the sand until she righted herself. Reaching the jeans, she lifted them off the ground and dug inside the front pocket, getting her phone out.

An impressive amount of blood water poured onto the sand. Lucy held it in two fingers until the last of the crimson mix spewed out. Placing the phone next to a rock, she stared at it with sorrow. Its sudden passing was the cherry on top of her day. She plopped down on the damp rock next to her, elbows braced on knees and chin in hands. Looking at the sea, she felt exhausted and dejected. She decided to lean back and lie on the rock. Watching the cave ceiling, she contemplated recent events.

The possible extinction of the human race by an extraterrestrial virus. Her mother's worsening condition, the utter disaster that was the entirety of last night. Her life in general. How it seemed to be veering off away from her. There was only one way out of this. Forceful, hard work. That was what usually got her through.

Stick to what you know.

Lucy remembered the stench of blood, the moans, and the rafters' clatter. The rock under her grew more frigid by the second. She jumped off and took a few steps back toward the ocean in hopes that the sunlight would cure her shivers. Stepping out into the sun and feeling the cool breeze did nothing. She shook without control. The boy's feral eyes flashed in her mind—the trashed room at Mrs. Rayburn's did as well. She imagined the room's floor covered with blood and Mrs. Rayburn hanging from the ceiling light, hands tied with the racecar sheets from the bed. Closing her eyes, she shook her head.

Where the hell is he?

Before her, the water rocked back and forth. A few hundred feet from the shore, something white poked through the swaying surface. Lucy moved forward to get a closer look. A white-beaked mask emerged from the water, followed by a black body. The Doctor walked steadily until the water was waist-high, then it exploded around him as he ran to her. He took great strides, which for a regular person would be considered long-distance jumps. When he reached the rocks in front of the cave a few moments later, he slid to a graceful stop.

"Hello, Miss Lucy," he greeted, half-turning to face her.

Good thing the rocks are tall enough to hide us here.

"Excuse the delay." He tipped his head forward in apology.

"Why did you suddenly pop up like that?" Determined not to be impressed, she kept her tone cold. "How exactly did you get here?"

He waved his hand at the ocean. "I walked."

"I guess you take the *power* in power walking literally then." Lucy arched her eyebrow.

"I do not follow."

"Mhm." She nodded. "No surprise there. Come on, let's get inside before anyone notices us."

They walked past the rocks and through the entrance to escape the scorching sun.

"So, what took you so long?" Her breathing had evened out after his arrival.

"I decided to do some reconnaissance."

"On what?"

"The surrounding area, the underwater portion to be precise."

"Wait, what? How is that even possible?" Lucy scrunched up her brow and rubbed her palms together.

"It is possible with the help of my equipment," he said, gesturing at his clothes. "The suit itself has been designed for extreme conditions because of the planet-trotting nature of my work. In addition to that, there is a life-support system in place if an agent ever finds themselves in a dire situation. Experienced agents rarely use that feature, however."

Well, look at him, all in a sharing mood. She smiled and rolled her eyes. "Why, because they're so good?"

"Not at all," he responded. "It is usually because they are dead." From the subtle fluctuation of his monotone, Lucy inferred that he was being sarcastic.

Biting her lower lip, she made no more comments but took the given opportunity to look him over, head to toe.

The surface of his overcoat was certainly slick, like black polished wood. Lucy speculated that the armband, now visible on his gloved wrist, was the driving force behind his blue, holographic screen. The sleek material covered his forearm as well. His overcoat hung loosely by his side, not restricting his movement. Lucy had seen him pull all kinds of things from inside, so it was bound to hold more secrets. The coat looked to be completely dry with not a single visible speck of water on it. Now that she thought about it, it didn't show even a trace of blood when they were in the arcade.

The black material must have hydrophobic properties. Or it's some sort of smart cloth, and he can change properties on the fly . . . ? Lucy wondered as she observed. The thought made her pine for her university classes. She was never going back at this rate.

His pants were, not surprisingly, black and made up of the same material as the rest of his attire. There didn't seem to be pockets, but what self-respecting advanced civilization would make pants without pockets. The continuous nature of his clothes gave Lucy the impression that he really was wearing a type of suit and not clothing as she understood it.

Moving past the pants, Lucy looked at his shoes. With disappointment, she realized they appeared to be regular shoes, their design clean and practical. Eyes back on his face, she saw the white beak bear down on her. Before she had a chance to react, it flicked her forehead.

"Hey, what was that for?" she asked, rubbing the spot between her eyes.

"It is quite rude to stare, Miss Lucy, also, I asked several times if you were okay, but you seemed entranced."

Lucy coughed. "Yeah, sorry about that." She stepped back and took a seat on the rock behind her.

The Doctor walked into the cave and leaned his back against the nearby wall. The rock beneath her offered comfort and a cold backdrop to the warm air. His mask seemed to linger on her legs.

Oh, crap, she remembered she was in her underwear. "Doc,

you still got the bag with the clothes?"

"Certainly, Miss Lucy." He stood back up, opened his coat, and unbuckled the white bag hanging off his waist.

"Let's see what we've got to work with." She shook the bag upside down until everything fell out onto the sand.

The article on top of the clothes pile was a black and red flannel shirt. The sleeves were stained with blood on either side. The girl who owned this shirt must've worn it tied around her waist, judging by the stains.

It'll have to do, she thought, dissatisfied.

Sifting through, she found almost everything else was heavily stained or sporting giant slashes. Lucy moved those aside. The last thing made her shoulders droop.

Just my fucking luck.

In front of her, in pristine condition, was a pair of denim cut-off shorts. They were so small that maybe they belonged to a twelve or thirteen-year-old girl. On that imaginary girl in her mind, perhaps they looked nice. On Lucy, they were definitely on the naughty spectrum. She stared at the shorts for a while, grabbed them, then the flannel shirt, and turned to the Doctor.

"Thank you," she said, trying her best to sound grateful, but her tone was still ostensibly venomous.

The Doctor, apparently oblivious to the mortal danger he had gotten himself into, nodded and said, "My pleasure, Miss Lucy."

She stood and walked onto the shore. The sun's rays didn't hit her back as hard this time around. *Must be getting late.*

Her feet slammed the sand as she walked, the ball of her foot sinking after each step. She got to the water with the clothes and knelt down to wash them. A gentle wave embraced her. Lucy sat there, feeling the ocean on her legs, and watched the horizon. The water was calm as far as the eye could see, birds flying in the distance. She wilted forward and let her hands sink to the wrists, her elbows resting on her knees.

On the pier, she could see the yellow tape along the side of the arcade. Her eyes followed people in all kinds of uniforms walking in and out. Police cars blocked the gathered crowd at the entrance to the pier, but something different caught her attention. She narrowed her eyes down at the wooden beams under the dock. A small shadow slid across the sand to the wood supports and crouched, staring back at her with green reflective eyes. A second later, Lucy shifted her gaze upward. More shadows appeared on top of the beams, close to the deck of the pier. All of their eyes glowed green, transfixed, and watching Lucy.

"Doc, get out here, now!"

Just as he cleared the rocks obscuring the entrance to the cave, all the small shadows moved in unison. Every glowing pair of eyes released Lucy and glued onto him.

"Did you see that?" As she spoke, the shadows fell to the water and disappeared.

"Yes, I saw." He nodded and stalked back to the cave. "Let us return quickly. We cannot remain in the open."

"Sure . . ." Still clutching the wet clothes, she knelt down and spread them on the sand to dry, then followed him inside.

The Doctor squatted, his back to the wall.

"Well done on providing us with the location of this cave, Miss Lucy," he said as she took her seat on the rock.

Lucy's eyes circled from the discarded box of condoms at one end of the cavern to the rusted cans of beer, half-shadowed a few feet away from the Doctor.

"Might I inquire as to how you came to know it was here?"

She looked down at the few feet of sand separating them and began drawing circles with her big toe.

"I was going out with this guy a while back. He liked to take me here. . . ."

She felt warmth crawl up from her neck to her cheeks.

"To have sexual relations?" the Doctor ventured, inflection rising.

"Sometimes." Lucy took a deep breath. "Most times, we'd just hung out at the beach because we weren't exactly flush with cash. Not that I ever am."

Lucy shut up, not wanting to ramble anymore. The Doctor made no further remarks, and she guessed he got the gist.

"Either way, not too many people come here, so we should be okay until the police leave. Are you monitoring their comms?"

"The unencrypted ones, yes. The non-essential officers were ordered to respond to other disturbances until the crime scene investigators arrive—" the Doctor stopped talking and tilted his head as if listening to a distant sound. "The investigators in question just arrived."

"Then we can leave soon," Lucy rested her elbows on her knees, and after a minute of excruciating silence, asked, "Can we talk about what happened in the arcade?"

The Doctor lowered his head to allow her some distant semblance of eye contact.

"Very well." He relaxed his shoulders, wrists loose between his legs. "Would you like to discuss the unfolding, larger situation or my actions in helping you and killing the host?"

Lucy suppressed her verbal outburst, but her upper lip drew back to reveal her teeth.

"Ah." the Doctor leaned his head back. "I see you would like to further discuss my assistance."

"Yeah, I'd like to discuss it." Lucy rubbed the skin of her forearm across her lips. "Matter of fact, there is nothing *to* discuss. I had it under control."

"Fascinating," the sarcasm in his tone made her eyes narrow. "What I observed was your hesitation in neutralizing a threat. A thing that was no longer human and was actively pursuing your demise."

"You saw wrong then because I didn't hesitate, and I certainly didn't need your help!"

"My apologies, Miss Lucy." He lowered his head so much that the beak of his mask scraped his coat. "Next time you are in a fight, I will not assist you until you request it."

". . . Good." She nodded, not sure how to react to the sincerity in his voice.

"I did not mean to offend you, Miss Lucy," he added. "Your well-being, as well as that of every one of your fellow humans, is my priority."

"Then we have an understanding," Lucy grunted and bore her gaze into him. "So what the hell is going on then?"

"I, myself, am not fully sure. The organism we are pursuing is unpredictable, which I need not mention makes it extremely dangerous. Especially when it lands on a planet with such an advanced civilization as yours. Therefore, I can only hypothesize what happened in the building you call *arcade*."

"Hypothesize away," she challenged, leaning as far forward as was comfortable.

"As you wish." He half-bowed his head. "Firstly, I must familiarize you with the organism itself."

Not expecting him to be so forthcoming, Lucy straightened her neck but otherwise remained quiet.

"The organism has several stages of development." He pushed some buttons on his wrist tablet, and a blue image of a microorganism appeared in the air. "The first stage is the mimic stage. The organism finds nearby organic matter to attach itself to, then it destroys all the original cells making up the host, replacing them with almost identical ones."

"With one difference . . ." His index finger shot up next to the screen. "Now every cell contains the original virus. This is known as the prime contagion. In our case, an orange." The microorganism image vanished, and in its place, a blue orange appeared.

She watched the strangely colored fruit make a complete revolution in the air then get sliced in two. The inside of the orange looked normal, but in a second, the image zoomed in, and Lucy saw its cells be overtaken by microscopic foreign bodies. The Doctor cleared the screen by touching his wrist.

"The second stage, the one we are presently in, is the transitional stage. It can be viewed as a metamorphic period in the maturation of the virus. The prime contagion has infected a host—the prime host—and will study its surroundings. Searching for an easy way to propagate. Unfortunately, that way seems to be through young children."

The image appeared again, this time a boy was walking on a street, after a few steps he found an orange on the ground and picked it up. Seconds later, the boy transformed into something else, something primal and dangerous.

"When a suitable child is found, the prime contagion infects it through direct contact, then the host is ordered to find more suitable candidates to infect," the blue boy continued to walk on the street until he encountered a little girl.

The boy dropped the orange in the girl's hand, and she transformed into something matching the boy's primal demeanor.

"Upon inspection of the failed new hosts, I can say with

confidence that physical touch is required for the process to begin. It would seem that superheated tissue joining the point of contact and the back of the skull is created. The tissue follows the quickest path available to reach the human cerebellum, at which point it seizes control of motor functions."

So that's why there were scorch marks on the bones. That's the trace of failure.

Lucy wanted to ask how tissue can be superheated to leave those marks, but she remained silent.

"The newly infected hosts have their natural abilities boosted. Strength, agility, endurance, even pain suppression is possible for the virus, given enough time. All of this is in preparation for the final stage."

"Let me guess." Lucy dropped her hand from her chin. "The final stage is apex predator infection?"

"In this case, yes. The third and final stage begins when the prime contagion develops the ability to infect the planetary apex species—adult humans."

"So does that mean it can jump species until it reaches the absolute top?"

"I'm afraid so," the Doctor answered, looking away to the sea.

"If it can do that," Lucy thought out loud, "then it had to be engineered by someone, right?"

"Very astute, Miss Lucy." He nodded. "This organism has been engineered for military purposes. One of the most terrible weapons ever crafted," he finished, voice bitter.

"Engineered by who? Why would they create such a sophisticated method of planetary extinction?"

"Very dangerous beings created it," he said, and his black pool eyes locked with hers. "As for why. They did it simply because they could." The Doctor's tone was grave, his hands clasped together, resting on his knees.

Awfully vague, Lucy thought as worry crept through the back of her mind. *This is it. This is where the trust ends, and he clams up.*

"Maybe they thought exercising supreme power would be fun," he continued, sounding deep in thought.

After those cryptic words, he looked up at the ceiling and spoke no more. The silence stretched out, and the air overflowed with dread. Lucy grabbed her knees until she could feel the fingernails dig into her skin; she took a deep breath.

"Okay then, I just wanna ask one thing." She tried her best to keep her voice steady.

He made a sound almost like a cough. "Ask away."

"Why were the adults strung up like that on the rafters?"

The Doctor touched his wrist tablet, and two people appeared in the air between them.

"I believe they were hung in such a way because that would give the infected hosts a clear three hundred and sixty-degree view."

The Doctor touched his wrist again, and the people began to rotate like they were on a vertical spit roast. Their bodies swayed, and Lucy could see their futile struggle to free themselves. The worst part was their eyes. Even though the image resolution was low, Lucy could see their pain and despair. Not being able to stomach it, she looked away.

"Please, shut it off," she whispered.

Once the terrible image had disappeared, a painful stillness filled the cave. Lucy got up and took the clothes out of the sun. They were dry enough, so she put them on, her unbuttoned shirt flapping softly at her sides.

She broke the silence. "So, why do they need to have a clear view?"

"I assume the prime contagion is learning all that it can about human abilities and limits. The children hosts study the infection process in the adults and deliver the information back to the prime host. They observe symptoms of rejection, like abrasions through which blood evaporates, discoloration of tissue due to higher body temperature, or anything particular they were instructed to watch out for. The whole process can be viewed as experimentation. The bodies we saw on the ground were failures. The ones hanging were still ongoing," he explained, and Lucy's fingers stabbed deeper into her palm.

The pain in her hand reminded her that she still lived. *And if I'm alive, I can help stop these things.* Tightening her fists, she pushed them into her knees. "So, what's the plan?"

The Doctor looked at her without saying anything. After a few seconds, he stood.

"Our course of action shall be as follows." He reached inside his coat. "The prime objective will be to evade capture by the authorities until we reach your residence." His hand came out, holding two of the alien syringes between his gloved fingers.

"Upon safe arrival, I will analyze the host blood contained in these." Shaking his palm, the syringes clinked together. "With it, I will try to pinpoint the location of the prime contagion. After that is accomplished, we deliver the information to the authorities, and with their help, wipe away the threat."

"What if we don't manage to find it in time?" Lucy asked, standing up as well.

"By then, the hosts should have caught the attention of the police, so it is safe to assume they would already be involved."

"Seems like a solid plan. How much time do we have before the prime contagion can infect adults? I know you're not sure"—

she raised a hand up to stop the Doctor from speaking—"so *hypothesize*."

"Without performing any tests, I cannot give you a reliable estimate, Miss Lucy. Suffice to say, the prime contagion's ability to infect suitable hosts is severely limited right now. It can only infect children through direct contact and still has to develop a method to infect adults. Thus, the best time to strike is during this transitional phase."

"If you don't know, you don't know. Can't be helped." Lucy frowned but nodded and extended her hand. "I promise to do my best to help you."

The Doctor paused as if skeptical, then grabbed it and shook it firmly.

The two of them stepped back. Lucy sat down on her rock, retrieved her dead phone, and watched the beach.

On the shore, a young boy stood close to the water, an orange in his hand. Lucy's eyes widened. She jumped to her feet and ran toward the shore.

"Doc, that's it"—she yelled as she ran—"he's got the prime contagion!"

The boy smirked. Turning, his feet blurred into a run that looked more like he was gliding across the sand. By the time Lucy reached the spot he'd stood on, the boy had already made it halfway back to the pier.

"Miss Lucy, wait," the Doctor yelled from her left.

He crouched behind the rocks.

"What do you mean, wait? He's right there," she shouted, pointing at the pier.

The boy disappeared into the shadows beneath the planks.

"We cannot leave now, Miss Lucy. The police have yet to depart the scene." He typed something on his wrist tablet.

The boy lingered beneath the beams. Shapes began to emerge. Children appeared behind the boy, some making their way down, others coming from the water. The boy with the orange stood in place and watched Lucy.

"Goddamn it! When are they leaving then?" She gritted her teeth, not taking her eyes off the children.

All of them knelt around the boy with the orange.

Wait . . . That's Johnathan!

"The crime scene investigators just arrived, but I cannot guess how long they will be. Maybe a while." The Doctor lifted his head from the screen.

She looked back at the kids. Johnathan hoisted his free hand up, and the children dispersed toward the crowd of gawkers on the boardwalk.

"We can't wait that long, Doc. They're on the move."

The children scurried atop the rocks around the pier.

They would be on the streets in a matter of seconds. Lucy rolled up her sleeves, pushed the phone into her damp pocket, and started to button her shirt.

"Miss Lucy," the Doctor began in a steady voice, "the prime contagion is obviously trying to bait us into a trap. Please, remain calm and let us follow the plan." He placed both hands on the sand, like a runner in a starting position. She couldn't go anywhere if he didn't let her.

Johnathan dashed up the stairs and onto the street.

"Fuck this," she said, doing up her final button and breaking into a sprint.

"Make your way to the streets, then follow me," she yelled back. "That little shit's mine."

ELEVEN

Johnathan sprung to the top of the stone stairwell of the beachside retaining wall. He turned and stood in place, watching Lucy struggle to find her footing in the sand. He then took one step back, blending into the gathered pedestrians. She ascended after him, surveying the crowd at the top.

Can't get through here.

She dashed right, toward an outdoor café. Jumping, she slid across one of the tables, circumventing the droves of people. Her landing was rough, but she hit the ground running. People began noticing her, so she slowed to a brisk walk until reaching the street. In the corner of her eye, she caught the Doctor climbing over the rocks. He gestured for her to get to the other side of the street. Nodding, she jogged across and waited while the Doctor waded through a throng of new onlookers. Anxious, she shifted her attention to the mass of people.

The pier's entrance looked like the prelude to a Black Friday sale. The police barely managed to keep the mob back. Lucy turned to check the Doctor's progress and saw a boy with an orange in his hand. He ducked behind a corner of an intersection half a block down. Not waiting for Emidius, Lucy pursued. Dodging the people in her way, she reached the intersection and scanned for her target.

She continued running, shoving people out of her way.

Halfway down the street, she still couldn't see a trace of her mark. Feeling her chest burn, she stopped to catch her breath. A hearse drove past her. Hanging onto its back door was the boy with the orange. Johnathan.

How—?

Furrowing her brows, she saw Johnathan's free hand holding onto the door, the fingers of his other, piercing the metal and keeping him anchored to the vehicle.

"You've gotta be kidding me," Lucy groaned through ragged breaths.

Not bothering to check both ways, she ran across the street. The angry shouts of drivers followed her all the way to the sidewalk. The hearse pulled away with increasing speed. She looked around for a cab she could hail but saw something even better—an unattended bike in front of a store. The thought of stealing someone's bike poked her heart with greater remorse than she expected, but she quickly pushed the idea from her mind.

Lucy drew in a breath and ran headlong, people jumping out of her way. The hearse reached the intersection, its left blinker flashing. Jumping on the bike, she leaned close to the wheel to avoid the tree branches shading the sidewalk. At the end of the street, the hearse made its left turn. Several people lined up, waiting to cross the intersection.

The hearse dipped out of Lucy's view, and she shouted, "Make way!"

The force of her growling made a few people shy away, while others jumped onto the road to allow her passage. A car stopped at the light to wait for a chance to turn. The people Lucy shouted at obstructed her path. The way forward was blocked by the vehicle, and the hearse was getting away.

She clicked her tongue. *Gonna have to go over then.*

Pulling the front wheel up, she braced for impact. The tire made contact with the hood of the stopped car. Leaning forward, she pulled the rear up, cresting over the hood. She landed on the other side, making a sharp left turn, the hearse once again in sight. It had gained some distance on her, but its right blinker came to life. Lucy slowed to steady her breathing. The sidewalk was too crowded, so she merged into the rightmost lane and followed.

Crossing the next intersection, she veered off from the road and onto the calmer sidewalk. The only junction from here on out was at the far end of the street, so she decided to reserve her strength for the obvious trap, somewhere up ahead. Half a minute later, the heartbeat in her ears quieted. Regaining her bearings, she caught sight of the Doctor on the other side of the road, his sprint matching her speed. When he saw she'd noticed him, he pointed up.

Children, in groups of three, ran on the rooftops above his head. The shapes of their bodies cast unusual silhouettes against the sun. She inspected the rooftops on her side as well and spotted more small figures. The hearse pulled ahead again, and Lucy peddled faster. With the number of pedestrians dwindling, she crossed over to the Doctor's side and caught up with him after a few seconds.

"Doc, I think I know where they're going," she said through ragged breaths. "If I'm right, we're definitely headed for a trap."

"Well, maybe next time you will exercise caution and stick to the plan."

She glanced up, taking a better look at the chasers' bodies, their outlines lumpy and grotesque. A cruel child's afternoon experiments with playdough. Arms too bulky, legs bent at painful angles. The sight made her queasy.

"I will not allow the hosts to harm you, Miss Lucy. Just stay close to me, and you will survive." His mask faced her.

She nodded, then announced, "If my hunch is right, we're getting close, Doc, so stop when I stop."

His beak dipped in acceptance. Lucy pulled ahead and crossed the street. The hearse got further away, but she kept the same pace. More and more deserted buildings bordered the road on each side.

Any one of them is perfect for an ambush. Let's see where the trap will spring.

The row of buildings on her right disappeared, and a high concrete fence emerged in their place. Since no one walked the street in this area, Lucy allowed herself to look only at Johnathan, whose glowing green eyes withstood her gaze. Without breaking his stare, Johnathan dislodged his fingers from the door. As he fell, he leaned forward. Keeping low, his shoes hit the ground, scraping the pavement, killing his momentum. He slid to a stop in front of a nine-foot-tall gate, back raised high, orange in hand, eyes still on her.

Lucy got within two hundred feet of him before he leaped into the air, grabbed the bar of the gate with his free hand, and scurried over it like a spider monkey.

Squeezing her rear brake, she stopped in front of it. The Doctor stood beside her a moment later. His black circle eyes regarded the children gathered on every rooftop bordering the building beyond the gate. Children—she shuddered—in height only. Some had skin as white as a full moon. Others had retained their fleshy tones, but now tumor-like bulges deformed and stretched the skin.

. . . And those are the lucky ones. She gulped.

Lucy made a point to skip over those wretched forms that bore jagged, white pieces poking out of their stomach, chest, and neck.

"Not all conversions are successful," the Doctor spoke in a sorrow-soaked tone. "As the prime contagion gets better, so will its creations."

Hundreds of infected stood and watched, not moving or attacking as if frozen in time.

"I guess this is one party we can miss," Lucy tried to battle the horrifying view with humor to minimal success. "You were right, I think we should get out of here, Doc. The odds are definitely not in our favor." Chills ran through her limbs.

The Doctor viewed the text streaming on his screen.

"Your best odds are with me, Miss Lucy. If we break formation now, the infected will hunt you down and kill you. It was your own decision to follow me through the trees. If you had followed my instructions, none of this would have happened," he said, then turned off his screen and stepped forward. "We might as well finish this now."

He grabbed the chain holding the gate closed with both hands and pulled. One of the links popped, and the two sides fell from his hands.

Now, that's just showing off. She rolled up her sleeves and followed him through.

The children on either side of them slid down the walls. Johnathan stood a hundred feet away from the entrance of an unfinished building right in front of them. The Doctor ran forward, Lucy in tow. Johnathan stood there, watching them get closer and closer. When the first of his infected reached the ground, he turned on his heel and ran inside.

"Miss Lucy, do as I say and remember, defend yourself. These are not children anymore," the Doctor instructed as they pushed through the entrance.

Infected dove into the first-floor windows.

"Roger," Lucy replied and focused on her surroundings.

The Doctor pointed to the shadowy outlines of stairs, and they ascended. The first-floor landing offered a door to the interior. A shape, the diminutive size of a child, flew out from behind it. The Doctor caught it and squeezed until it made a crunch. He threw the limp shape back through the dark doorway. Lucy heard the grunts of whatever it hit.

"Quickly, Miss Lucy! Go up."

Before he could finish, Lucy was already on the stairs.

"I will be right behind you," she heard him call.

She jumped over steps to cover more ground. One flight up, the elevation brought more light. Lucy could see another door after the next flight. A boy and a girl ran down at her. Lucy dodged right and drove her knee into the boy's temple. He flew off his feet and hit his head on the nearby wall. Lucy put too much force into her knee, and it dragged her around. Bony fingers clawed for her throat. Raising her forearms, she blocked the blow, and bones sunk into her flesh. She retaliated by pushing down until the girl slammed into the steps beneath. Blood flowed from behind the misshapen head. The Doctor's hand pulled the girl free from Lucy's arm and hurled its body at two advancing infected. The three of them hit the wall and stilled.

"For now, these infected hosts are only coming from behind. I shall remain here and guard while you go to the next floor and search for the prime contagion."

Lucy nodded and jumped up the stairs to the open void of the second-floor doorway. A single long corridor led both ways to many rooms with no doors. Lucy dashed to her right, glancing into each room she passed. *Nothing.*

She doubled back to the second-floor door. The Doctor stood in the same spot, bodies piled around him, the walls full of dents and craters. Running headlong, she left the sight behind. The rooms on the left side were empty as well.

Hands marred with open wounds and jutting bones caught the window, and an infected crawled through.

"Doc," she yelled, turning around and running back. "We have a problem!"

Before the words fully left her mouth, dozens of children clamored to get in. Every room she passed teemed with tiny, distorted bodies. She reached the second-floor door and ducked inside. Two forms flew after her. The Doctor swung his forearm like an ax and sliced both of them in the air.

"Up," he commanded, stopping the children's advance with both arms spread wide like the wall of a dam.

"Got it," she agreed between huffs.

Pushing off the wall, Lucy continued to lead.

A girl on top of the flight jumped down on her. She dodged, sticking her back to the wall. The Doctor caught the girl before she landed. He wielded the body like a whip, the short legs smashing faces and breaking bones. The horde slowed, hesitant in their attack. A boy jumped over the mass and drove the bony tips of his fingers into the concrete, sticking to the wall. It lunged at Lucy. Emidius had anticipated this, and the girl's body was already in motion. Her legs connected with the boy's waist in mid-air, and he plummeted down. Lucy continued up after seeing the Doctor discard his broken weapon on the steps. She made it to the top in a few jumps.

"Same as last time, Doc. I'll be right back," she said without turning and ran through the door.

This floor was empty. Only dusty hardwood and barren columns greeted her. She circled around the outside of the stairwell, and before reaching the doorway, she saw Johnathan at the far end of the hall. He hung from the edge of the upper floor, left hand limp by his side, still clutching the orange. Lifting himself up, he disappeared. Lucy dove past the Doctor as he unburdened himself of two infected and followed.

"I think he's leading us to the top," she shouted.

"How can you be sure, Miss Lucy?"

"He's buying time, probably, so the infected can swarm the building."

"Sound analysis," he agreed. "Then we must go to the top and confront it there."

"But then what? Do you have an exit plan?" said Lucy as she grabbed the railing and pulled herself around the next flight.

"I have several," he stated as if it were a stupid question.

"Do I live in those?"

"In most."

"How reassuring," Lucy huffed and leaped to the next floor.

She turned right and slowed her pace. The stairs were pitch black. No light anywhere. She stepped forward with caution, straining her hearing. Silence.

Sensing her hesitation, the Doctor said, "There is only one biological signature in our immediate vicinity, Miss Lucy, and it is on the roof above us."

"Understood. . . . Let's go then." She walked up the stairs and turned right.

The darkness deepened. Lucy crept forward as the noise from the horde below grew closer. She made out the outline of a door a few inches in front of her. Taking the knob in hand, she turned it, light streaming inside. Lucy squinted, threw the metal door outward, and slipped out onto the empty roof. The Doctor was right behind her. He closed the door, and she turned around.

Johnathan stood a hundred feet away from them. Lucy cautiously approached. His eyes glowed brightest of all the ones she'd seen so far. Even in daylight, they shone like gemstones. His body had no massive deformities, but there was something odd about his head. From this distance, the sides of his skull seemed bigger. His exposed arms had some sort of shell around the joints, which moved freely from the rest of the appendage. His neck was thicker, skin hardened into a tube-like shield.

He definitely didn't look like that when we were chasing him on the street!

"So, you got us here. What now?" she shouted, raising her arms.

The shout was more out of frustration than anything else. Expecting no reply, she continued toward him. His neck twitched. The thick skin on the side stuttered unnaturally, tremors climbing to his cheeks and mouth. His lips moved, but no words came out.

A loud bang sounded from the door behind her. The Doctor leaned against the assault from the other side of the metal, vibrating from the brutality. Lucy turned around and continued walking.

"Well, you got us here, kid. Good plan," she said with a taunting tone.

Fifty feet to Johnathan.

"You . . ." He forced the words out. His voice pained and ragged as if thrust from another world into ours.

"Yeah," Lucy picked up the pace. "We, what?"

Forty feet.

"You . . . die . . ." he said, stepping back, the edge of the building at his heels.

"We'll see about that."

Twenty feet. Lucy broke into a run.

"We"—he teetered over the edge—"live . . ."

His last word drifted to Lucy's ears like a flying autumn leaf. His disappearance was followed by two pairs of hands climbing over the edge. Two boys crawled to the roof and rushed Lucy. She took a half-step to the right. They both moved parallel to her, keeping the exact distance between them as before. Their plan seemed to be a two-sided simultaneous attack, keeping Lucy at a disadvantage.

Not if I can help it. She smirked, feeling adrenaline empower her.

Lucy chose the boy on the left and made a dash toward him. He pushed off the ground like an animal, flying at her. She pounced before outstretched arms caught her shoulders and squeezed. Lucy's knee connected with the boy's solar plexus. The hit loosened his grip, his hands falling to the side. They both descended, the boy hitting the concrete face-first, Lucy rolling to the right. Not fast enough. Something cut into the side of her right hip. She winced but didn't lose balance. Crouching into a defensive position, she lifted her arms to protect her head. The other boy ran headlong, trying to topple her. His added weight made her lose balance, and she fell back, grabbing his neck. The boy clawed at her wrist and forearm, sundering skin. Lucy screamed and twisted until the boy's neck broke.

His grip waned.

She seized the moment and kicked him in the stomach. As he fell away, Lucy heard shuffling steps approaching. She leaned forward, her right hand on the ground. The other boy sprang at her. His hand extended into a claw, sharpened, bony fingers grazing her neck. Instinct made her move back, saving her from losing a sizable chunk of her throat. Falling, she kicked her attacker in the chest and threw herself off balance. She hit the ground.

A second later, she was back on her feet, anticipating another attack. The boy she'd just hit took his time getting up. His chest sunken at the spot of her kick. Leaning forward, he prepared for another rush. Lucy heard wheezing from the side. The second boy struggled to breathe.

Broken bones aren't enough to keep them down, she noted, watching the gasping boy in her peripheral vision. Wincing, she felt around her neck with her fingers. Blood from the wound trickled down her back. She couldn't take any more hits; next time, she might not get off with just scratches.

"Miss Lucy!" the Doctor shouted from behind her.

The two boys used his shout as a signal, maybe thinking she'd be distracted. She ran right toward Broken Neck. Out of the corner of her eye, Kicked-In Chest did not run directly at her like last time. His stance was lower than before, targeting her legs.

Perfect, Lucy thought and pushed to go even faster.

"We have to leave," the Doctor's voice pierced through the savage banging on the door.

Lucy lost sight of Broken Neck and jumped. Extending her right leg, she kicked the boy in front of her. His head whipped back, and his limbs went limp. Broken Neck flew onto her from behind. Expecting this, she used the added momentum to spin in the air and position the boy beneath her. Before he could claw her back, Lucy's weight fell on his chest. Losing no time, she rolled forward, untangling from the boy. Lucy spun in place once she found her footing, then delivered a roundhouse kick to the rising enemy. He crumpled down into a sack of mangled flesh.

"Now!" the Doctor yelled, urging her to move.

Lucy spun around. The hinges of the door flew off one at a time.

"Ready," she shouted, glancing at the boy behind her.

Broken-neck's small hand vainly clawed the ground, reaching for her, but it didn't have the strength to move anything else. She refocused her attention, ran a few quick steps to the door, and braced it with her shoulder.

"Now would be a good time for that exit strategy, Doc!" the door shook beneath her.

Each hit almost threw her off. She dug her heels into the concrete, straining her shoulders and arms. Her vision quaked with frightening regularity.

"Then we shall begin," the Doctor said and turned his head to her. "Would you take a step back and to the side, Miss Lucy?"

She took a step back and pressed herself against the wall of the stairwell.

"After my signal," he began; Lucy heard strain in his voice for the first time, "you will have to run to the edge of the building." He gestured to the far end with his head.

. . . To the spot where Johnathan had fallen.

"You will need to run as fast as you can."

Lucy stared at the dark circles on his mask. They and the rest of it were sprayed with blood. He looked deranged, even before he explained the plan. There was no other way off the roof, so Lucy nodded reluctantly and got ready to run.

"Okay. Ready . . ." He moved his right hand near the knob and held the door with only his left.

"Go!" He said, ripping the door off its hinges.

"Oh—" Lucy began but thought better of it and ran.

The Doctor sailed through the air, landing near the edge of the roof. Door still in hand, he beckoned her. She ran as fast as she could. The children were almost upon her, the edge a few steps away.

"—Shit!" she finished her previous thought as the Doctor grabbed her hand.

They jumped off the building, soaring toward a triangular roof neighboring this one. A few moments before reaching it, the Doctor positioned the door underneath them. Lucy held onto his coat tight; their flight through the air both exhilarated and frightened her. Her muscles tensed and relaxed independently of her wishes.

The door hit the roof with a thud. Lucy felt a sharp pain in the left side of her torso. As the door slid down the side, every fiber of Lucy's being wanted her to go back. To go up. To go anywhere but down. She lost focus and closed her eyes. When she opened them, she saw the raised hand of the Doctor. It plunged down, breaking a hole in the concrete, which acted as a fulcrum, turning them toward the safe and very flat roof of the next building over. They skidded down the slanted roof, and Lucy was afforded a view down to the ground.

Johnathan's body lay motionless on the pavement below. Then his fingers twitched.

Impossible. He should've been splattered. She stared in disbelief.

Johnathan staggered to his feet and shambled forward with slow and tortured steps.

"Brace, Miss Lucy," the Doctor announced as they continued to slide.

Lucy turned her head but did not brace. The rough hit with

the adjacent cement roof made her thighs and stomach hurt. Sparks flew up as they and the metal door sped across. She cringed, and when she peeled her eyes open, she set them on the building they'd just escaped.

Children stood on the edge of the roof in a perfect double line, staring at the spot where Johnathan had just been. They all began to move. Those in the second row went inside the darkened stairwell while those in the front ran forward. Reaching the edge, they jumped. Some fell down to the ground, three-quarters of the way to Lucy and the Doctor. The others had managed to cover the expanse, colliding with the wall. Looking back ahead, the edge of the building they were on was getting dangerously close. But the door didn't seem to mind that.

"Doc, we're going to fall off!" Lucy noticed his right-hand fingers perforating the metal door.

"Not to worry, Miss Lucy," he said, which did not reassure her in any way.

They drew ever closer to the edge.

Standing up, he jumped to the side, letting the door fall away. Still holding Lucy in his arm, he landed on the roof and drove his free hand into it. Their momentum carried them for a few more blood-freezing seconds until they stopped right at the edge. Lucy's face hung over the street below for another terrible moment until the Doctor took a step in.

"Ah, all according to plan," he sounded pleased with himself as he let her down.

She continued shivering even after she felt a solid surface beneath her. Not even the five long lines the Doctor's fingers had dug through the concrete bewildered her. She just appreciated not being a smudge on the road.

"We should be safe now, right?" She managed to stand on

unsettled legs.

Walking forward, it felt like the ground was going to give way any second now, plunging her into another deep fall.

"I do not believe so," the Doctor replied, gazing down over the edge of the front side of the building.

She joined him hesitantly. All the children that had made the jump were slamming their hands into the wall. With their current speed, it would take some time before they reached them. Lucy lifted her gaze and met the Doctor's. Saying nothing, they both turned and ran in the opposite direction.

TWELVE

The rooftop stretched a few hundred feet in front of them. Along its length, knee-high concrete walls signaled where one deserted store below ended and another began. Lucy peeked over her shoulder as she ran. Small hands grappled the edge at the far end. Their fingernails were torn off, the skin peeled back to the knuckles.

Distal and intermediate phalanges, the terms from her schooling, came unbidden. Though the bones she saw no longer resembled the pictures from her anatomy texts. The skinless fingers were too thick to belong to the much slenderer hands below. Mutated into spikes that dug into the bricks, the fingers hoisted an infected child up. It glared at Lucy with feral eyes. Turning her head, she broke into a full sprint. No thought for rhythm, pace, or form. The children crossed the first wall. A single section lay between them and their pursuers. Lucy's extremities felt like they were submerged in boiling water. A surge ran from her torso to her arms and legs. She rushed headlong toward the nearby rooftop partition, jumped over it, and continued on. An antenna in front of her almost tripped her up. She avoided the fatal collision with a nimble sidestep. As she did, she glanced to her right again. The Doctor was gone.

Lucy slowed down enough to look back without falling. The Doctor jumped over the roof border she'd just passed. She stopped, giving him another second to catch up, but he just stood there. She gazed beyond him. Standing at the far edge of the building was Johnathan, watching from behind the ranks of his horde. At least fifty children closed in on them.

"Doc, what the fuck are you doing? We need to get out of here!" She screamed, backing away.

Sirens reached her ears, still distant but closing in fast.

She crouched, tensing her muscles. They responded well enough, but Lucy felt that one more exertion would take them past their breaking point.

Johnathan stared at them with his piercing neon gaze and tilted his head sideways. Lucy's heart thudded in her chest.

Then, he jumped over the edge of the roof and was gone, his infected running after him.

"What the fuck just happened?"

"We discovered the prime contagion's terminus." Emidius turned and casually walked to the end of the last sectioned piece of roof.

"And what does that mean?" Lucy allowed herself to breathe, her upper body folded over, hands braced on her knees.

"Not to worry, Miss Lucy. They will not follow us."

I guess we are back to vague.

Lucy came to meet him at the edge and saw an alley at the base of the building.

"Are we going down from the outside, or should I find us some stairs?"

"Stairs would be preferable as my equipment is . . . shall we say unreliable at this moment."

"Normal way down it is."

Relieved that they wouldn't be going over the edge, Lucy found an access door and tried to open it. Finding it locked, she stepped to the side and gestured at it. The Doctor pushed the handle through until it popped out the other side. Creeping through the unfamiliar building, they discovered a back door and used it to slip into an alley.

"Nice hot pants, angel," a voice came from behind Lucy.

She turned around slowly, too sore to be irritated. A homeless man covered in newspapers and leftovers of cardboard boxes rose from the ground using the dumpster behind him for support.

"Did heaven send ya? Heh heh," added the cardboard-clad hobo pickup artist.

"The fuck did you just say?" Lucy stalked closer.

The vagrant put his hands up to placate her.

"I'm jokin'." His eyes made nervous jumps from Lucy to the Doctor. "Didn't mean to offend ya, miss."

Lucy relaxed and watched the vagrant as his hand rubbed the back of his head. "Either of you got some cash to spare?"

He had to try his luck. Just look at that dumb smile. She shook her head and searched her pockets.

She pulled out a few damp dollars, emergency money hidden inside her phone case, then laid the sum in his outstretched palms. The dirty fingers curled around the cash, guarding the newfound wealth with vigor. The vagrant shuffled back, earnest nods of gratitude following each step. Slipping behind the nearest corner, he was gone.

Why did I give him money? I hate beggars. Looking at the Doctor and remembering what had happened made her realize why she'd done it. She couldn't help Johnathan or those other kids. Gory images still flashed in her mind. But she could at least give a few bucks to someone who might need it. After all, this could be everyone's last few nights on earth. What horrors were in store for him—all because of her.

She nodded to the Doctor and led him out of the alley with the modest flame of a good deed warming her. She smiled despite the situation.

They both walked onto the street, turned right, and continued at a brisk pace. There weren't many cars or people around them, but Lucy felt gazes slither up her legs to her obscenely small pants. Frowning, she walked faster.

"Miss Lucy, a vehicle is approaching," the Doctor pointed down the road.

"Okay. This way." She jogged across the street to a building with an open front door.

They slipped inside and stayed for about a minute until the car passed. As soon as the coast was clear, they were back on the street. Lucy kept catching the eyes of male strangers, but she just started to filter the lechery out. The sounds of police sirens and the nosy residents of nearby houses kept her attention. She was on the lookout for anyone watching them from a window for too long. Whenever she got suspicious of someone, she would drag the Doctor to the nearest alley or building entrance, all in the name of not drawing too much attention. In one such building, a cat sat on a window sill. It hissed at Emidius and swatted at his beak—eliciting no reaction from the Doctor's dark stare.

Lucy frowned. *Can the Doctor find the location of the prime contagion before things get out of hand . . . well . . . more out of hand?*

As they got closer to her apartment, she relaxed, but the relief washed away when it came into view. A crowd of curious people murmured around the small front parking lot that serviced the surrounding apartment complexes.

Police tape prevented the onlookers from entering her asshole neighbor's building.

She sighed, realizing what it meant. *They found the car I stole yesterday. What other possible reason could there be for such a significant police presence?*

"Doc, the building that doesn't have the yellow line in front of it? The one closest to us . . ."

"Your residence, yes. What of it?"

Lucy snapped her head toward him and threw him a confused look.

Nevermind. She massaged her forehead and continued.

"There's a back entrance in the alley where I saw you last night. Can you make it to that door without being spotted?"

"I would not be a very good agent if I could not, Miss Lucy."

"Oh, you've got jokes, do ya?"

"I have been told I am very humorous, yes."

Lucy raised an eyebrow and nodded sarcastically at the Doctor. "I bet you are, but for now, less jokes and more sneaking. I'll meet you in a few."

"Understood." He slipped past Lucy and crossed the road.

Emidius continued down the sidewalk until he found a side street and dove into it. Lucy took a deep breath, grabbed her shirt collar, and twisted neurotically. The fabric rubbed her wound, making her wince. Instead, she made sure her hair covered that part of her collar and rolled down both her sleeves. Confirming none of the damage could be seen, she began the trek home.

Reaching Mr. Wilson's shop, she stood in front of the entrance, watching the people gather behind the police line. The eponymous owner of the shop opened the front door and stepped out.

"Hey," she said, sounding glum.

"Hey yourself." His hands twisted around inside a dirty white towel.

Lucy turned to him. "Any idea what this is all about?"

"Nope." He shrugged his shoulders, his lower lip extended and curled downward. "Not a clue. But I've heard my share of hypotheses, you can bet." A bitter smirk peeked from under his mustache. "The best one, by far, has to be Mrs. Anselmi's." He chuckled and shook his head. "It's pure gold. Wanna hear it?"

"Sure, what's she got?"

"Well," Mr. Wilson perked up, not expecting that particular reply from her, "according to *trustworthy* sources of our dear Mrs. Anselmi, there is a special response unit that's affiliated with the CDC lab we've just outside the city. You know it?"

"First time hearing about it." Lucy shrugged her shoulders, the collar grazing her wound. Turning her head so he wouldn't see, she grimaced.

"Supposedly, there's a . . . what did she call it?" Mr. Wilson rubbed his forehead, trying to remember. "I think she said blacksite or some such nonsense. In any case, government spooks work there, ready to fight aliens or demons. She wasn't quite clear on that part."

Lucy chuckled and threw him a glance to see if he was joking. His expression was stony. A moment later, his mustache moved, signifying a smirk.

"Heh, that is something . . ." She nodded, hoping the worry she felt didn't extend to her face. "As fun as this is, though, I gotta run, Mr. Wilson. Thanks for cluing me in on the government's shadow operations."

"We serve hot conspiracy news every Monday." He quipped and turned to go in. "See ya, Lucy."

"Yeah." She waved, and the shop's door closed.

She stepped onto the pavement getting as close as she could without disturbing the thick line of people in front of her.

Officers stood every three feet making up a living "do not cross" line behind the tape. A few people in front got bored and made their way back. Lucy slipped between them, delving deeper. The officers closest to her strained their eyes, trying to catch glimpses of her legs and watch the crowd of people simultaneously. Lucy clicked her tongue and decided to go home. She threw a final glance at the stairs leading inside her neighbor's building. The door opened, and Richard walked down.

"Shit," Lucy said under her breath, slipping back into the crowd.

She stepped on someone's shoe as she turned. "What's the deal?" he shouted.

"Stop pushing. Hey!" another voice moaned.

Before she knew it, people around her were yelling and shoving. Gloved hands grabbed her arms and shoulders then hauled her away with incredible strength. Before she knew it, she was behind the yellow line, which one of the officers held up so the owner of the gloves dragging her could cross. Lucy didn't want to draw more attention to herself, so she just gave in.

The officer holding the police line smiled. "Don't worry, miss. We'll help you get through."

"Safe and sound," the gloves added.

When Lucy had more space, she freed herself with a nimble shake.

"Thanks," she turned and said with a bitter smile.

Both of the officer's faces beamed with the pride of having done their duty.

"This way, please," the officer who'd held her extended his hand toward Mr. Wilson's shop, nodding, she followed.

Her neighbor came into view just behind the officer's shoulders. His hands were handcuffed, and two men in tactical gear escorted him through the entrance of his apartment building.

"I fucking told you—" her neighbor strained and flailed against the dark-clad men holding him in unmovable grips. "It wasn't me! Someone stole my baby. I was here all night—you gotta listen to me!"

"Lucy?" Richard's voice drifted from behind, landing on her shoulder. "Is that you?"

Lucy squeezed her eyes shut, berating herself for being spotted. "Yeah," she turned around and smiled. "Hi."

"What are you doing here?" He stepped closer.

"Oh, I got into a little trouble with the crowd, and these fine officers helped me out." Continuing to smile, she waved her hand at the two policemen.

All the men's expressions lost their edge. They slowly melted under the pressure of her coquettish manner.

"That's good to hear. Thank you, gentlemen."

The officers tipped their hats and stepped back to their posts.

"Can I talk to you for a minute?" Richard asked, gesturing with his hand to the side.

His expression was less concerned than before, but still, something seemed to bother him.

"Yeah, sure," Lucy nodded.

"Come with me."

He took her to the staircase of the cordoned-off building, which lay near the center of the police-established perimeter. His eyes stared at the crowd, then returned to her.

"Are you sure you're okay?" The concern in his voice was more than Lucy expected.

"Yeah, I'm fine. Sorry for asking but, what are you doing here?"

"I can't tell you much, but suffice it to say, my work sometimes coincides with national security interests. Even being that specific might get me in big trouble." He smiled as if he were proud of the risk he was taking by telling Lucy these things.

She did her best 'I'm honored' impression and nodded. "I wouldn't want you to get in trouble."

"No worries." He waved her concerns away. "It's just . . . I really wanna get to know you. Even though we didn't talk that much yesterday, I think you're intriguing."

This is getting tedious, she thought. Out loud, she said. "I'm game if you are. Hand me your phone, so I can give you my number. Think of something for us to do and let me know."

A very unappealing smile of victory spread across his lips. Lucy's skin crawled at the way he behaved. He got his phone out, unlocked it, and handed it over.

Adding her number, she returned it. "Done."

"Thanks. Just one more thing." The look in his eyes changed from friendly to piercing. "How did you end up so deep inside the crowd that the officers had to help you out?"

"Oh, that," her mind raced. "Well—"

"I mean, Damien told me you lived somewhere around here," he cut her off, "but still, pushing your way so deep through those people. Do you live here?" He gestured at her neighbor's building.

"No, no." Lucy fake laughed. "I'm just interested in neighborhood safety. What can I say?"

Richard's eyebrow rose in suspicion. A honk came from behind him before he had a chance to prod further. He turned his head and gestured with his hand.

"Sorry, but I gotta go. I'll text you." He backed away, still focused on her until she waved him off, then he turned and made his way to the impatient, honking driver.

Richard hailed a nearby officer and spoke with him for a few moments. He got into the car and was gone. The officer took her to a spot in the crowd where other officials were crossing. She thanked the man, got away from the people, and made her way to her apartment from the other side. After she opened the back door, she didn't see anyone for a while. Then a white mask emerged from the shadows about seven feet in the air.

She motioned him over. "Let's go, Doc."

Moving quickly up the stairs, they reached her apartment door and went inside. Lucy left her keys and phone on the counter. The phone still had some moisture to share with the world. She knelt down and opened the small cupboard doors beneath the sink. There, she had her old phone stashed for just such occasions. With the new-old phone in hand, she opened the drowned one on the counter, took its SIM card out, and plugged it into the functioning one.

"Take a seat." She pointed at the couch with her chin.

The Doctor obeyed while Lucy waited for the boot-up sequence to finish. Once on, she dialed her second boss's number. The phone rang.

When he picked up, he chewed her out for a bit. After, she explained she had some personal matters to attend to.

"Fix your shit," was the last thing he said before hanging up.

Lucy closed her eyes and stifled a remark, the phone she left back on the counter. After rubbing her temples for a moment, she went over to the coffee table and switched on her laptop.

"We're gonna have to have a serious conversation, Doc. But first, I need a shower." She pointed to the bathroom door.

"I promised I'd teach you about the internet, but I think you can manage on your own." She leaned forward and opened a browser. "The flashing line over here means that's where you'll be typing. The buttons on the keyboard correspond to letters. The first one I'd recommend is 'How does the internet work.' That oughta be a treat for ya."

Leaving the Doctor to his own devices, Lucy went to the bathroom. When she removed her clothes, a musky smell assailed her nose. She frowned and kicked them into the corner. After unhitching her bra and sliding out of her panties, she crumpled them together and threw them into the sink.

Looking down at her stomach, she saw four big bruises on the right side. The skin wasn't broken, so there was no blood, but the pain was considerable. Next, she lifted her right arm to inspect the three deep cuts that ran half the length of her forearm.

They feel worse than they are, she concluded after finishing her inspection.

Her wrist had fared better, only displaying bruises in the shape of fingerprints. Moving it in a circle made her twinge. It was stiff but otherwise uninjured.

The final damaged area to check was her neck. She turned to the mirror.

Extending her neck to the side revealed the red lines on her throat. They weren't deep but had broken the skin. She shook her head and stepped into the shower.

Now that she wasn't in danger, she realized how tired her body was. Everything that happened caught up to her. Her knees gave out, and they hit the tiled floor. She braced her palms on the wall, regaining physical but losing psychological balance. Even under the hot water, her arms shivered.

She pressed her forehead to the wall, letting the cool tile ground her. It wasn't attacking children, or dirty looks from strangers, or the hands of a groping thug. It was sturdy and straight, something she could touch. Something she could hang onto. Closing her eyes, she let the water run over her skin. It stung terribly. Everywhere it flowed, the coagulated blood dissolved and streamed to the floor. She opened her eyes and observed the fresh river of red that oozed toward the drain. If she didn't hurt so much, she'd laugh at the fact that she was in an actual bloodbath. Smiling bitterly at the thought, she separated her forehead from the wall and sat back on her calves. The falling water felt warm this time. She opened her mouth, allowing the droplets to accumulate. Spitting the water out, she put her palms on the ground and pushed.

Feeling helpless doesn't get me anything; she strained her muscles, and the pain almost made her blackout. *This isn't on me. I'm doing my best in a fucked up situation. If we had better information, we'd do better. Scratch that. He does have that information. He just won't share it with me.*

She rose to her feet and hit the wall with her left fist.

I'm in control. Me—I'm in control. Yet, she felt the tug of her subconscious telling her that was a lie.

Turning her wrist, the sweltering droplets hitting her skin turned into a sobering icy stream.

Lucy remembered waking up, taking off her favorite onesie pajamas, and looking for something to wear to school. There were no clothes in her room except her underwear in the dresser. She put her pajamas back on and opened her bedroom door. The door to her mother's bedroom was open. Walking inside, she found no one there. The living room downstairs was empty, the kitchen too. The only place left was the basement. But Lucy would never ever in a million years go down there, where it was scary and dark. With concern for her mother mounting, Lucy gathered the courage to brave the first step to the basement.

She walked to the dreaded door then stood there, listening. The sound of the washing machine whirred from behind it. At least, she hoped it *was* the washing machine.

Gathering her courage, she yelled. "Mom! Are you down there?"

No answer came, so Lucy tried again. Still nothing. Now that she was in front of the door, imaginary cold fingers gripped her neck, making her shiver. Her fear, returning in full force, drove her back to the living room. With no one there still, Lucy went to the window. It was hard to see outside because snow had fallen the night before. The very first snow of the year, in fact. Lucy was excited about that. Wiping the fogged glass, she watched the wind throw sparkling snowflakes up and down. The swaying frozen crystals looked like mystical dancers riding the growing storm. As she watched, a solitary figure emerged from the howling winds. The figure was hanging something on the clothesline. Lucy's eyes grew wide, and she ran to the front door. Putting on her boots and coat, she burst outside. The wind bit into her cheeks, and her breath steamed up. She ran to the figure.

"Mom!" she yelled against the battering wind. "Let's go inside."

Her mother wore her usual home clothes, but for some reason, she had a sundress on top of the sweater and fluffy pants. The gale threw her braided blond hair into the air, stray golden strands twisted to the dance of the storm.

"Oh, Lucy, I'm almost finished. Help out and carry the dry clothes to the house, dear."

"Mom, please, we have to go inside. Why are you doing this?" Lucy grabbed her mother's arm, trying to pull her inside; tears welled up in her eyes. "Stop."

"Lucy, don't take that tone with me." Her mother stopped working and turned around. "I'm almost done. Now you take these clothes inside and no back lip." She pointed at the gathered laundry in the hamper.

Lucy's first instinct was to obey her mother's order, so she grabbed the hamper and carried it inside. Hot tears ran down her cheeks. The feeling of complete and utter powerlessness filled her heart. Once inside, she wasn't sure what to do. She didn't want to upset her mother anymore, but it was clear there was something wrong with her.

Lucy couldn't decide, and the pressure made her hands shake. The door behind her opened, and her mother walked in.

"My, my, why would anyone go outside? Right, Lu?" Her mother smiled, rubbing her hands together.

Relief washed over her. But that begged the question: Who was the other woman she'd just talked to?

"What was I doing, again?" her mother wondered out loud. "Oh, right! Laundry."

She looked at her wristwatch. "You get ready for school, missy, or you'll be late." She walked past Lucy to the basement.

"Okay, mom," Lucy took the hamper full of frozen clothes and dragged it upstairs to her room.

She searched in vain to find anything wearable. Every piece of clothing stung her skin when she touched it. With no other avenue of action, she pulled out the least frosted-over sweater and jeans and put them on.

The cold she felt then was biting and painful, while the one falling on her face now refreshed and rejuvenated. Clenching her fists, she chased the memories away and got out of the shower. When she had her own, non-bloodsoaked clothes on, she returned to the living room and stood in front of the Doctor.

"Can you stop for a second? I want to clear some things up with you." She took a seat on the chair opposite him.

"Of course." He cocked his head up and closed the laptop lid.

"When we were on the rooftop, you said something about the prime contagion's terminator."

"Its terminus, yes."

"Sure, that." She frowned and leaned forward. "We're not in mortal danger anymore, so you're gonna give me some answers."

She placed her forearms on her knees and balled her hands into fists. Her aggressive body language declared she wasn't backing down before getting answers.

"Certainly," he said, shifting his posture to face her better. "What would you like to know?"

The forthcoming attitude confused her. *I expected to have to pry or a verbal fight, at the very least.* "Let's start with this terminus. Explain that, please."

"Of course. We observed what I believe to be the prime contagion's terminus, the endpoint of its range of control. The prime contagion seems to have the ability to control hosts directly in an effective range of forty-five to fifty meters. Outside that limit, some sort of general command is followed, such as 'infect suitable hosts,' 'acquire additional information,' or in our case"—he pointed at Lucy—"it may have been 'kill non-infected human.'"

Lucy got her phone out. Apparently, he wasn't going to give her units of measure she understood, so she checked online. 147.6 to 164 feet, it said. Looking up, Lucy saw the Doctor had his palms on his inner thighs, shoulders square and beak pointing down with indignation. She raised her shoulders and gave him an apologetic frown. "Is that Johnathan's control?"

"No, Miss Lucy. Johnathan is the prime host, which is being

controlled by the metamorphosing prime contagion, the orange held in his hand."

"We just use morphing now," Lucy said, waving her hand in the air, "never mind that; all these different names are confusing. If we stop Johnathan and take the orange from him, we win, right?"

"Yes." The Doctor's beak rose up and down in a curt nod.

"Then we'll just call him Johnathan, so I don't get confused."

"Crude, but understandable. May I continue?"

"Yeah, yeah, go ahead."

"I expect that with subsequent mutations, the pri—ahem . . . Johnathan will be able to extend that range much farther. The whole planet is not out of the question. No one will be safe."

Lucy swallowed hard and sat back. "Well, we don't want that to happen, so we just need to get you a fresh enough sample like you said in the cave, right?"

"Correct. With it, I will be able to isolate environmental bacteria and biological residue from the DNA of the prime contagion in the sample, which will allow us to track it down." The Doctor mimicked her movement and leaned back, his height causing him to slouch.

"How fresh would the sample have to be?"

"Without running tests, I cannot specify exactly, but I would speculate that the host has to have been infected within 6 hours of sample extraction."

All the new information made Lucy's muscles tense again, so she cracked her neck to the side. "What about the one you got today?"

"Unusable, it would seem. I managed to test it in my craft while you were away, and the results I received were not helpful."

He raised a hand to stop Lucy's incoming question. "In the early stages of infection of a higher organism, the prime contagion's DNA volatility is exponential, which makes it extremely hard to track. Until it finds a viable way forward to infecting adults, that is why the sample needs to be as fresh as possible."

Lucy straightened. "So the contagion was engineered with counter-measures for cases like this—when someone tries to fight back."

"Yes. There are only a few such contagions in the same category five."

"And what's your excuse?" Lucy asked, shooting Emidius a sideways glare.

"Pardon?"

"You heard me. Why is it just you here? Why do you need someone like me to help?"

A deep, ominous, and dragged-out sound escaped his beak. "Treachery, I suspect."

"Care to elaborate?" Lucy extended her hand toward him, palm up.

A few moments of silence followed. The Doctor looked at Lucy and said nothing; his mask shifted forward to face her better. "I believe my mission was sabotaged, Miss Lucy. The threat level was altered before my departure. The target organism's data was doctored as well, so I would not get suspicious. Usually, in a situation like ours, containment vessels are afforded, at least one additional veteran agent, and clearance for heavy-duty weaponry. Much like the contagion we hunt, there are levels given to each threat, and as you might assume, a level five contagion requires level five response equipment."

"So what level gear did you get?" she asked, concern creeping up inside her.

"Level two."

Lucy bit her lower lip and leaned forward, her chin cradled in her right palm. Her stomach plummeted two stories down.

This is very bad, she thought; out loud, she said, "If we stick to your plan, do we have a chance?"

"Not a very good one, but yes, there is a chance I . . . *we* can prevent a global disaster, though I am afraid that your city is most likely forfeit."

Lucy's mind raced, and her breath seized. *Why am I so upset? I haven't lived here long, and I only know a handful of people. But it's still home;* the thought rooted itself firmly in her head.

My god . . . everyone living here could die.

She generally didn't care about most people, but the sheer loss of life that could follow was staggering. Even to a firm cynic like herself. She raised both hands to her cheeks and slapped them. "So we just follow your plan, and we have a chance. I can live with that. Come on then," she said, standing up, "let's go find the little bastard."

"We resume tomorrow," he said with a firm rise in his tone.

"Are you suggesting we waste time and do nothing?" Lucy's eyes narrowed, and her lips came together to form a small line.

"No, I am advocating caution, Miss Lucy." He gestured for her to sit back down.

Lucy looked away, refusing his invitation with a blunt shake of her head.

"We were almost caught by the authorities. You are exhausted, and we need to observe how the quarantine will unfold."

"What quarantine?" Lucy asked, giving in and sitting down.

"The one that was enacted seven minutes ago. I recently overheard it on the police's unencrypted radio channels. Leaving the city is strictly prohibited by inhabitants. Only officials and specially cleared VIPs may leave. A curfew will be announced soon, and the military official in charge will address the public."

"I guess that's good. At least the spread should be contained for now."

"Indeed, and to add to that, Johnathan is still only able to infect young children. This, as macabre as it sounds, is in our favor. The number of infected will not be so tremendous . . . for a time. Due to the unique biology of your species, namely having to go through puberty and the changes your bodies experience, the prime contagion will have to experiment until it finds viable ways to infect humans indiscriminately of age. This, in conjunction with requiring direct physical access to potential infected, will greatly slow down the spread."

Lucy's chin rested in her palms while her fingers massaged her cheekbones. "As great as that sounds, I bet it doesn't buy us a lot of time, considering it's a level five and all."

"Unfortunately, no." The Doctor sighed. "A generous estimate would give us about 120 hours if that."

"Five days isn't a whole lot, but better to be done with this sooner than later . . ."

The silence that followed felt like it contained the souls of the future dead, haunting the space between the people that set everything in motion. Lucy pinched the side of her thigh to keep her mind in the present, then broke the silence.

"Can I have a look at something on the laptop if you're finished?"

"Yes, of course." The Doctor pushed the computer over to her. "I have enough understanding to access the Internet on my own now. Thank you for that, Miss Lucy."

"Glad I could help," she said absentmindedly.

She wanted to see if something was posted about the

quarantine, but her homepage was already directing her to emergency news broadcasts and articles.

A picture of a man in his early forties, his hair cropped close with an immaculate uniform, caught her attention. The caption underneath said he was a military spokesperson. Lucy was reviewing the short summary of his achievements when a window popped into existence on the right side of the page. It read—*Quarantine official's address*. Lucy expanded the window to fill the entire screen.

"Good morning to all viewers tuning in," a well-coiffed young woman said. "In a few moments, you will be able to see the special announcement from General Baumer, who is currently in charge of the military quarantine over the city of Roan. Many citizens from inside the city are distressed by the fact that a state-of-the-art CDC laboratory, called 'Edge Lab' by its employees, is located inside the city limits. There is growing concern about the possibility of a biological disaster caused by the work that goes on inside the laboratory. Our social media analysts report that many people online believe the laboratory is a secret military testing ground for biological weapons. Some have even gone as far as to call it, and I quote, 'a CIA black site.'"

"These people," Lucy grunted and shook her head. "We've got much bigger fish than a fucking black site." She crossed her arms on her chest and leaned back.

The woman on the screen continued to prattle.

"Let us hear the fucking announcement already." Lucy grew more frustrated with each passing word the woman said.

"One minute remaining, Miss Lucy." The Doctor pointed to the right of the screen.

Numbers that Lucy hadn't noticed were indeed counting down from a minute.

"Our correspondents on the ground haven't been able to get inside the city, as all possible entry is denied by the military. On the quarantine's perimeter, we were assured that vital necessities are allowed inside, but only after thorough inspection. Further information will be relayed to you as we receive it." The woman's image faded, and a man appeared.

His hair was jet black at the top, gradually turning into pure silver just above his ears. His eyebrows were dark and wild. They threatened to overtake half of his entire forehead and made him look like a constantly disappointed father. The light of the camera hit his blue eyes in a way that deepened the color and reinforced his menacing presence.

"Good day, fellow American citizens," the general began. "My name is Frederic Baumer. I am a United States Northern Command general, and I have been put in charge of Roan's quarantine." He spoke directly to the camera, his voice smooth and stern, a perfect fit for the way he looked.

After the introduction, he glanced down and read from a paper in front of him.

"As of six hours ago, an outbreak of an unknown contagion inside the city limits of Roan has been registered by the local branch of the Centers for Disease Control and Prevention. Traveling beyond city limits is now forbidden to residents in an effort to better determine the cause and ensure the safety of neighboring cities and the state as a whole. Entry into city limits is severely restricted. Special cases may be made for extraordinary circumstances," the general paused for a second but did not look up from his pages.

"The following has been observed by specialists of the CDC. The main group of infected for now are children below the age of ten." The general twitched, almost imperceptibly, as if uncomfortable. Lucy, still on edge from events earlier in the day, caught the subtle movement. "Family members are advised that once infected, children may become rabid and extremely dangerous to others."

The general paused. Lucy rolled her eyes and said, "I'll say."

"Fellow citizens, we are facing a biological threat, unprecedented in our history. I urge you not to panic. The world's best military is at your doorstep, and we will do anything in our power to protect and help you."

He glanced up from the sheet of paper and looked right into Lucy through the screen. "Thank you for your time, and God bless America." The video ended there.

Lucy clicked the white *X* at the top and settled into her chair. The landline rang, and she closed her eyes and cradled her forehead in both hands. The Doctor shifted in place.

"I know," she said, dragging her words. "Let it ring. I'm not in the mood."

The phone continued to nag at her to pick up for a few more moments, then stopped, and the pre-recorded message played.

"This is Lucy. No idea how you have this number, but eh . . . leave a message after the beep."

"Hey, Lu, it's Val," her voice sounded raw like she had been crying. "I just heard about the quarantine, and I hope you're doing fine."

Pain seeped out of her words rooting Lucy in place.

"I don't know how to say this, and I'm sorry for piling on, but . . ."

Lucy's chest stopped housing her heart. Its beat died down, and in one horrible moment, the world around her ceased to be.

Just say it, Val, she willed the phone to speak, but it remained silent for that endlessly painful moment. She tried to get up, but none of her limbs worked. Only her ears remained inside the world while the rest of her disintegrated to somewhere else.

"Linda fell, Lucy. I'm sorry, I tried to get to her, but she's so damn fast sometimes." The anger Valentina felt at herself spewed out of the answering machine. "It's my fault, and now she's in the hospital. They said they need to keep her there for at least a week."

Lucy's breath exploded out of her. Her lungs filled with air eagerly as if she'd been drowning until now. Putting both hands on the table in front of her, she pushed herself up and turned.

"Good thing you didn't pick up the phone," Valentina whispered through the machine. "I'm not sure I could've told you directly. I'm so sorry . . ."

Valentina hung up. The machine marked the end of the message, a solitary, blinking red light signifying its presence.

"Apologies about your mother," the Doctor broke the uneasy silence.

He leaned to the side and watched the answering machine, then met Lucy's eyes.

"Are you not going to request further information about her condition?"

"I don't see the point." She shrugged her shoulders. "She's already in the hospital, and half the time we talk, she doesn't remember who I am."

"I see." The Doctor's beak bobbed up and down. "Some sort of degenerative illness?"

"Pretty bad one, yeah." She stood up and ran her fingers through her hair. "Can't be operated on. Can't be blasted with radiation. Expensive drugs only slow it down a bit."

"And those expenses are covered by your father or—"

"Me," she cut him off, her voice loud. "My dad's out of the

picture, so I pay for everything. That's why I'm in this fucking town in the first place." Her fingers dug into her palms.

The Doctor's black pools reflected her sitting there, looking remorseful and guilty.

That's because I am. I haven't been back to see my mom in I-can't-remember-how-long. I'm helping out, sure, but is that enough? Isn't it better for her to have a daughter that's present rather than a generous absent benefactor?

Blinking, she looked away from the sad and weak girl.

The Doctor's right hand plunged into his coat.

"Ah, this should brighten your spirits then." He got out a small leather bag and placed it on the table in front of Lucy. "As we agreed."

She didn't say anything. Opening it, she got a single gold coin out. It tasted the same as before. The metal was sturdy too. They were the real deal. Moving the cold, valuable coins through her fingers, she didn't feel the usual exhilaration from getting paid. Everything had changed in the span of a day, and she was drained. Standing suddenly felt like the hardest thing in the world.

"I'll catch a few winks, Doc, and thanks for keeping your word." She jingled the bag. "You came through for me . . ."

"My word is my bond, Miss Lucy." He tipped his mask forward in respect.

"Well said." She nodded as well and went into her bedroom. Climbing into bed, she drew her cover over her shoulders and put the leather bag close to her head.

I finally have everything I have wanted for so long. Then why does it feel this empty?

She knew why; the blinking light of the answering machine in the other room was a reminder. She had to see her mom—

take care of her—and now she had the means to do it. *The only thing standing in my way is the imminent end of the world . . .*

The storm of thoughts in her head subsided, and as sleep began to envelop her, she drew the bag closer, cradling it like it was the most precious treasure on the planet.

DAY 2

THIRTEEN

Lucy woke up with the round edges of the coins stabbing her chest. She pulled the bag up to her face; sunlight streamed in through her window behind it, illuminating her bedroom in a hazy morning halo. She drew herself up and placed the bag in her lap. The load of fortune weighed pleasantly on her thighs. Grabbing her phone, she grimaced at the loss of her old device.

I can buy a new one if I want to. No more hauling old emergency phones around. Turning it in her hand to get re-accustomed to its shape, she checked the time. 07:25 AM. Just in time for work.

She switched the screen off and stood up, stretching her perpetually tender muscles.

Wincing, she went to get some clothes. *I'm gonna need the mornings to recover if I'm tagging along with the Doctor. Mr. Wilson will be fine.* Still, it was only proper to let him know face to face.

Now dressed, she went into the living room. The Doctor remained in the same position she'd left him in. Head tilted forward as if gazing through the laptop's lid and into its electronic soul.

"Doc, I'm heading out for a bit."

He rotated his head slowly like a stone idol come to life in a forgotten temple.

"I'll free up my mornings and use them to rest since we'll be going around during the night."

He nodded.

"I'm not sure how long I'll be because I have some other stuff to do." Reaching for her keys on the table, she pointed a parental finger at him. "You keep out of sight."

"Understood, Miss Lucy. I will continue to get acquainted with the modern history of your world and try to mark out some locations we can investigate during our hunt."

"Hunt." Lucy tasted the word in her mouth. "Guess it is."

Taking a step, she was out of the living room and next to the bike rack. With practiced care, she slid the bike off and walked out the door. Stuffing the coin pouch into her backpack, she slung it on one shoulder. The wealth on her back made her lighter somehow. The slinking, moldy wallpaper that flanked her wouldn't hamper her mood today.

Pushing the bike down the stairs, she met a man who made it a point to tell her off as he retreated down to get out of her way. With the hint of a smile, she flipped him off and completed her journey to the ground floor.

She crossed the street, leaned her bike in front of Wilson's shop, and went inside. Seeing no one around, she quickly made her way to the counter. Rustling drew her eye down. Mr. Wilson sat on the floor, battling with an unraveled roll of register tape.

Lucy leaned over the counter and whispered, "They say the best way to catch a snake is to grab it quick—by the head."

"Oh! Lucy." His voice was gruff as if he hadn't spoken a word for ten hours. "You're early."

"Nothing to it." Lucy bit her lower lip and slid off the counter.

"Your newfound punctuality might be wasted. No one's come in yet. Can you imagine?" The frown of disbelief on his face was so deep it caused the rare appearance of dimples.

"Really? Not even Mrs. Anselmi?"

"Not a soul. Half the deliveries didn't even come in. Not to mention, no produce. Apparently, John's boss didn't have the right papers to get into the city. Something about government-approved vendors." His jaw clenched, its muscles vibrated like the strings of a guitar. "Thirty years in the business, and suddenly you aren't approved by the government. I tell you . . ." His mouth relaxed, and the burden of outrage was picked up by his shaking head.

They didn't let him in for other reasons probably, but I bet he can't talk about that.

"Pretty shitty, yeah." Lucy hugged herself, her palm sliding across the length of her left forearm. "Is it okay if we talk about something?"

Victorious over the tape, Mr. Wilson gave her his full attention.

"I won't be able to make it to work in the mornings from now on. Sorry to spring it on you like this." The flush of embarrassment ran up her neck, burning her cheeks and making her mouth dry. "I know I'm leaving you on your own without a replacement, but—"

Mr. Wilson put a hand up. "I'll manage on my own. As you can see"—he gestured to the desolate aisles behind her—"workload isn't exactly overwhelming. May I ask why?"

His eyes remained on hers while he piled one arm over the other in front of him and leaned on the counter.

"I've just been getting more work at my other job. Now that things don't move out of the city so much, we've got tons of deliveries," she spoke the words fast, hoping the lie would stick.

Mr. Wilson's chin moved up and down. His stare remained sharp, and his eyebrows furrowed in doubt.

"What happened here then?" He tapped his neck on the

matching side of Lucy's injury.

She instinctively covered the wound with her hand and chuckled away the worried look on his face. "I got pushed off the street by the police or the military. I'm not sure. They seemed in a rush." Each added lie tasted more and more sour.

"Mhm." He grunted and went back to working at the register. "You have to be really careful now. These boys are from out of town, so we may just be numbers to them. I'm gonna call the town hall today. They must have some instructions for proprietors. If work picks up, I'll have them assign someone to help. Don't *you* worry."

"If they can't send anyone, I'll be glad to help." She put both hands on the counter and drew in closer. "You won't even have to pay me. If I have some spare time, I'll be right over. You just give me a call."

The smile he gave her was so broad that it drew the mustache curtains over his mouth enough for Lucy to see his lips. His right palm rested over her hand, affectionately tapping several times.

"I'll manage, but thank you for the offer. The same goes double for you. If you need help, you know where I live." His dimples appeared again.

"I will," Lucy replied, even meaning it halfway.

"In any case, I'll try to help people as best as I can until this whole mess is sorted out. I am serious about being careful, though. Now more than ever. Okay?" He gave her a stern, downward look.

"Sure thing. I'll watch my back." Tapping both palms on the counter, she turned to leave, realizing her muscles had stiffened like sun-baked branches in the time she'd been standing there.

Bending her elbows back and shaking her neck, she had

released all the tension by the time she reached the door.

Outside, she pushed her bike on the sidewalk with one hand and called her other, and for the moment, single boss.

The line rang twice, then came the answer, "Did you fix your shit?"

She rolled her eyes to a passing pedestrian, who glanced around self-consciously. "Almost done. I just have a few errands to run today, and I'm good to go. I'm not calling about that, though."

"Why the hell are you wasting my time then?"

"Because I've got a business opportunity that only you can help me with."

"Go on," his voice mellowed out.

"Thought you might be interested." She smirked and made sure no nosy passersby could hear her. "I've come into some inheritance recently of the *gold* variety, and I was wondering if you had an associate that could help me exchange it for cold, hard dollars?"

"I'll get on it. Call you back if I hear anything."

"Thank you kindly." She terminated the call and got on her bike.

The streets were busier than usual. Judging by the number of people, Lucy would never have guessed that the military had cordoned off the city. The traffic was like the final day of a three-day weekend.

The machine has to keep chugging . . .

About ten minutes later, she arrived at her next scheduled stop, the bank. The long line in front of the entrance reminded Lucy of the insanity of an iPhone release.

"Are they giving away money?" She tilted her chin up in camaraderie with the last man in line.

His index finger tapped the wallet he held in front of his chest as if ATM withdrawal was a relay race. "ATMs in other branches are empty. This one still has cash in it."

The man faced forward again, and Lucy frowned at his odd behavior. Pushing past the line, heading to the front door of the bank, earned her some angry glances. Ignoring those, she chained her bike and went inside.

The first free teller she found had the eyes of a rifle-whipped doe. They jumped from the gathered mass outside the door to her coworkers behind the reinforced glass. Her hair was frayed on the left side, and her lipstick spilled beyond the edges of her lips. Lucy approached, noticing the lack of people inside while the horde outside the doors struggled to drain the husk of an ATM. She smiled at the jumpy woman and led with wanting her monthly payments to her mother changed. The woman's face brightened at the chance to do actual work. While her fingers typed on an unseen keyboard, Lucy rested her forearms on the counter in front of her. After the adjustment was completed, Lucy asked the teller if she could draw out any cash.

"I'm afraid not. We're nearing capacity," replied the woman, her designer suit making soothing noises as she gestured. "You saw what's happening outside. It's been hell this morning. "

"Eh, it was worth a try." Lucy shrugged her shoulders and gave the teller an understanding frown. "I'll try my credit card and hope it works. Thank you for the adjustments. Have a nice day."

The teller's face told Lucy she wanted to say something, but the rapid change in expression didn't bode well. Lucy closed her eyes in acceptance and pushed off the counter. Before she could complete her turn, the woman spoke again. "Wait here. I'll see what I can do."

Lucy nodded, leaning on the chest-high ledge in front of the plexiglass separating them.

The teller came back a few minutes later with six hundred dollars.

"I was only able to get you half your daily limit. Hope it helps." She pushed the necessary forms for Lucy to sign through the slot.

"Thank you!"

Wow. I didn't even try to finesse her, and she still helped me out.

The teller smiled, now in much higher spirits. "Glad I could help someone who wasn't so rude." She winked.

Lucy smiled back and pushed the form forward.

"Have a nice day," the teller said as she handed her the cash and waved goodbye.

With her money dealings done, Lucy went out of the bank, unlocked her bike, and set her destination for the nearest store she knew of that sold bladed weapons. Her phone said the trip would take forty-five minutes on bicycle. Plugging her ears with headphones, the music inside them set the tone of her journey, and she made her way downtown.

The entrance to the shop blended so well with the surrounding buildings that Lucy rode right past it. A polite, synthetic voice generated by her phone notified her of the error. Lucy's brakes screeched, and she turned around. Thirty seconds later, she was browsing an impressive array of weapons.

Most of the selection boiled down to firearms, and that meant a permit. *Out of the question.* Her eyes flowed over the assortment on the rack. *What I need is something fast, cold . . . and sharp.* She slinked to the back of the store, to a dimly lit single-row rack on the wall with a sign above her head that read 'Swords and Machetes.' The font for swords was appropriately medieval, while the one for machetes managed to evoke deep-in-the-jungle impressions with its stylized trees and shrubs.

The glistening edges shone with deadly gleam. Each one sporting a different size and type of guard, hilt, and handle. All of them looked presentable, but none were practical enough. Once the parade of swords finished, Lucy saw three machetes hanging at the far end. She picked up each and swung them to test their balance, making sure no one was around.

The first and the last weren't to her liking. Too big in size and too heavy for their hilt. The one in the middle fit just right in her palm. According to the all-knowing weapons rack, the machete's type was *barong*. Its handle was short, making a sharp downturn at the end for better grip. The blade, narrow at both ends, widened in the center as if some ancient god had inflated it with great steel lungs. The length and cutting edge were perfect for what Lucy needed. *This should keep me from being disemboweled.* With a final blade flick, she headed to the front.

The display case that doubled as a counter held a myriad of handguns that lay just under the glass. The black of the guns contrasted the harrowingly white background beneath them and gave everything outside it a haunted glow.

"How may I help you?" a male voice said, smooth and enthusiastic like someone on TV trying to sell you jewelry after midnight.

She peeled her gaze from the display case to find a man in a glaring green vest with a constellation of pockets along the front. A mess of dark blond hair hung over his forehead and light-blue tinted glasses.

"Uhm, yes . . . hello, I'd like to buy this." Lucy set her fingers on the weapon and gave it a meek push.

"Excellent choice." The man smiled and scooped up the machete in a single movement.

Scanning the shelves behind him, she asked, "Do you have any sheaths or scabbards, or whatever they're called?"

"I've got just the thing." The clerk's right index finger rose, and a moment later, he dove into the back.

He reappeared with a box in his hand and set it down on the glowing counter sliding the back of his hand over the lid with a showman's ease. "This is one of the last things we got in before the quarantine."

Inside the box were a dark-green camo belt, and a scabbard with a mechanical device attached to it. The clerk demonstrated how the device clipped to the belt and held the scabbard to it. The clasps latched to the green fabric, and the clerk attempted to pry it open until his cheeks and forehead turned strawberry-red.

"Pretty solid." He smiled and jangled the belt in front of her as his skin gradually returned to its previous color. "Give it a try." He thrust an eager fist in her face, almost hitting her nose.

Lucy pulled back to ensure no errant swings could reach her then tugged the scabbard. The man did not let go, and the device did not flinch. Convinced of the build quality, Lucy released.

"Now for the coolest part." The clerk left the belt on the counter and flipped a small switch near one of the latches.

The device loosened, and he turned the whole thing on its axis. Now the machete would be comfortable for a left-handed draw. Fastening the whole thing in place, he demonstrated its strength by trying to tear it apart again.

"Pretty cool, right?" He seemed overly happy for a person displaying only a blade covering and not the weapon itself.

Lucy leaned in, inspecting the device and looking at it from different angles. "How much for the two of them?"

"Three hundred." He set the scabbard down like an antique vase.

"Whew." Lucy whistled and hesitated by impulse. "That's steep."

"You can't put a price on protection," the clerk said with a trained retail smile.

Lucy tilted her head back and forth, feeling more at ease with the prospect with each nod. Getting her wallet out, she flipped through the bills and winced at Benjamin Franklin's disapproving glare before passing three of his likenesses over to the self-assured weapon's dealer.

I need this to stay alive. It's well worth the money.

"Do you offer any sort of bags?" she asked after he took the payment.

The clerk dove in the back again.

When he returned, Lucy chuckled at the multicolored souvenir bag in his hands.

"People get things from here as gifts, you know."

"Hey, man." She lifted both arms. "Not judging."

"So what's the difference between a scabbard and a sheath anyway?" she asked while watching the man tenderly tuck the blade away in its high-tech covering.

"Where the sheath is soft and elegant, the scabbard can help you crack somebody's head open . . . if you had to." He knocked on the hard surface with his right index finger. "A scabbard is more than pretty housing."

He put the belt inside the bag, machete and all.

On the ride back, traffic on the streets was laden with police cars zipping about, appearing and disappearing in an instant. Several military transport vehicles drove behind them or set up checkpoints along the busier city intersections. No one bothered

Lucy, and she minded her own business. A block away from her home, the phone vibrated in her pocket, alerting her to a text message she would have to check later.

Opening the door to her apartment, she spotted the Doctor at his usual spot on the couch. The sight made Lucy's heart flutter for a moment. Having someone there when she got back gave the stale, dusty air that met her at the threshold a different punch. It was as if her carcass of an apartment was showing the first signs of reanimation.

She hoisted her bike up on the rack and pulled out her phone, hoping the texts were from Sarah. Lucy needed an opportunity to apologize for what she had said the other day but didn't want to make the first move.

Two messages from Richard awaited her instead.

Nice running into you yesterday.

Lunch?

"Ugh!" she groaned so loud that the Doctor's head snapped up like a bird of prey on the hunt for a scurrying mammal. "Sorry," she said while massaging the bridge of her nose.

Gotta get rid of him. Her fingers began formulating a gentle letdown.

She sighed again when her tired mind refused to supply her with a cool and witty line. "Goddamn it."

"What is causing you such distress, Miss Lucy?" His movements lost their edge, but his beak remained pointed at her.

"My friend arranged a date with this CDC colleague of her boyfriend." She shook her head, not having the strength or willingness to make it clearer.

Lowering the mask down, his glassy eyes seemed to look at her from under invisible eyebrows. "You know a person who works in the Centers for Disease Control and Prevention?"

"The very same, and I don't know him, at least I don't want to. He's just some guy pestering me, and I'm gonna get rid of him."

Her fingers began to type again, this time crafting a much better excuse for why he should never talk to her again. The Doctor snapped up out of his seat, casting his impressive shadow over her phone.

"Might I make a suggestion before you reply?" He ripped the phone from her hands and held it above his head, beak pointing up as he stared at the screen and read what Richard had sent her.

Lucy hopped up and down like a flea next to the giant keeping her phone hostage.

The Doctor tilted his head with a predator's poise, his dark circle eyes settling on Lucy as a target. "Any government official that works in that institution could be immensely beneficial to the success of our mission. Why have you not told me about this earlier? This person might prove to be a valuable source of information."

"We have no reason to think that. Richard's just some guy." As much as Lucy wanted to believe her own words, she remembered that Damien had said he ran his own team. *And he didn't seem like just some guy when he was here yesterday. What kind of CDC scientist aids police with arrests?*

Giving up on retrieving her device, Lucy shuffled to the couch and threw herself down. Her aching muscles rejoiced. "What is it that you think he might be able to tell us . . . supposing I'd play along."

"Several things come to mind," he began. "For instance, experimental techniques for tracking infected, regions of the city with higher levels of infection, up to date sightings of Johnathan, upcoming routes of military and police patrols—"

"Pump the brakes." She raised both hands and rolled her eyes. "I got the picture. But aren't you a bit too quick at pimping me out, Doc?" The left corner of her mouth curled in a self-righteous smirk.

"Pimping?" Confused, the Doctor's head tilted, and he summoned the aid of his blue screen.

A few lines of unknown symbols flowed down, then he whipped his head back, shaking it like a WWII vet might, reading urban slang definitions. "Decidedly not!"

"I'm just messing with you." Lucy laughed and stretched her neck on the arching back cushion cover. "I'll go out with him then"—she sighed for dramatics—"and I'll try to get us some info."

"Good." The Doctor strode back to the couch and planted himself beside her. Once his attention returned to the laptop, he handed her back her phone. "Because I already agreed to lunch on your behalf."

"Son of a—"

The phone vibrated out of Lucy's hand. Picking it up off the floor, she saw her boss' name. "I have to take this. We are going to have a word when I'm done . . . hey, boss."

"Got some info about your inheritance."

"Hit me."

"Good news is I found someone still working that angle in the city."

Lucy looked over to the Doctor, his head tilted ever so slightly toward her. *Can he hear?* She shook off the invasive feeling. Leaving the comfort of the couch, she carried the conversation to her bedroom.

"And the bad?" she asked.

"It's Mike and his boys."

"Mother—"

She pursed her lips to prevent the slur. Her skin crawled from the memory of that muscled idiot's hands all over her body.

"I don't think so, man. Last time was . . . well . . ."

"Look. Do you need the stuff moved or not?" A heavy thud from a full cardboard box permeated her boss' phone and her ear. He lowered the receiver to growl at someone.

"I dunno," she said out loud, but in her head, she reeled.

This might be my only shot at cashing in. But the sheer stupidity of the risk gave her pause. *What if the Doctor fails at stopping Johnathan? Then we're all fucked, and stupid coins mean absolutely nothing.*

Looking at the vanity across from her, she saw her mother's hazel eyes stare back at her through the mirror. She'd vowed to go back, and that's what had to happen.

I need the cash, but I gotta be smart about it.

"No, boss. I'll find another way. Thank you, though."

"Don't do me like this, Castle. This wasn't easy to pull off—"

She hung up the phone before he could start his tirade and possibly convince her to change her mind. Smiling, she opened the bedroom door.

"Hey, Doc! Let me tell you about boundaries . . ."

FOURTEEN

The taxi drove her to the address that Richard had given her, a little cafe nestled between the CDC's Edge Lab and the Roan Zoo. While they drove, Lucy pondered on how she would pry information from the arrogant scientist.

It's not like I'm a master manipulator, and the more I think about this plan, the dumber it sounds. I have no idea how to get people talkin'.

The best she could come up with was seduction like the black widow in some classic noir detective movie. She had even rushed out to buy the appropriate outfit for the ruse. A yellow sundress complete with an oversized sun hat and airy scarf. What seemed like a good idea a few hours ago made her feel like a fool now. Grunting, she watched through her window as buildings passed by.

He'd probably be on his guard if she pried too much. *So what, should I sprinkle important questions on top of the banal ones? Guess that's the best I've got.* Cradling her forehead between her index finger and thumb, she shook her head. It was better than nothing. She'd just have to come off as air-headed as possible so he didn't get suspicious. *First step of the plan completed then. I would* have *to be stupid to agree to a second date after how he treated me on the last one.*

The remainder of the journey she used to channel Sarah—her

coquettishness and overt flirty attitude. Lucy moved her index finger and thumb along her jaw, relaxing it and tilting it side to side. Her spiritual seduction guru, Sarah, had a more easy-going manner of speaking, and Lucy hoped loosening her muscles would help. The taxi stopped, and the fragile persona she was constructing in her head almost flew out of her skin. Managing to keep hold of the Sarah-simulacrum, she paid the cabbie, then saw Richard walking down the sidewalk.

His footsteps were confident and measured as if stepping off-beat would mean him toppling over on the street. Before getting out, she thought this might be a good opportunity to act cute. She texted him saying *hey* and observed his reaction.

Lucy paid the fare and stepped out. Richard's attention was drawn to his phone, but he reached for it only when both feet were touching the ground. He took out the device with a smooth motion of a stalking wildcat. The text buzzed in her palm, but she didn't bother to look. He glanced up from his phone as she approached and gave her a smirk.

"I see you're trying to shame my fashion sense each time we meet," he said and laughed without a hint of offense on his features.

Got you looking . . . Now, all I have to do is get you talking, she thought. Out loud, she said, "You're fine, relax. I just went all out on the girly stuff today. What do you think?"

Knowing the answer, she gave him her most feminine side-to-side twist.

"You're pulling it off two for two, so I'll leave that part in your expert hands."

"You clean up nice yourself, but I accept your compliment. I will try to uphold my duties to the best of my ability." She raised her right hand as if swearing into office.

"Now that you've taken the oath, wanna head in?" He gestured toward the door behind them.

"You got it," she said and waited for him to lead.

As he walked, Lucy checked him out. He wore a t-shirt once more, its only redeemable quality being that he ironed it this time. In wild contrast, his pants were way too formal and looked like something a team leader would wear to work. It wasn't flattering to be on a date with someone who was putting so little effort into dressing up. *But it's a nudge in the right direction, at least.*

Glancing at his butt, she couldn't deny it pulled the fabric taut in all the right ways. Raising both arms to her cheeks, she gave them a quick slap. *Focus!*

Richard pushed the door open and walked inside without a second's pause for gallantry. Lucy furrowed her brows so hard they nearly collided. Almost losing grip on the character she tried to portray, she exhaled her animosity and followed. Inside, Lucy hung her hat on a clothes rack, and they took their seats. An attentive, middle-aged woman in a cream blue dress with an apron on top handed them two menus with the care of someone who might have handcrafted them. She thanked the lady, who rewarded her with another bright smile. Richard cradled his chin in his palm and tapped his right index finger on the closed menu. Lucy browsed through hers for no more than thirty seconds when the frequency of the taps increased. The movements irked her too much, so she pulled the menu up, obscuring the lower half of her face and allowing her lips to squirm in displeasure. Making her choice, she put the menu back down, revealing a now amicable expression.

"I'm ready," she announced, struggling to keep her voice level.

Richard swung away from his palm and called the waitress

over with an imperious wave. Before she reached them, Lucy looked around. The restaurant wasn't quite a restaurant, more like a bakery/coffee shop/fast-food combo. The walls were a not-too-bright shade of tan. Newspaper clippings framed in elegant black borders hung in strategic places, telling of world events or the story of a local individual's fantastic feat. She found it delightfully charming, even if some of the ceiling tiles had beige stains on them. The waitress arrived, and Lucy ordered a croissant with two chocolate muffins and green tea.

Richard opened his mouth, but the woman spoke before him.

"An omelet with extra bacon and the blackest coffee you've got."

She flashed a satisfied smile while Richard almost flung the menu at her.

"Yeah, that'll be all," he announced, not even moving his eyes to acknowledge the woman.

The muscles on Lucy's face worked overtime, keeping the corners of her mouth from falling into a frown that could break the table.

"So, a fan of chocolate then?" Richard's voice went from frigid to inquisitive neighbor too fast for Lucy.

She swallowed, then nodded.

"Yeah. I really like it. The worst thing about this quarantine, well besides people probably dying," she dragged the last syllable and leaned in on the airhead facade, "is that I like to get this chocolate syrup they import each week. So, since you're here, do you think they'll be able to bring it again cause I'd *really* love to get my hands on some." Tucking her arms closer to her body, she faked an embarrassed smile.

Studying his face, she saw no immediate signs of suspicion.

"Chocolate might be a stretch for now. We're letting in only essential foods." His eyebrows moved up a fraction to convey his sympathy. "No one will starve, though. The military will make sure everyone is fed and safe. Inside city limits, of course."

"Of course." Lucy nodded with a somber expression.

Richard's face gave no indication of his actual thoughts. Lucy focused on his eyes, constantly sweeping the room, too alert to belong to someone making their living watching microbes under a microscope.

"The waitress knew your order. You're a regular, huh?" she changed the subject.

"They do good food, yeah." His remark was so off-hand that she almost toppled backward. "Whenever I get actual free time, I come over."

Lucy took her arms off the table and twiddled her fingers. *Let's see if he bites.*

"Today at my second job, I was at the back of the store, and people were acting waaaay crazy. Hope you guys keep everything under control."

She held eye contact for too long because Richard's gaze sharpened. His irises honed in with predatorial accuracy.

Damn, overshot it. Her neck craned and stiffened, then moved back as if someone had pulled her hair.

Richard leaned forward in his chair, his arms closing in a ring atop the table. Ten interlaced fingers moved up and down in a dangerous rhythm. "I can't discuss work in detail. Mind if we talk about something else?"

"My bad, of course we can. I'm around people constantly, so it's all in your face. That's why I brought it up." She drew her hand between them and shook left to right with the fervor of a homeless car window cleaner.

"We're all in a tough spot, for sure," his tone was even and dry, making it hard to discern his feelings. "But we'll pull through."

Lucy agreed just as their food arrived. Each person took a bite, while the silence that settled between them grew as thick as a cinder block.

"TV or movies, what do you watch more?" Richard returned the date's tone to the mundane.

"Neither. Don't have too much time for that. I used to like a lot of sci-fi TV back in the day, but I think I've grown out of it now," Lucy replied with a sigh, then thought of something. "Wait, scratch that. There was a Predator rerun last night. You seen it?"

Richard's fork hit the rim of his plate, and he looked at her from under his eyebrows. "Is that a serious question?"

"Sorry, sorry." She chuckled genuinely. "It's not okay to assume anything, so I'm playing it safe."

"There's no need to be *that* safe." He tipped his head to the side, visibly intrigued.

"Got it. So I'm watching the movie, and you know how the Predator has like this *heat* vision?" she inserted the wrong word to bait him.

"Thermal vision, you mean," he informed her with a condescending smile that would prompt a punch to the face in different circumstances.

"Right. Thanks." She mustered all her remaining will, contorting her face into a thankful expression. "And while I'm watching, I realize we have this technology. Like, you could hook up one of these thermal thingies to a drone and let it fly around the city to search for bombs or other stuff. I'm not sure that's okay. I'm not crazy, right?" Her eyes pled for confirmation.

"Ahem," Richard began with a satisfying cough. "It is possible to equip a drone with heat-sensing equipment, but the power draw is too much to be feasible in any practical way. For now, you don't have to worry about this in particular."

Lucy narrowed her eyes in faux confusion, really selling the 'stupid girl' performance.

"You can't make a drone fly long if you strap too much stuff to it," he explained, sporting the same punchable smile.

"Guess it makes sense." She nodded with a thoughtful frown. "Still, I'm pretty proud I could imagine it."

"Yep, it's pretty impressive," Richard agreed with a magnanimous tone.

"How do you like them?" Lucy asked, prompting the lines of Richard's face to tighten. "Movies, I mean."

"Oh." His fingers raked through the right side of his hair. "They're good at making my mind go blank, and sometimes you need to wind down with some pretty pictures."

"Hundred percent," Lucy agreed for real. "Here's a question for you then. If you had the free time, what would you choose, the big screen or watching at home?"

"I'd go for a nap, to be honest."

"Don't be a baby and answer."

"Fine." He rolled his eyes and leaned back in the chair. "I can doze off at home, so I'll choose that."

His satisfied grin made Lucy want to retaliate. Their banter was going so well that she almost forgot the mission. *I'm here for a reason*, she thought and decided to change the direction of the conversation.

"Wanting to watch movies at home is perfectly normal, Richard. You don't have to pretend with me."

"Maybe I do." He tilted his head to the side, drinking in her reactions with his eyes.

The next moment stretched like they drifted on the event

horizon of a black hole. The tension broke when a sly smile spread across his lips.

"But watching with company is always better."

Lucy's mouth smiled on its own, and she leaned toward him. "It sure is."

She wasn't proud of how sultry her voice sounded, and even though she was on a mission, despite Richard's awful behavior, the inkling of chemistry made itself known.

Stop it! I'm not some fucking cliche, she reprimanded herself.

"Speaking of company. Let's say someone tries to schedule stuff with you in the future." She smirked, waiting for his reaction. "Would you be free during this time of day? Oh, and is this area safe enough for activities?"

His eyes didn't turn hard this time, but his mouth opened slightly. The only thing missing from his lascivious expression were strands of saliva sliding down the corners of his mouth.

Score. She returned the smile, putting the same intention behind it and acting receptive.

"What about you?" he pulled back the conversation. "You ride a bike all day, but what about your free time?"

Looks like he's feeling the chemistry as well but doesn't want to push it too far and make me feel easy. Sly and smooth, I can't be too careful around this one. Her shoulders stiffened, and she quickly rotated her joints to make it seem like she'd had a cramp.

"I'm more of an outdoor person," she answered, tilting her head side to side as if she had to think about it. "I don't like to stay at the apartment all that much."

"Okay." Richard leaned on his elbow without cradling his chin this time. "What about hobbies? After work and studying, of course."

He was paying attention last time. Placing her left hand on the table, she gently caressed the tablecloth with her palm.

"Well, I do like to train," she said. Richard's fingers interlaced, but his hands remained motionless on the table. "Like I go to clubs, dojos, all things related to martial arts are cool for me."

"Yeah, Sarah mentioned your job could get dangerous. Being good in a fight must come in handy." He nodded as if not to her but to something beyond their conversation.

"She exaggerates." Lucy rolled her eyes. "I haven't fought once on my second job or had to at all. It's just riding on a bike all day." The wave of her hand swatted away any and all credibility attributed to Sarah.

"Speaking of Sarah, did you get back to your apartment with them the other night or . . . ?"

"Damien was kind enough to drop me off." Her palm on the table froze then slid back until it was hidden under the edge.

"Where I ran into you yesterday?" He tried to stifle the hard light in his eyes but couldn't manage all the way.

"A few streets over, yeah." Lucy switched on her airhead mode once more, fluttering her eyelashes. "I got back, and at some point, I could hear helicopters. But it must've been my imagination."

"No, you heard right." Richard's face solidified into an unfeeling mask of stone. "That's why I'm asking. There was some trouble, and I was worried if you got home okay."

"That's sweet." She gave him an unassuming smile. "I went upstairs and dozed off just after I heard the noise."

Damn, what is this? Only I was supposed to be here to get information!

"That's really great to hear. With everything that happened yesterday . . . including the tragedy at the pier."

Why bring up the arcade? Is he trying to find out what I know about it? Her fingers under the table struggled against one another. *Good thing he can't see them fidgeting, or I would be busted. Just breathe and think. If he's asking about the arcade, he might just be reciting news, or he's digging for info.* Taking a long breath in through her nose, she dove back into the conversation.

"I hear it was bad. All those people dead," Lucy spoke with the appropriate sadness in her voice and on her face. "And then on top of that, quarantine!" She shook her head for added effect.

The features on his face softened.

"The clubs and dojos you go to"—his fingers detached, and he set both palms on the table—"do you do full-contact there, or is it something else?"

"Full-contact for sure. I tried kendo and other styles with weapons, but those weren't for me."

If he's asking all these questions about fighting ability, maybe I'm a suspect, and he's trying to gauge how many people they'll need to detain me.

The image of men in masks broke into her imagination. Their unidentifiable clothes shuffled as a black hood sped toward her head. Her face plunged into the darkness as strong hands carried her flailing frame. She disguised the burst of emotion as a sneeze. Pulling up her shawl, she hid half of her face.

"Sorry." She pushed the fabric closer to her skin and rubbed her nose to buy some time.

"Bless you," he said and offered her a napkin.

Reaching for it, Lucy studied his demeanor. Forward posture, nimble wrists. Shoulders relaxed but not idle. He was either the most alert scientist ever, or he was expecting her to make a move.

The door to the outside lay a few feet behind him, but his presence took up all the space in front of Lucy's eyes. He wouldn't let her get away if she tried.

So I won't. She smiled under the shawl.

"Thank you," she said, lowering the garment, and took the napkin.

Her face was relaxed and thankful, with no trace of terror. Richard's posture mellowed, and he reached for his phone.

"I've got a bit more time, so how about we help digestion with a little walk?" He raised his hand to call the waitress over.

Her mission so far was a bust, but there was still a chance to get some valuable information for the Doctor.

"I could go for a walk." She reached for her purse, but Richard tapped his left hand on the table, catching her attention.

"I'll handle the check. Don't worry," he said, his tone too confident to be argued with.

Lucy's hand fell back to her side. Her pride wanted to say something, but the mission came first. She didn't want to do anything that might antagonize him or possibly clue him in on her goal. *I can handle my own check, goddamn it.*

"I don't mind," she lied, allowing him to execute his obvious power play.

With the bill settled, Richard stood up, dispersing his presence even more, and got Lucy's hat. Donning it, she thanked him, and they both walked out. The 'Edge Lab' of the CDC stood on a gentle-sloped hill, looming over the street. The irregular edges and shapes of the building looked like a pile of discarded pieces of metal, once destined to make a groundbreaking sculpture. Richard walked in the opposite direction. Following him, Lucy felt the breeze on her lower thighs. The dress provided obfuscation from prying eyes and the bonus of bare skin on a pleasant day. Though the feeling was quickly dampened by the low dread that each successive step brought. Richard kept silent, and so did she.

Lucy drew her eyes away from him and noticed they were walking along a long fence that stopped at a tall archway. Above it, the sign read: *Roan Zoo*. Richard faced the double-winged bars of the entrance.

"Wanna go in?"

"Yeah," she agreed with eagerness. *Anything that isn't the silence.*

Lucy reigned in her tongue while Richard got them tickets, then they went inside. Looking at the lanes and concession stands, Lucy didn't see any people. Animals prowled cages, their bodies grazed the protective bars, and their heads swirled around as if looking for the missing visitors. Lucy stopped to watch two young bears playing with each other in their enclosure. One splashed the other, and in retaliation, was toppled to the ground. Friendly ear nibbles followed.

"They're very active today," Richard commented, standing beside her.

"How often do you visit?" she teased.

"Not as much as I'd like." His lips curled into a bitter smile. "But enough to know most plaques by heart."

"Mhm, okay busy man. Follow me." Lucy made a come-hither gesture and led him past a sign boasting the 'Penguin Plunge.'

Reaching the enclosure, she stepped to the plaque and pointed at Richard. "You stay right there. I'm gonna test just how much of an animal nerd you are."

"Running speed of penguins?"

"3.7 to 5.6 mph," he answered, his cheeks rising in a proud expression.

"Swimming speed?"

"Up to 22 mph."

"Length?"

"43 to 47 inches."

"Bah." Lucy waved her hand. "This is too easy. Everybody knows this stuff."

"You must hang out with a lot of ethologists then."

"I know what that word means." She pointed the finger at him, narrowing her eyes. "And yes, I do. Now, let's find some worthy trivia."

She spun in place and walked deeper in. Richard's knowledge didn't end with penguins. He continued to impress Lucy by knowing the bite strength of an American black bear—1200 pounds per square inch. Of a hippopotamus—2000 and, as a bonus, the megalodon shark at 40,000. He had other tidbits like what genus each animal belonged to, how they evolved, and from where. Nearing another enclosure, Lucy noticed the painted, happy face of a fox and decided to try her hand one last time. They walked through a wide, wooden arch, atop which limbs of crawling vines stitched together. Lucy waited for them to see an actual fox, taking a few strolls between the cages. The animals got accustomed to them and began poking snouts out of hidey-holes. Richard's attention fell on the inquisitively moving black nose, and Lucy set her play in motion.

"Do they usually get out more?" She kept her eye on the hesitant fox.

"More or less, yeah. People come through almost every day, and they're used to that, but now there's only us, and they're probably confused."

"Confused . . . I get that." Her chin moved up and down in slow, pointed nods. "Just like at the store. I missed a lot of faces I see every day."

"Everyone's scared right now," he said, shifting his face to look at her. "They'll start to trickle back in when things die down." He tried to sound reassuring, but something in his tone was missing.

"I'm not too sure about that." Her eyes broke away from the fox studying them and met his. "A lot of our regulars live around the pier," she exaggerated.

"A pretty affluent area, so your worry is a bit wasted on them, I think."

She frowned at his unexpected comment.

"What I mean is"—he raised a hand to stop her question—"rich people weather adversity in comfort, while the less fortunate get the brunt of it."

Lucy didn't stop her neck in time before she gave an eager nod of agreement.

"I think so too. Like, I'm sure the Rayburns won't want for anythi—"

Richard's face became smooth and still like a block of ice, and she acted confused at the change. "What's with the look?"

"That name. Rayburn, how do you know it?"

"Mrs. Rayburn comes to the store all the time." Biting her lower lip, she leaned into the airhead within. "Yeah, she's a bit pretentious, but at least she doesn't throw money around like some of her neighbors."

Trap set. The satisfaction in her belly threatened to burst out and throw her dress to the wind. *Let's see what he does . . .*

"You know anything about her son?"

Bingo.

"He's come with her a few times. Johny or Johnathan, right?"

"Johnathan," he confirmed, his tone cautious and flat as a freshly minted penny.

"Johnathan, that's right. He's kinda shy and small, but he's an okay kid, as far as I've seen." Lucy covered her mouth, painting her features in the shade of distress. "Why do you ask? You know the family?"

Richard's face stood frozen for a moment, then his cheeks drew back in a queasy frown. "The only thing I can say is that it's nothing you'd want to know about."

Lucy tried to push for more, but his phone rang, scaring the fox back into its den.

"Yeah," he picked up, turning away from her. "Right now? Yes, I know. I was just on my way. There's no need for that . . ."

He stopped talking for a few seconds, then nodded and said. "I'll be right there."

"Is everything okay? I'm sorry if I'm keeping you."

"It's alright, not your fault. I was just told that my ride is waiting out front." He gestured to the entrance with his chin. "Come on. I'll walk you there."

Lucy urged him forward by raising her eyebrows. At the entrance, she saw three idling Humvees. Four soldiers stood with their weapons ready. When they got close, one of the soldiers handed him a vest.

"I'm really sorry about this," he said while he put on the Kevlar vest.

His forearms tensed under the shirt, making the fabric stand up with an appealing bulge. He fastened the clasps with practiced ease, and a confident smile brightened his face.

"I hope we can pick this up another time."

". . . Yeah, sure," Lucy said, dumbstruck, "bye."

Richard nodded then went inside the vehicle. Ten seconds later, the whole convoy had disappeared.

FIFTEEN

Walking through her apartment door, Lucy took off her hat and hung it on her bike's handlebar.

"Welcome back, Miss Lucy." The Doctor, still busy on the laptop, had managed to make it to the other side of the couch in all the time she'd been gone.

She ambled to the chair and sat across from him. "Hey, Doc."

"Was your mission successful?"

Lucy looked down and raised her eyebrows. "Nah, I wouldn't say that, but at least I didn't get arrested." Her eyes met his. "Richard didn't tell me anything, and instead, he grilled *me* for information. Asking what I did the night I met you and if I knew anything about the pier. You know, general stuff that someone asks on a second date. . . ."

The dark circles on his mask elevated slightly to look at her. "I am glad you were not arrested, but it is unfortunate that we have no additional information."

"Sorry for not being a master spy!" She threw her hands up in the air, pushed her chair back, and stood. "I'll try to do better next time I have to get information from a near-complete stranger."

The Doctor's hands stopped flying over the laptop's keyboard. "That is not—"

"Save it." Lucy put her palm between them. "I'm gonna do

something useful while you merge with the couch." She turned and went into her bedroom.

Taking utmost care, she took off the dress and opened her wooden wardrobe. Shoving her other clothes aside, she put the dress on the empty coat hanger and slammed the door closed. She then yanked her home attire out from the hamper. As she climbed into her old sweatpants, that same old ketchup stain from the other night caught her eye. No more than two days had passed from her disastrous dead drop, and still, she couldn't find twenty minutes of free time to do laundry. Fate had spoken, and cleanliness was out of the question for now.

Going back to her bed, she drew her backpack close and retrieved the machete. She examined the scabbard and found the mechanism to latch it to the belt. The scabbard clicked into place. Lucy tried to wiggle it with all of her strength, but it didn't budge. Nodding to herself, she inspected the side facing her and found the rotating switch; she turned it. The whole thing unhinged, and she moved to the opposite side, setting it for a right arm draw.

She got up, fastened the belt to her waist, and took a stance. Throwing a few practice jabs, she tested out her overall balance. *Could be better, but it's salvageable.*

Just in case, she did a few sharp movements, imitating dodging and repositioning.

Resetting her stance, she took her right hand and placed it on the handle of the machete, then drew it out as fast as she could. The added weight tipped her to the side, and she clicked her tongue with dissatisfaction. Repeating the same motions, her leading foot buckled. Adjusting her shoulders and torso to the left, she tried again, this time almost falling flat on her face. Agitation ran up the back of her hands to her neck. Huffing, she jumped up and down a few times to dissipate the feelings of inadequacy.

The first thing I'll need to learn is to get the machete out fast and efficiently.

Hours of concentration and weapon drills tensed her forearm muscles. The voice of her short-lived Kendo sensei rang in her head. *Familiarization leads to success.*

Following that adage, he'd filled an entire wall of the dojo, floor to ceiling, with certificates of excellence. Lowering her hands to her sides, she relaxed and set her mind to proper breathing. Her mindset flowed from unrest to determination. Drawing the machete, her form was good, even though she missed her imaginary target. Pulling back her hand, she smacked her elbow on the wardrobe. Swallowing the pain, she stepped to the side and swung again. This time her left foot caught on a corner of the bed.

Fuck this small apartment!

Grinding her teeth like a windmill after harvest, she put the belt and machete in her bag and left the room.

The Doctor's mask couldn't move down quick enough to cover up that he was watching the door. Lucy glanced at him, said nothing, then headed out of the apartment and up the stairs to the roof. Forcing open the rusted door hanging on a single hinge, she looked over her shoulder to make sure it didn't topple down to the street. The hinge creaked like a dying coyote but held firm. Lucy left the bag by the door, clasped the machete to her back, then bounced up and down one more time to shake off the last of the tension. The ten flights of stairs had got her heart pumping for the upcoming drills.

Up on the rooftop, Lucy towered over every other building, giving her a gut-clenching view at the height of each jump.

Landing, she took a few steps around. She found nothing that might injure her if she were to fall, and with that done, she placed herself in the middle of the roof and began.

First, a hundred draws and resets. At twenty, she got rid of her left drift. At fifty, her feet ceased to wobble, adding to her accuracy. At one hundred, she had eliminated all unnecessary movement. Satisfied, she relaxed her posture, her shoulders back, weight leaning on her lower spine. Rubbing the sweat off of her brow, she eased back into stance.

She unsheathed the blade and felt its weight. First in one hand, then the other. Moving it left to right with her wrist created an invisible crescent. It dragged her hand to each side like a cinder block was tied to it. Angling the machete's edge down, she pulled back, then made a clunky downward chop. Rotating her wrist, she tried the same thing from different sides and angles. She couldn't stop her swings because of the weight.

Gazing at the glinting edge, she worked on a strategy in her mind. Taking in all the factors, she decided what to do. The machete went back into the scabbard, and she focused on a point in space. Grabbing the handle, she drew the blade so quickly that it cut the air with whistling speed. Recovering, she did it again and again until her wrist went rigid and her accuracy fell dramatically.

Stretching her shoulders and spine like a cat waking from a nap, she allowed her muscles to recover a bit.

So the best I can do now is hit, dodge, second hit if possible, if not, flee. It's an okay plan, but it's risky, she thought while leaning forward and squaring her feet. *Let's make it a bit safer.*

A hundred more draws and resets followed. The strain on her wrist lessened, and she no longer missed, but the pain remained, making her grimace at each strike. Pushing through the discomfort, she willed her body to work as she wanted it to.

Taking a minute to rest, she grabbed the handle with both hands and slashed, pulling back at the last moment. The blade hung in place just where she intended. She tested out different angles and found the control was there, but two hands would slow her down enough to allow an infected to disembowel her two times over.

For the sake of covering her bases, she unhitched the scabbard and affixed it to the front of her pelvis. Drawing, grasping with both hands, then slashing still was slower than using only one hand. Frowning, she returned the weapon behind her back.

Going back to her single-draw plan of attack, she tried to do a follow-up strike after the initial one. Losing her footing, she fell, stopping herself with her left hand. The rough tiles covering the roof scraped her palm, reminding her that this was a stopgap solution. She pushed off the ground until her shoulders mirrored the horizon. Bending her knees, she settled into stance and resumed training, her only prospect of survival.

The door to the roof hit the bricks behind it. The Doctor stood at the entrance with his fist before him mid-knock, looking embarrassed if such a thing were possible. She spun the weapon in her hand and returned it to its home.

"Mind if I join you, Miss Lucy?"

"I guess."

He closed the door, watching the single straining hinge with typical alien curiosity, then stepped to the side and became still like a statue. He kept a silent watch, hands clasped behind his back. Lucy was unnerved for about a minute, then allowed the dark blot to fade into the blue background of the sky. The exertion became routine again until she felt her breath catch in her dry mouth.

Damn, I wish I'd remembered to bring some water. Her eyes drifted to the Doctor, who held a bottle in his hands.

"Hope I did not infringe."

"You're fine." She made an impatient gesture with her hand. "Gimme."

He handed her the bottle, which she drained after a few thirsty gulps.

"I would like to apologize for my words, Miss Lucy. I know this afternoon was a lot to ask from an untrained operative."

"Don't worry about it. I had to let off some steam anyway, so it's all good."

He offered his hand to her, she shook it, accepting his apology and putting the matter behind them.

"You have impressive form," he complimented after the handshake ended. "Your agility is admirable as well. And speaking of that, when we pursued Johnathan through the building, I had an idea about a sort of combination maneuver. Would you like to hear it?"

"A combo? Like from a video game?" She snickered. "Sure, hit me."

His head tilted back. "I would rather not. The goal is for us to hit the enemy."

"Not like that, dummy. It's an expression. It means, lay it on me, like laying a hit on someone but instead its information. Got it?"

"Modern vernacular. I understand. Now, if you would kindly step as far back as is safe."

Lucy strode back until she neared the railing on the edge of the roof.

The Doctor twisted his neck in a motion imitating the letter S, then said, "What I propose is that we use you as a decoy since you are weaker and slower than me, hence a perfect target for the infected."

"You sure know how to make a girl feel special, Doc," she said with half-closed eyes.

The beak of his mask plunged down, his neck craning.

"Don't sulk now. I'm just joking."

His posture remained rigid, so she added, "Say your piece."

Raising his right hand, he coughed like a broken radio. "In short, you lure the infected toward me, and I run through them. Allow me to demonstrate."

He knelt down like a sumo wrestler preparing for a match.

"Now, run forward and surmount me."

Lucy blinked in confusion. "Like vault over, is that what you mean?"

His beak moved down in a curt nod. Lucy threw the bottle to the side and rushed forward. Once near him, she put everything she had into her legs to jump over his impressive stature even when kneeling.

"Great. Again." His wide strides carried him six feet forward.

He kept close to the center of the roof, so Lucy wouldn't be in danger of meeting the pavement below after one of her jumps.

Good thing we have a lot of room, she thought before making her dash.

This time, the Doctor didn't kneel so far down, and Lucy had to use his shoulders as support as she launched herself over him. He made no complaints and simply took his place on the opposite side once more. Again, she ran. This time when she jumped over, she felt the wind rush underneath her. Emidius lunged forward as if to attack a pretend entity chasing her. They practiced the maneuver a few more times until Lucy was winded. The Doctor stood there as collected as he was when he first stepped on the roof. "Shall we continue?"

"I get the idea," she panted, her pride the only thing keeping her from keeling over. "I think it should work."

"Glad you agree, Miss Lucy. Be mindful that this can be done the other way around, depending on our needs in the confrontation."

"You mean you jump over me?"

"Yes, precisely."

"Something tells me you will have a much easier time of it than me," she said, looking up at his silhouette, towering above her with the late afternoon sun setting behind him. "Let's give it a try."

The Doctor nodded. Lucy backed away then ran forward, jumping into a roll a foot away from him. He crested over her with ease. Uncoiling from her roll, Lucy grabbed the handle, and the machete's edge sang in the descending twilight. Releasing her concentration, she exhaled and dusted herself off. The improvised hit felt like the right conclusion to their combination.

The sun had hidden behind the skyscrapers in the distance, leaving the sky painted in a deep shade of burning red.

"Time sure flies when you're having fun. Let's go inside so I can catch a few winks before we head out."

The Doctor picked up the thrown bottle and followed her through the door.

Going down the stairs sent needles through her calves, lower back, and arms. Just opening the door to her apartment made her biceps scream at her. In her bedroom, she unbuckled the belt, then crashed onto the bed. Setting her alarm to after curfew, she closed her eyes and fell asleep. A few moments of respite later, it began to buzz.

"Whoever's calling is dead," she growled and grabbed her phone.

No one was calling. The alarm had gone off at the appointed time—10:30 PM. She drew herself up and sat on the edge of the bed.

Proper darkness had set outside, and the street below was silent. She shuffled to the living room. "Are we leaving soon?"

The Doctor peeled his black hole eyes away from the corner he'd been staring at.

"As soon as you are ready, Miss Lucy," he said and stood. "My craft has been monitoring several locations in the city, which we should investigate tonight."

"Right." Lucy rubbed her eyes. For the first time since she met him, the Doctor had changed his clothing. The usual color of his coat had gone from slick black to night-sky blue.

Understandable, we do want to blend into the darkness. She had just the thing in her bedroom.

"You get those locations on the laptop, and I'll put on something appropriate." She gestured with her chin to his clothes. "I don't have the exact same color, but it's pretty close, don't worry. I won't give you away."

"Much appreciated, Miss Lucy," he said as he dragged the laptop closer to himself. "But please do not delay. As I mentioned before, I need a sample of a host that was infected no more than six hours prior."

"Yeah, yeah," Lucy shouted from the other room. "So you can isolate the environmental pollutant and pinpoint the newest mutation of the prime contagion. I got it."

She found what she was searching for, a dark blue shirt with no decals and loose-fitting sweatpants in a lighter dark blue than the Doctor's hue. She kept these for just such clandestine night operations. With the clothes on, she clasped the machete belt around her and fished out a couple of bills stashed deep in her wardrobe.

Bernard knows everything that happens on the street. If I find him, he's gonna want his fee.

Stuffing the bills inside her pocket, she walked out. The Doctor spun the laptop around and showed her several locations on the map. They weren't very far from her building, and they could probably check them all out tonight.

"Got it." She nodded after saving the locations in her phone. "I can take you there."

They both strode for the entrance, Emidius ahead of her. When he reached the door, he stepped to the side, waiting with the patience of a classically educated butler.

Eyeing him, Lucy grabbed the doorknob. "So, I have to ask. What's this craft you keep talking about? Like your spaceship?"

"Heavens, no." He shook his head. "My vessel is in orbit on the far side of your moon, so I can avoid detection. And it's fortunate I took that precaution as your technology has advanced far enough that I would have been caught immediately."

"Far side of the moon, huh?" Drawing in a breath, she got ready to take advantage of the easy setup, but his earnest tone made her reconsider. "Great. This is normal now."

The Doctor tilted his head, and she just shook hers.

"Nevermind. Let's go."

Twenty minutes of sneaking later, they met one of Bernard's people warming his hands on a trash fire. Lucy raised her open-palmed hand and gestured for the Doctor to hang back. He melded with the shadows while she approached the rusted barrel that hosted the life-preserving fire. The tramp's eyes shifted from her face to the spot where the tall figure had disappeared.

"There a place for good food nearby?" she asked, arms caressing the edges of the flames.

The tramp's shoulders relaxed, but his eyes stayed sharp.

"Depends on what you're willin' to spend," he replied, edging back a bit, ready to bolt at a moment's notice.

"I've got a twenty," Lucy continued to watch the flame, her face placid.

"Can't get shit for that much." The tramp pushed one nostril closed, then cleared the other with a loud push of air.

Lucy looked at him with eyebrows raised. "And if I scrounge up forty?"

"Could help you out then." The tramp scratched the side of his chin. "Let's see 'em."

Lucy drew two bills out of her pocket and held them just above the licking tips of the fire. The tramp's eyes went wide, and he dove to snatch the currency.

"Tell me where first. You can see I'm good for it." Lucy raised her chin so that the light would cast dancing shadows over her features.

"Somewhere on 5th street. I'm not sure where exactly."

Lucy nodded, taking one bill out of her hand and putting it back into her pocket.

"Hey," the tramp yelled. Anger made the underside of his scraggly beard bobble like a ship in rough waters.

"Bad info gets you half," Lucy's tone was as cold as the night beyond the edges of the fire.

The tramp took a step closer. The Doctor emerged from the darkness behind him, grabbing his neck and arresting his advance. The tramp looked up to see the white mask slowly shake from side to side. Gloved fingers released the shivering vagrant, who abandoned his fire and ran into the depths of the streets. Lucy nodded in thanks, and they resumed the journey.

On the way to their vague destination, they encountered a massive number of people breaking curfew. The regular police patrols took care of those. She and the Doctor wouldn't have that kind of problem because she knew how to go from place to place without being seen. The patrols got more frequent, so Lucy led the Doctor through more back alleys and decrepit buildings. Even though the refuse obstacles slowed them considerably, back doors or missing windows provided a veiled way to their destination. After an hour, they neared the building Lucy knew Bernard used as a meeting spot on 5th street. They stepped on the pavement toward it, but halfway across the street, headlights appeared from their right. The Doctor shot forward, jumped in the air, and crashed through one of the boarded windows. Confused for a moment, she then realized why he'd done that.

All the windows are boarded up; he made me a way in.

She jumped, grabbed the edge, and pulled herself up. Once inside, she crouched under the window.

Spotlights pierced the dark above her head, the light projecting shimmering lines on the walls. The window above her was now the biggest source of luminescence.

The Doctor stood on her left by a door frame leading out of the room. He watched the street through the boards.

"Two police cars, Miss Lucy. Four officers in total. One has just reported this position for suspicious activity," he spoke without turning or moving his head.

"Shit," Lucy cursed through gritted teeth. "So much for evasion."

"I could disable them easily, but our presence would be known. It is paramount that our search remains *unimpeded.*"

Lucy clicked her tongue then peeked over the edge to the

outside. The officers were out of their cars and pointing their flashlights directly at her hiding spot. She ducked back down.

"Lucy is that you?" a voice from the other side of the room said.

Lucy spun around, her hand on the machete. "Who's there?" she asked in the general direction of the voice.

The Doctor's fingers pointed behind him. His focus on the officers did not waver. "A man. Cowering in the corner. Approximate distance, three meters to our left."

"Yeah, no shit." Lucy squinted her eyes.

There was indeed a shape of a man kneeling down on the opposite side of the room. The sound of a bottle dropping followed by a soft grunt told her all she needed. "Bernard, asshole. I was looking for you. Didn't they tell you?"

"Sure they did, that's why I'm . . ." he tried to speak normally, but the quiver in his voice gave him away. "I'm fuckin' here, a-ain't I?"

"Well, don't just stand there." Lucy swung her hands in the direction of the light. "Get rid of the cops, and we'll talk cash."

"Whatever you need, Lucy. Just don't—don't let the birdman *disable* me," he said and scurried over to her in a frantic crawl.

He made a point of going around the room, as far as the walls would allow, steering clear of the Doctor. Coming into view a few seconds later, Lucy could see the array of food stuck to his beard, the smell of him as fragrant as ever. His eyes were bulging.

"Go!" Lucy's chin shifted in the direction of the door, urging him on.

"Quickly," The Doctor's tone blew through Bernard like an icy wind.

Bernard didn't move. With a knowing sigh, Lucy got out a twenty-dollar bill and gave it to him.

Ever the businessman.

He nodded with appreciation and crawled past. There was no way around the Doctor, and when he got close, his whole body trembled. Reaching the front door, Bernard rose, got a small bottle from his pocket, and unscrewed the cap. He took a big swig then sprinkled some of its contents on his shirt and jacket. Returning the bottle, he spun and charged through the door.

"What the—" one officer managed to say before they all yelled in unison. "Freeze! Hands on your head!"

"G'morning, officers," Bernard slurred, loud enough for his hidden audience to hear.

"Stay right there and no sudden movements. What's your name?" one of the officers yelled.

Three of them had their hands on their holsters. The one that had just shouted did not.

"I'm goo' 'ol Berny, officer! Ask anyone around." He made a grand wave at the buildings behind them. "They'll tell ya."

He pretended to lose balance from the wave and staggered in place. The officers relaxed. Only one left his hand on his gun.

"Who broke that window?" the yelling officer asked.

"Some punk-ass kids, that's who. They threw bottles at the winda. Empty bottles, can you believe that! People live here," Bernard said with his index finger pointed up, his arm swaying in the air. "Damn hooligans." He added in a quieter voice, then leaned closer to the yelling officer.

The man used his baton to poke Bernard in the chest, keeping him at bay. Bernard looked down at it then back up at the policeman, who was at least a foot taller.

"Officers, I wanna thank all 'o ya." He lifted his right hand and, in a sweeping motion, pointed at everyone.

"For all the har' work ya do to keep us safe. These fucking

brats got no manners, I tell ya. A fella can't sleep in peace anymore." Bernard shook a fist up at the skies, then staggered back from the baton.

"Fucking kids, man," one of the officers said, shaking his head. He spoke to the one in front, "Come on, Steve, this guy's sauced to high heaven. We've got bigger fish." Having said his piece, he returned to his car.

Officer Steve took a step forward, placed his baton on Bernard's shoulder, and said. "Better go find someplace else to sleep this off, 'ol Berny. No one's supposed to be out after ten. There's a curfew. Get out of here."

He pushed Bernard to the side. The homeless man staggered and turned down the street. Officer Steve looked at the building and ambled up the steps. Lucy held her breath. The front door closed with a slam. He walked down the stairs and got into his car. Thirty seconds after the vehicles left, Bernard came back inside. Fright contorted his cheeks and forehead when he saw the Doctor.

"Don't worry, Bernie, the Doctor's cool. He's with me." Lucy stepped forward, standing between them as a safeguard.

Bernard nodded, still unconvinced. His shoulders slumped down, creating a slight forward bend in his neck.

I won't be able to convince him, might as well not waste my breath.

"That was one hell of a performance out there," she congratulated, hoping her impressed smile would alleviate the tension somewhat.

He perked up a bit, but still, he only made eye contact with Lucy for a few moments before his gaze drifted back and up to the white mask in the darkness behind her.

"A great performance deserves a great reward," she said and

got out a twenty-dollar bill. "So you can replenish your stock." She tapped the pocket on his chest that held his flask.

He grabbed the bill and turned to leave. Lucy coughed, getting out two one-hundred-dollar bills and waving them for him to see between her index and middle finger.

His eyes sparkled at the sight of the currency. "What'd ya need?"

"I've got three addresses, and I need you to tell me if there have been infected children around there."

"Sure thing." His head followed the gentle movement of the bills in Lucy's hand.

Taking out her phone, she showed him the map.

A dirty digit, poking out of fingerless gloves, prodded at the screen. "This one over here, I told everyone to steer clear. The other places I haven't heard anything about."

Lucy extended her hand forward, and Bernard attempted to pull the cash from her fingers.

"If anyone asks?" She tugged the bills with minimal force.

"I ain't seen shit," Bernard fired back immediately.

She smirked, then let go. "Good man."

Bernard scurried out before she could say anything else.

"Come on, Doc." She turned on her heel.

They delved deeper into the building. Lucy tried the back door, but even after two kicks, it refused to open. Stepping aside, she gestured with both hands for the Doctor to remove the obstacle. He crashed through with a gentle push. Thankfully, no one came to check on the noise.

Lucy watched for lit windows, which gave little illumination, but at least showed her where not to set foot. Jumping from yellow imprint to yellow imprint, they navigated the dark urban pathway. Outside the exit, trash cans overflowing with garbage provided the perfect observation spot. Lucy knelt down and scanned the street. Patrol after patrol passed, making it difficult to cross. Lucy and the Doctor waited until a nearby break-in left a chance for infiltration through the tight net of the authorities.

With each passing street, the number of derelict buildings increased dramatically. The structures with signs of life in them looked no better than the vacant ones. Lucy watched for lights in windows to indicate where it was safe to walk. The other shelters, enveloped by darkness, usually housed unsavory and dangerous individuals. Those were to be avoided at all costs if they wanted their mission's lifespan to last longer than one night. Lucy wasn't certain if the Doctor's special suit could handle ballistics, and she wasn't all that keen on finding out tonight.

This part of the city seemed to be patrolled far less. In opposite proportion, shady people popped up everywhere they went. But tonight, Lucy wasn't too bothered by their presence. Whenever someone spotted her, they would try to stalk closer, then a moment later reassess their decision when a pale, white mask floating behind her appeared in the night. As the Doctor's giant frame broke free of the shadows, all possible hostile or lecherous intent vanished, and would-be assailants disappeared after it.

The cars along the sidewalks were missing tires, windows, and other critical components. A lot of them had found their terminal parking spaces. One had its door open a fraction; two legs hung out, unmoving. Lucy hoped whoever the legs belonged to was sleeping off a night of drinking and not something else. She slowed, turned her head back, and looked at the Doctor. "Anything out of the ordinary?"

"Only human signatures, Miss Lucy. Nothing odd detected yet." He looked at the buildings and to the people on the street.

". . . Except for extreme poverty."

"Yeah. Not the most fun part of town, I admit."

They continued to walk, now on the street.

"May I inquire about something, Miss Lucy?"

"An inquiry," she said with exaggeration, then threw him a glance. "Sure, go ahead, inquire away."

"Why do you have extensive knowledge of, judging by its outward appearance, such a dismal part of the city?"

"Hmm, short answer is my job takes me to places like this often."

The things she did while working ranged from immoral to federal felonies, so her mind made several attempts at constructing an explanation, but none presented her as a person with moral character.

"I believe we will have time for the longer version," he replied, words sounding quieter than before.

She walked a few steps forward and felt the Doctor wasn't behind her, so she looked back. The building that had caught his attention appeared over a hundred years old. Accumulated grime had subsumed whatever color it had been before, turning it into a dark, dirty obelisk of progress.

Treading back over, she asked, "What's up?"

The Doctor studied his screen.

"This building meets several of the search criteria for Johnathan's hiding place." Blue light, invisible to others, threw a cerulean shade over his white mask.

He walked to the door of the building and tried pushing and pulling. The door was stubborn and stayed locked. Lucy was about to suggest they try the back, but the Doctor pushed the lock until it gave way and fell on the other side.

"So what do we do now?" she asked after their twenty-seventh consecutive forced entry.

The room they were in had a single piece of furniture, a couch in the exact middle.

"Now we wait for my equipment to finish a thorough scan of the premises for any traces of the infection." The Doctor walked to the couch, taking a moment to adjust the cushion like a bird fretting over its nest.

Lucy suspected that these cushions had seen more bodily fluids than a motel bed, so she crept closer but remained standing.

"Well, we've got some time now." Lucy shrugged. "You still want the story, Doc?"

She looked at the sitting figure, mask still illuminated by the flickering screen on his arm. Concentrating her gaze on his neck and head, she tried to see some form or shape, but it looked like the mask was floating in the darkness. If not for its whiteness, the Doctor would appear like a shifting shade, a trick of the light.

Until he grabs and crushes your neck from the shadows that is.

Lucy shivered. The Doctor looked up from his screen a moment later.

"If you would, Miss Lucy," his tone was soft and pleasant, almost urging.

"Okay." She sauntered a few steps and leaned on the wall opposite him. "Every day, I work four hours at Mr. Wilson's shop . . . well used to. Then I squeeze as much as I can out of my second job, official title: bike courier." Her eyes darted everywhere except the middle of the room where the pale mask floated.

"The deliveries I mostly make on my bike. But sometimes we get a 'walking delivery,'" Lucy made air quotes and paused, expecting him to ask what that was.

He didn't say anything or tilt his head, so Lucy decided he understood the gesture.

She pushed off the wall and moved to the window on her left, boards blocking her view of the street. She grabbed and pulled one of the top panes. It groaned and gave way slightly. Bracing her foot on the window frame, she pulled back. The board came out, and she almost fell backward with it. Regaining her balance, she threw the board to the other side of the room. Moonlight streamed from outside and almost made the Doctor pop out from the darkness. He was no longer a disembodied mask floating in mid-air.

Much better.

She walked back to her original spot, leaned on the wall, breathed in deep, and continued.

"So, walking deliveries—how do I explain without self-incrimination . . . ?" Lucy wondered out loud.

"What do these walking deliveries entail?" he attempted to help her out.

"I go to work, my boss says we have a special job. I take the package and deliver it to the given address."

"Then, you are not allowed to use your bike?"

"Not really. I can if I want to. It's usually easier to disappear while you're on foot," she said thoughtfully.

His head tilted. "What is the connection to the underbelly of the city?"

"Here's where it gets tricky." She looked at the ceiling. "The delivery itself is normal enough, usually. But we don't know what's inside the package. Could be cocaine. Could be a severed finger. The possibilities are endless. Most times, it's a hot object. Something the clients can't or don't want to move themselves."

"How is the temperature of the package relevant?" He shifted on his cushion, beak still askew.

"The package is not literally hot." Lucy tilted her chin up, rubbing her forehead. "It's just usually highly illegal, and the client doesn't want to be associated with it at that moment."

"I see." He nodded after a few seconds. "And this is done to supplement your income, or is there another reason?"

"My boss does it because he owes debts, or he wants to keep breathing, or he just likes to do it . . . to be honest, I have no fucking clue. But to your point, I do it because the money's good. It helps me out a lot."

"Also—" The words stubbornly tried to retreat, like shy children at a new playground. "I like the thrill. Like when you're on a delivery, and it goes wrong, it's your life on the line. Everything boils down to you surviving. You have no obligations, no sick loved ones, no constant worry about money. It's pure and simple. Either you make it, or you don't."

Silence hollowed out the room.

Why did I blather all that out to him? The intense vulnerability baring her emotions brought was like running naked through the streets. In front of a 4th of July parade.

"I would not wish to cause offense, Miss Lucy, but that sounds incredibly dangerous and self-destructive. Believe me, I understand the allure of a challenge. My species thrives on it. But you have others that love and care for you. Have you ever thought about the pain and loss they might feel if you do not"— his monotone became frightfully low—*"make it out?"*

With his back stiff, he kept a watchful, dark eye on her when he added, "Testing yourself is all and good, but care for your life, please. After all, it is the most precious gift any of us living things have."

More silence followed. Lucy leaned her right shoulder near

the windowsill, her fingers wrestling each other like one would win a world championship.

"I apologize for sticking my," he said, pointing to his mask, "beak into your business. It is not my place."

"Yeah, it isn't," she said, still glued to the wall, giving him a sideways glance.

He nodded, allowing the conversation to die out. Lucy mulled over his words, angry at their truthful sting.

He doesn't know me. Fuck what he thinks. She pushed off the wall. "Is that thing done already?"

"Yes, it is, and it even picked up trace DNA from a host."

"Nice, so how do we proceed?" She stopped next to the couch, sure to not let it touch her.

"We follow its general direction."

"Then let's get out of this dump," she said and walked to the door. "You lead. I'll suggest better routes if we wind up in trouble."

"Understood." The Doctor opened the door, taking point.

The street was barren. There weren't even abandoned cars with people sleeping in them. The Doctor set a quick pace, and Lucy followed close behind. The streets got smaller as they neared their destination. Alleys formed a labyrinth around them. Buildings became more and more decrepit and neglected as they went.

Definitely not a place to wander alone at night.

They stopped in front of an alley. Shapes danced about in the shadows. The Doctor looked up from his screen, relaxed his hands by his sides, and made a single step toward the interior. The shifting darkness calmed, and the night became still again. The shapes seemed to return to whence they came, swallowed by the dark hole they crawled out of. Lucy was glad she wasn't on the receiving end of the Doctor's intimidation walk. He had the power to make the air freeze in place. He pivoted, rechecked his screen, then continued down the road past Lucy. At its end, they turned left.

The street turned out to be a cul-de-sac. At its wide circular ending sat regal houses, lost in time. When they got close, Lucy marveled at the façades. Columns on the first and second floor, small statues by the windows, and the embellished front edge of the roofs. The windows, however, were all missing. The boards in their place diminished the prestige of the houses by an immense margin. The Doctor stopped at the gate of the house in the middle, its front door facing the street head-on.

"We have to check inside." He opened the gate and walked up the stairs.

Lucy trotted after him. The front door was or had been a deep blue color a long time ago. Now streaks ran from top to bottom, like time itself had sundered it. The Doctor turned the ornamental doorknob, which Lucy was surprised had not been stolen. The lock popped, and the door opened with a sad groan.

"Shame," the Doctor said as he looked at the locking mechanism in his hand.

Throwing it to the side, he walked in, Lucy following behind. Light passing through the boarded windows revealed the interior.

Down a narrow hallway, they found themselves in a giant room with a colossal staircase. On each side of it were corridors to other parts of the house. The corridors led into impenetrable darkness, while the stairs led up to a landing that branched left and right. Above it, a railing stood in front of a whole wall of windows. Former windows. Currently, they were just rectangular, boarded holes trying in vain to replace them.

Lucy followed the stairs to the second floor and leaned on the railing. The walls adjacent to her held still intact doors leading to forgotten rooms. While she explored the house with her eyes, the Doctor walked up the stairs and stood beneath her on the landing. The top of his head reached her knees just barely. Watching him from above for a change felt nice. Lucy missed being taller than people.

"There are strong signatures in the vicinity, Miss Lucy. We will have to remain here for a while."

"At least the location is nicer this time. Breathe it in, Doc. That's the smell of former wealth."

"Mold?" he asked, puzzled.

Lucy took a deep breath in, then added, "And despair."

"I see," he said.

Pretty sure you don't.

"So we have a good lead or what?" She knelt down, put her chin on her knees, and looked at the Doctor.

"Most promising, yes." He turned around and surveyed the second floor. "This house belonged to people with means, correct?"

"I suppose." She puckered her lips in thought. "The taxes alone could buy you a normal house, so I guess someone wealthy must've lived here. Why'd ya ask?"

"I was wondering. What happened to this region of the city. Almost no one lives here, and those who do are—"

"Of ill repute?" a bitter smile spread across her lips.

"No." He glared at her. "I was going to say, of unfortunate circumstance."

"Some are, yeah." She nodded in agreement. "As I was told, this neighborhood used to be home to people who worked at the old factory."

"But some time ago, the factory closed down, some sort of financial crisis, misspending of funds, bad management, the

Illuminati, take your pick. I've heard it all." She looked at a spot above his head, imagining three children running up and down the stairs, irritating their peace-seeking father.

The phantoms vanished, and she returned her gaze to the Doctor's mask. "What I do know for certain is that more than a thousand people lost their jobs. So that's a thousand families with no money for mortgages, schools, and in some cases food."

"So they left in search of greener pastures, as they say," she stood up and walked to the landing.

"Very saddening," the Doctor said when she reached him.

Lucy shrugged. "That's what I've been told by Bernard and his friends."

"I wanted to ask, how did you make his acquaintance?"

"He knows his way around, has information, and I have money. He scratches my back, and I do his. That's the arrangement. He's like my . . . street adviser, let's call it." She smiled at her words.

"I see." The Doctor's beak bobbed. "Very helpful of him."

"Helpful, my ass," she said, flashing the frown of the fleeced. "He lives on the street, and nothing's pro bono on the street, Doc."

She continued to shake her head and felt a very palpable two-hundred and twenty dollar-shaped vacuum in her right pocket.

"The merchants of Venice would be proud of the commercial savvy applied in this century," he praised, arms on his chest, beak swaying up and down.

Lucy grunted in agreement.

"This old factory building you spoke of, Miss Lucy, do you believe it warrants a look?"

"Nah," Lucy's tone and the shape she made with her lips were skeptical, "don't think so, Doc."

"Why?"

Lucy looked at him with disbelief.

"Come on. If I were an intelligent space contagion, I wouldn't hide in a place so obvious and tacky." Her eyes narrowed.

The Doctor's forearm made a sound. He quickly brought the screen to life, information streamed down the holographic projection.

"What is it?" Lucy's gaze jumped from the screen to his mask.

"We have to move." He leaped down the stairs.

Lucy ran behind him, having to jump steps to keep up.

"An organism match has been made," he said and flung open the front door.

"How close?" Lucy asked from behind him.

He slid to a stop and stepped to the side. "Extremely." Lucy scanned the surrounding houses. Small figures stood motionless on every roof.

"Which one do we need?" The number of infected made her voice quiver.

Despite her efforts, fright crept through her veins. The Doctor looked down at his screen, then up at a rooftop to their right.

"That one." He pointed to a group of repulsively deformed children, one of which was Johnathan.

SIXTEEN

Lucy recognized Johnathan by his bulkier neck and misshapen hand. The other two forms beside him looked even less human. Before Lucy could formulate a plan of action, the Doctor jumped ahead. His body broke through the second-story wall of the building across the street. On the roof, Johnathan spun on his heels while the two deformed shadows ran forward. The Doctor's form sprang up through the ceiling. Debris flew out of higher story windows accompanied by the clamor of concrete breaking. Lucy clenched her jaw and followed.

The pain of getting left behind stung more than she expected. *So much for being a team.*

She put all her effort into gaining speed as the infected slid down the surrounding walls.

Gotta make it out of this cul-de-sac, or I'm dead meat.

She made it back to the street proper and found two girls touching down on ground level at the same time. Lucy continued forward but soon heard small taps behind her. Glancing back, she saw the misshapen form of the girls right on her tail. She wouldn't be able to outrun them. Lucy slowed then pivoted. The girl on the right extended her arms forward, bony fingers poised. Lucy unleashed her blade, slicing through those fingers and into her neck. The little head fell to the ground with a plop. The other girl slid on the pavement, spinning inhumanely fast.

Lucy was ready. Switching her grip to two hands, she angled the tip down and skewered the girl's spine. Her tiny fingers, almost reaching Lucy's abdomen, now fell limp.

Many forms low to the ground drew closer. Pushing garbage cans with long stifled embers to the side, they flowed closer. Freeing the machete, Lucy raced to the entryway of the cul-de-sac. Five distinct grunts bit at her heels. Fleeing with a drawn weapon wasn't great for balance, and since it had performed so well, she decided to try taking the pursuers on.

Not here, though. I have to find a better spot away from this death trap.

She sprinted toward unfamiliar buildings, using all the energy she dared to spare. Their rooftops were clear, so she focused on escape routes. The quiet intersection she passed wasn't well suited, so she kept going. One block down, she reached a road artery with enough alleyway capillaries to facilitate an emergency escape if she needed it. Sliding to a stop, she readied herself.

Once the first warped creature was in range, Lucy swung down and severed its right arm. The other four slowed their attack sensing a new type of danger. She gave them a crooked smile and dashed toward the nearest one, decapitating it before it had a chance to retreat. The last three spread out evenly and attempted to encircle her. Moving forward, Lucy tried to get the one in front. It dodged back, then stopped moving. Without hesitation, she decapitated it with a horizontal slash. The other two took a position at each side, and they lunged. Cursing herself for falling for such a rudimentary tactic, she chose the right side and plunged her machete into the lower back of the infected flying toward her. She tried to get the weapon out but wasn't fast enough. The last infected jumped and caught her left hip. Losing balance, she tumbled. The infected swung for her chest, and just as its claws connected, Lucy's free hand pushed it back, narrowly avoiding her ribcage being torn apart. Pain blazed across her chest as three lines opened on her skin and oozed blood. The infected continued to flail its arms.

Missing its opportunity to kill her gave Lucy enough time to angle the machete and stab into its swollen belly and twist. A flood of entrails gushed over Lucy's chest as she yanked out her blade. Her blood mixed with that of the infected. Her eyes grew wider, and she pushed the lifeless body off her. Scrambling to her feet, she looked down at her blouse. A gash ran from her collar almost to her solar plexus. Panic tried to take hold of her mind, but her instincts took over instead.

You're still under attack. Worry about infection later!

More infected stalked down the street and from nearby buildings. This wasn't going to be as easy as she had mistakenly believed.

Move. Her mind commanded. *You have to move!*

She sheathed the machete and ran in the vague direction that the Doctor had gone. As she neared the first intersection, something occurred to her.

If the Doctor was going after Johnathan, she should go the other way, away from Johnathan's range.

So instead of going right as she first planned, she went left. More than two dozen infected did not waver and continued behind her. There were too many. Fighting was out of the question this time.

She searched for a house, preferably a two-story. One that she could enter unnoticed. If not, she could bait some of the infected inside and try to get out through the second-floor window.

That's too simple. They won't fall for it. They're not just dumb kids anymore, Lucy chastised herself as she frantically tried to come up with something else.

The infected were still on her tail, but some trotted slower, their heads bobbing around.

Confused, maybe?

The display of strange behavior stirred Lucy's curiosity, so instead of searching for an escape route, she kept her eyes peeled for a place to hunker down and observe. Reaching the corner, she ducked into an alley at her right. Inside, she found a few boxes stacked for shelter. She arranged them around herself and crouched down, feeling like yet another piece of refuse piling high into the darkness. The patter of small palms slapping the sidewalk, getting close, told her their numbers were large enough to classify them as a herd. The incoming mob of hunched-down death made her redouble the effort of steadying her breathing. Something underneath her was wet, and she cringed, hoping it wasn't bodily fluid left behind from the last resident. Lifting her hand from the damp cardboard, she inspected it in the moonlight, coming in through a tear in her makeshift roof. *Yup, blood. Knew it.*

Her boots, blouse, and pants secreted droplets that hit the cardboard with thunderous thuds. The thirty-odd infected lurched to a stop just beyond her view. The fear of being discovered made her skin crawl, and her heart beat faster.

The infected stomped in place then dispersed. One, however, stayed and took slow steps toward Lucy. It stared at the ground, following the red splotches leading straight to her hiding place. She drew breath and held it, all the while slowly getting her machete out and not taking her eyes off the infected's silhouette of lumps sticking out of its neck, shoulders, and arms.

Just like Johnathan's, Lucy remembered and altered her plan of attack. *Body shots it is then.*

The infected was close enough now, and Lucy sprang out from her pallet haven. It did not try to defend itself but instead gave Lucy the chance to tackle it. She felt bony fingers prod her abdomen, piercing her skin. The pain made her see stars, but she managed to pin the thing's legs to the ground with her thighs. Pushing her elbow into its neck, she felt a tubular growth snaking around the throat. Machete out, she stabbed its abdomen twice. Unrelenting, it thrashed its arms until Lucy stabbed it three more times, ceasing its struggle. She dragged the infected back under her cardboard cover. One more infected appeared at the mouth of the alley just as Lucy settled back into her hiding spot. It stalked inside, not looking at the blood on the ground, prowling the nooks and crannies.

She couldn't stay there any longer. Gripping the small body, she threw it at the one searching for her. It hit the unsuspecting infected, toppling it.

Lucy got up and poised the tip of her blade to lance both but stopped when the living one started screaming—a gurgling howl like a goat being choked. The infected on the ground stared at the head of the one on top with its eyes wide and twitching. Lucy put her knee on the corpse, immobilizing the one thrashing on the ground. She moved the head of the dead one toward the one below. It whimpered and writhed under her weight. Pulling the head back had the opposite reaction. The living infected stopped whining and focused on Lucy. Malice contorting its face, the thing tried to claw its way to her. Having seen enough, she plunged the machete through the top infected's back and into the lower one's abdomen. The alley was still as blood pooled beneath Lucy and her recent kills. Standing up, she dragged the top infected away. Bracing her knee on its neck, she chopped.

These aren't like the ones I fought before. The Doctor might be acting like a right asshole, but he'll need to know about this.

Grabbing the infected by the hair, she slashed its neck, expecting to make a clean cut, but the blade got stuck. Straining, she freed the machete from what looked like cartilage and struck again. The round growth protecting the neck did an outstanding job at slowing her down. She made a final cut, pulled the head up by the hair, and stared into its dim green eyes. Inspecting the severed head, she discovered that the growth went all around to the base of the skull like an obnoxiously sturdy turtleneck. Pieces of meat and blood splattered on the corpse beneath her.

And this is just after not even two days in the wild. Category five contagions are no joke.

Lucy sheathed the machete and made her way in the direction the Doctor had disappeared. The streets had no infected on them, and no one pursued her, so Lucy picked up the pace wanting to be rid of the morbid baggage she'd acquired. Three streets over, two figures noticed her. Shuffling on legs bulging with pustules, they blocked her path. Stepping to each side, they prepared for a two-pronged attack, then froze in place. Their eyes fixed on the head Lucy carried. She raised it up like a gruesome lantern, pointing it toward them. Their teeth clattered, and they ducked into a nearby alley. Lucy crept to the corner, weapon ready, and checked to see if they had gone. To her surprise, the alley was empty. She looked around for another couple of seconds, and when nothing jumped out at her, she continued on her way. The sound of rapid gunfire pierced the air, coming from the same direction that the Doctor had run off to.

Figures, she scoffed and hurried onward.

Arriving at the commotion, she saw infected swarming military and civilian vehicles from all sides. Hundreds more flowed down the buildings' walls like a waterfall. Lucy was too close to the fighting, so she leaned back behind the corner. Something in her periphery caught her attention. A black figure leaped from a nearby building and crashed down on the pavement beside her.

"Glad you made it, Miss Lucy," the Doctor said almost nonchalantly.

His remark irked her beyond belief. The only thing keeping her from exploding into a ball of shouts was her upper incisors biting down on her lip.

"Yeah, no thanks to you, asshole." She pushed the severed head into his hands. "Have a look at what you left me to fight by myself."

The Doctor spun the head to inspect it, stopping when he noticed the strange growth.

"That thing around its neck caught my attention too. On top of that, it was smarter than the rest. The ones that don't have the growth seemed to be afraid of it."

"Very useful, Miss Lucy. Remarkable work. It seems my trust in you was not misplaced."

Lucy had enough of him acting like he didn't abandon her to a horde of monsters and the haughty attitude like she didn't deserve an apology.

"Why did you—"

"Fall back," a cry from the soldiers cut her off. "Down the street, over there!"

With no time to argue, Lucy dragged the Doctor inside the building next to them. Like a giant black bird, Emidius perched himself near the entrance and watched. Lucy knelt down and took a breath. Crawling deeper inside the house, she found all the windows boarded up and draped with sheets. She made her way to a window that let in the moonlight and knelt beside it to observe.

The military vehicles had made a blockade on the street, and the soldiers shot from behind it. Sprinkled between the men in uniforms were civilians, cowering under the gunfire. Infected poured out of buildings, alleys, and rooftops. Automatic weapons cut them down with methodical precision. The line was holding.

Good. They'll have their hands full here, and we'll slip by unnoticed.

Then she heard the *clacking* sound of weapons being inspected before a fight. She shifted to the window next to her with a small space between the boards she could peer through. The window faced an alley leading directly to the flank of the firing line. Around ten men stood guard, spread out to the sides. A moment later, small footsteps came from the darkness of the alley.

"Open fire," the man in front of the line shouted.

Lucy raised her hands and covered her ears. The men fired, but she couldn't see if they hit their target or not.

Are they winning? she wondered as she struggled to get a better vantage on the situation.

The firing diminished, and several men cried out. Lucy caught one of the fatal exchanges as an infected threw itself against a soldier and killed him, getting peppered with bullets in the process. Two, three, four men fell, one right after another. The infected sliced through their exposed skin and killed them on the spot. A second later, they themselves were dead, but the flank was now exposed.

Dark figures rained down on the surviving soldiers. A flood of living, breathing shadows filled the alley. The murderous wave smashed into the firing line and engulfed it. The tide of death continued down the street and crashed into the other men. The carnage rendered Lucy's legs to gelatin. Not able to move an inch, she could only watch the unfolding horror.

There are so many of them!

The infected first went for the legs, breaking them and toppling the soldiers left standing. On the ground, the infected continued their spree, slashing anything in reach with their claws.

Seconds after the tiny beasts swept through, almost all soldiers were dead. Some weren't so fortunate. Their terrible moans made Lucy shudder. The infected had done their job in haste and disappeared just as quickly. The Doctor came and knelt next to her. She tried to ask what they were going to do, but he put his index finger beneath his beak, asking for silence, and she followed his gaze back to the street.

Groups of four infected circled the bodies, locating soldiers still alive and dragging them off. One out of each group moved differently than the rest. Stiff and unsure. The three others dealt with the soldier, while the stiff one just walked close behind them. Soon, no living person was left on the street. Then, to Lucy's utter shock, they began unloading the trucks. Her eyebrows furrowed as two small figures carried away every box within.

What could they possibly need with military weapons? She watched in amazement at how efficiently they unloaded the cargo.

All that gear is worth a fortune, she thought out of reflex, doing the math in her head. She salivated as thoughts of millions of dollars worth of gear titillated her mind.

The Doctor tapped her on the shoulder and pointed to the outside. Lucy nodded, and they both went out, Emidius still carrying the head in his hand. The last of the infected had just gone around the corner when Lucy turned to speak. But the

Doctor jumped in the air and scaled the façade of the nearest building, letting the head he carried drop with a splat on the ground. Looking up, her eyes met those of a thick-necked infected.

"Asshole," she said, watching the climbing Doctor in disbelief. *He left me. Again!*

Fuck him then. . . .

She knelt down and grabbed the severed head as added protection and quickly snuck away along the street, slipping between the shadows to keep from being seen. Up ahead, she spotted the military trucks, now almost entirely stripped clean, save one that had all its doors still closed. The streets appeared barren of both living men and prowling children. Overcome with curiosity, Lucy crept to the truck and tried the back door. Locked. Instead of deterring her, the lock fed her motivation to discover the vehicle's secrets. She ran to the driver's side door, and after a quick look over her shoulder, tested the handle. It clicked open.

Pulling herself inside the tall cab with a hop, she crawled over the driver's seat and into the back. Three cases of assault rifles lay along the left wall. Not as much as she was hoping for but still worth a pretty penny.

If I get these back to Cher Ami, I'm sure we could sell them off to a fence for a hefty finder's fee. And if push comes to shove, there should be some arms dealers I could get in touch with.

The thought made her gulp. The carefree manner with which she contemplated making the monumental jump from petty crimes to federal offenses unbalanced her world. Shuffling back to the cab, she gripped the wheel and focused on a manhole cover in front of the truck. "Beggars can't be choosers," she said aloud to push her nagging doubts aside.

She planted her butt into the driver's seat and fist-bumped the air when she saw the keys in the ignition. A cry made her freeze. It was one of those desperate womanly cries they put in movies. Lucy opened the door and stepped out of the truck, turning in the cry's direction. A woman carrying a small girl rounded the corner. Relief shined on her face at the sight of the vehicles, then a moment later, she noticed the bodies, and despair washed over her features once more. She ran toward the truck as Lucy got her machete out.

This must be a trap.

The woman's braid flung left and right from the exertion. Strands of her bright golden hair flowed through the air as if in a wild dance. For a brief instant, images of a different shade of blond flashed through Lucy's mind. Shaking her chin, she chased away the thoughts of her mother.

"Please help us! They're chasing—"

An infected leaped out of a nearby alley and toppled the woman over. Lucy dashed to them. The woman took the brunt of the fall on her elbow. Bone claws cut through her skin, trying to break her grip on the child. Lucy bisected the attacker's head with a clean two-handed swing. A torrent of blood, brains, and viscera spewed on the young mother, staining her clothes and wide-eyed features.

Lucy tried to assess the damage to the woman. The wound on her arm was deep, and she seemed to have another one on her abdomen. Shock began to set in, but she never released her protective hold around the child.

"Come with me," Lucy said, helping the woman to her feet. "I'll get you out of here."

SEVENTEEN

The woman let Lucy drag her to the truck. The arm she'd used to shield the child was so severely injured, Lucy could see bone. They'd nearly reached the door when four infected appeared down the end of the street.

They're probably here for the last of the cargo . . . Lucy helped the woman inside and turned around, gripping the severed head by a fist full of hair. . . . *My cargo.*

Raising the head in front of her, she took steady steps toward the infected. The fear in their glowing eyes grew as the head neared. Some collapsed. Others cowered behind trashcans and lamposts. Lucy drew her blade and cut down the nearest one, clavicle to hip, flesh split like a flower in bloom, crimson lifeblood hitting the dirty pavement. Kicking the dead infected to the side, Lucy stalked closer and hacked the rest to pieces, taking out her frustration on their grotesque forms. She wiped the blood off the machete on the nearest corpse, then grabbed a loose garment and wrapped the head.

It could still come in handy.

Climbing inside the truck, she left the shrouded head in front of the steering wheel and inspected the woman. Her skin was pale, and she couldn't move her right arm. She used her healthy hand to stroke the little girl's head.

The girl took in a big gulp of air and steadied her shaking lips.

"Is mommy going to be okay?"

Blood dotted the girl's porcelain doll face like freckles. Lucy looked at both of them, then grit her teeth.

I have to get this woman some help, but I can't risk being spotted in the truck. Fuck!

The girl kept her widening gaze on Lucy, not letting her wiggle her way out of an adult's responsibility.

"Don't worry." She gave the girl a smile. "Your mommy will be just fine."

She started the truck, and they headed to the nearest hospital. The girl unrelentingly peered at her, but that didn't bother Lucy as much as the memory of the pain she felt when her own mother was in trouble.

This time, there's someone to help.

They met more and more patrols the closer they got to the hospital. Lucy's breath caught in her throat each time oncoming traffic passed them by. The adrenaline in her veins diminished each moment, leaving way for stress to assert its tiring presence. Yanking the wheel, she turned the key and let her arms shake in the darkness for a few moments.

That's far enough. We can make it on foot from here.

Meeting the girl's apprehensive eyes, she said, "I'm Lucy. What's your name?"

The girl looked at her mother.

"It's okay . . ." The woman's eyes fluttered in a brief moment of lucidity.

"Samantha."

"That's a really pretty name. Do you like to be called Sam?" Lucy spoke with a gentle tone.

"Yes." She nodded energetically.

"Okay, Sam, take my hand so I can help you down, and then

I'm gonna get your mom too. We have to walk from here on out."

After helping Sam, Lucy grabbed the head atop the dashboard and tied the cloth to her belt. Climbing up once more, she helped the woman down, mainly carrying her.

"Now, Sam, grab my belt over here." Lucy pointed to the left side of her waist. "Hold on and don't let go, okay?"

"Okay." Sam nodded so hard that her chin almost hit her chest.

"Great." Lucy dove under the injured woman's arm and heaved her up.

They ambled down the street, Lucy's thigh colliding with the strapped head as she went. The balmy, decomposing skin stuck to her pants after each hit. Goosebumps ran up her forearms as images of decaying flesh sliding down her leg filled her mind.

One block down, the woman passed out. Lucy felt blood on the arm she had around her waist. A few minutes later, the right side of Lucy's body burned. She leaned the woman on a rusty car and tried to catch her breath.

We're not gonna make it at this pace. Her eyes moved to Sam, who still diligently held her belt even while they rested.

"Hey, Sam."

The girl looked up.

"How about we let your mom rest here for a bit while I take you to the nice people at the hospital and then—"

"No," Sam's reply was adamant. "I'm not leaving mom!"

The words clutched Lucy's heart and hurt her more than anything the infected had managed in two days. This little girl showed more bravery than Lucy had in her entire life. The world was crumbling, men with guns shot at living shadows, and this fragile girl refused to abandon her mother.

"Yeah, you're right." Lucy patted her head. "Why would anyone do that?"

Confusion ran through the girl's darkened features.

"Thank you for reminding me of something, Sam. You're a very good girl." She lifted her mother once more while Sam smiled proudly.

"Let's get the fu—heck outta here."

Lucy ignored the burning pain in her right side and, with renewed vigor, dragged the bleeding woman two more blocks. Remorse nibbled at her soul all the way there.

The bright lights of the hospital's entrance almost made Lucy cry. Walking through the front door, she must've been a sight. Three long tears running down the front of her blouse, hair a mess, and an infected's head dangling in front of an unconscious woman.

Lucy took one step inside, and the fatigue caught up to her. Sam ran ahead.

"Please, help my mom!" she tried her best to shout but only managed more of a squeak.

Despite that, a nurse noticed them, called an orderly, and rushed over. They grabbed Sam's mother and took her away. Sam hugged Lucy's thigh then trotted after them. The cold around Lucy's heart melted when she saw the girl's slight form run like a kid instead of a malicious monster. No one paid her any mind as she slipped back into the night.

Police and military presence got too intense for her to keep on the street, so Lucy had to duck inside buildings until it was safe to move again. With nothing to do, she dimmed the light of her phone's screen and typed a message.

Hey, sorry about how I acted. Are you okay?

The message traveled to Sarah.

I mean, with the whole quarantine business, everything okay? she added.

The reply vibrated in her hand.

It's cool, Lu. I need a dose of reality now and again, so thanks for that.

Sarah was dancing around the subject.

You do, but I'm sorry for the thing I said about you being rich, I know you're not like that, it's just I'm high-strung right now, and you were the only outlet available.

Bitch, don't call me an outlet.

Lucy smiled as she read.

That's gross, and apology accepted. I'm waiting on some good news tomorrow. You get ready, okay?

What for?

It's a surprise. I won't spoil it. The message ended with an emoji sticking its tongue out mischievously.

Fine, talk to you soon, Lucy typed and ended the conversation.

Weighing the option of going back for the truck, she let five police cars and several armored transports roll by before deciding it was too risky. Slipping out of her shelter, she set course for her apartment. The level of involvement the officials showed made her jump into shadows every minute or so. Once the danger had passed, she pacified her anger, only allowing an irate exhalation to escape her throat. After evading authorities for an hour, her fury at being left behind only grew. Thirty more minutes passed until she arrived at her half-dead abode. The time on her phone said 1:11 AM.

The sound of bending metal made her look up. The Doctor slid down a drainpipe and met her at the entrance to her apartment building.

"Fucking finally. Why did you run off? Twice!" Her

questioning eyes grew twice their size. "Do you have any idea how deadly those things are for someone like me?" She pulled the collar of her blouse down to expose her brand new claw marks.

"Not here," he said, walking by her and going into the alley.

She followed as he summoned his screen into view, then typed something. The space in front of them shimmered. Lucy blinked, and a small structure that looked like a pumpkin appeared where there was only garbage before. Lucy rubbed her eyes as that seemed the appropriate reaction. The space pumpkin did not disappear. A small platform extended, leading up to the shining interior.

With tentative steps, she climbed inside. The platform retracted, and an opening above the door released a mist-like vapor that descended to the floor. Touching it, it became a slab of solid material, sealing them off.

"I was pursuing Johnathan in an attempt to save your race," he spoke a few feet away, down the only available corridor. "What were you doing?" His tone rose uncharacteristically high.

"So was I, asshole." She swung the wrapped head, slamming it into a nearby surface. "And I managed to help a woman and her child along the way."

"Very admirable, Miss Lucy, and what about the approximately eight hundred sixty thousand other inhabitants of your city? Do you believe your momentary compassion helped them?" Ignoring the bundle, he took a step forward. "Are they safer now than they were a few hours ago?" He sounded petty, making Lucy's fingers prod her palms.

"At least two are safer, yeah," she said defiantly. "What about you? Did you gather some actionable intelligence or a viable sample?"

"No," came his muted reply.

"Well, I did." She pointed at the head again. "The head that you so diligently forgot belonged to a more advanced infected. It looked like it was in charge, or they were afraid of it. And those two I saved, I did because, unlike you, I have to sleep each night."

She blinked, and the Doctor had closed the distance between them. His arms by his side, fingers spread wide. It looked as if he were about to tear her in half like a piece of paper.

"Do not presume to know what horrors haunt my dreams while I hibernate. I, too, have lost comrades, good beings that were embroiled into events beyond them."

"Check your fucking attitude then." Lucy was too mad to be afraid or heed reason. "Because I'm the only one who can help you work this shit out fast enough. You could probably do your mission without me, but not in time. Without me, people are dead. Hell, maybe everyone is dead, and I *know* that's not something you want. So you need me alive!"

"And what do you suggest?"

"I don't fucking know; get me one of your suits. Even if I can't use it properly, it's gonna be some help. Otherwise, I won't last one more night like this." She pulled her shirt off, revealing her battered torso.

Rivulets of blood slid down her skin from the reopened cuts. The Doctor looked up and down her neck, chest, arms, and the small round wounds on her abdomen.

"I cannot do that, Miss Lucy," he said after finishing his visual inspection.

"Well, then you're gonna lose the only person that actually carries out *your* mission." Her fingers closed around the shirt hem, and she pulled it back down so forcefully that threads frayed with an audible snap.

The dark pools on his mask studied her for a moment. He turned and moved with a new purpose. Unwrapping the head, he placed it in an open, square space. Mist vapors fell around it and became dark blocks when they reached the flat surface beneath the pooled gore.

"The new strain is evolving faster than expected," he said while gazing at the information. "The analysis is not yielding the full results. Even so, at this rate, adults may be infected within sixty hours. Soon, Johnathan will break free of the bottleneck imposed on him by the juvenile biology of his host."

Spinning in place, he faced a fully tangible wall that rose ten feet from floor to ceiling. "This changes the parameters entirely."

Lines etched into the wall carried a liquid down it. The Doctor walked the corridor, holding his forearm close to the walls. Moving his arm to different spots on the etchings, the display changed color and lettering. The screen always hovered in front of one of the many indentations that filled the solid surfaces at regular intervals. The walls looked like they were shot with high-velocity bullets and never repaired.

The liquid in the etchings flowed to the center of the indentations.

Stepping closer to one, she pointed to a nearby nexus and asked. "What are these?"

"Information distribution units." The jerky motions with which he went from spot to spot made his coat ruffle. "Now, please stop distracting me."

He moved further down and continued checking the 'information distribution units.' Lucy followed, inspecting the floor and ceiling. The ceiling was white, soft light exuding from it. Refocusing, she noticed the Doctor had stopped and was now typing something. The symbols that appeared looked more and more aggressive. Lucy came closer, and a new flow of characters elbowed their way onto the screen. With two streams to deal with, the Doctor's fingers moved and bent in ways humans weren't designed to. Lucy didn't have to understand the symbols to recognize a warning sign when she saw one.

Twirling her index fingers around each other, she asked, "Is everything okay?"

The ceiling changed to a color that made Lucy's legs buckle. Observing the odd hue froze her eyelids open, and she couldn't blink. The Doctor pushed his left elbow into her side. Returning her agency, she dashed back to the door without thinking. The door loomed over her with monolithic indifference.

"What's going on?" she blubbered, her head turning in different directions as if recovering from a ghostly slap.

Every nexus she could see projected a screen like the Doctor's, and on each were the two streams.

"What are you doing, Doc?" Claustrophobia crept up her spine and began to squeeze. *Is he going to kill me?* The thought froze her blood. "Can't we talk about this?"

The warning signs began to flash with higher frequency.

"Time for discussion is over, Miss Lucy," the Doctor spoke calmly, not moving from his spot. "I need to bypass some security protocols, and I will be with you in a moment."

The nearest warning sign changed—the font of the new message was bigger than before. Under the sticks and squiggles that the Doctor typed, appeared a new breed of incomprehensible character. With each passing second, a character changed.

"Is this thing counting down to something?" Lucy felt her throat tighten, her chest got too small for her lungs, and her breathing got as shallow as a prehistoric riverbed.

"Fifteen seconds to release of atomizing mixture. Pardon me, ten seconds now." The Doctor was frantically swiping windows that popped up on his screen.

The light changed to soft white again, the strange color vanished, taking some of the room's tension with it. The screens disappeared, and the nexus in front of the Doctor blossomed, pushing forward a white rod. A gust of mist shot down to the floor, materializing into a white cube. The Doctor's finger traced a circle on top of the new structure. Once done, the circle split down the middle and retracted into the sides.

Is that a fucking space drawer? The thought made her chuckle, despite the near-atomization.

The Doctor took out a small black case with his left hand. Then he touched something on his screen. The drawer became light again and flowed back up into the rod, which retracted inside the wall. He walked to Lucy with the case.

"Got it." His tone was jolly. "Much faster than expected even."

The wall slid up, and Lucy tumbled out of the ship. Her vision shook from the frightful experience. The Doctor's silhouette appeared in the doorway.

"What the fuck just happened?" Her voice and legs shook in tandem.

"I had to bypass some bureaucracy, Miss Lucy."

"You don't want me dead then?"

"Not particularly." He tilted his head to the side. "If I'd wanted that, you would have been atomized to carbon just now."

"Yeah, I got that part. What in the fuck did you just do?"

"Decrease the profanity, please, Miss Lucy. I got a piece of equipment out of storage." He pulled the case up and showed it to her.

Anger quickly overcame fright. "If your ship was gonna go haywire while I was inside, you could've told me to leave before getting it."

"Your presence was not the issue. It appears that the tampering of my equipment goes far beyond landing coordinates and time of arrival."

"You already said." Lucy raised her eyebrows in irritation.

"So I did, but the sabotage seems to run deeper every time I investigate."

"You know what, never mind. I don't care." She threw both palms up. "Just keep me away from that death trap, and I'll be good."

The Doctor walked down the ramp then looked around his ship. "Hardly, Miss Lucy. We just take security very seriously."

"Keep joking, ass," she mumbled under her breath.

The fear of the Doctor hadn't left her body yet, so she didn't want to push it. Her phone vibrated. A message from her boss. It had a location, a time and at the end was a golden coin with the words: *last chance.*

"You know what?" A smile spread across her lips. "I don't need this right now. I've got stuff to handle."

"But, Miss Lucy—"

"But what? You said we're a team, right?" Indignation burned on her cheeks.

"Yes, of course—"

"Then you left me." Her palm slapped her chest, making her wince from the pain. "A person who can die any minute of any day while walking around with you."

"I was completing the mission." He squared his shoulders. "Like you eloquently brought up earlier, we are here to do what needs to be done. Is that not the reason you are here?"

"I . . ."

"Indeed. You said that you are vital to my success, and that is fairly accurate, but do not so grossly overestimate your importance. I can do things your underdeveloped mind cannot begin to grasp. So I would suggest, in the friendliest of fashion, that *you*, should check your fucking attitude." His synthetic voice crept so low that Lucy could swear it came from the darkness around them.

"A team, Miss Lucy, is made of individuals coming together to complete a common goal. It is not a race to see who can do the most. You would do well to keep that in mind the next time I save your life."

The Doctor pulled both hands behind his back and stood tall and proud, verbal victor over a foe at wit's end. Lucy's lips shook like waves at high tide. Turning her back, she flipped him off and disappeared around the corner.

EIGHTEEN

Lucy barely reached the destination on her phone in time. Leaning on a stone wall, she slid down until she sat on the ground. The coins, secure in her backpack. Taking a few moments to catch her breath, her eyes explored the surroundings.

Tall residential buildings stood in a perfect row down the street across the factory's yard. Figures dashed past the few lights still on in the higher floors. The inhabitants of the rooms behind the desiccated walls were a far cry from the optimistic and hard-working men and women that put all their hopes into their workplace.

By the number of lights on, there can't be many people around. Figures. Standing up, she dusted her hands off. She had to get off the street before a patrol saw her.

Sliding the rusty fence forward, she ducked inside. The moon illuminated old buildings that ran on each side of her for as far as she could see. Shattered windows gaped like dark punctures through which the night could penetrate. No artificial light gave Lucy her bearings, so she got her phone out and illuminated the old pavement. Piles of slick refuse reflected her bright light. Rats scurried away from the unforeseen guest's cautious steps. Walking by the mound recently vacated of rat presence, fumes of rot made Lucy's nostrils close up. Continuing forward, each unfamiliar sound froze her in place.

Fuck, the Doc was right. This would be a great place for Johnathan to hide. And all these unlit buildings are perfect for raising a horde of infected.

Putting her right hand on the machete's handle, she continued forward. *Let's hope I won't have to eat my words about this shitty factory.*

Three dead buildings flanked her on the right and two on the left. Their doors stood frozen mid-swing, nothingness peering back at Lucy. Moving faster, she reached a bend in the unkempt road. In front of her stood a behemoth of a building, stretching to both sides, dwarfing the ones she'd just passed. The road beneath her feet now led to the left, into impenetrable darkness and vague outlines of other deceased houses of industry. The right side didn't offer a much better alternative. At the far end of the colossus towered another building to rival its size. A beige and crimson dome stood on top of two floors of neglected steel and concrete.

What could possibly have been made in a building that looks like that, she wondered as she got closer.

Sounds came from behind the corner. Lucy slowed her pace and listened for a moment.

Humans, she realized, relaxing and took a breath.

Driving her heel into the ground, making sure her steps were loud enough, she turned the corner. Two men stood in front of doors fit for battleships. Throwing one last inquisitive look at the mysterious dome, Lucy continued toward the men. Soon they heard her and made their way over. Shining her phone light at their torsos, she recognized Frank, both hands in casts. Lucy allowed herself a quick smile before a flashlight beam hit her face.

"Well, looky here," Frank's voice grated her ears.

"Hey, Frank. I see you've got some trouble with your hands." She arched her right eyebrow, and her face grew concerned. "Are you okay?"

"You think you're funny, eh?" He pushed his face almost into hers.

"People have said as much," she continued with a smug tone. "I hope you get better soon, and since you can't frisk no more, I'll make it easy for you."

She took the machete out with one quick motion and pushed it flat against his chest. "Here you go. Oh, oops, I forgot." She drew it back, handing it to the man beside him.

"Come on, Frank. Mike's waiting."

A crooked smile distorted his darkened face.

"Yes. He. Is." The satisfaction in his voice made Lucy weary.

Frank stepped to the side and gestured with an immobile hand for her to go on ahead. Lucy grabbed the straps of her backpack and walked to the immense door. The space beyond the door stretched to the side and further in. Beams of steel speared the darkness above; the edges of the nearest two towered over a flickering fire that cast erratic shadows across five men. One face Lucy recognized. Mike.

In the few feet she walked to reach the edge of the light, she noticed vast outlines of machines, their shapes huddled together like dying beasts on a freezing night.

"Ah." Mike smiled when she stepped into the faint firelight. "Here's our gold trader." A wave of chuckles ran through those gathered around the barrel.

Lucy noticed several other figures lurking in the dark, just beyond the reach of the feeble light.

Two on the right and at least one on the left, hiding behind the columns.

The darkness beyond Mike held more steel beams. Moonlight from a crack in the ceiling made their metal gleam appear like knives poised to slice a giant to pieces. The relatively small gallery everyone occupied still looked big enough to accommodate aircraft.

Maybe that's what they did here. Build planes, the thought piqued her interest, and her mind strained against the fatigue of the long day like an ant trying to pull a slice of pizza.

"Come on then, get closer so I can see ya," Mike urged with a wave of a hand that jingled with gold bracelets.

Lucy came closer, unslinging her backpack. The folded-up sleeves on Mike's silk shirt touched the side of his chest while he collapsed his hands behind his back.

"It was Lucy, right?" He pointed a finger at her while she retrieved the coins.

"Yup." She stood across the ring of fire and handed the bag to the nearest man.

"Let's see what you've brought me, Lucy." The coins were passed along to him.

Without moving his eyes away from her, he took them and dropped the bag on the ground. The coins jingled with the sound of broken dreams. The men spread out, creating a ring around her.

"I was told you were on the level," Lucy's voice was low and tired. *I'm not going to be intimidated.*

"I am." Mike nodded. "And I was when I got the call that someone needed to move some gold."

"But when I found out *who* that someone was." His head fell forward and stopped as if caught on a string. "I got to thinkin'. Would a man in my position, a leader of others." He swung both his arms to encompass everyone around Lucy.

". . . allow a nobody like you to set him up?"

"I didn't—"

A hand grabbed her chin and an arm coiled around her stomach. Mike moved his index finger from side to side.

"I know you didn't. You're a nobody." His finger beckoned someone from behind. "That's why I got the one responsible."

A man made of muscle was shoved next to Mike. The corners of Lucy's mouth twitched when she saw her boss, face beat to a pulp, his eyes almost invisible under welts and swollen skin. The two men that brought him in looked to have had a rough time of it. One's nose was smashed in, while the other's mouth bled onto his out-of-season Hawaiian shirt. Lucy's eyes returned to the taller face, and her boss gave her a puffy smirk, which rewarded him a hit to the liver.

Lucy tried to wiggle free. "We didn't do anything, asshole. Let him go!"

Mike's right hand opened, and he gestured for her to calm down. His other hand dove behind his back, pulling out a knife.

"This is now a holy place of business. Do not desecrate it with lies, please." His eyes fixed on hers, the intention to kill clearly visible. "I'm here to discuss matters with your employer, so you keep quiet."

The arms holding her tightened, and she winced in pain.

"Thank you." He nodded to her then turned. "Patrick, welcome. We don't know each other that well, but I never thought you'd do me the way you did."

Another hit to Patrick's liver followed. He only grunted in reply, eyes trained on Mike's.

"Not gonna say anything? Offer me a deal, negotiate. We're businessmen here." Mike smiled as he tapped the flat of the blade against his chest.

Her boss didn't reply, and more blows rained down on him. Standing tall, taking the punishment, he said nothing.

"I see you're no fun." Mike sighed, his head tilted to the side. "What about now?" He strode to Lucy and put the knifepoint against her stomach.

"It wasn't us," Patrick coughed, his words hard to discern. "You're looking the wrong way."

Mike's jaw stiffened, and he lunged at her boss. The knife's blade touched his throat.

"And are you the one to show me where to look?" Mike spoke through his teeth.

A shuffle went through his men. Lucy noticed them lean forward like they were getting ready to tackle someone or jump away.

"I ain't tellin' you shit." Patrick tilted his chin down to look, the knife cutting his skin. "You said you're here for business, right?" His lips drew back as far as they could, showing red-stained teeth. "Go ahead then, do your business."

Mike nodded to the men beside Patrick, who raised his head and looked Lucy dead in the eye. The knife went in his stomach three times. On the fourth, it pierced his heart and remained there.

In the quiet of the warehouse, the last breath of a man dying on his feet drifted above the crackling fire, then disappeared in the hall of past industrial glory.

This isn't the way it was supposed to go, she tried to wiggle out, but the crushing grip of her captor made it too painful. *We did illegal shit, yeah, but never something that would get anyone killed!*

She focused her mind on his glassy eyes and maintained her breathing pattern. *Not gonna fall apart, don't fall apart, Lucy.*

Mike flicked his head, and his men released Patrick's hands.

The body did not fall. With an impressed frown on his face, Mike put his left palm on Patrick's chest and pushed until the body fell to the ground, his knife now free. Turning to Lucy, he came closer.

"People outside of this building"—he spun the downward-facing knife in a small circle—"and not involved in our business, might take my actions as barbaric."

Glaring at her, he raised his hand.

"But you and I . . ." The knife moved like a metronome between them. "We know better. You know why I did that, right?" His chin moved down.

"A message," Lucy said, trembling.

"Yeah, sure," Mike continued, "but this is more of a warning. The warning being . . ."

He lunged at her and grabbed the back of her hair. "Do not fuck with me. And speaking of fucking . . ."

His stare turned nasty. A tick made the right corner of his mouth twitch. "Here's what's going to happen. I'm taking your gold, and that's that. What you have to decide right now is whether you want to live or not."

Stepping away, he walked back to the flaming barrel.

"If you don't want to live, we can be done in a couple of seconds." Puckering his lips, he watched the fire with raised eyebrows.

Her machete found its way to her throat from unseen hands.

"But if you want to live for *some* reason." He shrugged his shoulders, prompting a laugh from the men. "Then I'll have to make you an example . . . and Frank's already volunteered."

Grunts of affirmation filled the quiet air.

"What's it gonna be, little gold trader?" Mike looked her in the eye, both hands on the outside rim of the fire barrel.

The heavy steps of Frank came from behind.

What am I even doing here? she wondered. *I wanted some cash to help out my mom. Maybe save a little bit for me. Enjoy life. Live!* Her legs itched to run, to get as far as possible from these people that wanted to harm her.

"Let's hear it," Mike prodded for her answer.

The circle of men tightened in expectation of the show Frank would give them. Lucy's extremities felt numb as if every ounce of liquid from her veins was missing. *But that's not it. I just ran away. It was easier to send money and not worry about it. Easier to forget how it was growing up. It was easier to just leave her there to rot away. . . .*

Her lips trembled when she tried to agree.

"She's shakin' like a leaf, Boss."

Lucy licked her dry lips. "I . . . I want to live."

The corner of Mike's mouth twitched into a smirk, and he gestured with his chin. Her captor pulled her away from the light.

I can make it. I will make it. I have to see her and apologize, even if she doesn't know who I am.

A scratching noise and a figure moved above Mike. The darkness fractured into a compact shadow that jumped down. A bony claw cleaved the top of Mike's head, the limp hunk of flesh landing on a nearby henchman. Mike's eyelids opened and closed with the speed of a hummingbird's wings. Grunting, he raised the knife, but a slender hand scraped the inside of his skull, scooping pink globs of brain out. Mike tipped forward and fell face-first into the fire. His hair caught the flames, then his clothes. The barrel tipped over, spilling more fuel on his body. The air filled with the nauseating smell.

Lucy grabbed the hand holding her machete and bit into it.

The man yelled and tried to hit the back of her head. Shielding it with her hands, she increased the pressure, feeling blood spray into her mouth. The machete fell, and Lucy followed.

An infected slammed into the man's chest. Lucy grabbed her weapon and rolled to the side. She collided with Frank's feet, toppling him to the ground. Flailing his arms, he attempted to get up. A claw sliced his head halfway through. Lucy looked at the flame engulfing Mike. It reached her bag and set it ablaze. One of the turtleneck infected stepped out of the shadows. Not losing any more time, Lucy stood up and ran.

Men cried out from everywhere. Those that had waited in ambush were being dismembered just out of sight. In front of her, a normal infected ripped a man's forearm and began to beat his convulsing body with it. Sidestepping them, the arm of a man grabbed her. The henchmen pulled down, her shoulder hitting the floor. Groaning, Lucy tried to spin on the ground and kick his feet, but three infected swarmed him. Fingers ripped open his stomach and throat. Lucy pushed off the ground, her right shoulder throbbing with pain. She took two steps before ducking.

Someone shot at her, the bullet bouncing off the beam she took cover behind. Glancing back, she saw the shooter being swarmed. The wrist behind the gun got severed by a turtleneck. The hand fell to the ground. A moment later, the head followed.

Lucy dashed for the door. A shoulder crashed into her right knee. Her foot buckled, and while she toppled, she hacked the attacker's back, not knowing if it was a man or an infected child. Getting up, she dragged her hurt leg and slipped outside.

Every visible surface crawled with nimble figures. Bands of infected hounded the living, dropping down from rooftops, slashing out from crevices, and pursuing those fleeing. Lucy's peripheral caught a small shadow lunging for her Achilles tendons. Striking blind, she shaved off a piece of skull. The clawed fingers gouged out a chunk of flesh on her lower calf. Clamping her jaw to keep the tears of pain away, she limped along the wall to the building's nearest corner and peeked around it.

The remains of Mike's gang were going through a meat grinder. Men discharged handguns while infected scaled their flesh, clawing it open. The way she came was blocked, so she pushed off and did her best impression of a run toward the domed building. Distant police sirens and even more distant helicopters joined the carnage cacophony in the night air. Her leg ached with each step, so she leaned on the doorframe. The colossal dome now out of sight, she tried the door. It didn't budge. She strained as hard as she could, wounds all over her body reopening like a perforated dam, ejecting crimson waters. The metal gave way, and Lucy squeezed inside.

Before she could close the door, a claw slashed her left shoulder blade. Her fury flared at the bone that stole from her body. Spinning, she swung the machete down, severing the arm at the elbow. The appendage was pulled back, and an infected's head pushed through the opening in its place. Lucy raised her weapon and jammed its point into the bobbing forehead. More infected piled on top. She hacked and hacked until the feral swarm became a mound of meat. Pushing the door shut, she ran to the interior. The whir of the helicopters neared, but the tapping of feet was already inside the building.

Giant machines set in rows upon rows filled the rooms she passed. Ducking into one, she glued herself to the wall and waited. Four sets of feet ran by. Stopping a few yards down, the figures swayed their heads, searching for her. Lucy took care not to make noise as she approached, her right leg giving her immense trouble. One head turned and saw her. Swinging wildly, not aiming for any specific part, she sliced the infected to pieces. Kicking the remains of her slaughter away, she made unsteady steps forward.

The first floor afforded no safety, but the upper ones might. Gunshots rang from behind, then only the steady splat of the blood dripping from her body kept her company.

The second floor opened to empty workshops and offices. Infected hadn't reached it yet, so she searched for a place to hide—to crawl inside and disappear. A figure flew through the gaping windows on the wall behind her. It rolled in front of her. Before it could stand, she managed to hit its back three times. More gunshots came from the outside this time. Lucy looked at the broken window and saw a sea of red and blue lights. More and more were coming, and the steady sound of propellers neared with each passing moment.

Infected vaulted over the windows. Pushing her palm into the wall, she ran, only stopping to check which door would take her away. The figures behind her got closer as the doors became fewer. At the end of the walkway, she reached a path that led elsewhere. Finding a wide room filled with drawing boards, Lucy slinked to one corner and hid behind a bookshelf. A pursuer's steps came close. She dove out, grabbing the infected and stabbing it in the heart. Falling to the ground, she rolled to the side, throwing the body. Two of its comrades came to investigate. The body drew their attention while Lucy dashed forward, decapitating both in a single strike.

Leaning on the wide door frame, her eyesight blurred. She staggered out the room, energy seeping out of her wounds with each breath.

She tip-toed to the stairs leading up. Two figures dove at her.

One she kicked, the other caught her leg, making her fall. Hitting the side of her head on the lip of a stair, she swung the machete on instinct. The blade made two cuts. When her focus returned, she saw the infected's face was missing a nose, and a straight red line went from cheek to right eyebrow. Undeterred, the thing drove a claw into her left leg. The pain moved Lucy's arm, the machete cutting through its wrist, leaving the hand stuck inside of her. She kicked the infected down the stairs using her other leg, its neck breaking at the bottom. Pulling the claws out, she released a quiet scream and continued to stumble upward.

The stairs seemed endless. The mass of infected following her shook the metal beneath her feet. Reaching a door fit for a central bank vault, she tumbled inside, then quickly stood and slammed her right shoulder into it. Claws and feet stuck out of the last space between the door and the frame. Their number was too large for her to overcome in her depleted state. Not about to give up, she swung her weapon down, cutting off what she could. The sound of the helicopter filled the room. It would be her saving grace if she could get its attention.

The domed ceiling had a few windows still intact. Leaning on the door, she reached over and grabbed a severed body part. Throwing it at the glass, she managed to hurl one more before the mass beyond the room pushed her off the door. Running with all her might, she soon reached the end of the tiled floor. All the doors she tried were locked or rusted shut. Each breath burning her throat, she turned, weapon extended forward. At the forefront stood one of the turtlenecks. The glow in its eyes looked triumphant to the near-bloodless Lucy.

A cylindrical object fell between them. Lucy shielded her eyes from the white flash. Her feet gave out, and she leaned on the door behind her. As she slid to the ground, men descended down dark ropes. The flash of automatic fire made no sound as the infected became pin cushions full of lead. Lucy closed her eyes, then a moment later, a shake on the shoulder woke her.

"Lucy. Lucy!" a helmeted man shouted—his words sounded worlds away.

He took off his headgear and pulled the balaclava down, revealing his face—Richard's face. The horror in his eyes grew with each piece of Lucy he inspected. Thankful for his concern, she felt an ember of heat light in her chest.

He pulled her up under her arm and dragged her out of the room. Infected attacked them on the stairs sporadically, and each time, Richard covered Lucy's head with his arms. The protective embrace smelled of gunpowder and oil, making her weak cheeks rise in a smile.

The ground floor was a battlefield. Lucy's hearing returned only to be hammered by the intrusive sounds of automatic fire and people dying. A figure slammed into them. Lucy fell. Trying to move, she found none of her muscles worked. She could only watch as three infected caught Richard. Grabbing his combat knife, he crouched forward and rolled to avoid an assailant flying through the air. Coming out of the roll, he cut one throat, then a second. The third infected recovered and attacked again. Richard angled the knife down, and when the infected's claw hit his Kevlar vest, he stabbed its brainstem.

After holding to make sure nothing more would attack, Richard recovered Lucy and carried her to the courtyard.

"The Doctor," she mumbled.

"Every hospital is full, and no one will treat you at the triage," his voice strained from the exertion, "but I'll think of something, don't worry."

"Apartment," her mouth was too dry for talking, but she still managed to give the address, "just take me there. I have a friend who's a doctor. He can help me."

"You need a hospital, Lucy. No one can help you at your apartment," the sadness in his voice poured out.

Lucy focused her eyes on his face and saw he believed her as good as dead. A door opened, and he let her down on the backseat of a car.

"I just want to see my mom," she spoke as loud as her failing vocal cords allowed.

"Fuck." Richard slammed the door closed, and Lucy lost consciousness.

NINETEEN

For a brief moment of consciousness, she opened her eyes to see a giant, black blob. Its white, ghastly face loomed over her. Drawing nearer, the shade lifted a round part of itself and left it on her chest.

"The remorse I feel for your condition is indescribable, Miss Lucy. I can offer no other assistance than this," the shade spoke, pointing a swath of darkness at the sphere on top of her.

"If you manage to interface with the suit, you have significant chances of survival. The choice to give you this was not easy.... In the beginning, I contemplated eliminating you because you steered my mission toward catastrophic failure, but now I feel you are deserving of a chance, at least. We may not see eye to eye, but I believe our goal is finally aligned.... Good luck, Miss Lucy, and fight to the very end."

Lucy blinked, and the shade was gone. She felt the weight of the sphere on her chest, then moments later, it grew warmer and liquified, spreading its heat across her breasts and stomach. Soon her whole body loosened. She tried to see the substance, but she didn't have the strength to lift her neck. The ceiling faded as her eyelids began to close. The darkness that followed resembled a lucid dream.

What is this?

The ceiling was gone. Everything had disappeared, darkness

facing her wherever she looked. Lucy tried to move her hands or feet, but nothing obeyed. The vast body of gloom pinned her down. She couldn't tremble, even if her life depended on it. The darkness started to push. Her chest rose and fell faster. She tried to slow it down and then realized she wasn't controlling it. She *was* breathing, but the process had become more autonomous. She tried to hold her breath. Her chest expanded and took in air. She tried to hold that air in, but it left her lungs and the process repeated. The terror evaporated, only to be replaced with deep annoyance.

That's an improvement, her thoughts were as grim as the darkness surrounding her.

She attempted to breathe on her own for a while longer, with no better results. No fatigue came from her attempts, just added frustration, so she stopped. While struggling to figure out what was happening, she'd failed to notice the diminishing feeling in her extremities. Hands and feet had dissolved into her surroundings and no longer sent back signals to her synapses.

Lucy struggled to lift her thigh, but nothing came into view. She turned her gaze up in the darkness.

Or is that down?

Concepts like horizontal or vertical didn't exist in the shapeless abyss.

So what happens when the loss of feeling reaches my head? the question burned through her mind and kept it sharp.

She concentrated, feeling liquid creeping up her skin. Inch by inch, swallowing her body into the void.

Do I die like this? Eaten by fucking alien sludge? That can't be. Did he say something about a suit and interfacing? Maybe this is the process?

She wanted to calm down by taking a deep breath, but it

did not belong to her. The restlessness in her mind had to be fought another way. All of her doubts, creeping and otherwise, were pushed back. She imagined her small childhood home. Knocking on the front door, she heard the rustle of clothes. Valentina opened the door, her pint-sized stature pushed past Lucy. Nearby, a woman sitting on a couch turned her head. Lucy's mother smiled warmer than the midday sun.

She froze the picture there. That image remained in her mind while the dark wave slowly drank her body. If she focused on the scene, her mind stopped racing. Gruesome thoughts didn't disturb her. Doubts couldn't hinder her. The darkness grasped at her chin, and before she knew it, she had no mouth to express futility with. The wave went up relentlessly, engulfing her nose and cheeks. Only her eyes remained. She unfroze the scene, allowing her mother to rush over. Familiar arms embraced her in a blindingly bright hug.

Like being sucked into a black hole in space, the image condensed. *Please, no,* she begged the dark before everything disappeared.

Her eyes opened to the painful light. The Doctor was kneeling on top of her. Right hand on her throat, left hand restraining both her wrists above her head. The muscles in her arms were exhausted as if she'd tried to lift a washing machine for a good half hour.

The Doctor inched closer, his tone dubious, "Miss Lucy?"

Lucy saw herself in his glass eyes, her hair ruffled, nostrils flaring, and spit dried on the sides of her mouth.

"I'm *alive!*"

He looked at her for a few more moments, then said, "Welcome back."

In a single, swift movement, he let go, jumped off the bed,

and turned around.

"What happened?" Her dry throat screamed for water.

"You interfaced with the suit. . . . Congratulations. The eyes are the hardest part," he spoke in a low voice, keeping his back turned to her.

"Stronger subjects tend to be violent when the suit bonds with the visual organs. I had to restrain you. My apologies." He showed the side of his mask, then bowed forward.

"Why are you acting—?" Looking down at her naked skin, she realized the answer.

"Didn't you say this was a suit? What happened—? Ugh, never mind! Just hand me my clothes from over there, please."

"Clothes are no longer necessary, Miss Lucy. All you have to do is think about what you wish to wear, and the suit will accommodate."

"What . . . ?" Confusion made her mind fuzzy. "If you're not gonna help, just leave then. I'm not comfortable."

"Apologies, but I cannot. This is a very traumatic time, especially for someone who has not undergone training. I will not turn around until you are ready. You have my word." He knelt down on the spot.

Too disoriented to argue, Lucy dragged herself to the foot of the bed. The Doctor sat between her and the door, arms crossed as if awaiting intruders. For a few seconds, she basked in the ability to control her breath. The memory of the darkness still lingering on her skin.

"Did I hear you right? You said something about undergoing training." Her voice still sounded foreign.

"Correct. Recruits are given fabric that mimics the properties of the suit. They put them on their arms and legs, then train their mind to alter its shape, density, and structure."

While he talked, Lucy lifted her forearm. Her wounds were gone.

At least you get some perks for nearly dying.

Concentrating, she tried to will clothing over her skin. Nothing happened.

The Doctor continued, "Then, after physical preparations are complete, mental training follows."

"Would that be training that helps with interfacing?" she sneered.

"Correct." His head sank forward. "While training is useful, it is not a requirement for interfacing. I elected to attempt to preserve your life. You were going to expire—"

"From bloodloss," Lucy cut him off. Glancing at her teammate sideways, she managed a smirk. ". . . Still, that was some reckless risk-taking, Doc."

He said nothing, so Lucy pushed further.

"What were my chances anyway? Good, bad, average?"

"I estimated your interfacing chances were just above 30% without the wounds. With them, below 10%."

"Wow." Lucy crossed her legs. "No wonder you were surprised to see me. Those are some shitty odds."

The numbness this information brought filled Lucy's stomach with cold dread.

Gathering the courage, she asked, "What happens to those who don't interface?"

"Brain function slowly deteriorates until the subject reaches a state best translated as *cerebral calm*. The brain would wind down, so to speak, until vital functions ceased. Death is the final outcome," he paused for several moments. "The condition is quite rare but not unheard of."

She looked at his back. Shoulders slumped forward, neck

bent, and head facing down. She felt the habitual hot sting of hate spread through her body as he talked about gambling her life. But after his last words, the fire in her mind faded. She remembered the people on the street, the soldiers in the alley; they all were people trying to forge some understanding even if it cost them their lives. She let her breath out, allowing all animosity to fly out with it.

"Is that why you refused to give me the suit before? You thought I might not make it?"

"I did my best to protect you." His monotone sigh afterward hurt her ears. "The suit was a final resort I did not wish to use. We may have differing opinions, Miss Lucy, but your safety has always been a prime concern for me. The negatives far outweighed the benefits of the suit."

Something occurred to her. "Wait a minute! Was that what happened in your ship? You were stealing the suit for me?"

The white beak swung down as if to snatch a wily worm. "Yes. I had planned for this contingency."

Frustrated at herself, Lucy tapped a fist into her forehead. *Stupid! And I thought he wanted to kill me. . . .*

"Sorry I ran off," remorse dragged behind each word. "And sorry you had to steal tech for me. You're probably gonna get in a lot of trouble for that one, aren't you?"

"You do not need to worry about that, Miss Lucy." He waved away the concern with a casual gesture over his shoulder. "And your apology is accepted. I only hope now you will put your trust in me." He tapped his chest.

"I'll do my best," she promised.

They both remained silent for a time.

"I think I'll be fine, Doc. I'll try to work the suit for a bit, but could I have some privacy?"

He gave her a curt nod, then stood and left the room.

Lucy imagined wearing clothes. Nothing happened. The image always disappeared after a few tries, fading into the abyss that she'd escaped minutes before. She opened her eyes.

This is fucking stupid. Only little kids are afraid of the dark. Slamming her lids down, she tried to imagine clothes once more.

They vanished into the all-consuming dark. This time, she pushed back. She pushed and pushed until the image of her clothes became clear, and the black, sticky feeling of the darkness was tucked neatly into a small corner of her mind. Fighting this fear was going to be an uphill battle.

Examining herself, she now wore her dark blue blouse and jeans from the other night. There was no sign of battle damage or wear and tear, yet the clothes looked identical.

At least it works intuitively, she judged, as she focused on fine-tuning the length of her sleeves.

She managed to move the very end of the sleeve a fraction of an inch up and down after a lot of straining. Keeping her focus was difficult, but getting the suit to do what she wanted was reasonably easy once she had it.

Instead of returning her arm to the side, she decided to try something. Centering her vision on her forearm, she rolled up her sleeve and touched her skin with a finger.

Feels normal.

She dragged her finger up until it hit the elbow. The skin-on-skin contact felt the same as it always had.

Okay, let's try this . . .

She placed her left palm on her right forearm, squeezed, and dragged it down toward her wrist, trying to see if it would hurt. The skin moved, then turned red, and she felt real pain.

Weird.

She stared at her red skin for a while until it changed back to its regular hue. After testing that out, she got up and walked around the room for a time. The clothes stayed in place, even when she didn't think hard about them. She also noticed that when she wasn't thinking about her footsteps, their sound disappeared.

It's like I'm makin' sounds when I expect to hear them. Now, this is some cool tech!

She tried her theory out by walking to the door while she thought about her favorite ice cream. Stomping as hard as she could, her feet made no sound. She opened the door to see the Doctor standing next to the table looking at her.

"So what about the head?" She swung the door behind her, and it closed on its own.

"Pardon?"

"Something for my head." She patted the top of her hair. "A helmet or something? Or better yet, one of those fancy armband screen projectors."

"Ah, unfortunately, I do not have any spares." Emidius spread his arms to the side. "They are issued only with an agent's main suit. The one you are wearing is a replacement."

"Too bad." She gestured for him to sit down and took a seat by his side after he did.

"What time is it anyway?" She yawned and looked out of the window.

"6:23 PM."

DAY 3

She threw him a side-glance, her mouth frowning in disbelief.

"A young man left you in my care approximately fourteen hours ago."

That's right, she remembered, *Richard brought me here!*

Suddenly, the events of last night flooded her mind. The disastrous exchange, the look in her boss' eyes as the life drained from them, the attack, and finally, Richard pulling her to safety.

"Where's my phone?" she asked frantically, and the Doctor pointed to the table.

A knock on the door stopped her hand. Exchanging glances with the Doctor, she stood up and went to the peephole. Dark clothes obstructed her view. She turned the knob and opened the door.

Richard's face swung to the side so suddenly that Lucy worried he might break his neck. "You're. . . alive? I-I came to make arrangements. You were in such bad shape this morning."

The bags under his eyes looked like healing bruises, and a large amount of stubble signified he hadn't slept.

"Come in," she said, stepping aside. "Let's talk."

Richard walked by and stopped in the middle of the living room, next to the table. His eyes scoured Lucy's neck, the patch of skin on her right forearm.

He's looking for my wounds, but the one on my neck I got days ago.

Narrowing her eyes, she asked, "Why were you in the factory last night?"

"Come on, Lucy, you're not serious," he scoffed, then drilled into her eyes with his, waiting for her to find the page he was on but gave up. "Okay. I had you followed after our date."

Lucy tilted her head to the side, her upper incisors gnashing her lower lip.

"Don't act dumb. The wounds consistent with infected attacks, your mysterious presence at almost all major sightings, the car next door?" He leaned in, smirking. "You probably ditched it after you went to the crash site, right? Oh! And don't forget your cameo on the arcade security footage." His eyes sparkled at her. "I told you I like movies. Best one I've seen all year."

Lucy took a step to the side, positioning herself between him and the door. The Doctor rose to his feet.

"Hey, hey, let's not do anything stupid now." He put his palms up to placate them. "I work for the government, and you two obviously don't want it involved, or you'd have sought help already. I'm just trying to wrap my head around the situation."

"So you had me followed?" Lucy's tone could freeze rain. "Obviously, you think you know something. How about sharing it with us?"

"Look, I wanna help—"

"Talk," the Doctor's monotone cut Richard's words clean off.

"Sure thing." He nodded, taken aback. "I think you two were one of the first to get in contact with the infected. You knew more than you let on, and that's why I had you followed. According to the report, the agents lost you and the big guy at some point during the night, then they caught up at the abandoned factory. There were unconfirmed sightings for the vector, and we marshaled a response."

"He probably *was* there," Lucy growled under her breath.

"Excuse me, *he?*" Richard's chin dove down.

"It, Johnathan, whatever you wanna call it." Lucy looked pleadingly at the Doctor. "Let's tell him. He might be able to help. We're nearly out of time either way."

The Doctor kept silent for a few seconds while Richard's eyes darted between them. Raising his arm, the Doctor projected an image of Johnathan in the air. Surprised, Richard stepped back, almost tripping on the TV stand.

"The prime contagion's first successful conversion was of a child named Johnathan," the Doctor explained. "In the interest of brevity and clear communication, Miss Lucy and I have agreed to refer to patient zero as Johnathan."

Richard smacked his lips as his eyes did their best to pop out of their sockets. Lucy locked the door and walked to the couch while the colorless head of Johnathan made revolutions above her table. The prime contagion made alterations to its body. It now had sharp teeth and hardened bone mass around the neck and back of the head. The skull had reformed almost to a point, reminding Lucy of a shark. It wore a too-large Kevlar vest that covered it from chest to groin. The last thing she noticed was Johnathan's shin bones, sharpened to a blade's cutting edge, the skin on the legs drawn back to allow the filed bone access to the outside. The image made Lucy want to throw up.

The Doctor switched off the hologram and sat next to her.

"Looks like he's been busy," she said, deep in thought. Noticing Richard still standing, she gestured for him to sit on the chair. "Sorry, but we don't have time for you to be surprised. This thing is close to infecting adults."

Richard swallowed. "I think I'll stand." His eyes jumped to the door.

"You won't make it." Lucy shook her head and pointed at the Doctor with her chin. "He's stupid fast and strong. He was sent to get rid of that thing, but it got away."

Lucy poked the Doctor's side with her elbow. "Come on, show 'em that thing you do with the quarter."

Emidius tsked, crackling like a radio searching for a station. "We really do not have time for coin tricks, Miss Lucy."

"You're right. Enough horsing around then. Doc, I assume you haven't been wasting your time until I woke up."

"I have formulated a plan, yes." The dark circles of his mask did not move away from Richard's face. "Allow me to explain."

"After reviewing the data my craft has acquired and using additional terrestrial video resources, I have managed to make some discoveries about the infected, which will be instrumental to our success."

The Doctor sat back and straightened his coat.

"The large number of hosts that Johnathan has amassed— that I will henceforth refer to as 'the horde'—has grown very large. This is due to the way that Johnathan constantly keeps them in operation. By that, I mean scouts, feeler infected as it were, scour the city to find hotspots of defensive activity during the day. Additionally, from what I have observed, I believe the normal hosts have some sort of low-level psychic connection with the prime contagion."

Meeting two faces with confused expressions, he lowered his head and elaborated. "Johnathan possibly has a psychic way to give commands, such as *attack, infect, return,* and so forth. Once those are completed, the normal hosts seem to converge back to Johnathan, so infection can be carried out by him, and further tests can be done in search of viable ways to infect adults."

Richard's index finger sawed along the underside of his chin. "You're saying the prime contagion has to be in the same space as the victims for a successful infection?"

"Correct." The Doctor's beak bobbed up and down.

"This doesn't explain the slow pace still," Richard spoke again, "there should be more numbers of infected by all metrics."

"My current hypothesis"—the Doctor's palm touched his chest—"is based on the fact that I have caught reports of infected leaving the sphere of influence. It could mean either Johnathan is readying an expansive push outward, or he is testing new strains of the infection, given to select hosts who venture beyond his control. In the first case, we are in for a fight. In the second, the special strain-carrying host has to complete its mission then return with results. This would be a gamble for Johnathan because it takes valuable time and resources but does not guarantee success."

"But if the strain succeeds," Lucy cut in, leaning forward. "Everyone will be vulnerable to the infection."

The stark truth of the stakes they faced filled the air between them. No one spoke further for a few moments, their thoughts almost tumbling out from their features.

"If I may expound about the hotspots I touched on a moment ago." Grabbing the laptop, Emidius opened a map and pointed to several red dots, all of which represented large buildings.

One of the dots on the map, Lucy recognized as a nearby school. Richard knelt beside the table.

"All of the locations attacked by the horde are large, spacious, and not easily defended against highly agile opponents. Each target thus far has been densely occupied with those fleeing the poorer areas of town. Simply put, Johnathan seeks places where people have huddled together to protect their children." moving both hands to his knees, the Doctor looked like a statue of Thoth, having just imbued humanity with the knowledge of its fate.

The cold, tactical part of Lucy's mind admired the prime contagion's plan. The empathic part screamed with the pain of all who had lost their lives in Johnathan's murderous expansion.

"These attacks serve dual purposes, the first and most obvious one: to infect more suitable hosts, the second seems to be the abduction of adults for experimentation purposes. This I gathered from the growing news reports of whole families disappearing."

"How long before the infection of adults is feasible?" Richard's fingers scratched the side of his chin with nervous frequency.

The Doctor's neck moved in his direction with a slow and deliberate turn. "I speculate no more than thirty hours. Now, please ask your questions at the end of the presentation."

Richard's features rippled with surprise. Saying nothing, he drew his elbows closer to his torso.

Emidius resumed, "With that information in mind, I believe the next major attack will be here." His gloved finger pointed to a large building a bit outside the city limits. "Church Lake."

"The manor!" Lucy and Richard said in unison.

"You know of it?" the Doctor asked, pointedly looking only at Lucy.

"That's Sarah's address."

"A friend of yours?"

"Yeah." Lucy moved the map up and down to confirm. "It's the same place."

"Then the next open tab will be of interest to you." He gestured with his beak to the screen.

Richard read the headline out loud. "Crowning day of Grimaldi Sanctuary, the manor in Roan which now houses five-hundred quarantine refugees . . ."

"It's like they're making a buffet for Johnathan." Lucy's freehand fingers rested on her lips. "I gotta call Sarah and warn her."

"Um . . . Miss Lucy?" The Doctor's long arms formed a dark *X* across his chest. "A moment. Before you act rashly, please know that I have checked the location, and the Grimaldi family has hired a small mercenary force to protect the estate. This in itself is not reassuring enough, I understand, especially when a friend's life might be in danger," his words ceased for a moment while he deliberated, "but consider the tactical advantage we possess if we know where the attack will happen."

Richard's forearms struck the table, and he raised his voice, "We have to warn those defending the manor! Give them a fighting chance. Even if we use them for a trap, it isn't right to not try and prevent some of the casualties."

"If we do, Johnathan might get wise to it and not attack. Then we won't get a sample," Lucy spoke her thoughts out loud.

"What sample?"

Her irises slid away from the screen down to the Doctor's face. "The Doc needs a sample from a fresh host, infected no more than six hours earlier. They mutate too fast, and without it, he can't get a trace for Johnathan. The whole point is for us to find and kill him, then this thing ends."

"The hope being that he will be there, and you kill him." Richard rocked his head back and forth, attempting to piece together what was going on. "Or you snag a recent infected and Birdmask over there gets a sample that will lead you to him. Sorry to say, but that sounds like a terrible plan."

"It's the only one we have," her tone bordered on a whisper.

"Fuck," Richard cursed, his right palm dragging through his hair. "Then I'll have to agree with Birdmask. Knowing where you have to fight is a great advantage. Keeping it contained at all costs is all that matters."

"So use all those people in the manor as bait." Lucy's hands moved to her thighs in indignation. ". . . or do nothing and lose the war?"

"Not bait, Miss Lucy. A final battleground."

Lucy appreciated the Doctor's use of semantic gymnastics to

alleviate her reservations, but the end result remained unchanged.

Feeling abhorrent and dirty, she nodded in agreement. "Let's get this done."

TWENTY

TWENTY

"I'll try to get you some backup." Richard's eyebrows framed determined eyes. "Gotta work my superiors a bit, but I'll do my best."

Images of him in tactical gear, and the smell of him when he dragged her out of the factory, swam inside Lucy's head.

"If you're not coming, can you get me a ride to Sarah's? I'm assuming traffic's a shitshow."

He nodded, then made a phone call.

"Be down in fifteen. I'll wait for you there." Opening the door, he lingered, then gave Lucy a short goodbye wave.

"Do you trust this man, Miss Lucy?"

"Probably not," she dragged out the words. "Only about as far as I can throw him. He's government."

Turning her head, she added. "He might be able to help. We're too close to catching Johnathan to be tripped up. What bad could a little added help do now?"

"A tremendous amount," his tone dipped low. "If we are not careful, all living things on this planet are forfeit."

Locking her fingers together to keep them from fidgeting, she exhaled. "I know that, and we'll keep an eye on him, but for now, he might be useful."

She stood. "I'll go ahead and change, be back in a few."

She went inside her bedroom and sat on the bed. Getting her

phone, she texted Sarah, asking if it was okay to swing by. While waiting for the reply, she practiced with the suit. Eventually, she found out that if she concentrated on her hand and made the suit appear there, the rest of her clothes were much easier to maintain in full form. She pictured gloves and laid that image over her hands. The suit responded, showing her wearing the gloves she imagined. After some attempts, she managed to make the look stick and appear pretty authentic to boot. As an added bonus, her shoes seemed to work the same way. With two points keeping her suit in check, she wouldn't have to worry about the rest of the outfit.

I'll be around people, and the machete will stick out like a sore thumb. Gotta think of a way to cover it up.

Getting up from the bed, she slowed down her breathing and focused on an image of a jacket she had in her wardrobe. Her blouse changed color and shape, becoming the jacket. Lucy got the machete from beside the bed, fastened it in place, and checked to see if it was visible. Sadly, half of the scabbard poked under the hem. She closed her eyes, focused her mind, and altered the dimensions of the projected cloth. Meeting considerable difficulties, she gave up and raised a disappointed eyebrow to herself in the mirror.

The blouse was so much easier. Why isn't it working now?

She abandoned the idea and imagined a jacket of a different style, color, and length. A triumphant huff came out of her mouth when she achieved the desired effect. A knock sounded on the door.

"Ten minutes have elapsed, Miss Lucy."

Taking a final look at her clothes, she clicked her tongue and walked out.

As she did, Emidius raised an open-palmed hand, then said,

"Before we depart, I have something to share with you."

Lucy acknowledged with a nod.

"The suit allows two-way communication between fellow agents so you can contact me at any point. Focus your mind on wanting to speak to me, and the suit will oblige."

Lucy concentrated then spoke. "Like this?"

"Yes," the Doctor's head jerked to the side, "but please lower your volume. The suit can pick up on even the slightest sub-vocal vibration."

"Sorry." She frowned while he cradled his head.

His long fingers on the sides of the mask made him look like a giant human, fighting a severe migraine.

"You know what, Doc? I think you should find your own way to the manor. I mean, infected might be watching already, and if we arrive together . . ." Her wrist twisted in a circle, and she gave him a meaningful frown.

"Understood. I will remain hidden until we spring the trap." He took one stride and wound up at the window. "Take care," he said and slipped out onto the fire escape and disappeared.

"I'll try," she half-whispered and left the apartment.

Four military vehicles waited downstairs. Three were poised to go right, and the solitary one pointed left. Richard's gaze searched Lucy's vicinity for a moment. Not seeing the Doctor didn't make an impact on his features. He slid the Kevlar vest over his shoulders, checked the straps, then gave Lucy a curt nod. Lucy's chin rose in response then she strode to her assigned vehicle. She let a soldier fasten her vest, and they were on their way. Sarah texted back a picture of an excited puppy and told Lucy any time was okay.

On the ride over, she saw the chaos gripping the city. A man tried to pull out a plank on a window. Two others ran to him, dragging him to the ground. The would-be protectors spared no savagery when defending their chunk of concrete. Army and police vehicles sped by in a constant stream, zipping from one spot to another—the fires of unrest burning down the very fabric of the town. Lucy closed her eyes to the horror.

The escalating, needless violence twisted in her chest. *This isn't home anymore*, she tried to remind herself.

The angle of the road changed to a soft incline.

Looking out again, she saw a vast forest surrounding a sprawling old manor.

Barbed wire clung to the top of the wide fence like sharpened tumbleweed. The old brick, laid to perfection, denoting the splendor behind it, now had to stand like a shield crowned with bladed edges. Soft, closely trimmed grass went up the incline all the way to the grand building overlooking the snaking road. The vehicle stopped. Lucy took off the vest and stepped down. Handing it to the soldier, she thanked him. The men guarding the gate exchanged stern glances with those escorting Lucy. She rolled her eyes at the banal display of machismo. The soldiers returned to the vehicle and drove off.

In front of Lucy, a man with his torso clad in Kevlar and littered with ordnance held an assault rifle at the ready, finger deadly close to the trigger. Another man stood a few paces away. His weapon poised for action, muzzle pointed halfway toward the ground.

These people are no joke. They're here to kill when necessary.

"My name is Lucy Castle." She raised her arms above her head. "Sarah Grimaldi is expecting me."

The man closest to her nodded and let his weapon hang on his neck. The other did not.

"I'm going to do a weapons check on you, then we will verify your identity, ma'am." His tone had an apologetic ring to it.

"I'm carrying a machete on my back. I'm reaching for it now." She extended the fingers on her left hand and lowered her right, slowly.

Drawing the blade, she lifted it up in the air. When they both had a good look at it, she let it swing down, holding it in two fingers. The closest man took it, examined it for a moment, then let it drop into the dirt beside the road. The corner of Lucy's mouth twitched, and her nostrils flared, but she kept quiet.

"Any other weapons to declare, ma'am?"

"No."

He nodded and patted her down. She winced at his touch. The violent hand that held her last night felt like it was around her mouth once more. Closing her eyes, she set her jaw and withstood the nauseating feeling. Her mouth quivered, and her eyebrows shook from the strain. The soldier sensed this, hastening his work.

"Thank you, ma'am. Apologies if I was too rough."

"It's fine." Holding her head high, she spoke with a voice that shook only slightly. "Do you need an ID or something?"

"No, ma'am, you're expected." He snatched her machete off the ground and handed it back. "Please go ahead and have a pleasant evening."

He tipped his head and signaled for the door to be opened.

The other man followed her until Sarah met them on the road. She wore a white dress that went to her knees. A wide black belt with a golden buckle framed her upper body, and long flowing sleeves ran down her shoulders.

Days away from the apocalypse, and she still looks like a model fresh off a photoshoot. She shook her head.

"Lu!" Sarah cried out. She slammed into Lucy, throwing her

arms around her waist.

"Hi, there," Lucy patted her head. "It's nice to see you too."

"Oooh." Sarah's excited trembling almost wiggled her out of the hug. "I'm so glad you're here! Come, come. Let me show you around."

She pulled Lucy's hand like a stranded sailor hanging onto a lifeline.

"Fine, I'm coming. Just don't tear my arm off."

"No promises. Keep up."

The man escorting Lucy retreated back to the checkpoint.

"What's this?"

Lucy turned to see Sarah gesturing at her gloved hand.

"Had an accident yesterday, the gloves stay on until my cuts heal, I scraped them real bad on the ground when I fell. Now, you." Lucy used her free hand to wave at the men patrolling the ten-foot stone walls. "What is *this?*"

Sarah spoke over her shoulder at her. "Oh, I just asked daddy to make a refugee camp."

"I read as much," Lucy replied as they reached the halfway mark to the manor. "*Why* would be the better question then?"

"I was helping in the community center." Sarah's right hand waved while she reminisced, "and I kept seeing all these people running away from their homes because they'd been attacked. Some kids were left on the street. Can you believe that? People abandoning their children to save themselves. Despicable." Sarah clenched her fists and shook her head, lips pursed.

She looked too cute for Lucy to take her seriously, with her perfect dress and dainty, prim footsteps.

"Philanthropy, eh?" Lucy nodded her approval. "It suits you."

"Everyone needs help, Lu. The world doesn't run on *I*'s. It runs on cooperation. That's why I'm always in your face, trying to get you to accept some."

"Thanks for that," Lucy's tone was even.

Sarah took a deep breath in preparation for an argument.

Lucy smiled and cut her off, "You're sweet to offer help, and in the future, I promise, I'll try to take it."

Sarah stopped in her tracks, immense pride spreading across her features.

"Well, here's your chance." Forearms on her stomach, she laced her fingers together. "Daddy got mom and me VIP passes out of the city, and since you're practically family, he got you one too."

Sarah turned her face to Lucy, her lips bunched together, satisfied with herself. Lucy straightened her back at the unexpected news. The opportunity to get away from the city glowed as brightly as Sarah's styled hair.

I can see my mom! Her first thought cheered then quickly saddened her. *But what about all these people? I can't run away now. We're almost there. Besides, she just said cooperation makes the word turn.*

"You're a jewel," Lucy hugged Sarah, matching her fervor.

Sarah nestled deep into her chest. "And you're lucky to have me."

"Enough sappy shit." Lucy unhooked her arms. "You've got stuff to show me."

Sarah held her hand until they reached the manor. A giant entrance opened right when they were in front of it. The butler holding one wing of the wide door led them into a giant hall. The wall extended about thirty feet to her right, ending with a small staircase leading up, its railing in perfect harmony with the surrounding walls. They reached the stairs, where the hall branched left and right.

Sarah led her to a sliding door. Next to it, two wooden columns framed a long hallway leading to a steel-reinforced glass gate. Sarah pulled Lucy through the sliding door and into a massive hall that looked like it could have once been a ballroom.

My apartment can just about fit in here. Lucy picked up her jaw and shuffled after Sarah past two giant couches flanking a walnut table and onto a small terrace.

A woman sat in a cushioned chair peering out over the terrace to the yard below.

"Hey, mom. Lucy's here. You remember my mom, right?" Sarah finally let go of Lucy's hand.

"Yes, of course." Lucy took the woman's extended hand in hers. "How are you, Mrs. Grimaldi?"

"I'm fine, dear." Smiling, Mrs. Grimaldi shook Lucy's hand. "Welcome to our home. Please, call me Margot."

Margot looked as stylish as her daughter in a long-sleeved cobalt dress.

Lucy knew she was an older woman, but that could hardly be gleaned from watching her face or demeanor. When she smiled and talked to you, you felt at ease. As she sat in her chair, she exuded an air of respect. Comfort streamed out of her, and you couldn't help but feel it too. Her movements were so refined and inviting that after only ten seconds of talking, Lucy felt perfectly welcome.

"Let's go," Sarah said and grabbed Lucy again. "We'll check with daddy, and then you can catch up."

"Bye," Lucy managed before being dragged back. Margot waved her delicate hand.

Coming out of the room, they went down the long corridor and through the reinforced gate. Lucy and Sarah walked beneath a large, overhanging terrace that protruded out of the back of the main building. Clearing the last vestige of the manor, Lucy noticed an odd shadow fall in front of them. Behind the marbled railing stood an anti-personnel, mounted machine gun. She turned her head back, about to ask the obvious question when the sight of five hundred tents struck her.

Sarah waved her hand. "There it is!" she said with no small aplomb.

The grounds here were a level lower than the rest of the building. Tents that went to the far end of the property littered the plot of land like mushrooms. Men with rifles patrolled all around the perimeter close to the three walls. Barbed wire crowned the tops of the left and right wall while the one at the back had yet to be coronated. Two watchtowers offered protection there instead of wire, and only the forest stretched beyond.

Usually a dependable barrier on its own, but not against Johnathan.

Lucy swallowed a feeling about these defenses. They relied too much on the walls.

Don't these people know that the infected can scale anything?

Lucy almost crashed into Sarah, who stood still in the middle of the path. Her petite blonde host asked where the commander was, and an armed man pointed at the infirmary tent. Sarah thanked him and signaled Lucy to follow. When they made it to a tent marked with a red cross at the end of their current row, Sarah ducked inside.

A group of kids sprinted around the tents like hungry animals looking for food. They came close to Lucy, their swarm disappeared around her, then reformed one tent down. She saw a familiar head of hair running by her. When the kids returned, she tapped a little girl on the shoulder.

"Hey, Sam."

The girl turned, looking at her with eyes wide and full of surprise.

"Lucy!" she gasped breathlessly and slammed into Lucy's pelvis, her tiny arms squeezing her legs.

She put her palm on the back of the silk-haired head. "Is your mom okay?"

"Yup." Samantha nodded, her eyes following the kids running down the next row.

"I'm glad to hear it." Lucy smiled and urged the girl on with a gentle push. "Go play."

Sam took off like a rocket. When she made it back to her playmates, the gaggle of children exploded with laughter and resumed running around. Sarah returned to Lucy's side a few seconds later.

"Daddy is finishing up," Sarah said and turned around to wave at a passing woman.

The flaps of the tent opened, and a tall, thin, older man stepped out. His eyes focused on Lucy, and recognition fled through them. With arms opened wide, he strode over. His hug was almost as loving as Sarah's. After he locked his arms around her, he followed the movement with a gentle squeeze. The embrace reminded her of her mother's—parental and caring.

Another man stepped out of the tent. He was much shorter than Sarah's father and wore the clothes and equipment of the other mercenaries. His shirt sleeves were filled to bursting with muscle, and he moved like fifty pounds of gear weighed nothing. He saw the hug and waited it out at a respectable distance.

"Welcome, welcome!" Sarah's father relaxed his grip. "I'm so glad you came by."

It'd been years since Lucy had seen him, just shortly after

saving Sarah from the bar hound the day they met. He had remained his handsome square-faced self, the only difference being the years had added a little weight to his cheeks, but nothing to ruin his sharp features.

"Thank you for having me, Mr. Grimaldi." Lucy smiled.

"Please, Mr. Grimaldi was my father," he said his dad joke with such candor that it almost didn't make Lucy cringe. "Call me James." His right cheek rose and stood as a slight smirk appeared on his lips, revealing the ends of straight white teeth.

"Sorry." James shook his head. "Where are my manners? This is Commander Andreas. He's in charge of the protection force I've hired."

Commander Andreas gave her a curt nod but remained in place.

"He is the head of security for the estate." James lifted his right index finger and tapped his cheek. "Or is it compound now?"

"It's whatever you like, sir," Andreas stated in a high, soft drawl.

Lucy shot a glance at Sarah. She'd expected a more intimidating person to be in charge. Catching herself judging a book by its cover, she stopped that train of thought immediately. In recent days that type of thinking could get you killed.

"Yes, I suppose." James lowered his hand back down and gestured for them to follow. "Let me show you around."

He began to explain how the idea came to him with the aid of Sarah. How it was morally bankrupt to allow your children to be subjected to infection by leaving them to the whims of fate and so on. Lucy drowned him out and focused her hearing on the more exciting exchange happening through Commander Andreas' shoulder-mounted radio.

"Radio check," he ordered.

"Main gate secured," a voice reported.

"East wall fortifications complete, ingress deterrents in place, continuing patrol," a new voice spoke.

"West wall fortifications complete, deterrents in place, continuing patrol."

"North wall perimeter secured, scouting party sent further out, continuing patrol."

The radio stood silent for a moment. Lucy noticed a group of kids hiding behind tents following her. When they made the jump from cover to cover, she saw Sam among them.

You don't want to be near me. Go away. She cut the air with a sharp movement of her chin.

A yell from three tents down finally made the children leave, but Sam remained, hands resting on the tent fabric for support. Ignoring the girl, Lucy pictured the situation according to the voices on the radio. West was the left wall, and east was the right, north was the one that wasn't fortified yet. That particular wall did not face north, but Lucy appreciated the simplicity of the setup.

"One minute to nightfall, stay sharp, over and out." The commander released the radio and focused on his patron.

Lucy really wanted to talk to the commander about the defenses and how they wouldn't be adequate against the horde.

"Don't you agree?" James looked at her expectantly.

"Sorry?" Lucy gave him an apologetic smile.

He continued, "The way that this whole quarantine has been set up."

"Miss Lucy," the voice of the Doctor materialized in her ears, "a large force of infected is headed toward the manor. Estimated number: 170."

The amount echoed in her head.

That's too many, even for us.

Her eyes grew, and panic began to grip her mind. She looked around to find Sam hiding behind a nearby tent.

"Commander," the shoulder radio came to life, "multiple hostiles spotted inside the forest. Motion sensors indicate at least fifty in number."

"Sanders, what's the bearing?"

"North wall, sir," Sanders replied.

"Fall back. Do not engage the enemy. Fall back to the west wall and regroup," the commander's voice became steel. "Everyone on sanctuary ground, get civilians moving toward the manor. We'll set up a defense line there. Move!"

"Sir," the commander turned to James and spoke with his polite voice, "we have to get you inside as quickly as possible."

"Nonsense," James said, offended, "I will help you round up my guests. Their safety is our only concern."

By the look on his face, Andreas wanted to comment but held his tongue. He just followed silently behind as James roused people from their tents. Getting her phone out, Lucy texted Richard.

ETA on reinforcements?

People stumbled out of tents, dallying to take belongings or finish dressing. Waiting for Richard's reply, she watched James tell his guests there was a special surprise at the manor and that everyone should go there. Two of the mercenaries made it to them from the front. Lucy swung her head in a circle, trying to see where the others were, but no one else approached.

The evacuation wasn't moving fast enough. The people were not told to drop everything and run but were left to move at their own pace. A large line of civilians formed and snaked its way back up the stairs.

Richard's text buzzed in her hand.

I couldn't get a full response together, but I'm coming over with some people I trust. Be there soon.

Lucy clicked her tongue as she read.

The influx of civilians coming out of their tents prevented the mercenaries from spreading out in correct formation.

"West and east wall," the commander spoke into the radio. "Once you've linked up with everyone, make your way inside the grounds. Five men to each wing on overwatch of the front gate. I don't want any surprises coming from over there. We're buttoning up." Andreas spoke ten names, and the men on overwatch confirmed they understood.

All the refugees were now moving. The mercenaries managed to push through the mass and form a defensive line behind the shuffling feet. Lucy's fingers moved back and forth, urging Sam to come. The girl trotted over. Picking her up, Lucy jogged to catch up with the other refugees. James and Andreas walked at the very back of the group. Behind them was only darkness and automatic weapons.

Lucy looked back and saw a shadow crest the wall. Muzzle flashes illuminated the surroundings. Samantha buried her face in Lucy's neck.

"Contact," a man near her yelled and continued to fire.

The commander shouted orders to anyone in earshot. "Close in on flanks, return fire."

The line of men tightened, becoming a crescent. Their weapons fired ceaselessly as more and more small bodies made it over the wall.

Lucy observed the tactics Johnathan employed, only sending one or two of his horde over at a time. A bad feeling closed its fingers around Lucy's stomach.

"Someone get me some light!" the commander barked, and floodlights destroyed the night around them.

Lucy's arms shot out, trying to reach the commander's shoulder and stop him from forfeiting their tactical advantage. A large number of infected sprung over the wall, and the true attack began. Until this moment, in the dark of night, only the commander knew the layout and how to exploit it. Now, so did Johnathan. The new wave of infected dropped down to the ground. Their bodies darted between the tents, and the mercenaries' bullets cut through tents and stone but rarely caught the nimble shadows. People panicked, broke rank, and began shoving each other.

"Hutchens," the commander yelled over the gunfire, "cover fire, short bursts."

"Wilco," came the reply as the anti-personnel gun announced its existence to the infected.

The large-caliber rounds shredded tents and infected alike. Hands, fingers, and organs flew through the air. Lucy managed to count about twenty small bodies dismembered by the deafening weapon.

Something's wrong here. Losing that many just to get the layout of the place? She couldn't put her finger on it, but Johnathan wasn't this rash with his forces. They always had a goal set.

"Contact left," a man nearby shouted.

Three infected lay down on the barbed wire side by side, paying no mind to the sharp prongs digging into their skin. Lucy had a terrible realization and turned to make the commander stop using the mounted gun. Too late. Figures scurried over the other wall already. Johnathan had boxed them in from two sides, sealing the compound's doom.

We'll see about that.

She let Sam down, taking her hand instead, and pushed her way to the commander. "Listen, you don't know me, but I know those things. I've survived them for the last couple of days. They're here to kill everyone, and the only way we'll have a chance is if you deny one of the sides they're attacking from."

The commander said nothing and continued to survey the battle. The look on his face showed he did not like what he saw.

"Talk fast," he ordered.

"Burn the tents; use incendiaries if you have them. They've got us cornered now, so we need to stop the biggest source." Lucy pointed to the north wall. "If we stop them from there, you just have to worry about the other two walls."

Lucy hoped he saw that if the north side rush wasn't stemmed, their whole sorry group would be smashed against the walls of the manor. Andreas scratched his shaved face, the muscles on his forearm jumping up and down, betraying his displeasure in being talked to like that.

He let the hand drop and set his jaw before giving the order. "Incendiaries on the tents. Stop them in their tracks, then focus on west and east wall once the fires have started."

Black canisters arced over the tents and lit the ground with bright fire where they landed. The effect was immediate, infected falling to the ground with agonizing screams. Some were caught on the edge of the inferno. Those that remained upright pushed forward, bodies burning. The automatic weapons made short work of them. The situation began to look salvageable, the wings of the defensive formation huddled down back to the manor. The horde clashed with the mercenaries but did not penetrate very far, their job much harder now when facing an organized force.

Lucy pressed in tight to the back end of the fleeing group, one hand holding Sam, the other gripping her machete. The smell of burning flesh wafted over from the firewall behind them. Lucy gazed at the blazing bulwark and saw infected throwing themselves inside, using their flesh to douse the flames and make a path. The commander noticed this as well and issued appropriate commands to the newly arrived men from around the compound. Bullets continued to cut down infected, but that simply sped up their effort in snuffing out the flames. Lucy stepped to the side, concentrating on the Doctor in her mind.

"Doc, if you can hear me, we could really use a hand. I can't protect all these people by myself."

"We are not here to protect, Miss Lucy. We are here to end the fight," his tone had finality with which Lucy couldn't argue.

She set her jaw and looked west. The biggest wave of infected tumbled down the west wall. The commander's radio confirmed that the east wall was in the same precarious position. The mob of people behind Lucy had been pushed against the manor, clawing at each other to get to safety.

"Get as many civilians as you can inside," the commander spoke over his radio and fired off a burst at the shambling infected.

Lucy stepped as close to him as she dared.

"Tell them to stop," she urged, and the commander gave her a look of disgust, but she continued, "those things are stronger indoors. This is probably why they're attacking so boldly. They're trying to push everyone inside where they'll have the advantage. Trust me."

"I don't," the commander said flatly, "I'll trust my combat experience and my men over some gangly girl I met twenty minutes ago."

"A gangly girl who's fought more battles with these things than your whole group combined!" Lucy came into his personal space, her face towering over his. "If you want to save lives, you'll listen to my advice."

"I'm in charge here," he didn't flinch, "and whatever I say goes, so stop playing soldier and shut up."

Lucy realized this wouldn't go anywhere. She turned and sprinted over to Sarah, Sam's little legs struggling to keep pace with Lucy's long strides.

"Now, Sam, you're gonna go with this nice lady. She'll keep you safe." Lucy transferred the girl to Sarah's arms.

She nodded, still showing the same courage as the other day. Lucy stood up and met Sarah's frightened eyes. "Stay outside, close to the soldiers. Do not go inside for any reason."

"What about you?"

Smiling with the side of her mouth, Lucy took a few steps back. "I'll try my best to help."

Sarah opened her mouth, but no words came out. Leaving before her friend could stop her, Lucy made her way back to the main building. The manor behind her overlooked every wall, so this spot gave her the best tactical vantage. People pushed past her as she established contact with the Doctor.

"Doc, the mercenaries are a lost cause. We gotta step in now."

"If we involve ourselves now, we risk letting Johnathan slip away. Help as best as you can. I will join you when the time is right."

Her jaw muscles danced as she looked at the nearby west wall. The bodies of the infected continued to construct a corpse bridge, allowing them to jump over to the west wall of the manor itself. The east wall did not have bodies strewn so close to the building. Making a decision, she shoved people out of her way and rushed inside. Going up the stairs, she plunged deeper into the corridors until she reached a room full of covered furniture facing the west wall. An infected crashed through the window, and another one followed after it. Lucy grabbed her machete and decapitated the first home invader, the second she kicked in the ribcage, its small body flying through the window and out of the room. Lucy stepped closer to the window, which had now become a gaping wound, droplets of blood running down its transparent surface. The infected writhed on the ground, refusing to die. She waited until several bullets made its movements stop. Glancing over, she noticed Sarah at the back of the line with her father, still not inside. More shadows leaped over the wall, breaking the mercenaries' flank.

Nothing else tried to intercept her again. All the infected landed in the courtyard and cut into the crowd instead. One managed to kill two mercenaries and then topple a civilian to the ground before getting shot. Lucy wanted to go down and help, but the entrance under the terrace was clogged by people trying to get in. She wasn't going to penetrate through there.

Window it is then.

She cleared the remaining glass and stepped on the pane. Focusing her mind on protection, she ordered the suit to comply and jumped toward the nearby shrubbery. Her abdomen and forearms took the brunt of the hit, the momentum severing weak branches. Before hitting the ground, she rolled. Getting her bearings, an infected jumped at her. She slammed the flying body, her forearms still hardened by the suit. Its skull shattered, and it fell to the ground. Scanning for more attackers, she made her fists hard as steel and zeroed in on the nearest ones. Closing in behind them, she drove her fists into heads, necks, and rib cages. Most hits maimed her targets but did not kill; she didn't have time to get bogged down. They just needed to be out of commission for now.

People noticed her making quick work of the foes and clumped up behind her, seeking safety.

"Don't rely on me," she yelled without turning. "Go find soldiers!"

With the infected diminishing in number, she needed to find out what was happening on the north and east fronts. She finished the remaining infected on her side and made her way back to Commander Andreas.

I cleared the manor, so our back should be safe for a few minutes at least. Maybe he's ready to listen to fucking sense now.

The blaze from the tents had died down, but the smell was still as repugnant as ever. Lucy had made it halfway to the commander when a dark figure flew over the west wall. The Doctor landed in the sea of fire, something in his hand unfurling to the ground. He raised the whip in his hand in a single motion and sent out a black line that cut through a dozen infected. He turned right and faced a small figure standing at the junction of the north and east walls.

Perched there was Johnathan, his deformed hand in front of his face like a shield. His glowing eyes, conducting the movements of an abhorrent orchestra. The power to end lives contained in a simple wave. His body had undergone additional changes since the recording of the image the Doctor showed in her living room. First, the hand holding the orange had hardened around it, creating a bony bludgeon. Sharp pieces of metal driven into the skin covered the other arm all the way to the wrist, where his slender digits had become five white talons.

The Doctor pulled his hand back and delivered a devastating blow that cut leaves off their stems. Johnathan blocked the popper with his stump. The noise from the impact hurt Lucy's ears. Johnathan fared much worse. The force of the blow liquified his eyes and flung his hair back. Emidius rushed him, Johnathan jumping down at the last possible moment. The Doctor flew over the wall and into the trees, but Johnathan ran through the fire toward the defensive line. Skin melted off his face when he stepped out of the flames. In a few moments, it regenerated, and he opened his eyes. Two brand new lights outshined the fire behind him. Lucy tracked his movements from her vantage as he ran next to the east wall, infected trailing behind him.

Lucy turned her attention back to the refugees. Over half had made it inside the manor. Like fish in a barrel, and Johnathan was a fisherman who had traded in his rod for a shotgun.

Not good, not good.

Halfway down the hill between Andreas and the manor, she turned to follow Johnathan.

Nearing the entrance, she caught sight of him again. His trail of infected snatched children from the crowd as they sped past. Their high-pitched wails like nails on Lucy's spine.

The mercenaries opened fire as Johnathan leaped into the air and crashed through a second-story window.

"Doc," Lucy said through huffs, "he's inside the manor. I'm on him right now, but he may circle around and flank the defenders."

Lucy slowed and threw a backward glance. More infected emerged from the flames, blackened and blistered, they loped toward the north wall.

He's creating a vice! Lucy steered away from the people and jumped through the nearest window. The well-furnished room housed no living beings.

"Doc, I'm gonna work my way on the ground floor, you go

up, and I'll meet you there," she said as she grabbed the door leading out.

"Understood," the Doctor replied.

Lucy found herself in a hallway. People shoved and pushed, so she hardened her suit once more and plowed through them, making sure not to use any more force than needed. The hall led to the front of the manor. A door on her left swung open, and she dodged back, an infected's claws missing her by a breath. It crashed into the wall. Lucy regained balance and kicked its neck, sending it sliding across the floor. Inside the room, more infected climbed in from the outside, one of them with a fleshy bulge around its neck.

She slipped inside, closing the door behind her and locking it. *None of you are walking out of here.*

The infected spread in a circle immediately.

"You've learned," she observed out loud.

The first to attack was the turtlenecked lieutenant. Lucy steeled the fabric on her arms and grabbed it mid-air. She drove her knee into its solar plexus and threw it aside. Buying herself enough time, she went for the nearest infected, swinging her machete. It managed to jump back. Lucy followed its downward arc. As it landed, she skewered it. Letting go of the machete, she rolled away, the other two infected a claw swipe behind her. As she found her footing, she took a breath, hardening her torso. She received two hits, one on her left hip, the other on her chest. Lucy feigned a stagger, then drove her heel into the closest infected's chest. It flew to its lieutenant. Lucy turned, poised for a grab. A window broke by her side. A new lieutenant sunk its claws into a sturdy bookshelf, eyeing Lucy. The other turtleneck jumped to its feet, leaning forward for a strike.

Realizing how bad her odds were, she recovered her weapon,

then jumped out a window. Ten feet away from the east wall now, she saw a large wave of infected pushing toward the manor. So many squirmed and climbed over each other that they had suffocated the fire beneath their mass. An infected tumbled out of the window after her, metal gleaming in its hands.

That's a knife!

Before Lucy could formulate a plan, glass rained down. Shielding her head, she jumped back. Johnathan's body hit the ground, cratering the surface. The Doctor plummeted down and slammed his fist into his neck. The knife-wielding infected jumped on the Doctor's back and stabbed maniacally. Two more dropped from the window above. Each ripped a piece of piping from the drainage system of the building and hammered at the Doctor's leg joints. His left leg buckled, and Johnathan was able to slither away from the crushing weight.

Now free, Johnathan's sharpened fingers grabbed his broken neck and set it back in place. The angular head popping back like a repaired toy. He leaned forward, preparing for a dash.

Lucy stepped to the side, using her body to prevent a new attack on the group of civilians inching their way inside. Johnathan tilted his head in what looked like amusement, then dashed forward. Lucy hardened her torso as much as she could. The deadly shadow sped past her. Eyes wide, Lucy turned. Blond hair bobbing at the edge of the refugee line caught her attention.

"Sarah. No!"

Johnathan landed, rolled once, then sliced through the three men protecting the women and children. Lucy ran for them as Johnathan pushed Sarah to the ground and placed his deformed hand on her neck. Claws collided with Lucy's back, knocking her to the ground.

Sarah flailed, using everything she had to keep her attacker from reaching the little girl she protected. Johnathan roared with rage, prying Sarah away from Sam. A hand caught Lucy's ankle and pulled her even farther from her goal.

Johnathan yanked Sam up and laid his hand on her neck.

"No!" Lucy screamed as bone-claws assaulted her body and infected surrounded her.

Rage filled her mind and ran through her limbs. Rolling, she crushed one infected under her, then caught the nearest other by the throat, ripping it out. A gleaming pipe rose then fell toward her face. Black, gloved fingers stopped the blow, bending the metal. The Doctor flung the infected up and over the wall.

"Made it, I see," she growled at the Doctor while he pulled her to her feet.

"At the appropriate time." He nodded.

Both turned and ran at Johnathan, the Doctor keeping pace with her.

Infected formed a ring around Sarah's group, cutting off any path to safety. People near the edges were pulled into claws that ripped the unsuited to pieces. The horde stepped over the discarded, tightening the circle.

The Doctor's whip flew through the air, cutting down several small figures. Lucy did not wait for him to clear a path and jumped into the ring of butchery. She angled the machete, aiming for Johnathan, who continued to lean over Sam. Lucy scored a solid hit on his forehead. Or where it used to be. Between the Doctor's clash with Johnathan by the window and now, his face had gained a thick, white, bony mask. He growled, right hand slashing Lucy's chest.

The Doctor's fist hit Johnathan's mask a moment later, sending him tumbling back. Recovering, he spread both arms and screamed. Infected swarmed around them. Horrifying faces bunched together, and sharpened bone was poised at the fighting duo. Lucy's mind cleared as she stared her death in the face. Burning fabric and flesh made her want to vomit. Cries of fear and screams of dying agony turned her hot blood cold. The end was all around, residing in deformed faces and children's hunched-over bodies.

Gunfire of higher caliber reached the circle of death from above. Yellow droplets of accelerated lead destroyed part of the circle.

Johnathan's throat thumped, producing a few sounds of displeasure before he lunged forward. Another burst of fire pinned him to the ground. A helicopter ruffled Lucy's hair, and she looked up. A black chopper hovered deafeningly close above them; its familiar gunner kept Johnathan pinned until his ammo ran out. Richard smiled down at Lucy and winked before reloading.

The horde dispersed, bodies were thrown above Johnathan's position in order to shield him. The pile of infected around Johnathan tried to move away, but Richard had the leader in his sights and resumed his onslaught. Johnathan retreated with his horde toward the north wall. Fire and bullets their farewell wishes. The commander and James placed hands on the straggler refugees, almost throwing them to safety.

Lucy crawled through the bodies in frantic search of Sarah. Her fingers caught on hair and clothes, blood painted the entire corpse mound. Her heart pounded in her chest and threatened to burst any moment until she found her. Sarah sat next to a stout man with spilled-out guts. She cradled Sam's head in her lap.

"Are you okay?" Lucy's fingers explored Sarah's head for wounds.

"I couldn't do anything, Lu," her friend mumbled, shock setting in.

Lucy stroked her hair and cheek. "Not your fault. Don't think about it."

She checked Sam for a pulse, feeling only the slightest beat announce the girl's failing heart. Her right shoulder sagged, the bones inside twisting into a new shape. Her body twitched while her insides transformed. The skin on her hands was pale, already rotting away at the fingertips. Lucy's heart seized in her chest for a painful moment, and she stood, turning away from the sight. Her mouth quivered.

"Come on . . ." She helped Sarah to her shaking legs.

Beckoning the Doctor over, she gestured with her chin at Sam. He nodded, picking up the girl.

"Let's get you some water." Lucy led Sarah to the nearest corner of the manor.

Her white dress was stained with crimson streaks, blood splatters on her face. Men with weapons rushed around them, going in the opposite direction. Lucy heard Sam struggle to breathe. Convulsion caused by pain and change made her body tremble in the Doctor's arms.

Her hands on Lucy's shoulders, Sarah tried feebly to see around her steadfast friend. "What is happening—? Sam!" Lucy held her in a tight embrace, shielding her from the sight.

"I'm sorry. It's going to be over soon," Lucy said, struggling to hold her petite friend in place. She was stronger than she looked. When the Doctor reached them, Lucy gestured for him to go around the corner and out of sight.

Sarah railed against her and wriggled free. "What is he doing to her!"

Catching up to her, Lucy held her close, leaning on the

manor wall for support. "She is going to become one of those things, Sarah."

The syringe device in the Doctor's hand plunged down into Sam, extracting what they needed. He laid her down, and a bright, white flash followed. Lucy covered Sarah's eyes; she still trembled, but her body steeled.

"I couldn't do anything. They were in my fucking home!" The underside of her fists hit Lucy's hips, making her wince.

"I know the feeling," she reassured as the Doctor's beak moved down almost to his chest, confirming the deed's completion.

"There you are." Richard jogged over. "Everyone okay?"

"Yeah, we're fine . . . mostly." Lucy's eyes darted to Sarah, then returned to his.

The Doctor neared after putting away the syringe. "I have what we need, Miss Lucy. Let us depart."

"Depart?" Sarah looked at the white mask. "Who is this guy?" Her head moved from Lucy to the Emidius, fright clouding her eyes.

Lucy sighed. "It's a long story, and now's not the time. We'll have this whole mess sorted, though."

Standing there in her blood-covered dress, she planted her feet and glued her arms to her torso. "Let's go then."

Lucy put both palms on the sides of her neck. "You're in shock," she said, shaking her head. "You're not going anywhere."

"The hell I'm not!" From the tone of her voice and the ice in her eyes, Lucy could tell no amount of argument was going to dissuade her stubborn friend.

"Fine," Lucy's hands fell from her neck and went limp by her sides. *The Doc should love this development.*

Turning to Richard, she gave him a thankful nod. "You really pulled through."

"You're welcome." He narrowed his eyes and smirked at her for a few moments before he continued, "What's the plan now?"

The Doctor settled between Richard and Lucy, making her step back to create space for his large frame. "We return to Miss Lucy's apartment where I examine the sample."

"We can just take it to my lab," Richard offered. "It's closer."

Sarah leaned on the wall behind her and watched with confusion as the three talked.

"Rudimentary equipment will not suffice. We need my landing craft."

"Rudimentary? That's a bit hurtful." Richard tilted his head and looked at him from under his brows.

"No fighting, let's just get it done." Lucy put an arm forward. "Won't we be wasting time going back, Doc? Can't you just bring it here?"

"I could, but thanks to the timely arrival of reinforcements, air traffic has increased significantly."

"Yeah, you're welcome too, Birdmask." Richard patted the Doctor on the back, but his face contradicted the friendly gesture.

"In short," the Doctor continued as if nothing were said, "it would be a waste of time to wait for my craft. Just like this conversation."

"Fine, fine." Lucy rubbed the bridge of her nose. "Sorry to do this again, but can you get us a ride?" She looked up at Richard, who stepped closer, his hand grazing hers.

"I can, but I'm coming with. No discussions."

Lucy glanced at the Doctor, who gave a nod of agreement.

"Better go let your dad know, Sarah."

Sarah pushed off the wall and shook her head.

"Nah, he'll worry that way. Let's just go."

Lucy raised her eyebrows and gestured for Richard to lead. Going to the front of the manor, they got inside one of four parked black SUVs. Richard and the Doctor sat in front while Lucy and Sarah strapped into the back. There, Lucy relaxed her shoulders and melted into the seat. Her eyes began to close on their own.

Young faces appeared in her mind. Their bodies thrown over barbed wire, others climbing over them to bring destruction. She remembered her efforts to defend herself. Her hands hitting and stabbing tender flesh malleable to the point of disgust. Cutting into meat, severing it without remorse because her life was on the line had caught up with her.

She opened her eyes and looked at her gloved black hands. Not a single speck of blood on them. The only evidence of those she killed remained on the blade of her machete. She didn't even remember sheathing it. When she lowered her right hand, she felt the handle there, expecting her, ready to slice through things. Things that a week ago had been children, with no care in the world, their biggest fear, something crawling under their bed or hiding in the closet.

The fear of what lay behind the basement door of her childhood home bubbled up from the dark recesses of her memory unbidden.

Lucy's stomach turned.

TWENTY-ONE

The government plates on the SUV allowed them access through numerous checkpoints. People fought in the streets, broke into buildings, and fled from infected everywhere Lucy looked. She let her thoughts go out of her head, leaving it calm and vacuous. The vehicle was quiet except for the occasional muffled screams or bursts of automatic fire from outside. The SUV pulled over in front of Lucy's apartment building.

"I will need some time to examine the sample." The Doctor opened the door and left.

"That's that, I guess," said Richard with a shrug.

The interior seemed too small all of a sudden, and Lucy's arms shook. "I need some fresh air." She opened the door and leaped out onto the sidewalk.

She breathed in a lungful of city smog. *Much better.*

Releasing her breath, the pressure lifted from her chest. She stretched her neck and lifted her gaze to the topmost summit of her building. The darkened, dying structure that held her apartment within its bowels didn't seem so bad tonight.

"You doin' okay?" Richard leaned over the roof of the car.

"Fine." She waved him off. "Just gotta run to the bathroom."

"Wait up. I'll bum a glass of water."

She shrugged her shoulders and went up the stairs. Inside the apartment, she locked the door to the bathroom and slid down to the ground. Her hands shook, the wrists on her knees kept the tremors down her forearms somewhat contained. She clasped her hands, trying to stifle the embarrassing, uncontrollable fountain of fright gripping her.

She had always taken unnecessary risks. And somewhere deep down, she knew that death could be waiting for her as a consequence. It was different now. It never felt real before.

But after what happened to Partick and her brush with death in the factory, all she could think of was everything she needed to live for. The responsibility of it stifling her muscles and keeping her down on the ground. Bony fingers assailed her from all sides. Beyond their deadly reach was a small house, her mother at the doorstep. Golden hair in a braid, resting on one side of her chest.

"Sure you're okay?"

Lucy jolted and stood, walking over to the sink and splashing water aimlessly before answering. "I'm fine, just drink your water, and let's go."

"You got it."

Lucy waited a few seconds for his footsteps to recede before coming out. Richard pretended to drink, following her with his eyes. The blinking of her answering machine caught her attention, but she didn't have the heart to listen tonight. Instead, she watched the dark through the living room window.

A hand rested on her shoulder.

"You know, when I got to the manor, I saw you going in to save Sarah . . . and I thought you weren't coming out." The way he touched her sent shivers down her spine.

He turned her around. "It's okay to be scared. Those things are fucking scary!" His tone lightened the mood, and she smiled, raising a mocking eyebrow at him.

"Glad to have you back." He smirked and lifted his hand to push a stray hair behind her ears. "You and Birdmask are a great team, but with Sarah and me on your side, you can't possibly lose."

Lucy chuckled at the thought of Sarah fighting in that dress. Richard pulled her close, putting his arms around her. Breathing in his smell, she moved her hands over his back while his fingers went to her neck and chin. He tilted his head and pushed his face closer, stopping just inches from hers. There, he waited. His warm breath tickled her lips, and she stared into his deep brown eyes that shone with the distinct gleam of mischief.

She closed the gap between them and pressed her lips onto his. He tasted like sweat and metal, and the combination lit a fire in her pelvis. All the pain and hurt evaporated as she slung her arms around his neck.

With short pauses to see where they were going, they edged into the bedroom. Richard threw the Kevlar vest to the side while Lucy undid his belt. Lifting his shirt over his head, Lucy pushed him down onto the bed and sat astride him. While the shirt obstructed his vision, she ran her hands over her body. Wherever they went, a trail of flesh appeared. Once Richard pulled his shirt the rest of the way off, Lucy dove in for another kiss. She leaned to the side, trying to reach her drawer, when Richard grabbed her waist and flipped her onto her back.

Smiling, she opened a drawer and got out a condom. Passing it to him, she grabbed her pillow, moving it away from her head and placing it at her lower back. He put his lips to hers again, and moments later, Lucy angled his shaft inside her.

Moaning in pleasure, she flung her head back, hanging off his neck. He began to work away, unearthing wondrous pleasure from Lucy's body. She got lost in the experience, gripping him so tight her arms ached. He lowered himself onto her; her cheek pressed against his neck, and she felt his pulse rising. His breathing grew rougher as her peak grew closer. She pulled his face down and kissed him again, his engorged shaft filling her to capacity until she could barely breathe. His final thrusts pushed her body as warmth washed over her in waves of euphoria.

The two laid there for a moment to catch their breaths before pulling to the side. Richard tied off the condom and inquired about the trash can. Lucy pointed to the kitchen, and when he left, she imagined her clothes back on. The aftershock of pleasant exertion ran through her muscles, tightening them for a moment, then releasing them to the blissful relaxation they'd more than earned.

When Richard returned, they put their clothes back on in silence. Lucy watched him, how awkward he seemed, stumbling as he pulled on a leg of his pants.

The anxiety she had felt since the manor seemed silly now. She decided Richard was right. As a team, maybe they could prove victorious. For the first time since she could remember, the idea of leaning on someone brought her comfort.

"Ready?" Richard said as he grabbed his vest from the floor.

Looking up at him from the bed, she nodded. Both stepped out into the living room.

The Doctor met them as they came out. Lucy's right palm slid across the crook of her left arm while Richard tried to tame a few jutting clumps of hair.

"Terrible news. I was not able to examine the sample."

"Shocking." Richard rolled his eyes.

"Shush." Lucy waved him off. "Why? Someone tampered with the testing equipment too?"

"Afraid so, Miss Lucy. I followed the required procedure

according to the milestone we've reached in the mission. The necessary equipment is missing."

Silencing a remark from Richard with a stare, she said, "What's our play then?"

His white mask swayed from side to side in hesitation. "I can *attempt* to use the facility at the CDC for my examination."

"Oh!" Richard's eyebrows rose mockingly. "You mean the rudimentary one?"

"Precisely," the Doctor replied in an equally mocking monotone.

"Stop bickering like children," Lucy chided. "Let's go then. The sample's wastin'."

The Doctor and Richard exchanged glances. Finally, Emidius conceded and waved his hand to the door, allowing Richard to lead. He walked by with a smug look on his face. Lucy shook her head all the way to the hallway.

"Took you long enough," Sarah said with an angry look in her eyes when Lucy opened the car door.

Her hands crossed over her chest, fingers tapping away, blood still splattered across her face. Her gaze shifted from Lucy to the back of Richard's head. The obvious bed hair on both made her mouth form a silent *O*. Lucy sat down, and Sarah poked her ribs, giving her a thumbs up.

"Not a word," Lucy spoke through her teeth.

The SUV began moving and soon breezed through the main gate of the CDC. The cars parked in parallel along a narrow road, and everyone disembarked.

"Come on." Richard strode to the automatic doors.

Lucy watched the far left edge of the building as they walked. It looked like a tipped glass pyramid. Beyond the doors in front of them was a staircase that went up in a dangerous-looking slope. Military guarded the entryway, and some patrolled the lobby. As soon as their group neared, two armed men came to life and ambled toward them. Richard raised his hand and held up a badge, which made the men go back to standing like statues.

They didn't even ask about the blood on Sarah's face. Must be a regular occurrence around here.

"We'll head to my lab after we've deconned," Richard said as he walked straight to one of the elevators in the lobby. "As you can see, security is very tight. I won't have any trouble from you, right?" He turned on his heel and stared pointedly at Emidius.

"None whatsoever," the Doctor replied solemnly.

"Deconned?" Lucy tried to assuage the tension.

Richard gave her a backward glance as if he'd just remembered she was there.

"Sorry, decon is short for decontamination. After that's done, we can go to the lab." He pushed the elevator button, and it flashed, acknowledging his request to go down.

While the elevator made its way to them, Lucy looked up at the giant glass column that seemed to encase all four available elevators, one of which was as big as the other two put together. The elevator dinged and opened its doors. Inside were two other people. Richard didn't greet them or didn't know them, but either way, the party of four got in and kept silent throughout the downward journey.

Richard turned right as soon as the doors slid open. "This way."

He led them through a long concrete tunnel. Colored lines went in different directions on the lower end of the wall. At junctions, they took turns and pointed at other corridors. After a hundred feet, Lucy spotted the legend explaining what the different colors meant plastered on the wall. Richard stopped in front of a wide door to the left of the sign.

"One by one now." Richard beckoned with his hand for them to step up.

The Doctor went first. He stood in front of the wide door as it began to depressurize. The air wheezing out, sounding like a machine's sigh. The Doctor stepped beyond the threshold, and the door's seals turned in the other direction.

"There's an observation deck outside the laboratory," Richard said to Lucy and Sarah. "You'll have to wait there. Without proper qualifications, I can't let you inside."

Richard entered next, and when he made it to the other side, the door unlocked and opened. Lucy stepped in to repeat the process. Once done, she found Richard, now wearing a white hazmat suit, and the Doctor standing a few feet away.

"You can watch from there." Richard pointed at a window down the hall.

"Thanks," she said to their backs as they entered a door to Richard's right. The keypad beside it displayed the word 'Lockdown' in red lettering.

Lucy went where she had been directed and stopped at the viewing window. Sarah made it through decon, strands of her hair pointing every which way.

"That thing really gave it to ya, huh?" Lucy said with a wide stupid grin on her face.

"Almost as good as Richard gave it to you," was Sarah's petty response.

Coming over, she readjusted her hair. They didn't speak for a few minutes while they watched Richard zip between different devices, the Doctor stepping away each time they were about to collide.

"Listen," Lucy began, "I'm sorry for the way I treated you, and I don't just mean now, I mean since we met. . . . I've been a pretty shitty friend."

Sarah said nothing but nodded her head in agreement, puckering her lips.

"I didn't want you to get involved here. This is super dangerous stuff, and I don't want you to get hurt."

"Tough." Sarah's eyes shifted between the Doctor and Richard. "I'm here because we're all involved, and I want to save the city. If we don't help each other, those things will tear us all apart." She hugged herself, one hand rubbing her shoulder.

"I'm here because I love you, and I couldn't let you do something so dangerously stupid alone. I'm your friend, and you can rely on me!"

"Even against space aliens?" Lucy leaned her head and opened her eyes wide.

"Especially against those," Sarah confirmed with a firm tone.

They looked at each other for a moment and laughed.

On the other side of the window, Richard jerked and dropped the glass vessel he'd been carrying. The sound echoed through the room. His eyes darted to the right and lingered there as if he were listening to someone speaking.

The lights above their heads switched colors from *scientific white* to *get-out red* before ear-piercing alarms flooded the building.

TWENTY-TWO

Richard raced out of the lab. "The building is under attack," he said, his voice muffled from inside the hazmat suit.

Raising an arm, he pointed at his ear. "I just received the news. All personnel are to evacuate to designated emergency quarters."

The Doctor strode past him, came to a stop by the large entrance door, and waited there. Lucy and Sarah stayed by the lab entrance, their attention on the talking hazmat suit.

"Condition has been set to black. It's the highest one we have!" Richard spoke the words too fast, then his tongue grazed his lower lip from side to side.

Lucy grabbed his arm and squeezed. "Show us the way then."

He looked at her, blinking. His head shook, and his gaze grew sharper.

"Okay, follow me." Richard turned on his heel and went to a keypad near the decontamination chamber.

He typed on the console, and the doors slid open.

"Go inside, all of you." He hurried them with his waving palm.

The decontamination procedure sprayed them with white gas, and ten seconds later, the doors opened again. Lucy and the Doctor walked out first, caution in their step. A crowd of ten people moved through the corridor. Their bodies huddled together, packed in close by fear. Their hasty feet almost tripping over each other.

"Where to?" Lucy asked Richard, who pointed to the elevators.

As the group neared the metal doors, they began to screech open. White claws slipped through, bullying the metal mechanism back, its screams of anguish making the crowd pause.

"Back!" Lucy's hand swatted the air, trying to pull everyone closer.

The Doctor stepped next to her. The infected ran through the group of people, attacking any part they could reach. She and the Doctor sprang into action. Lucy ran left. Her target had pushed a woman to the ground, claws poised for a downward strike. Before Lucy could reach them, the infected plunged one hand into the woman's chest. A moment later, the small eyes shot up, zeroing in on Lucy. As the infected's soaked fingers left the woman's spurting chest, Lucy's machete whistled through the air, separating neck from body. She slipped on a small lake of blood on the floor and almost fell to the ground. The Doctor stood over the body of the other infected, the left side of its skull concave. With a sharp tilt of her head, Lucy pointed to the elevators. The Doctor nodded, and before they continued, Lucy glanced back. Richard had positioned Sarah behind his bulky back, from where she now peeked. No attackers were coming their way, for now, so Lucy followed the Doctor, taking care not to slip on the blood-slick floor again.

Lucy counted seven corpses before they reached the half-open doors of the elevator. Seven more dead because of the nightmare she'd started only a few days ago. Smothering the guilt, she leaned on metal and listened. Sharpened points broke through concrete. Grunts and the shuffling of clothes came closer after each piercing thud.

"They're climbing down the wall, coming fast!"

Lucy spun, catching the Doctor's eye. Behind him, a sign pointed to the direction of the stairwell down the other end of the long corridor. Pushing off the wall, she scurried past, tapping him on the shoulder to follow as she went by. Reaching Richard, she urged him in the right direction, swinging her chin. He fell in line, Sarah glued to his back.

As they got closer, screams came from everywhere, the floor they were on and the stairwell leading up. One of the stairwell doors was open. She heard gunfire, flesh being torn, but what made her heart race was the sound of tiny feet pattering down toward them.

She turned to Richard and Sarah. "Run!"

Lucy slowed her pace for a second to jump over the bodies and blood. The Doctor ran close behind. Junctions of corridors sped past her, screams echoing from each one. Three branchways later, the noise died down.

"Richard, stop," she panted. "We need to make a plan."

Richard slowed and leaned on a nearby wall.

"Which floor do we need to reach?"

"The floor above is where the shelters are," Richard pointed to the ceiling.

"Impossible," Lucy shook her head, cutting the idea down. "It sounded overrun."

"The infected are coming down." Lucy sheathed the machete and continued, "They must be sweeping floor by floor. Is there anywhere else we can hole up?"

Sarah's breaths heaved roughly beside her. The sides of her pale neck were bright red from the exertion. Despite that, the features on her face showed a will to live, not resignation. *Good. I need her alert.*

Richard's right hand went to his wide plastic visor. Looking at the hand, realizing he couldn't touch his face, he rocked his head back and forth a moment. "We can go to the isolation chamber. It's in a separate wing from everything, independent water and air supply."

"Great. Is it on a deeper level, cuz we need to go down." Lucy's right index finger pointed to the floor.

Richard nodded.

"Okay, let's go." Lucy urged him on with a pushing motion.

He led them down a hallway until they reached another stairwell, went through the doors, and began to descend. A woman in a billowing lab coat flew past them down the well. Her screams met the cold ground below with a splat and ceased. The back of Lucy's left forearm was touched by a gentle hand. Looking over her shoulder, she saw Sarah walking behind her. The small woman's fingers trembled, so Lucy gave her a reassuring smile and nodded that it was okay for her to hold on.

The ventilation shafts carried more screaming and gunshots to them. Blood dripped on the railing from the floors above. Lucy kept a step behind Richard, the Doctor guarding the rear. The sounds of destruction accompanied them two floors down where they exited the stairwell, entering a corridor almost identical to those above.

Richard took them to the right. A minute later, the sounds of automatic weapons and inhuman howling caught up with them. The doors leading to other rooms got fewer and fewer. The brightly colored lines that were abundant on the upper floors disappeared as they went. Soon, only a single yellow arrow adorned the wall. They took another right; the new corridor had two doors in it. The first, at the midpoint, led to a staircase. The second, down the far end of the hall, stood tall like the king of containment doors.

"That's the isolation chamber." Richard pointed to the metal regent.

The two wings of the stairwell doors flung open. A group of infected sauntered in. Lucy and the Doctor immediately stepped next to Richard, shielding Sarah. Bone claws clutched the arms of corpses. White spikes pierced through flesh, pulling the bodies behind them like they were trash bags on the way to the dumpster. A new line of saturated red was being painted on the floor by the bodies.

These infected looked different from any Lucy had seen so far. All five of them wore Kevlar vests that reached their knees. Military helmets protected their heads while the bulges underneath their chins braced their necks. The fingers on their free hands curled into a ball, deformed into a bone-bludgeon made to resemble Johnathan's diseased appendage.

The one in the front of the group heaved the body it was holding forward. It slid across the floor like a curling stone down an icy lane. It came to a rest at Lucy's feet. The infected crouched like hungry beasts. The sheen of their eyes shined yellow-green.

On the ground, the corpse's chest filled like a bellows, and Lucy noticed the flesh on its fingers rot away.

The hairs rose all over her body. *An infected adult! We're too late. . . .*

The Doctor tried to step in front, but the crouched figures were on the move. Three slipped past him, two for Lucy. One for Sarah standing behind her. Trying to shield Sarah, Lucy's feet were kicked out from under her. Two infected pounced on top. The third toppled Sarah, white daggers meeting soft fabric.

Sarah's dress entwined with Kevlar as she and the infected tumbled down the hall. Lucy slashed one of the attackers but lost her balance and fell.

The Doctor took a step toward them a few feet away, but a bludgeon smashed into his knee. Staggering, another infected jumped on his neck. Lucy wanted more than anything in the world to look back. With a desperate swing, she tried to finish the infected in front of her. The blade found no flesh. Armor covered all the vulnerable spots, but caution made it back away. Forsaking her fight, Lucy twisted her body, one foot on the floor. The infected on top of Sarah scraped its fingers through her torso. Lucy launched herself at it. The claw fell and fell and fell, throwing blood and viscera on the walls, Sarah's diminutive form spasming after every blow. Lucy swung the machete into the back of the neck. The weapon stuck there, and it slashed out its arm, claws slicing her forearm. She tackled the attacker, her fists hardened by fury and sorrow. Forgetting the corridor behind her, she straddled her foe and hit its chest, head, arms, and any part within reach. Soon the infected was nothing more than ground meat in Kevlar packaging.

Even after the total decimation of her target, Lucy continued hitting. When her fists met the floor, two arms slid beneath her armpits and pulled her up. Lucy tried to break free; there was more damage she could do.

"Calm yourself, Miss Lucy," she heard the Doctor's voice from far away. "We have to help your friend."

She realized he was speaking in her ear. His arms were holding her at bay, a few inches off the ground. Her vision cleared, and she saw Sarah sprawled in blood. Richard was kneeling next to her with a large red gash in his suit, trying to find a pulse.

"Let me go," Lucy's calm voice made the arms holding her

unlock.

Landing, her feet buckled, and she fell to the floor.

"Fuck. I can't feel anything through this suit." Richard began throwing pieces of his hulking attire.

Lucy's shaking fingers touched Sarah's neck just next to a gaping wound. They detected nothing. She shivered and moved her hand down to Sarah's wrist, where she felt a faint, feeble spark of life. Lucy released her bated breath.

"We need to reach the isolation chamber," the Doctor's voice brought her back to reality.

He was standing by Sarah's feet, the dark pools on his mask scanning the corridor for other attackers.

"Take your friend while I gather these," the Doctor pointed to the infected around the floor.

Bracing her foot on its mutated back, she used all her strength to free the machete from the thing's neck.

"Take the corpses too," she told the Doctor as she sheathed her weapon then gently picked up Sarah. Her eyes were closed, blood dripped from everywhere on her upper body. It looked like she had been through a shredder.

Richard, now undressed, heaved himself up while putting pressure on his open wound, releasing blood in a steady trickling stream. He hobbled to the pad and opened the behemoth door.

The Doctor, holding all the bodies at once, looking like a many-armed abomination, joined them in the decontamination chamber. Once through, they found themselves in a vast circular room filled with equipment. At its center was another chamber with viewing windows.

Richard opened the door to the inner room, and the Doctor flung his infectious cargo on the pure white tiles. Lucy carried Sarah farther in after them. The Doctor took a spot between them and the pile of corpses while Richard remained by the door, near the keypad.

Lucy kneeled on the floor with her friend in her arms. Sarah twitched, and Lucy looked down to see hazel eyes staring into hers.

"It's going to be okay," she whispered, holding her close and stroking her hair.

Sarah's eyes focused, and her mouth formed a weak smile. She tried to say something but didn't have enough air. Only guttural sounds escaped her throat. Lucy leaned in and turned her ear to hear better.

"Please, stop . . ." Sarah said in the faintest voice, ". . . the pain."

That was all she managed before heaving for air. Tears filled Lucy's eyes. Her head hung low, forehead almost touching Sarah's cheek.

"This is all my fault," Lucy whispered. "I couldn't protect you, but don't worry, we'll get you help. You'll be good as new." Her voice broke.

Her tears poured off her cheeks and ran down Sarah's face. She felt a squeeze on her left hand. Sarah tried to move her head, but all she managed was a delicate sway. The wounds on her throat bloomed red like flowers.

"Please," Sarah strained and mustered all her strength to squeeze Lucy's hand harder.

Her eyes closed when the grip waned. The world around Lucy seemed covered in blood.

Why is she still conscious? Why won't her body give her peace? the thought igniting grief and pain throughout her, the edges of her mouth twisted down in a quivering, powerless frown.

"We can fix her up, right, Doc? Give me one of your

probability of survival statistics!" Lucy begged, looking up at him.

"All we can do now is release her from suffering, Miss Lucy," the Doctor said in the saddest tone she had heard from him yet. He gently raised Sarah's hand to show her the withering flesh.

The pain of her failure was so much greater than what she'd ever felt before. The world before her eyes turned so dark, she couldn't even see the pristine tiles behind the Doctor anymore. Air stopped coming into her lungs. Her body was giving up, and her spirit was being stuffed into a small black box, never to be opened again.

And why should it? No one would feel the difference anyway, she resigned herself to the darkness.

"Lu . . ."

Her vision cleared, showing her Sarah's ravaged torso.

"Don't . . ." Sarah panted for breath. ". . . blame . . ." The struggle to form words nearly knocked her unconscious.

The last word she couldn't manage, so she just kept panting, but Lucy felt Sarah's wrist turn up toward her.

"How can I not blame myself?" she sniffled, trying to keep her hands from holding too tight and bringing more pain to the broken form she cradled.

Despite her injuries, Sarah smiled like she always did when butting her head into Lucy's life, trying to help a jaded woman that fought against the world every day.

"The choice is yours, Miss Lucy." The Doctor stood, leaving her to make it.

Trembling fingers pulled her machete free. Lucy raised the blade and angled it over Sarah's heart.

"I'm so sorry," the words hurt so much that her forehead and temples almost exploded.

Willing the weapon down, it did not move. Its edge shook in place, stubborn in its refusal to sever the life of the dearest person Lucy had. The inside of her skull came under attack from thumping blows. Pushing her teeth against each other until they nearly broke, Lucy tried again. The machete moved only a fraction, invisible resistance keeping it from its target. A sharp point touched her other elbow. Shifting her shaky gaze, she saw flesh fall away, revealing bone as pale and white as a full moon. Lucy's lips trembled, and she tried to force her hand down once more. A large, gloved hand gave her shoulder a squeeze.

Lucy looked up at Emidius pleadingly, and he nodded. He placed his hand over hers, and they pushed together. The machete went through Sarah's heart in one smooth motion. The blow ended her struggle, relaxing her features back to the face of an optimistic and happy friend.

Lucy drew the blade out, letting it fall with an echoing clang. She sat back on her calves and watched as the small ocean of Sarah's blood encroached over the flawlessly white floor.

The pile of corpses behind the Doctor shuddered. Pale hands scraped the tiles with long, bony fingers. The newly infected rose with slow, jerking motions.

Richard pressed the keypad next to him, entombing the doomed trio with their now adult-sized enemy.

TWENTY-THREE

The Doctor pounced on the nearest infected adult, kicking it aside. The others lurched forward, but he moved through them like a whirlwind. Lucy ran to the door and tried to force it open while torn limbs and bodies flew around. The Doctor made quick work of the adult infected.

Having no luck with the door or its keypad, Lucy knelt beside Richard. His chest rose and fell at odd intervals. Blood still hemorrhaging from under the tear in his suit, Lucy's mind conjured images of skin falling from fingertips.

"What did you do?"

"I locked us in," he wheezed, neck twitching. "All of us except Birdmask could be infected. We shouldn't go anywhere."

The Doctor's forearm rose. Alien writing appeared on screen, then he leaned his mask to the side, facing Lucy.

"Your suit is counteracting the infection, for now, Miss Lucy," he announced.

She dragged her palm over her forearm, letting the dark skin of the suit reveal itself.

"I see how it is. So much for being a team," Richard coughed. "Sit tight and wait for them to get you out then."

"Open it up," she commanded, her voice hard.

"No." His paling face moved left to right. "It's infecting adults now, you saw for yourself." He turned his head and weakly gestured to Sarah's body lying on the ground.

"There are a hundred more upstairs," Lucy yelled, both hands raised.

"We don't know that they carry the same strain, and I can't do shit about those." Richard hacked spittle from his throat. "But I can make sure that this information at least never gets back to Johnathan."

"We don't have time for that!" Lucy hit the wall next to him. "We have to get out there and kill that little shit."

"I have footage of the code he used, Miss Lucy."

"Don't bother," Richard convulsed. "That works only for lockdown. They designed it like that."

Disregarding his words, the Doctor input the code. Nothing happened.

"Told ya."

"This will not stop me." The Doctor went to the nearest door.

Richard grimaced and lifted himself up as much as he could. "Maybe, but the big one we passed through is gonna slow you down. You can't tell me you'd risk infecting others."

"To save your young world, I would risk all the lives in this room." The Doctor began hitting the door.

Dents soon turned to craters. The metal gave way, and he was through.

"Nothing personal," Richard peered up at Lucy with drowsy eyes. "I had to do it, and you should try talking sense to him." He lifted his hand to look at it. The skin rotted from his fingers, exposing the bone underneath.

"Guess this is it for me. It's been fun, Lucy." His lips went crooked, and he nodded to the blade in her hand. "Would you do me the courtesy?"

This time she didn't hesitate. Lucy's machete sliced through his throat. Watching the light fade from someone she'd been intimate with made her arms tremor with unpleasant anxiety. She set her jaw against the emotional discomfort and joined the Doctor as he tapped the keys on his screen with evident frustration.

"Did you mean that?"

"Mean what?"

"That you were ready to sacrifice all of us to complete the mission."

His fingers stopped. "Yes, I did."

"Good." Lucy nodded and crossed her arms. "Because we have only one play left."

He turned his mask to face her. Soft light colored the silence.

"If you're right about the psychic connection, every second we lose brings a lieutenant that may have successfully infected an adult closer to Johnathan. That is if he doesn't know already. You need to infect me so I can lead you to him. That's the only thing we have time for. This is the final stage. We win or go extinct."

"I may not be able to cure you after the infection, Miss Lucy. The suit will offer some protection and slow down the transformation, but beyond that . . ."

"I accept the risk. Get us out and call your ship. Playtime is over."

The Doctor nodded then went back to the circular chamber.

"Allow me to dispose of these, Miss Lucy," he called from inside, prompting her to lean her back on the still intact door.

She heard him rustle around in his coat. A second later, brilliant white light came rushing out of the room. As the light streamed, a projection of the Doctor's silhouette appeared on the wall. It knelt down, venerating something on the ground.

The light died. Having removed all hazardous materials inside the room, the Doctor left.

Lucy mouthed a silent thank you for the final respects he paid to Sarah's body. Going back to the main door, he flung his coat out behind him and unhitched several dark, round devices with gray etched lines that went around indentations like buttons.

Arranging them in a wide half-circle on the metal, he said, "Take a step back, please."

The devices began to burrow into the door, sounds and smells of gouging metal fell over Lucy. When they were about midway through, they began to spin wildly in place. The drills hissed and sprayed a liquid into the surface. As they turned, the fluid that slowly ate away the door steamed and bubbled around them like molten lava. The deeper down they went, the quicker they spun. A few seconds later, there was a giant gaping hole in the middle of the behemoth door.

Slipping out of the opening, his report came in her ear moments later. "Clear."

Lucy plunged through the melted door, rolling to her feet on the other side. Linking up, they stalked forward.

"My craft is en route, Miss Lucy. Now we need to navigate the battle upstairs."

Through the double doors, they raced up the stairs. The infected didn't oppose them until they reached the ground floor. Chaos engulfed the lobby. Security and army forces crouched behind improvised cover, firing at armored figures. The Doctor led Lucy around fallen pieces of rubble to overturned furniture, their main goal to avoid this fight.

Reaching a ten-foot-tall window, the Doctor swayed his hand indicating where Lucy should take cover, then ran through it. Huge chunks of glass broke on his shoulders and head. Worried that the commotion would draw someone, Lucy looked back. The gunfire continued the same as before, so she made her way out, stepping onto trimmed grass. The space pumpkin from the alley waited for them just a few feet ahead. The ship's door shifted away like a heavy stone slab, revealing an entryway. Lucy jogged over and climbed in.

The Doctor stopped halfway through the corridor then began typing something on his screen. When Lucy got to him, a door on the wall opened with the backward slide of an avant-garde bread cupboard. The cylindrical moving sheet was at least two inches thick.

"A large contingent of military forces has been sent to pursue a group of infected fleeing the attacked laboratory," he read off his screen. "I will follow on foot, attempting a visual confirmation."

"Is that for me?" Lucy pointed to the opened cylinder.

"It will serve as containment while you give me directions to the prime contagion. You will have to be restrained for your own safety as well as mine."

"I understand." She stood inside the opened cubby. "Do it."

He pressed a button, and the door closed. Clasps caught her wrists and ankles, pinning her to the wall. Looking down, she saw more clasps grab her knees, elbows, waist, and finally, one gripped her around the neck. Trying to move yielded only bruised skin from the restraints.

"Do your best to give me directions when we get close to Johnathan," his voice came in her ear.

The wall in front of her turned into a screen, and Lucy saw the bulging cell she resided in from the Doctor's perspective.

"I'll do my best." Her throat dried up. *Damn it, when's the last time I drank some water.*

Lucy felt a sting on her neck. The device responsible then

retreated back into the wall.

"Farewell," he told her, standing at a door leading to the clouds outside the flying ship.

"Try not to kill the soldiers, okay. They're only doing their jobs," she said with a tongue quickly transforming into a lump of sand.

"I will do my best," he replied and fell through the sky.

Her thirst began to fade. Now only the heat remained. Sweat dripped from her eyebrows. Trying to wipe it away, her right hand made a clanking sound by her side, the clasps holding tight. The muscles in her arms throbbed with pain. The heat they emanated made her skin feel like it was melting. Her hearing worked in waves, but she heard screams echo off the walls each time it did. Her right leg muscle began to heat up after her arms, joints throbbing like someone was hitting them with a hammer. A bout of hearing overcame her.

"I am here with you, Miss Lucy," the Doctor's voice boomed inside her head, overpowering her screams and drowning them out.

"Focus on Johnathan. Do you feel him?"

Somewhere behind the Doctor's, Lucy heard another voice in her head. It dragged the syllables and spoke nonsensical words. It wasn't intrusive. Rather it sounded like a TV you had on in the background while you were trying to concentrate. She didn't know what it said, but it moved further away.

"Wrong" was the only word that came to her mind.

The Doctor turned and moved in a different direction. Lucy course-corrected when she could use her mouth. Her vision became spotty and worked in intervals like her hearing. Her left leg joined the choir of pain. She screamed and slouched forward, the clasps preventing her from falling. Her feet no longer moved when she struggled. She tried to do what the Doctor told her. She focused on the curved screen in front of her.

It displayed the Doctor running down streets, which he seemed to cross as fast as Lucy could peddle on her bike. A Humvee collided with him. He fell on the pavement. The pain in her stomach pushed a grunt out of her and made her close her eyes. The secondary voice grew closer. Lucy moved her lips to say they were on the right path, but her ears heard nothing. When she opened her eyes again, the Doctor was standing on top of a vehicle. He pried open its roof like a sardine can. Five men raised their weapons. He grabbed the driver and the man next to him, hoisting them up and then flinging them back down on top of the other men. The Doctor dove inside the roofless vehicle. His hands pawed at the soldier's vests, taking them off and grabbing grenades.

Her extremities disappeared. The pain was still there, but it no longer overwhelmed her. The Doctor jumped out of the vehicle. Kevlar vests strapped around his arms. A blockade of three vehicles obstructing his forward path opened fire on him. The Doctor threw a smoke grenade then shielded his upper body and head with his hands. His barrier reverberated from the force of the rounds, forearms jerking as if from kicks. A giant ball of smoke billowed from the feet of the soldiers. The gunfire lessened, and Doctor lowered his hands. He jumped in the air and dove into the smoke. His enhanced vision showed clear images, unhindered by the gray shroud.

He took a sharp right turn. Cresting the hood of an SUV, he landed behind two soldiers, slamming both helmeted heads on the side of the vehicle. Shouts came from his right. He followed. The closest soldier on the street he kicked in the chest, sending him flying through the smoke. He dashed at a man preparing to fire. A black line sprang forward, coiling around the rifle. The Doctor pulled the weapon with his whip. Others rallied around the fallen soldier, but Emidius spun the gun around, hitting all three of them.

Lucy's lower abdomen began to itch and burn. Thousands of needles poked her insides. Her stomach spasmed, and she threw up. While she struggled to see, the smoke around the Doctor lifted, dispersed by the end of helicopter blades. He ran left as yellow-bullet streaks rained down on his position.

The burning sensation moved up, engulfing her torso. Its severity made each gulp of air escape back out as if an unrelenting boot were stomping her chest. Tears ran down her cheeks. The small amount of moisture they left on her face felt like the most wonderful breeze. Her tears ran out, and Lucy felt them slip away. She looked down and saw two respite-giving teardrops fall to the floor. Their loss made her want to cry more, but there was nothing left. Her lips quivered from pain as even air touching her throat burned.

Close, we're close, she felt but only managed to say. "Clo—"

The ship turned in the wrong direction, and her legs ached with a new type of pain.

"Wrong," she whispered as a helicopter flew over the Doctor's head.

He turned right, meeting a military armored personnel carrier. The Doctor rushed it, throwing smoke and flashbang grenades inside as the APC's door opened. He kicked back the first man in the doorway, then slammed the door and locked it with a metal-bending hit to the handle. He waited a few seconds, then ripped the door off its hinges. The men from inside staggered out, falling to the ground disorientated.

Lucy's ears rang from the screams. Every attempt to take a

breath was met with her throat locking up. She focused all her efforts on forcing air inside to no avail. She was suffocating. The ship changed course with a violent jerk. Lucy's throat unlocked, and she took a big, loud gulp of air. Every nerve ending on her skin fired signals of desperation to her brain. Even the hairs that touched the restraints or the wall behind her brought discomfort and nausea. A moment later, finally, she passed out.

When she came to, the whole inside of the ship blinked a familiar but indescribable color.

Like when he stole the suit. Is it picking up my infection?

Her arms and legs had a strange numbness to them. She tried moving her left hand, and the clasps groaned.

Must've loosened them while I was thrashing about.

The extreme pain had vanished, which meant they were close. "He's around here somewhere, Doc."

"Understood," the Doctor acknowledged.

"I'm good to fight. Let me out so I can help."

The clasps released her without argument. She opened her feet wide to avoid her vomit, but looking down, she didn't see anything on the spotless black floor. The door opened, and Lucy almost fell, her feet still adjusting to unrestricted circulation.

"I will be with you shortly, Miss Lucy," the Doctor's voice boomed in her head.

"No need to yell. I'm coming to you."

The room spun. Her legs buckled. Trying to brace herself, her arms gave way as well, stopping her just before she slammed her face on the wall in front. Turning, she walked to the door, her balance and composure increasing with each step. The door opened, and light hit her face. Her joints and muscles throbbed like after a martial arts final, but a growing sense of power energized each new movement.

It's probably the infection eating away. It gave the infected enhanced abilities, so it's probably the same for me. A carnage-welcoming smile spread across her lips. *The Doctor might have some fancy tech to save me, but even if he doesn't, I'll make damn sure Johnathan pays for what he's done.*

An overturned APC slid across the ground. It slammed into a group of five infected, crushing them into a wall. The door of the armored vehicle opened with a slow and lazy arc. Two infected sailed through the air, mid-jump at a snail's pace. Standing at the door of the ship, she noticed the sluggish movement of retinas observing her presence. They readied themselves for an attack. A helicopter's blades beat the air with rhythmic blows just out of sight. A soldier made it out of the armored vehicle and climbed down to the ground. When his boots hit the pavement, Lucy heard the slowed words coming from his shoulder radio. Before the soldier was able to reach his gun, she exhaled and sprang into motion.

The infected ran past her, not able to switch targets fast enough. The soldier fired and killed one of the rushing figures. The other rammed into him. Lucy used the distraction to run to the building fifteen feet in front of her. Johnathan was near.

"Doc, inside!"

She dashed through a courtyard and up five steps. Through all the loud noises in her head, she heard tiny, incessant footsteps behind the gaping doorway to the ground floor. They leaped off the ground. She bent her right leg in preparation. The infected sailed at her, and Lucy's knee collided with its neck, throwing it back inside. Her speed was much greater than she intended, and she flew through a narrow hall, walls laced with doors on each side. Tucking her chin, she rolled then turned, weapon ready. The Doctor landed, rousing a dustbowl around him in the doorway. Observing her, his beak went up and down. Lucy returned the gesture. Her enhanced hearing picked up the clacking of automatic rifle bolts being pulled back.

"Take cover!"

The Doctor broke through a door on his left, and Lucy jumped after. Firing mechanisms of the converging army forces outside pushed out casings. Yellow-hot lead cut the air above her head.

"The military has followed me here, unfortunately," the Doctor's voice spoke in her head. "After our departure from the CDC, it seems we have become persons of interest."

"You think?" Lucy's cheek scraped the muck of the floor as more bullets diced the building.

"I presume you have put us in this tough tactical position for a reason?"

"Reign it in, Doc," Lucy growled from the floor. "And yeah, Johnathan is here. Up, it feels like."

Nodding, he dashed out of the room. The beige plates on his arms taking a few stray shots. Lucy cursed. Pushing off the ground, she crouched behind him. Squat walking, hands over her head, she saw him going up a stairway. Plaster rained down on her head until she reached the stairwell going up.

On the second step, a high-pitched whistle came from outside. Lucy glanced at the door just as a burst of fire ran through it. Flames bloomed all around, embracing the dry wood like an old lover. Debris hit her back, and she raised her hand to shield her face. She hurried up while the stairs still held. At the top, she saw the Doctor bulldoze four infected. Behind her, the impossibly loud blaze burned closer and closer. The sounds were getting too loud for her to handle. As she struggled to make her way to the Doctor, the infected clamored over each other, piling onto his limbs and torso. Two sharpened pipes burst out from the decrepit walls on either side of him. The left pipe was angled down toward his chest, the right up at his head. Slamming his head forward, he destroyed the sharp implement. The pipe broke, its back end lodging into the attacker, poking through. The other pipe landed a blow on his shoulder. The Doctor used the momentum to spin in place, the dark form of his limbs cutting through and annihilating everything around him. Lucy weaved to the side as a thrown arm threatened to put her back on the ground.

She pointed to the stairwell, and they continued up. Soldiers came through the smoldering front entrance and opened fire. Chairs, tables, and half-rotted pantries were clumped on the steps leading to the third floor. The Doctor groped the pile in an attempt to clear a path, the Kevlar plates tied around the back of his arms, making the job that much harder. Footsteps neared, prompting both of them to turn around at the same time. Vision swimming, Lucy pivoted on one foot and, sailing through the air, unleashed her blade. The machete sliced through one skull, then the whole arm of the trailing attacker. Her heartbeat hastened, making Johnathan's voice louder, and her tightened muscles ache with deep and unfamiliar pain.

"Going through here is a waste of precious time. We have to find another way," the Doctor said as he dashed back down.

Walking the corridors of the second floor, he studied the ceiling.

"We need to find a weak point."

"Y . . . e . . . es," Lucy struggled to use her mouth.

The voice in her head grew more powerful with every step. The Doctor whipped around to her after she spoke. His reflective stare leveled at her, and she saw her messy hair and wild eyes.

Words are hard . . . thoughts are hard . . . hurt . . . is easy.

Thinking felt like trying to catch mist. Instincts took over. The Doctor moved, and so did she. Each room they passed had figures that climbed in through windows or demolished in through the wall. They stood at the ready, not pouncing or making other threatening moves. Gunfire was constant on the floor below, but no soldiers made it far enough into the building to reach the staircase.

"Here," the Doctor pointed to the door on their left.

Vociferous noise hit the room on their right. Fire erupted behind the door, moving like a ghost through the wall, then the room exploded into a million pieces. Lucy's ears stopped working for a brief moment before a wailing ring grew louder and louder. Heat began to run up her skin. She could feel herself breathe, the air wafted around her, but no sound was loud enough to drown out the terrible squealing. Losing one of her senses made the others quickly compensate and adjust. Heat, she now felt with greater intensity. Burnt flesh expunged other smells. Then she felt the *pain*. Not her own, but the response of the bodies all around her. She felt the vibrations in the air caused by the desperate movements of their burning limbs. Their agony was so great even the prime contagion's pain suppression wasn't enough to quell it. The infected were not immune to pain, she realized with horror. The heat and the overwhelming feeling of death made her legs sway for a moment. The skin inside her suit began to boil.

If it wasn't for this suit, I'd already be dead, the dim thought appeared in her mind.

A black arm wrapped itself around her waist. The Doctor held her tight and jumped up through the ceiling. Another explosion hit the rooms below them. As soon as the Doctor landed, Lucy broke free of his grip. The floorboards behind them tilted and fell to the story below, so she ran. The Doctor touched the back of her left shoulder and ducked into a room. Lucy made a half-turn and dove in after him. Heat came from the hallway behind her. The boards outside the room were obliterated into brown dust. Lucy couldn't hear it, but she felt the vibrations through her feet. Across the expanse, Lucy spotted the stairwell leading up. She grabbed the Doctor by the material of his coat's shoulder and ran down the once hallway, now cliff edge around the fiery pit. Pressed against the walls, they circumvented the crater, making one last daring leap to the stairs. Her feet buckled on the landing, and she fell to her knees, not sure if she could continue. The closer she got to Johnathan, the more her life seemed to slip through her fingers.

On the next floor up, Lucy smelled something just outside. She never realized touch and smell were such powerful senses before. Her eyesight blurred, perceiving the movement of her limbs in slow motion. The Doctor joined her snail-paced crew. Once she blinked, the world moved at its normal pace. Johnathan's presence moved away from this floor. She tapped the Doctor's shoulder as a slight breeze hit her cheek. The smell of gasoline oozed through the walls a moment later. The rhythmic nature of the near-imperceptible draft told her it was caused by spinning blades outside.

"Helicopter!" she screamed, not sure how loud.

The Doctor pointed to the nearby stairwell and ran. Bullets ripped through the walls just as she cleared the third step. The Doctor reached back, grabbing her by the shirt collar, then throwing her up over the railing to the next flight. He crested the railing right after. The bullets and gasoline smell followed them. Lucy ducked her head and lay down on the stairs.

The rain of bullets relented, giving them the chance to climb. The building shook from another impact. Lucy ignored it, not missing a step. Vitality drained out of her with each muscle contraction. Her limbs tried to go limp like they'd done when her blood spilled all over the abandoned factory. Johnathan was within reach, and no bad memories or blood loss was going to slow her down. Stepping foot on the last floor, all doors flung open. Some doorways were insufficient for the mass of diseased children, and clawed fingers dug through rotted wood and decade-old plaster. They scurried over each other in their attempts to reach them. Johnathan had orchestrated this whole situation, leading her by the nose again, but there would be no hesitation this time. She and the Doctor were here to slaughter, circumventing traps, or doing clever gambits were out the window. Lucy's life was ending, and now, so would theirs.

The Doctor disrobed from his makeshift Kevlar armor. The plates hit the floor with a dull thud. Lucy raised her machete and shielded her face with her hardened free hand. Swinging wildly, she crashed into the infected. Hacking away without a target, her blade rose and fell, sliced then skewered. Pieces of young bodies flying around and behind her, she butchered her way through the horde.

Her blood boiled as it pumped through her heart from the excitement of the carnage. The sprayed blood fuelled her lust. Mincing her foes, she was elated, but her insides struggled to keep up after each successful kill. The violence she brought reflected on her muscles and nerves, making them flare up as if she were the one getting battered. The Doctor covered her back and flanks. All the infected she missed, he diligently put down. The attackers stood no chance. No matter how many came at her, Lucy cleaved them to pieces. The toll on her body grew heavier with each new spray of crimson.

She heard the voice louder. "He's close."

A new scent wafted over that of working engines, gunpowder, and blood. She marched toward the end of the hall with the Doctor at her back. As they neared the room from where the voice came loudest, Lucy held her nose against the reek of human filth, urine, feces, blood, and rot. The cocktail of scents Lucy was all too familiar with, living and working in the poverty-stricken areas of the city. But now, the stench of degradation overpowered her senses like never before. If she'd had anything in her stomach, it would already be on the ground. She reached for the doorknob and opened the door.

Johnathan stood crouched at the far end of the room. The stump braced on the ground between his knees, clawed hand, taking soft jabs at the air. Daylight coming from a skylight above his head bathed his malformed silhouette. Shadows covering his masked face, two points of light stared right at Lucy. He jumped up through the opening. As they ran through the room, Lucy realized why it smelled the way it did. Those young enough to be infected were brought here. To a room with covered windows and no light, where a monster holding an orange took their life. With no one to call out to for protection and no possible way of escape, they were turned into creatures of malice. Scared and lonely, their last conscious moments were spent in an awful and stinking room.

The Doctor reached the skylight first and jumped through it. Lucy grabbed the ledge and followed him up. The Doctor's body flew past her. Johnathan dove toward her. Lucy blocked a blow from his sharpened tibia. The Doctor attacked with his whip, coiling it around the bony neck. Johnathan pulled him off his feet. Colliding, they each hit the other once, then jumped back.

Three helicopters surrounded the roof. Johnathan reached the edge and jumped to the adjacent building. Lucy heard the chain guns of the helicopters begin their revolutions of death. The Doctor pursued with Lucy trailing close behind, and the helicopters opened fire just as she jumped. The bullets that ripped the air as she flew made ripples of sound that she felt more than heard. The Doctor's coattails disappeared over the far edge of the building. She rolled on the roof, and without a second thought, got up and ran headlong for the edge.

Lucy mimicked what the infected did and both hardened and sharpened her fingers. Falling down, she plunged both hands into the wall. Her unpracticed fingers dug too deep into the brick, slowing her to a crawl. Unsure how far out to pull her hand, she went down in bursts, a few feet at a time, but she made it down with no broken bones. The Doctor smashed through a door on the ground floor of a building across the street. Lucy ducked behind a car as bullets tore it apart. When the rain of lead stopped, she tumbled across the street, her feet giving out right before the door. Rolling, she made it inside the building. Her boosted senses told her it was filled with moving beings.

Movement, fourth floor.

She made her way there, finding a giant hall full of infected. Johnathan's stumpy arm leaned against a column. The Doctor ran at the mass. His hands went through faces and smashed heads into pulpy goo. Johnathan used the distraction to edge away. Lucy's smell picked up the stench of rubber or cable insulation. Taking a step forward, she heard a button click in Johnathan's hand, and the bloom of a yellow explosion rolled over her, eating all available oxygen.

Not moving, she tried to tinker with the sensitivity of her hearing. The sound of the explosion stopped her ears from working again. Instinct made her raise her arms. The heatwave ran through her forearms and singed the ends of her hair. Peeking from behind, she saw dozens of charred bodies around the Doctor, who stood near the column at which the explosion originated. The Doctor twisted toward Johnathan, who fled. Focusing, Lucy heard his voice in her mind. He was angry that the trap hadn't killed Emidius. She smiled as she went after him.

Down. No . . . up, baffled, she went back inside the hall.

The floor shook, then shifted, then slanted, making Lucy's inner ears urge her to get far, far away.

"Not this again," she moaned, not hearing herself.

The column showed cracks running from the huge chunk missing in its center. The Doctor stood close to it. The whip in his hand glowing red hot. With a flick of his wrist, he wound the black line around the column's crack. Concrete began to melt. The Doctor released the whip then curled it in another spot just above the one he'd melted. He braced his body and pulled. The building stopped swaying, but the column continued to fracture. Infected encircled him.

The breaking column and the skewed floor made Lucy realize what Johnathan had wanted to do.

He's baiting us to the top, and he'll collapse the building!

She cut her way to the Doctor, slashing left and right.

"We're fucked, Doc," she managed to say with effort.

Lucy searched for the bloodlust inside her. She allowed the smell of blood and the burning flesh of her enemies to fill her mind. The first three infected in range she cut down in a single swing. The next group came from her right. She collided with them, stabbing, cutting, and slashing. Infected encircled them from all sides. Lucy stood up and pivoted off each leg in turn, moving like a razor-sharp acrobat around the Doctor. She found opportunities to cut anything jutting from the mass of bodies. The tactic worked for another orbit before the infected got cautious. Groups of four began to come from different directions. While Lucy dealt with the first, the second piled on the Doctor and tried to pry him away. Soon they surrounded her, putting a fleshy wall between her and him. She managed to get one or two, but they pushed her back toward the windows. Her movement away from the column wasn't barred, but going forward, trying to reach the Doctor, prompted the infected into action. They appeared like a giant dog's head, protecting its territory. Infected buried the Doctor while Lucy found herself at the far wall. The pile of bodies that used to be the Doctor began to glow red. A moment later, the mound exploded, and a shockwave pushed Lucy out the window, movement slowing to a crawl once more.

A frightening moment later, her view flipped from inside to outside, from glass to concrete. She reached out, her fingertips scraping the surface, then slipped away with more glass. The second-story window ended, and she saw another fragment of wall. Pushing her fingers forward, they slowly but surely began to cut into the concrete. Her speed decreasing, she pushed her feet down and gave the same hardening command to her toes. The suit obliged. Lucy swung her feet in midair, planting them in the sill of the window below her.

Time resumed as a deep exhale escaped her lips. Her fingers trembled inside the holes she'd made. Above her, infected flew out of the window, headfirst toward her. The rain of mutated bodies neared. Lucy pulled her right hand out, hardening it. She swung—her fist colliding and pushing the infected's body to the side. The added weight made the punctures in the wall grow into crevices. Leaning forward, she kept from falling. The moment of imbalance made her whole body shiver. The other infected missed their mark. Her fear fell away with them, and anger seeped into her veins.

Her muscles contracted and expanded, ready for action. Pain radiated from every fiber of her being, nearing critical mass. The suit hardened around her hands and feet. She pushed herself up with an explosive burst of strength. Time slowed down again as she flew up. When she neared the fourth-story window, the wall moved away, and the building tipped. Her speed gave way to gravity. The receding window showed her a black shadow running up the slanted floor. Even with her heightened senses, she still barely recognized the speeding shade as the Doctor. He jumped to her, then pushed her abdomen with his left palm.

Lucy's trajectory changed as she hurtled backward toward the nearest building. Tons of steel and concrete crumbled down in front of her. The Doctor caught a nearby lamp post with his whip and swung down safely. Lucy shielded the back of her head with her arms and hardened as much fabric as she could manage before crashing through brick and glass into someone's kitchen.

Trying to stand, her left knee lifted then fell to the ground. The breath in her chest burned hot like the exhaust of a speeding car. She gazed at the lethal fumes rising above the adjacent former building.

For a brief moment, everything turned black. Panic made her sit back on her haunches. Blinking, color and picture returned to her.

Johnathan's voice beat inside her head like a war drum. Allowing his influence to take hold, her muscles obeyed the alien command. She rose to the sight of hundreds of dark figures answering the prime contagion's call. They penetrated the inhospitable smoke on a protective trajectory to their leader.

Lucy focused on the fast specks, diving into the spreading, virulent cloud.

Her blood boiled in her veins, and she gnashed her teeth. With everything she had left in her quickly weakening body, she broke free of the call. Drawing her index finger over her nostrils, she leaned forward, ready for one final confrontation. Jumping over the edge, she raked the wall with her fingers, landing hard on her trembling legs.

"Just like . . . we practiced, Doc," she panted when she found her footing.

"Understood. I will funnel the target to you," came the reply as she drove ahead.

A small figure bumped into her. Before it had a chance to attack, Lucy twisted its neck and pushed it away. Johnathan stopped in place and turned. Her cracked lips curled up, bleeding all over her smile. The smoke lowered visibility to zero, but she didn't need to see. Picking up as much speed as her failing body would allow, she ran past a shadow, her hardened fingers obliterating its skull. Another shadow turned, but Lucy had already rushed past it.

"I'm close," she wheezed through failing lungs. "I . . . I might not make it. I need your help."

Infected caught her presence and followed along the strewn rubble.

"Up or down?" the Doctor's voice cut through the sounds of concrete climbing feet.

". . . Down!" Lucy took her last breath, and the outline of a bird-masked figure rushed toward her and flew over.

She could taste Johnathan's malignant presence—three feet away. Putting all her remaining strength into her feet, she jumped. Her machete sliced clean through protective cartilage and neck. A frightened hum came from all around her. With no control over her limbs, she fell face-first onto a slab of concrete. Her lungs gasping for air that wouldn't come.

Before her eyes fluttered to a close, she saw the Doctor's outline take a defensive stand at her dying feet.

DAY ???

DAY 222

TWENTY-FOUR

Waking up was something Lucy did not expect. Yet her eyes opened, and she found herself in a vast room. Hulking dark columns reached down from the shadowed roof and culminated right above her head. Cables or something similar to them snaked around the columns and delivered a thick substance between them. She appeared to be on a raised platform that could be reached from several staircases. The floor had specks of light to show the way, resembling the inside of the Doctor's pumpkin.

Lucy could feel some sort of power flow through the entire structure, like a car engine revved up, its invisible energy roaring under the hood. A large section of the wall in front of her showed twinkling stars. At the bottom of the panorama stood the Doctor, gazing out into the vast expanse. His wrist beeped, and he swung his head toward her. Running over, he almost collided with the contraption holding Lucy in place.

"Miss Lucy," his monotone sounded as surprised as she was to find her awake.

"Did we win?" her mouth almost couldn't form the question.

Trying to move any part of her body yielded no results. Only her eyes and mouth seemed to work.

"Assuredly so." He nodded. A soft wave of his hand drew a flying screen to him that displayed letters with the speed of falling rain droplets. "How are you feeling?"

"Not dead," she replied, raising her eyebrows.

"It gladdens me to see your sense of humor has been preserved."

"Stop yapping and get me some water." The dried, dead thing masquerading as her tongue seemed to consume all of her saliva as soon as it made it into her mouth.

"In a moment, first get yourself acclimated."

She threw him an angry look. She would not be restrained again. That was an experience she did not care to repeat. Her hands wouldn't move. She tried and tried, commanded the muscles to do their job, but nothing obeyed. Her legs, feet, shoulders, neck, all of it numb and distant. Clenching her jaw, she exhaled then took a breath.

What is this? she shot the question with her eyes.

The Doctor projected a hologram above his forearm. It showed an image of Lucy, submerged in an upright vat. She couldn't move her neck, but she could feel liquid all around her.

"I had to put you in stasis while I synthesized a vaccine. You have been here for quite some time, I'm afraid . . . we have almost arrived back at my place of work."

Place of work. That means space. Space . . .

Her mouth quivered despite her firm resolve to not be too emotional. Flaring her nostrils, she blinked a few times as that was the only physical outlet she possessed right now.

"My mom, I wanted to . . ."

"I made sure your mother would be financially secure before we departed. It was a trivial matter to shuffle around some capital." His hand dove into his coat, and he pulled out her phone. "I took a final memento for you."

He showed her a picture of two women standing side by side,

smiling without a care in the world. Lucy felt her chest grow lighter. Moisture blurred her vision, and having no movement in her fingers to wipe the tears away, she let two streams glide down her cheeks.

"Thank you," she said, looking up at his dark eyes.

"You are very welcome." He left the phone on a nearby piece of alien furniture.

He typed something onto his screen, and Lucy felt a jolt of energy run through her. The vat drained, leaving her upright. Her suit, covering everything from the neck down, now dripped with the strange-colored liquid. Lucy tried to walk, but her feet were wooden stumps, disconnected from her circulatory system. Allowing a few moments for the drug the Doctor had given her to reach them, she then wiggled her toes. Being successful in that, she dragged her sole across the floor. It wasn't quite a step but a successful forward movement. These minuscule half-steps soon took her nearer to her target, the phone. Using her hands to pull her thighs, she managed to amble the last three feet. Grabbing her phone, she looked at her mother again. The image warmed her. "Did they ask why you were there instead of me?"

"Miss Valentina did. I explained you were accepted with a scholarship for excellence in a rigorous higher education program."

"Yeah, that sounds nice. I like it." She switched the screen off, embraced the phone on her chest, and threw him an appreciative smile. "What happened to the infected?"

"Without the prime contagion's leading influence, the infected were gathered in a few days. Losing their propagation method has simply turned them into feral and dangerous creatures. I opted out of destroying them."

The lost lives of countless children went through her like

the scythe of the grim reaper, yet a larger concern troubled her. "You're not afraid us humans might reverse-engineer the virus?"

"If I had such a worry, your whole city would have been excised. Your current level of technology is inadequate for that feat. I cannot interfere beyond my mission, which with your assistance, I have completed." Interlocking his fingers, he kept his hands at belt level.

The mission, huh?

Images of Sarah's bloody body flashed before her eyes.

You didn't die for nothing, Sarah. I made it count! Her fingers strained against the surface she used as support.

"The loss of life was regrettable," the Doctor read the emotions on her face. "But we were victorious, and you should be proud of that."

"What about me? What happens now?"

Raising his mask and letting his hands fall to his sides, he replied. "Now, I will have to take you to my superiors."

"Couldn't you just tell them I died and you lost the suit?" She furrowed her brows in confusion at the obvious and easy solution.

"Not possible, unfortunately."

"And why pray tell?" Tilting her head to the side, she mimicked his speech pattern, adding her own sarcastic twist to it.

"First, your blood contains a mutated strain of a virus dangerous enough to be labeled a world-ender. The falsification of my landing time and coordinates might have been for that express purpose. Moving on, the suit you interfaced with is not standard issue for young agents. It is actually a regulation suit for high-ranking members."

Lucy stared at him. Expression placid, her mouth open only a fraction, completing the dumbfounded visage.

The Doctor puffed out his chest and clasped his hands behind his back. "This part of the burden falls on me because I made a decision on the ground that keeping you alive and safe was paramount to the success of the mission. And as it turned out, I was correct, but the suit once interfaced is yours until death."

Lucy's eyes grew wider.

"As you can see, you are not the only one, as is your expression, *bearing crosses*. But more importantly, this leaves you in a very precarious position, Miss Lucy. Not to mention that I have unseen enemies, which only you are trustworthy enough to help me root out. The organization I work for now effectively owns your skin and blood," he said, pointing his index finger at her nose. "So the situation has you backed into a corner, and I *will* have to take you to my superiors."

"The single bright side you have is that your mind"—he touched her forehead gently—"is owned by no one but yourself."

Lucy felt rage sting her recovering limbs. All this misfortune had been thrown at her, and she had little recourse in the matter. Rage tightened her fists, but as soon as they had closed, she relaxed her grip.

"So, if you allow me to help you, I believe we may find a way out of this." He drew the finger back.

Lucy studied him for a few moments. This sometimes goofy acting alien life form had been there for her more than most people she'd met in her life. The odd mannerisms and his pursuit of doing the right thing spoke to her in a way nothing before had. His mission became hers, and he did his best to help her out even when it wasn't easy. Thinking on it now, she wouldn't want anyone else to have her back in the whole universe. She extended her hand, grasping his.

"Okay. We're on your turf now, and I'll need all the help I can get. Partners?"

He shook her hand as a colossal floating structure appeared in the panorama window. "Partners."

The floor shook as if the ship had been caught in the maw of a deep-space void monster.

"Ah, we have arrived!" He turned on his heel and walked down the hall.

Raising her arm, Lucy willed the suit to harden into a bludgeon that could break concrete. The imposing walls of the space superstructure loomed over her as she released her concentration and dripping vat-fluid hobbled after him.

"Let me do the talking," he said when Lucy ambled to his side.

Descending from top to bottom, the door opened. Bulky armored suits engraved with threatening markings clattered as energy weapons were aimed at their heads. Behind them, endless white walls cradled the figures like clasping palms about to coalesce into a cosmic cage.

She gulped. "Sure thing . . ."

ACKNOWLEDGEMENTS

Thank you to Hristo and Nikola, who suffered through my early attempts at writing. The value of their honest opinions and the time they graciously devoted is beyond what I could express with words.

ABOUT THE AUTHOR

NICK NIKOLOV used to read fantasy in high school and play a lot of video games, emphasis mainly on games. First encounter with amazing storytelling was in a game called Legacy of Kain: Soul Reaver for a hard-to-come-by Playstation console, you read that right, the very first Playstation. The importance of amazing stories became starkly apparent since that encounter. In the coming years up until graduation from University with a bachelor's degree in Automation, games were the main source of gripping narratives. Upon entering the workforce, the need to create grew so great, that a change had to be made. The choice being, either suffocate the creative drive or attempt to get good at writing. And here we are, after seven years of struggles, two and sometimes three jobs at once, and a lot of hard lessons learned, finally, an actual book that can be read!

Learn more at *www.nikolovstories.com*

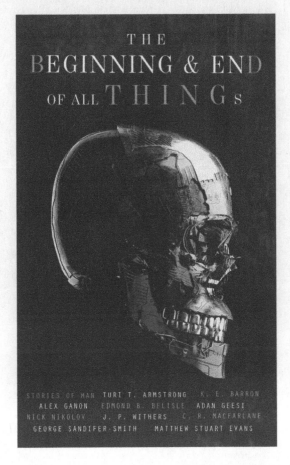

9 781989 071182